BEWARE THE LAW OF THE JUNGLE . . .

Kevin Grunfeld was a hulk of a man, a good six and a half feet tall with dark, deep-set eyes that would have done credit to a pit viper. He stared at Gloria for a few moments, slowly taking her in from head to toe and back again.

"Gloria VanDeen," he said. "Welcome to my town. And to my planet."

"Thank you, Mr. Mayor. You won't need your bodyguards," she said, indicating the two men with a short motion of her head. "I probably won't hurt you."

Grunfeld snickered. "That's just Karl and Hank. They won't hurt you none, neither, 'less I tell 'em to."

"That would be exceptionally stupid, even for a small-town oaf like you." The mayor's eyes widened a fraction at her words. "Let me make this as clear as possible, Grunfeld. You may be the biggest fish in your little puddle here, but the tide is coming in and you are about to be swamped by the Empire. My team will arrive in a week, and we will begin registering voters. If you get in our way, a shipload of Dexta Internal Security forces will follow shortly to make travel arrangements for you and your Neanderthals."

"Well, ain't you somethin'!" Grunfeld declared. A full-scale smile, or something like one, spread across his face. "Heard about you, but I never quite believed it. Emperor's ex-wife, they say. You sure sound like it, and ain't no doubt you look like it, but ya know, this ain't no Imperial palace you're in now. This here's Greenlodge, Territory . . . . law around here. In f . . . . ay goes, and that's all th . . . . of you, Miz Gloria, the . . . . to find. . . ."

ALSO BY C.J. RYAN
DEXTA

GLORIOUS TREASON

C. J. RYAN

BANTAM BOOKS

GLORIOUS TREASON
A Bantam Spectra Book / December 2005

Published by
Bantam Dell
A Division of Random House, Inc.
New York, New York

Bantam Books, the rooster colophon, Spectra, and the portrayal of a
boxed "s" are trademarks of Random House, Inc.

ISBN-10: 0-553-58777-3
ISBN-13: 978-0-553-58777-7

Printed in the United States of America
Published simultaneously in Canada

www.bantamdell.com

OPM 10 9 8 7 6 5 4 3 2 1

GLORIOUS
TREASON

chapter 1

THEY CALLED HIM OLD ABEL, AND HE HAD BEEN there since the beginning—before the beginning, really. He wandered freely, almost randomly, through the valleys and forests, finding shelter when he needed it in natural caves and depressions or in the flimsy lean-tos he built, then abandoned as his moods and whims dictated. No one knew his age, but it was considerable, and it was a mystery where and how he obtained his food, clothing, and other presumed necessities of life. Not that he needed much.

He was a small, stoop-shouldered man with a scraggly white beard, long, tangled hair, and sharp, suspicious eyes the color of the evening sky before a storm. His voice, on the rare occasions when he used it, sounded like a stick being dragged through dry leaves. He appeared and disappeared without preamble, and although he was recognized throughout the mining camps and sparse clusters of tumbledown shacks that dotted the slopes of the valley, no one could claim to know him. He seemed neither alien nor entirely human—a species unto himself, indigenous and mysterious.

Sylvania was his world, as far as it was anyone's, and even the nabobs in the Lodge and the swaggering boom-rats in the town and the camps treated him with a wary, deferential respect. When they saw him coming, leaning heavily on his wooden staff and lugging a sackful of Spirit-knew-what over his shoulder, the miners paused in their work and nodded to him. Some even ventured a greeting, perhaps receiving a nod of recognition in return; perhaps not. The bolder souls among them occasionally invited him to share their dinner, and sometimes he did. He might even engage in something that passed for conversation, exchanging a few words about the weather: a topic on which he was considered—in the absence of meteorological satellites—the ultimate local authority. He knew to the hour when rain would begin or end, and precisely how high up the slopes it would turn to snow. On other subjects, he had little or nothing to say, but he listened carefully to the words of the boomrats about the progress of their diggings, the latest troubles with Grunfeld and his thugs, or the new whore down at Elba's.

He rarely bothered with the town these days, and when he did, people made way for him and whispered behind his back, telling the newcomers—and there were many of them now—that this strange, threadbare apparition was just Old Abel, the local "character," as if that explained everything that needed to be known about him. Elba gave him food and drinks and some-times joined him at his table. He was even believed to spend time in the rooms upstairs—but if he did, the whores didn't talk about it. Some of the older boomers might buy him drinks in return for a few minutes of his almost wordless company. And then he would be gone again, quietly retreating to his silent wilderness.

A few of the boomrats actively sought him out in the forests, convinced that Old Abel knew better than any-one just where to find outcrops of the glimmering green crystals whose discovery, three years ago, had lured them here across the light-years. But Old Abel could seldom be found unless he wanted to be, and he had nothing at all to say on the subject that obsessed the boomers. His silence only served to convince them that he was in possession of secret knowledge that, if they had it, would make them wealthy beyond calculation. But it was no easier to find Old Abel than it was to find the crystals themselves; in fact, it was more difficult, for the Fergusite crystals rimmed the broad valley and littered its streambeds, but there was only one Abel, and he moved as he would.

Exactly what Abel knew, or might know, was a subject of endless debate around the campfires and cookstoves. Some advanced the opinion that he knew nothing at all and was, in fact, simply the ignorant, witless old hermit he appeared to be—but they could not really bring themselves to believe that. Others were convinced that Old Abel had a secret cache somewhere up in the mountains, and lived a life of luxury and ease when no one was looking. A few even suggested that he was really an Imperial agent, spying on the boomrats for the Empire, or for Dexta. Or for the Lodge, or one of the corporate titans.

The oldsters—men like Bill McKechnie and Amos Strunk—knew better, but made no attempt to dispute the opinions of the latecomers. They kept their own counsel and merely smiled as they listened to the theories come gushing forth like water through a sluice. But Bill and Amos had heard the Voice, and most of the newbies hadn't.

They didn't talk much about the Voice. Those who hadn't heard it were convinced that the Voice was simply the delusion of men who had spent too much time in the silent hills of this lonely world, and some of those who had heard it feared that the doubters might be right. The easily frightened among them had taken heed of the Voice and quickly packed up their meager belongings and left the planet as soon as they could. Others, with stronger spines and a more resolute nature, had defied the Voice and remained at their diggings, but kept an ear to the wind and tended to jump at sudden noises.

The Voice seemed to come from everywhere and nowhere, and whispered to them at odd moments as they squatted in the cold, rushing waters, panning for crystals, or sat among the high crags, fussing with their plasma drills. It came to them in the dead of night or in the blaze of noon, on the shining outcrops of the cliff faces or in the gloom of the forests, and it spoke different words to different men. To most, it breathed in soft, insistent tones, "Go away. Leave me alone." To Bill McKechnie and Amos Strunk, it had said only, "Don't hurt me."

Old Abel wouldn't talk about the Voice. "I hear what I hear," he had said one night at Bill McKechnie's campfire. "And you hear what you hear."

WHAT ABEL HEARD ONE MORNING IN MARCH of 3217, as the Empire reckoned time, was not the Voice, but a cry of pain and outrage. It echoed down from the high reaches of the slopes, up near the snow line, where some of the newbies had been testing their luck. Abel peered upward from the edge of the forest, where he had spent the night, and saw two men he recognized even from this great distance, and a third that he didn't know—and never would.

The two he knew were Karl Cleveland and Hank Frezzo—big, tough, distinctive men who worked for the Mayor, the Honorable Kevin Grunfeld, tsar of the town of Greenlodge and anything else he cared to be tsar of. Cleveland and Frezzo held a third man between them, grasping each arm at the shoulder while their victim's feet kicked frantically at empty air. With a minimum of effort and only a final dying scream to mark the moment, the two tossed the third over the edge of the cliff face, sending him pinwheeling downward a hundred meters or more to the jumbled pile of scree at the base of the precipice. They peered over the edge for a few seconds, evidently satisfied with their work, then walked away and out of Abel's line of sight.

Abel waited a while to be sure they were gone, then laboriously picked his way upward through the scree to the place where the shattered body of the newbie had finally come to rest. Even if Abel had known the man, he would not have been able to recognize the smashed face that stared sightlessly upward toward the cold sun of Sylvania. Abel didn't touch the body or attempt to scavenge anything useful from his kit, although others undoubtedly would when they found him. Nothing was easy to get or hold on to on this planet, and even life itself was but a slippery possession.

He liked the newbies even less than he liked the oldsters, but Abel found himself feeling sorry for the dead man. Somewhere, perhaps a thousand or more light-years away, at the other end of the Empire, this man had once had a home, maybe even a family. When they heard the news—and they would eventually, for Dexta was remarkably efficient in such matters—they would be saddened and mournful. Or perhaps not; perhaps the dead man was a good-for-nothing son of a bitch, like so many of the boomers, and the Empire would be a better place without him in it. Abel didn't know and didn't really care.

But he cared about Sylvania, and was disheartened by what this and other such incidents must inevitably mean for his world. Sooner or later, the Empire would have to do something about it. More boomers were already on their way, and now they must be joined by the grim, gray bureaucrats of Dexta, who ran the Empire and enforced its rules. And Dexta, in turn, would soon be followed by the corporate behemoths, who would rape this quiet valley, then kill it, as surely as Grunfeld's men had killed this sad specimen crumpled at his feet.

And what, Abel wondered, would the Voice have to say about *that*?

chapter 2

THE TWO MOST POWERFUL MEN IN THE EMPIRE stared at themselves and each other in the gently rippling waters of the reflecting pool, the replica of the Taj looming above them in carefully crafted splendor. The original had been destroyed in an alien attack during the Second Interstellar War, more than seven hundred years earlier in pre-Imperial days, before the men of Earth had come to dominate this corner of the galaxy. Reconstructed as one of six Imperial Palaces scattered around the terrestrial continents, the Taj Mahal no longer seemed a monument to love but to human persistence, ingenuity, and arrogance. The two men embodied those same qualities.

Norman Mingus was the first to break the spell of the reflection and look away. Tall, spare, slowed but unbowed by his 130 years, Mingus had a face that was pink and unlined and might have belonged to a retired and much-loved schoolteacher. Instead, it belonged to the Secretary of the Department of Extraterrestrial Affairs.

The Emperor Charles V, forty-seventh in an unbroken line stretching back nearly seven centuries, lingered another moment with his reflected image. When at Agra, he affected garb of flowing white robes and rather fancied the way they set off his athletic frame and regal features. He imagined that Alexander the Great, when he came east, might have cut a similar figure. With his closely cropped beard, longish curling locks of dark blond, and pale blue eyes, he knew that he *looked* like an Emperor, just as Mingus, 102 years his senior, with his dark business suit and beady, censorious eyes, looked like a bureaucrat.

"I do love it here," Charles said, finally looking away from the reflecting pool. "Next to Rio, I think Agra is my favorite Residence. Of course, Paris has its own particular charms, as well. And there's much to be said for Colorado. Tell me, Norman, which do you prefer?"

"I suppose, Highness," Mingus replied after a moment's thought, "it depends on what business brings me to them."

"It's always business with you, isn't it, Norman?" The Emperor shook his head regretfully. "Very well, then, business. We may as well go inside, lest we be distracted by this beautiful day and magnificent setting. Four walls and a couple of chairs will do, I suppose."

CHARLES LED THE WAY INTO THE RESIDENCE, slowing his normally brisk gait to accommodate a man who was nearly five times his age and had been Secretary of Dexta ten times longer than Charles had been Emperor. Mingus followed at his own pace, feeling no need to match the Emperor stride for stride. He had been walking with Emperors for forty years and was no longer impressed by their company—never had been, in fact.

Charles was Mingus's third Emperor, and probably his last, although even that was far from certain, given the casualty rate in that office. His first had been Darius

IV, bumbling and benign, who had somehow managed to die of old age in spite of his occupational hazards. Dour, dark-visaged Gregory III had come next, his brief reign cut short by a botched coup known as the Fifth of October Plot, which had swept the Emperor and the next five in line to the throne from the board, leaving the callow and untested Charles to carry on in their place.

It was far too early to judge Charles in any historical sense; it was entirely possible that he might yet wind up with "Great" affixed to his name. Possible—but in Mingus's view, unlikely. Still, Charles's flaws—self-absorption, self-indulgence, and outright selfishness—were the flaws of youth. If he lived long enough, he might outgrow them. But the early signs were not encouraging and Mingus didn't much care for the young Emperor. He had a streak of meanness in him, more appropriate to a small-town bully than the leader of an Empire encompassing a sphere of space two thousand light-years in diameter, with 2645 planets populated by three trillion sentient beings. And Charles had surrounded himself with a retinue of truly detestable young chums, who lent the Household a pungent and unmistakable air of decadence.

On the other hand, Charles was intelligent, reasonably industrious when motivated, and had an excellent grasp of the complexities and realities of his realm. What he needed was guidance—which Mingus was prepared to offer but which Charles was just as prepared to reject. Mingus knew that Charles resented him, just as every Emperor resented every Dexta Secretary, but at least Darius and Gregory had been willing to listen. And today, of all days, Charles needed to listen to what Mingus had to say; the very future of the Empire might depend upon it.

THEY SAT OPPOSITE EACH OTHER IN COMFORT-able chairs, surrounded by a profusion of elegant tapestries and opulent bric-a-brac, which they ignored as completely as they ignored the tea that had been brought by silent and quickly vanishing servants.

"As you know, Norman," the Emperor began, "I asked you here today to discuss the situation on Sylvania. We had expected to commence large-scale mining operations there at least six months ago. In that expectation, we have been disappointed. We would appreciate an explanation."

When Charles said "we," it was not necessarily the Imperial We. In this case, Mingus knew, the use of the plural pronoun referred to Charles and his coterie of intimates from the Big Twelve corporates, who were drawn to him like iron filings to a lodestone. Or like flies to shit, Mingus thought. It was an unworthy thought—but in this case, entirely apt.

"Highness," said Mingus, "it is a complicated problem."

"Of that, I have no doubt. I was hoping that you would uncomplicate it for me."

"Very well, then. In a nutshell, Sylvania—in a legal sense—is neither fish nor fowl. It is, at this moment, still an Unincorporated Imperial Territory. Normally, that would entitle you to make whatever deals you wish with the corporates and begin mining operations at your pleasure. However, the planet has been continuously inhabited by a population of over one thousand for nearly twenty years. Under the provisions of the *Imperial Code*, those residents have certain rights that date back to the Homestead Acts of 2697 and supercede the provisions of the *Code* which would otherwise apply here."

Charles nodded vaguely.

"However," Mingus continued, "because the population is still under five thousand registered voters, you have no legal authority to incorporate the territory and appoint an Imperial Governor, thus bringing it under the aegis of other provisions of the *Code*. Specifically, the Eminent Domain Statutes. Without Eminent Domain, large-scale mining operations of the sort you and the corporates envision would not be permissible unless you could somehow gain the consent of the entire resident population, as defined by the Homestead Acts."

"Which I'm not going to get," Charles acknowledged. "I understand all of that, Norman. What I don't understand is why, in spite of the economic boom that has begun on Sylvania, we don't yet have five thousand registered voters? I gather that people are flocking there as fast as they can. A rough count of the freighter traffic implies that there are already at least seven thousand people on that planet." Charles leaned forward and smiled unpleasantly. "So why hasn't Dexta been able to get them registered?"

Mingus pursed his lips for a moment. He didn't quite sigh.

"I confess, Highness," he said, "to a certain amount of embarrassment in that regard."

"Why is the Imperial Historian never around when I need him?" Charles wondered. "Certainly, this must be a historic first. Norman Mingus, embarrassed?" Charles gave a snort that might have been a genuine laugh, of sorts. Whatever his shortcomings, Charles did, at least, have a sense of humor.

Mingus shrugged. " 'Embarrassed' is the only word that applies, I suppose. The awkward and, yes, embarrassing truth, Highness, is that at the moment, the Department of Extraterrestrial Affairs has not a single representative on the planet of Sylvania. You see, sire, they keep quitting on us."

"Quitting?" Charles raised an eyebrow.

Mingus nodded. "We send people there, and before they've been there a month, they come down with what you might call gold fever. All around them, they see people striking it rich. Dexta staffers are as human as anyone else, and sooner or later—generally sooner in this case—cupidity trumps institutional loyalty. They stop shuffling papers and start digging for Fergusite. We can't chain them to their computer consoles, you know. Every Dexta staffer we've sent to Sylvania in the past year has resigned and headed up into the hills to make a fortune. And I gather that some of them have done just that, which only encourages the others to follow. I can't really blame them, I suppose. If I were a young man, I'd probably do the same thing."

Charles got to his feet abruptly, shuffling his sandals on the glistening tile floor. He walked around behind his chair, leaned against it, and peered at Mingus. "I have difficulty picturing that," he said, a bemused smile flickering across his handsome features. "You as a young man, I mean. Somehow, I always imagined that you were carved from a block of marble, fully formed."

Mingus returned the half smile. "I wasn't," he informed the Emperor. "I just feel that way. Complete with cracks."

"You know, that gives me an idea. I'm going to have the Imperial Sculptor do a bust of you, Norman. I'm going to put it right behind my desk in Rio. You'll be there forever, staring down at me and all my successors, like Poe's raven, croaking 'Nevermore' at us whenever we get a notion that you'd disapprove of. Keep us honest, I'd think."

"Forgive me, Highness, but that's what I'm trying to do now. The problem we have to deal with is not the Dexta staff on Sylvania or getting voters registered. The problem is the damn Fergusite itself—and you know that as well as I do, Charles."

Charles cocked an eyebrow at him. "Do I, Norman?"

"Well, dammit, you should," Mingus responded, raising his voice slightly.

"Whenever you call me 'Charles,'" the Emperor said, "I get worried. Don't try to get fatherly with me, Norman. I had a father once, and he was a scoundrel and an idiot. As for the Fergusite, it's not a problem. It's a once-in-a-lifetime opportunity!"

"Gold fever!" Mingus sniffed. "You've got it, too, I see."

"What if I have? Spirit's sake, Norman! A quadrillion

crowns' worth of Fergusite, and you want me to leave it in the ground?"

"That's where it belongs, Charles," Mingus said evenly. "For the sake of your Empire, leave it where it is."

FERGUSITE WAS THE STUFF THAT MADE THE Empire possible. First synthesized in the twenty-second century—atom by atom and at great expense—the precisely structured latticework of Fergusite focused the immense energy generated by fusion reactors inward upon itself, until the strain ruptured the very fabric of space-time and formed an eleven-dimension membrane of Yao space, which squirted through normal space at transluminal velocities and thus made the dream of interstellar travel a reality.

It was long believed that Fergusite could only be created artificially, but three years earlier, in 3214, the Imperial Geological Survey had stumbled upon a vast deposit of Fergusite on the small and neglected world of Sylvania, 542 light-years from Earth. Natural Fergusite could form only when the most precise combination of factors came into perfect alignment—mineral content, time, pressure, temperature, and gravitational force, all as delicately balanced and tuned as a symphony orchestra with a billion different instruments all playing the same music at the same instant. The Sylvanian deposit of Fergusite was nearly as pure as the artificial version that the Big Twelve corporates had been brewing in their factories for eleven centuries. With a minimum of processing, it could be used in the Ferguson Distortion Generators that rode on every starship—at a tenth of the price of the artificial Fergusite. The discovery would dramatically reduce the cost of interstellar travel, and might usher in a new Golden Age for the Empire.

But there was a problem . . .

• • •

"IT IS NOT A PROBLEM!" CHARLES INSISTED VEHE-mently. "It's a minor . . . *inconvenience*, nothing more."

"You call being crushed into a soup of subatomic particles an *inconvenience*?" Mingus demanded.

"There's no need to overdramatize it. Yes, a few more ships may—*may*—be lost. But what of it? Boats have always sunk, aircraft have always crashed, starships have always disappeared. It's just the price of doing business, and everyone accepts that. Except you, apparently."

"Using the Fergusite on Sylvania would raise that price significantly, Highness."

"It would do just the reverse! Dammit, Norman, just look at the figures my economists prepared. The Empire spends 30 trillion crowns on interstellar trade each year. Fergusite production represents nearly a third of that cost. Using the Sylvanian Fergusite, even allowing for processing costs, would save something like seven trillion crowns—a 23 percent reduction! Think of what that would mean. Reducing the cost of interstellar travel by nearly a quarter should lead to a 50 to 100 percent increase in the total volume of trade. How can you claim that would be bad for the Empire?"

"I have economists too, Highness," Mingus reminded him. "And they've factored in some things that your economists didn't bother to include. The loss of an additional ten to one hundred starships each year would cost—here, let me bring it up on my pad." Mingus reached into his pocket.

"Oh, don't bother," Charles told him. "I've seen those numbers. I just don't believe them."

"All right, then. But there's another factor that you cannot assign a number. The loss of confidence in the safety of interstellar travel would have devastating consequences for the entire Empire."

"Spare me, Norman. Do you really think anyone would care—or even notice? How many notice now, when we lose a ship? There are 3 trillion people in the Empire, and fewer than one-hundredth of 1 percent of them ever get anywhere *near* a starship. A few more losses—and it will be a lot closer to ten than a hundred, my people assure me—won't make a damn bit of difference."

"Except to the people who are on those ships," Mingus replied. "And their families. And the insurance carriers; rates will go up substantially, you know. Did your economists bother to mention that? Then there's the cost of replacing the losses and training new crews. But the *real* cost—"

"Is unknown! No one knows—not your economists and not mine. Why must you assume the worst?"

"Because of the consequences. Highness, if I am wrong, there are no consequences. The Empire simply goes on doing business as it has always done. But if *you* are wrong, the consequences could be catastrophic. If—"

"Nonsense."

"Dammit, Charles, just shut up and listen!"

No other person among the 3 trillion in the Empire could have told the Emperor to shut up. Even for Norman Mingus, it was a close call. Charles stared at him in suppressed rage for a moment, then crossed his arms, balanced his right ankle on his left knee, and sulkily sat back in his chair.

"All right, Norman," he said. "I'm listening. Make it good."

Mingus took a deep breath. "Highness," he said, "as you pointed out, it is impossible to determine with certainty the quality of those Fergusite deposits on Sylvania. The initial reports suggest that the level of impurities lies in a range between one and ten parts in a billion, but we have a very limited number of samples. And, as you know, we cannot test every piece of Fergusite that comes out of Sylvania because the very process of testing destroys the sample and makes it useless. So all we have to go on is a statistical procedure that, by its very nature, is suspect. The process we use to fabricate Fergusite is rigidly controlled, but nature is random and sloppy. One chunk of Fergusite might be perfectly pure, and another chunk right next to it might be dangerously impure. There is simply no way of knowing except by putting it to work in a distortion generator and hoping for the best."

Charles nodded. "Go on."

"Any impurity in the structure of the Fergusite can cause the bubble formed in the FDGs to become asymmetrical, resulting in the collapse of the bubble and the destruction of the ship. Even with the process we use now, impurities are believed to result in the loss of some ten to twenty ships each year. We can live with that. But could we tolerate the loss of one or two hundred?"

"It would be nowhere near that high," Charles protested. "Maybe another ten or twenty, worst-case."

Mingus stared at the Emperor. "You said you'd listen."

Charles retreated back into his chair.

"As you know," Mingus continued, "a trickle of Sylvanian Fergusite is already being sent off-world for processing and has reached the commercial market. And in the past year and a half, two starships known to have employed the Sylvania Fergusite have disappeared."

Charles gave a derisive snort. "I hope you're not going to try to tell me that *two* constitutes a statistically significant sample."

"No, but it does constitute a warning. What I recommend is that for the next five years, we restrict the use of Sylvania Fergusite to unmanned messengers and couriers. That *would* give us a significant sample. If the loss rate remains acceptable, we could then initiate large-scale mining operations and approve the Sylvanian crystals for general use. But it would be nothing less than foolhardy to open the floodgates now and inundate the market with unproven Fergusite of dubious reliability."

"Five years? Out of the question. I won't wait another five months, Norman."

Mingus ignored the interruption and continued. "Aside from the direct consequences," he said, "consider this. Of the Big Twelve, only seven actually manufacture Fergusite. Prizm takes 70 percent of the commerical market; the others make it mainly for their own use. Now, what happens if tons of Fergusite start flowing out of Sylvania? For one thing, Prizm would take a huge loss and be forced to shut down most of their Ferguisite facilities."

"That's their problem," Charles said. For hundreds of years, emperors had routinely pocketed vast sums in "contributions" collected from the Big Twelve. Charles pursued the practice with more diligence and enthusiasm than most of his predecessors, but his relations with Prizm were not especially close. What he lost from Prizm, he would more than make up with revenues from whichever corporate wound up with the Sylvania concession.

"It could become *everyone's* problem, Highness," Mingus pointed out. "What happens if, after Prizm shuts down its fabricating plants, we find that the level of impurities in the Sylvania deposits is simply too high to be sustained? The Empire would be crippled for years, perhaps decades. Without reliable interstellar travel, the Empire might very well break up. You couldn't even depend on the Navy to hold it together, because they'd have the same problems as everyone else."

"Purely hypothetical."

"Hypothetical or not, it is a consequence that cannot be ignored. And," Mingus added, "there's this. The confidence of the population in the reliability of interstellar travel would be ruinously, perhaps fatally, weakened. They would turn inward and rely upon their own resources, pursue their own goals. The very concept of the Empire would come into question. You want to run the Empire on the cheap, Charles—but if that's the kind of Empire you want, you may find yourself with no Empire left to run."

The Emperor nodded thoughtfully, then leaned forward again.

"Is that it, Norman? Anything else you care to say?"

"Not just now, Highness."

"Good," Charles said, a cold edge coming into his voice. "Now, *you* shut up and listen, Norman, and listen very carefully. In the first place, exploiting the Sylvanian deposits will not weaken the Empire, but strengthen it. Do you know what per capita interstellar trade amounts to? Barely ten kilograms per year. Ten kilograms! That's a pittance. It could—and should—be ten times that. The only reason it's not is because interstellar travel is so fucking expensive. We're going to change all of that, and the key to doing it is those Fergusite deposits on Sylvania. The geologists tell me there's enough to last at least a century. And that century—*my* century!—is going to see a historic increase in trade, prosperity, and Imperial strength. It's going to be a fucking Golden Age, Norman, and I am not about to let you stand in the way of it."

"I see," Mingus said.

"Just in case you don't, let me paint you a picture. You are going to get those five thousand people registered in the next three months. And about ten minutes after that, we are going to begin large-scale mining operations on Sylvania. If you try to drag your feet on this, or employ your usual bureaucratic bullshit to obstruct, delay, or impede this operation, I'll drag your ancient ass before Parliament and have it booted out of Dexta once and for all. There are plenty of MPs who would like nothing better than to have one clean shot at you, and by the Spirit, I'll make sure they have it. I'll go public with this and let the people of the Empire know that the only reason they can't have cheaper trade, lower taxes, and a chocolate fudge sundae with cherries on top for breakfast every morning is because of *you*, Norman Mingus. You understand me, Norman?"

Mingus locked eyes with the Emperor for a long moment, then nodded slowly. "I believe that I do, Your Majesty."

Charles's body, as tight as an old knot, abruptly relaxed. He sat back in his chair and offered a thin smile. "Now then, Norman, suppose you tell me how you intend to solve our mutual problem on Sylvania."

Mingus returned the smile. "I have a possible answer, Highness," he said. "But you won't like it."

"If it works, I promise you I'll love it."

"I doubt that, Charles," Mingus said. "I sincerely doubt it."

chapter 3

GLORIA VANDEEN, LEVEL X DEXTA BUREAUCRAT,
Director of Dexta's Office of Strategic Intervention, heroine of the recent Mynjhino Crisis, the most wildly popular
and glamorous woman in the Empire, and the twenty-
four-year-old ex-wife of the man who was now Emperor
Charles V, lay naked on the grass in Central Park and
gazed languidly upward at the fleecy white clouds drifting
through the sunny skies. Lying next to her, separated by a
now-empty picnic basket, was her assistant, Petra Nash,
equally naked but far less comfortable about it.

This was a Visitation Day, when devout Spiritists
throughout the Empire celebrated one of seven appearances by the Spirit, exactly eleven hundred years earlier.
Petra was not especially devout, and wasn't really sure
that she was a Spiritist at all, but was content to tag along
with her boss on this beautiful day. She told herself that
this wasn't really quite the same thing as being naked in
public, not when she was surrounded by thousands of
other celebrants who were wearing no more than she.
Still, the sight of all that bare flesh was a little unsettling.

When she thought about it at all, Petra supposed that she agreed with those who claimed that Spiritism was based on a clever and audacious fraud. Weary of centuries of religious warfare, a small band of twenty-second-century scientists and advertising copywriters had supposedly invented the Spirit and her gospel as an antidote and alternative to the bloodthirsty deities worshipped by most of the existing religions. The beautiful, ethereal, and nude Spirit, forty feet tall, who had announced herself to the world in seven spectacular Visitations, was really, the cynics claimed, just a holographic projection, and her Seven Seeds of Wisdom no more than a collection of slick catchphrases and slogans. Whatever the truth of the matter, Spiritism had swept the world, ushered in an age of global harmony, and put an end to religious warfare. Currently, 70 percent of the Empire's population considered themselves to be Spiritists.

Part of Spiritism's appeal lay in the fact that it was a gentle and even sensual religion, which found neither sex nor the human body to be shameful. Thus, for more than a thousand years on Visitation Days—weather permitting—devout Spiritists had assembled here and elsewhere throughout the Empire for a frankly carnal celebration of their faith. Not ten meters away from her, Petra saw a couple enthusiastically demonstrating their devotion. Hundreds more were doing the same all around the Park.

Well, Petra thought, at least it's not as ridiculous as some religions, like the ones that insisted a woman's body should be covered from head to toe, or which engaged in festivals of public self-flagellation. She believed that all religions were pretty silly, one way or another, but at least Spiritists didn't go around slaughtering infidels and imposing their beliefs on others.

She glanced again at the copulating couples surrounding her, then turned back to her boss. "So," she said, "we've got a mission, huh?"

"Yup," Gloria replied. "The Office of Strategic Intervention is officially open for business."

"And we're going to Sylvania for . . . a voter registration drive?" Petra found that a little difficult to believe, and perhaps a bit disappointing.

Gloria turned and grinned at her diminutive assistant. "What's the matter, Petra? Not glamorous enough for you?"

"Well," Petra said, "it just sounds sort of, you know . . . routine. It's not quite what I expected the OSI to be doing. But at least it should be easier than Mynjhino."

Just four months earlier, Gloria and Petra had made their triumphant return from the planet Mynjhino. Gloria was then a Level XIII Coordinating Supervisor for Mynjhino's jurisdiction, and Petra her Level XV assistant. What had first seemed to be a nativist uprising among one of the two intelligent species on the planet had turned out to be something far more complex and deadly. But Gloria, using her wits and wiles, had averted a tragedy and emerged from the affair as the heroic darling of the media and nothing less than the Sweetheart of the Empire. The fact that she was the Emperor's ex-wife and probably the most beautiful, sexy, and desirable woman in the Empire only added more luster to what had been, by any standard, a courageous and noble performance.

Upon their return to Dexta Headquarters in Manhattan, Norman Mingus had promptly promoted Gloria to Level X (and Petra to Level XIII, Spirit be praised!) and appointed her to run the newly created Office of Strategic Intervention. Mingus had realized that Gloria was a unique asset for Dexta—even though she had managed to embarrass, outwit, and thoroughly annoy her ex-husband during the Mynjhino Crisis—and he sought to employ her to maximum advantage. So he created the OSI, intending to use Gloria as his chessboard queen, dispatching her to hot spots throughout the Empire where the existing bureaucratic machinery of Dexta was inadequate to deal with the situation.

But four months had gone by without a single call for Gloria and the OSI. They had kept busy for a while simply setting up the office, recruiting staffers, and generally getting things up and running. Once all that had been accomplished, there had been little for them to do, so Petra was glad that they were finally getting an assignment. Still, a voter registration drive was not exactly the sort of role she had envisioned for OSI.

"It won't be as easy as it sounds," Gloria told her. "It's a complex situation, and there's a lot more involved than just signing up a bunch of boomrats. Mingus gave me the basics on the comm, but I'm going to meet with him this afternoon to get the full story. It seems that Charles is very eager to get those voters enrolled."

"Aha!" cried Petra. "And how did he react when Mingus told him he was sending you?"

Gloria laughed and sat up. "Well, according to Mingus, Charles didn't quite have a stroke. But I gather that he was not a happy Emperor. Still, he didn't really have a choice. Voter registration is Dexta's business, and not even Charles can tell Mingus how to run his shop. Anyway, at least we'll be on the same side as Charles, so we shouldn't have to put up with any of his Imperial bullshit this trip."

"I just love it when you say nasty things about the Emperor." Petra giggled. "It makes me feel like I'm in on some subversive conspiracy."

"Charles thinks *I'm* a subversive conspiracy, all by myself. The thought of me getting involved in this Sylvania business will probably give him hives."

"Well, it serves him right," Petra declared. "After all the problems he made for you on Mynjhino."

"It went both ways, you know," Gloria admitted. "I publicly embarrassed him and made the whole thing a personal battle between the two of us. I probably shouldn't have done that, but what's done is done. I'll just be happy if we can handle this Sylvania thing without another public pissing match with Charles. I mean, he *is* the Emperor, after all, and we're just Dexta drones."

Petra looked at her gorgeous, naked boss and sniffed. "Some drone!"

Gloria was the product of DNA from six different continents, plus some refinements added by twenty-ninth-century genetic sculptors. She was of medium height, but seemed taller thanks to her long, silken legs and slim, athletic waist. Her breasts were not large, but firm, globular, and tipped by dark, jutting nipples that seemed perpetually erect. Blond above and below, her skin was a rich cocoa color, like a Euro with a great suntan or a Polynesian who had been under the weather. Her eyes, as intensely blue as polished turquoise, were set at a slightly exotic angle suggestive of Asia; her broad cheekbones tapered down to a narrow, delicate chin, and her nose was short and straight. She escaped perfection only in her somewhat thin lips, which looked, perhaps, a little too determined, but curved slightly upward at the sides, suggesting a permanent bemused smile.

Having been raised in and around the slightly overripe Court of Darius IV, she had no inhibitions about displaying her charms, and famously failed to restrict her nudity to Visitation Days. She had confided to Petra during their Mynjhino adventure that she carried specially crafted genes that endowed her with an enlarged pleasure center in her brain and enhanced nerve structures that made her nipples and navel much more erotically sensitive than those of any normal woman. She had also hinted that she possessed some additional nerves and musculature— inside and out—that made sex a thoroughly spectacular and satisfying experience for both her and her partners. If the sexual fires within Gloria burned hotter and brighter than for most people, it was hardly a wonder. "I'm not a slave to it," Gloria had told her. "I can control it—most of the time, anyway—but sometimes . . ." Gloria had trailed off with a smug, contented smile, leaving Petra to wonder about those "sometimes."

Petra, who had a "cute little body," according to interested observers, and a face that was pretty bordering on plain, couldn't help feeling jealous of her boss at times. In fact, the general resentment of "enhanced humans" had put an end to the twenty-ninth-century fad of genetic sculpting—publicly, at least—and prevented a dangerous cleavage of the human race. Still, it was commonly supposed that a favored few—including, it was said, the Emperor himself—possessed certain genetic advantages that were not available to the common run of humanity.

But Gloria couldn't help being a genetically superior, beautiful, privileged, rich girl, any more than Petra could help being the product of a broken, impoverished home in nearby Weehawken. What mattered was what they had done with their lives. Gloria had joined Dexta after her divorce from Charles because she didn't want to be just another useless rich person; Petra had joined, after twice failing the qualifying exams, because she aspired to be more than just a cute little nobody from New Jersey. All things considered, she thought, they had both done pretty well so far.

Merely surviving their first year in Dexta had been a major challenge for both of them. Dexta, by design, was a Darwinian jungle where only the strong survived and the weak were ruthlessly weeded out. Every form of physical, psychological, social, emotional, and sexual abuse was fair game for the new Fifteens, and fully 20 percent of them never made it past their first year. Gloria had survived only by becoming a Tiger, and Petra by becoming a Dog.

Over the centuries, a metaphorical but very real menagerie of distinct species had evolved within Dexta. They were known as Lions, Tigers, Dogs, Moles, and Sheep. The numerous Sheep formed the backbone of the bureaucracy, and found safety only in numbers and anonymity. Moles were bureaucratic infighters who tunneled under the surface and emerged at opportune times and places to trip up the unwary and establish their own niche.

The Dogs came in two breeds, Pack Dogs and Lap Dogs. The Pack Dogs—often frustrated Sheep or failed big cats—were bureaucratic street gangs who roamed Dexta's lower levels and savaged the weak and unprotected. Lap Dogs were Sheep who had attached themselves to a superior and gained a measure of security from the roving packs.

Lions, mostly male, were the natural leaders, fierce and determined. They sometimes formed prides for mutual support, but often hunted alone, surviving through their strength, ability, and sheer force of personality. Tigers, mostly female, were sleek and beautiful, and prowled the Dexta jungle using sex the way Lions used strength. Both Lions and Tigers could rise high or fatally fall in the high-pressure environment of Dexta.

Petra knew that Gloria had endured an especially harrowing first year, because as the ex-wife of an Imperial— although Charles was not then the Emperor and seemed unlikely ever to be—Mingus had made her a special target for the savagery inherent in Dexta's lower levels. He didn't want Imperial dilettantes polluting his organization, and had let the right people know that he wanted this VanDeen person to receive the full Dexta Treatment, in the expectation that she would soon retreat to her life of privilege and luxury rather than face the fires of Dexta's lower levels.

Instead, Gloria had survived and flourished, thanks to the tutelage of Viveca Kwan, a successful Tiger who had advised her to become predator rather than prey. Using her stunning beauty and sexual prowess to full advantage, she had escaped the hellish attentions of the Pack Dogs and ascended the Dexta ladder swiftly. Gloria learned, as well, what some Tigers never understood— that sex was only the lubricant, not the machine. What truly mattered was how well she performed her job, and that she did with skill and, as on Mynjhino, courage and brilliance.

Petra had also begun as a much-abused Sheep, and might have succumbed to the fury of the roving packs, but found protection by becoming Gloria's assistant. As Gloria's Lap Dog, she gained a degree of security and the patronage of a powerful superior. Their shared perils on Mynjhino had cemented their relationship, and now Petra was not merely Gloria's assistant, but her best friend.

Being so close to a woman like Gloria was not always easy. Petra often felt invisible in her company, and Gloria's wealth, glamour, and stunning sexual presence could be more than a little intimidating. Petra was, in many ways, just a kid from Weehawken, and was still a little unnerved by the high-powered and sophisticated world she had come to inhabit.

As if she had read her thoughts—and Petra wasn't convinced that she couldn't—Gloria turned to Petra and said, "Why don't you go for a stroll and find yourself a guy? A little grope in the grass might be good for you. You haven't had anyone since Mynjhino, have you?"

"Well, I've been kind of busy . . ."

"So have I, but you don't see me letting that stop me, do you?"

That was certainly true. Before Mynjhino, Gloria had been downright reserved in her sexual activities. But since their adventure, she had been the highly public companion of famous men from every walk of life: actors, athletes, scholars, politicians, writers, artists, even a Spiritist bishop. Petra, like the rest of the Empire, had watched in fascination, envy, and admiration.

"I don't know, Gloria," Petra said. "I'm not quite as much of a free spirit as you are."

"C'mon," Gloria coaxed. "It's a Visitation Day, for Spirit's sake! And your mom is in Weehawken and will never know a thing."

Petra grimaced. That was a sensitive point with her.

In the glare of the media spotlight that had been focused on Gloria, Petra had enjoyed some brief fame of her own, centered around her intense but tragic affair with a young Dexta staffer on Mynjhino who had been killed during the troubles there. She had gone along with the media show up to a point, but when she returned home, she found that her mother was shocked and disappointed by her daughter's behavior.

Of course, her mother was shocked and disappointed by practically everything. She made it clear to Petra that she did not approve of her association with a person like Gloria VanDeen—although her opinion was mollified somewhat by an invitation to a lavish dinner party at Gloria's new Manhattan penthouse. In her mother's view, the Emperor—any Emperor—could do no wrong, and Gloria's public altercation with him was shameful and unworthy. And, for that matter, Gloria's sexual charisma was a little much for a woman who basically disapproved of sex and, more to the point, men. Mrs. Nash—Mr. Nash had fled twenty years before, when Petra was six, and had not been seen since—was not exactly a Spiritist, or much of anything else, exactly. She had sampled various religions over the years, but found them all disappointing, as she found virtually everything else in her life to be—including her daughter.

Gloria noticed the frown on Petra's face and said, "Hey, Petra, repeat after me. 'I am a grown-up. I can do whatever I want.'"

Petra smiled and said, "I am a grown-up, and Gloria can do whatever she wants."

Gloria returned the smile. "So can you, kiddo. Look, *my* parents didn't exactly do handsprings when they found out that their darling daughter wanted to be a Dexta bureaucrat. They thought I should have gone on being a rich parasite, the same as them. But I think they've accepted it now. After Mynjhino, they didn't have much choice."

"We keep saying that, don't we? After Mynjhino, before Mynjhino. I guess that really changed our lives."

"If it hadn't," said Gloria, "there would be something seriously wrong with both of us. Spirit, Petra, you lost a man you loved and I was nearly killed more times than I can count. Things like that are *supposed* to change you. When I got back here, I realized that I could never go back to being what I was before—and that I didn't want to. Why should you?"

"I see what you mean. I suppose I've changed too, but that doesn't mean I stopped being Petra Nash. I know you think I should be more of a Tiger and less of a mutt, and I'm not exactly against that, but I don't think I could ever, well . . . just go wild, the way you have."

Gloria pursed her lips. "You think I've gone wild?"

"Well, maybe not wild, exactly, but you sure have turned yourself into—I don't know—something between a sensation and a scandal. I mean, the orgy in that nightclub last month? You were all over the vids, Gloria."

Gloria grinned at the memory. "Okay," she said, "maybe that was a little over the edge, but dammit, I don't regret a single thing I've done since Mynjhino. When Mingus asked me to run his Office of Strategic Intervention, I realized that what almost happened to me on Mynjhino could actually happen at any time. If I'm going to go hopping all over the Empire putting out brush fires for Mingus, sooner or later I'm going to get seriously burned. Incinerated, maybe."

Petra involuntarily shivered and clasped her arms around herself. "Don't even say that, Gloria! I hate it when you get fatalistic."

"Sorry, but you know it's the truth, Petra. I don't know how long I have, but however long it is, I want people to remember that I was here. I want them to say, 'That Gloria VanDeen was quite a gal, wasn't she?' "

"She still is," Petra offered. "And I'd prefer to keep it in the present tense, if you don't mind."

Gloria reached for Petra, took her hand, and

squeezed it. "Make you a deal," she said. "I'll concentrate on staying alive if you'll try to let yourself live a little more. *Dum vivimus, vivamus*—which I think is Latin for, 'Let the good times roll!' "

"I think they're about to start rolling for you right now," Petra said. She nodded toward a young man who was approaching them. She recognized him as one of Gloria's many ardent companions—an athlete, she thought. It was already becoming apparent that he was glad to see her.

"Johnny!" Gloria cried out. "Over here!"

"Well," said Petra, collecting her clothing, "I think it's time for me to get back to the office."

"Hey, stick around. Maybe you'll pick up some pointers."

Petra considered it for a moment, but decided that she didn't really want to watch Gloria making love in the middle of Central Park.

"No," she said, "I wouldn't want to inhibit you."

Gloria shrugged. "Okay, have it your way. And would you tell the staff that I want to meet with everyone as soon as I get back from my meeting with Mingus?"

"Will do," Petra said after she had pulled her dress over her head. "Have fun."

Petra resolutely marched off, threading her way through the writhing bodies in the Park. Almost against her will, she stopped and looked back at her boss. Gloria and her friend had wasted no time. She watched for a moment as the muscular young athlete thrust himself into the golden body of Gloria VanDeen, and Gloria arched her back in primal ecstasy.

Petra forced herself to turn away, but not before Gloria spotted her and gave her a cheerful wave in the midst of her erotic endeavors. Petra shook her head and mumbled to herself as she walked on.

What would Mom say? she wondered.

chapter 4

GLORIA RETURNED FROM HER MEETING WITH
Mingus, feeling the weight of the Empire on her shoulders. She walked through the outer office, noting that Petra was away from her desk. Entering her own office, she closed the door behind her and plopped down into the chair and ran her hands through her long, Dura-styled mane, then leaned back and closed her eyes.

Spirit! How could Mingus ask such a thing of her?

In the months since her return from Mynjhino, Gloria had grown enormously fond of Norman Mingus. And she knew that Mingus was more than a little smitten with her. Despite his great age, antigerontological drugs had preserved his patrician good looks and he had the vigor of a man half his age. He had been married five different times, so he was a man who appreciated women. Yet their relationship had remained chaste and proper, more by his choice than hers; Gloria knew that Mingus didn't want to risk compromising her position in Dexta by having an affair with her.

Sleeping one's way upward within Dexta was an accepted practice for both males and females; it was simply part of the ruthless games that were played in the sprawling bureaucracy. But Gloria's status was already unique because she had once been married to the Emperor. That made her suspect; using Imperial influence to get ahead would not be tolerated by those who had no such advantage, and would have made her a special target for the take-no-prisoners tactics often employed by Dexta staffers. Her public contretemps with Charles had been sparked, in no small measure, by Gloria's desire to assert her independence and make it clear to one and all that her Imperial connection meant nothing to her.

On the other hand, sleeping with Norman Mingus, while a purely intramural matter, would not have endeared her to her fellow bureaucrats. Dexta's culture, although brutal and unforgiving, was also highly sensitive to appearances and propriety, as defined by the expectations of the Dexta masses. Gloria could have a highly public sex life, sleep with her fellow staffers if she chose to (which, for the most part, she didn't), or prowl the corridors of Headquarters in a state of near nudity (which, for the most part, she did), all without offending against Dexta's odd sense of decorum. But having an affair with Norman Mingus, the one and only Level I, might very well put her on the wrong side of some invisible line that separated the acceptable from the unacceptable. At least, Mingus feared that it might, and chose not to take that risk. Gloria respected his wishes, but regretted the necessity.

But now, Mingus was asking her to do something that was infinitely more dangerous and discreditable. His argument was compelling, his logic unassailable, and the need absolute. Gloria overcame her shock and, in the end, agreed to do what he had asked of her. Still, she had left his office with a feeling of bleak dread in the pit of her stomach and a sense of foreboding and outright fear.

As she sat next to him on the sofa in his immense office, Mingus had explained what he wanted of her, and why. Low-grade Fergusite from Sylvania, according to Mingus, would threaten the stability—and the very existence—of the Empire. Her mission would be to prevent the large-scale exploitation of that Fergusite and, if necessary, to destroy it.

Charles, in his usual greedy and shortsighted fashion, was determined to reap the profits he believed would flow from the Sylvania Fergusite. To that end, he had instructed Mingus to register five thousand voters on that distant backwater world—as quickly as possible—so that he could appoint an Imperial Governor, invoke Eminent Domain powers, and strike a deal with the corporates to begin mining operations on a massive scale. Gloria's job—ostensibly—would be to do as Charles desired and get those voters registered.

Her *real* job, Mingus informed her, would be to prevent a quadrillion crown's worth of Fergusite from reaching market. There were two possible ways in which she might accomplish this rather remarkable feat. First, she could somehow prevent a vote on Eminent Domain from reaching the required 60 percent approval, thus precluding the corporates from evicting the boomrat prospectors from their claims and beginning large-scale strip-mining operations. In this effort, she could expect help from at least one of the Big Twelve; Prizm, which stood to be the big loser if Sylvanian Fergusite flooded the market, was sending a representative to Sylvania who would work with her to assure the failure of the Eminent Domain vote.

But even if Eminent Domain passed, there was still a second way to prevent the suspect Fergusite from reaching the distortion generators of the Empire's starships. It was theoretically possible, Mingus assured her, to destroy the entire Fergusite deposit before it ever left the ground. Gloria blinked a couple of times when she heard that, but said nothing.

"You'll meet with the Sector Imperial Geologist, Stuart Eckstein, before you reach Sylvania," Mingus told her. "I've met with him already, and he described a method by which it might be possible to sabotage virtually all of the Fergusite on Sylvania and render it useless. It won't be easy, but Eckstein believes that it can be done. He'll fill you in on the details when you meet him. Naturally, it would be preferable to avoid that necessity, but if the corporates get their Eminent Domain petition approved, we'll have no choice in the matter. One way or the other, we *must* prevent the large-scale exploitation of that Fergusite."

Mingus had given her a hard, no-nonsense stare when he said that, impressing her with the depth of his commitment. Gloria understood that her own commitment would have to be just as fierce as his. Far too much was at stake for half measures and playing it safe. Whatever the risks, Gloria must find a way to succeed in her mission.

Worst of all, she could tell no one—not even Petra— the true nature of their mission to Sylvania. She would have to tell a lot of lies, or half-truths, to her OSI staff, which didn't strike her as the best possible way to begin their bureaucratic life together in Dexta. OSI's very existence was an anomaly, and a potential threat to some people in the organization. If there was a need for a Strategic Intervention, that could only mean that the existing Dexta structures had failed in some important way. Well, that was certainly the case on Sylvania.

Petra opened the door and stuck her head inside Gloria's office. "Good, you're back," she said. "How did it go with Mingus?"

Gloria gave a weary shrug. "It went."

"Everyone's in the conference room waiting for you."

"Good. I'll be along in a couple of minutes."

Petra nodded, started to leave, then paused and looked carefully at Gloria. "Is everything okay?" she asked. "You look kind of upset."

"Oh," Gloria replied, "I'm just collecting my thoughts."

"Hmm," said a skeptical Petra, who knew Gloria's moods well by this point. "Is there a problem?"

Gloria shook her head. "No problem. See you in a few minutes."

Petra nodded, then disappeared, closing the door behind her.

The first lies, Gloria thought. They sure as hell won't be the last.

No problem? Well, not really, Gloria supposed. Treason wasn't a problem—it was a capital crime.

GLORIA ENTERED THE CONFERENCE ROOM AND heads snapped to attention, not simply because she was the boss. She was wearing a nearly transparent white blouse, wide open to the waist, and a black miniskirt that provided an absolute minimum of coverage in front, and somewhat less than that in back. She took her seat at the head of the table and smiled at her troops. They smiled back.

They were a good group. There were fifteen of them, counting Gloria. She had recruited a number of her fellow staffers from her pre-Mynjhino post in Sector 8, along with a smattering of people she had known or heard good things about. There were a few Lions, several Tigers or Tigers-in-the-making, and some solid, dependable Sheep. She had avoided bringing in any Moles, although you could never be sure about some of the Sheep. And Petra was her loyal Lap Dog. She hoped they would work well together, but their first assignment was likely to be a disappointment for most of them.

"As you've probably heard by now," Gloria began, "the Office of Strategic Intervention has officially received its first assignment. There is Imperial interest in this matter, so I want us to look sharp, especially since this is our first mission. Basically, our job will be to register voters on Sylvania, although there's a lot more than that involved. I'll give you the details in a moment, but first, I've asked

Grant to give you a backgrounder on Sylvania." She nodded toward Grant Enright, her second-in-command, at the opposite end of the long table.

Grant Enright, a handsome, capable Lion, enjoyed the distinction of being one of the few human males who had ever said no to Gloria. When he was her superior in Sector 8, she had made a run at him and was shocked when he turned her down. He was a rarity in Dexta, a happily married man; Dexta actively discouraged marriage in its lower-level personnel. Moreover, Enright didn't engage in the sexual stratagems so often employed by Dexta staffers on the make, believing them to be a distraction and, not infrequently, self-defeating. So he had resisted Gloria's advances and become her friend instead of her lover. When she was offered the OSI job, she recruited him to become her Office Administrator and had him bumped up a peg to Level X.

"Dina has it," said Enright, turning to his Deputy Administrator.

Dina Westerbrook cleared her throat and glanced at a sheaf of papers before she began speaking. She was a willowy blonde in her early fifties, which meant that she looked no more than about thirty. She was beautiful, but had a withdrawn, haunted air about her. Before Gloria picked her for OSI and promoted her to a Twelve, she had been a Level XIII for more than twenty years, with no hope of advancement. Dina was a Tiger who had made one big mistake early in her career, and had been paying for it ever since. Gloria didn't know the details, but presumed that Dina had slept with the wrong man, or men, or had used her sexual appeal and prowess for the wrong ends. That was the danger of being a Tiger in Dexta; sex could cover up a multitude of sins, but it could also be responsible for creating them. The wonder was that Dina had stayed at Dexta instead of just leaving in quiet disgrace. But she was experienced and dependable, so Gloria had rescued her, realizing that someday she might find herself in the same position.

"Sylvania," Dina began, "is an Unincorporated Imperial Territory in Quadrant 3, Sector 15, 542 light-years from Earth. Its current population is estimated to be about seven thousand, although we don't have precise figures yet. There are no indigenous intelligent species, but it has a very well developed ecosystem, classified as a Group One-C.

"It was first settled by humans about twenty years ago. Until the end of the war with the Ch'gnth Confederacy, forty-three years ago, it was in disputed territory. Humans couldn't get near it, and the Ch'gnth ignored it because the climate is cooler than they prefer. Following the war, the first settlement was established by a private group from Palmyra, which is the nearest Empire world, about thirty light-years away. That group, which consisted of a few wealthy business leaders, built what they called the Lodge on the southern coast of the planet's only major continent. They used it as an exclusive vacation retreat and brought in a number of workers to serve as staff. They, in turn, built the only real town on the planet, called Greenlodge, a few miles from the Lodge itself. Over the years, the permanent population gradually rose above a thousand. It stayed there until three years ago, when the first naturally occurring deposit of Fergusite was discovered. Since then, there has been an influx of people seeking to strike it rich, which quite a few apparently have. Along with the miners, there is the usual mixture of speculators, merchants, prostitutes, and assorted hustlers. In short, a typical boomworld."

"I hear it's an incredibly beautiful planet," put in Patrick Gilhooley, the OSI Coordinator for Agriculture.

Dina nodded. "That's what attracted the group from Palmyra in the first place. The only continent is about the size of Australia, situated in the northern hemisphere. Sylvania's sun is a yellow dwarf that doesn't put out much heat, so only the southern part of the continent is readily habitable. Along the southern coastal plain, the climate is generally Mediterranean, with rainy and dry seasons. A high mountain range rises just inland from the coast, with dense forests in valleys that have a temperate rain forest climate. Beyond the mountains, there's a broad savanna stretching northward to a tundra region and more mountains, but the entire human population is restricted to the southern coastal plain and the nearby mountains—which is where the Fergusite is."

"I don't understand why the population is still so low," said Kristen Kim, the Currency Coordinator. "You'd think it would have soared by now."

"The main reason," Dina answered, "is that it's not easy to get to Sylvania. There's still no Orbital Station, although one is now under construction. That means that you have to get to Sylvania via Palmyra, since it's impossible for a starship to refuel or perform routine maintenance at Sylvania. And the Palmyrans have mixed emotions about the whole Sylvania boom. Their wealthiest leaders, who established the Lodge, are reluctant to see their vacation retreat turned into a mining camp, and so they have done what they could to slow and control the traffic through Palmyra. Specifically, they imposed a whopping big 'transit tax' on anyone using the Palmyra Orbital Station as a way station to Sylvania. Also, they hope to control whatever development does take place on Sylvania, so they have limited the freighter and passenger traffic from Palmyra and given preference to their own people who want to go there. And finally, the likelihood—inevitability, really—of the Big Twelve taking over the whole shooting match on Sylvania has tended to discourage any significant migration. Mostly, it's just individuals who have managed to scrape together enough crowns to make the trip in the hope of making a killing."

"Thank you, Dina," said Gloria. "Anything else?"

Dina smiled. "Just that I'm looking forward to seeing Sylvania," she said. "When do we go?"

"Uh . . . *we* don't." Gloria offered a lame smile that failed to soften the frowns that appeared around the conference table. Her team was willing and eager to go, and it hurt her to have to disappoint them on this, their first job together.

"Here's the situation, folks," Gloria told them. "At the moment, there is not a single Dexta representative on the planet of Sylvania. More than a dozen have been sent there in the past year, but every one of them quit to go off into the hills to mine Fergusite and get rich. And as much as I respect you all and trust your loyalty, I don't intend to subject you to the same temptation. Mingus feels the same way about it. So we're going to try something different."

"Hmmpf," snorted Arkady Volkonski, the Coordinator for Internal Security. "You want to make this the Office of Strategic Impoverishment, I see."

"Arkady, dear," cooed Althea Dante, the Imperial Coordinator, "you would never let yourself get your hands dirty, digging up old rocks. Nor, I hasten to add, would I. And I, for one, am relieved that Gloria does not intend to dispatch us to some dreary backwater on the far side of nowhere."

"Not so fast, Althea." Gloria gave her a malicious grin.

Althea had been a Level XIII, along with Gloria, in Sector 8. A glamorous and notorious Tiger in her midthirties, she had been stalled at Level XIII for years, despite her intimate knowledge of affairs in the Imperial Household. Althea's sexual maneuvers had become an end in themselves, and although she had proven herself useful to Dexta on many occasions, her overall performance had been considered by her superiors to be too self-serving. She and Gloria had enjoyed a bitchy rivalry back in Sector 8, but when advancement to OSI came, Gloria took pity on Althea and brought her along, with a promotion to Level XII.

Althea's mouth opened in shock and unspoken protest, but she reined herself in and sank back into her chair in wary apprehension of what was to come next.

"Here's what we're going to do," Gloria continued. "Basically, we'll fight fire with fire. We're going to recruit a team for Sylvania composed entirely of Dexta staffers who are already independently wealthy. Presumably, that will make them immune to the lure of the Fergusite. At least, that's what we're counting on. And to ride herd on our crew of rich recruits, of course we'll need someone who is familiar with the whims and ways of the wealthy. Someone who has spent her entire professional career in the company of people who think they hold the mortgage on the universe. Someone who—"

"Oh, Gloria, darling!" Althea moaned. "You can't!"

"Sure I can. You're it, Althea."

"Spirit!" Althea buried her face in her hands. Gloria grinned to see her old rival in such a state of chagrin. It would do her good, Gloria told herself.

"In the meantime," she said, turning back to the rest of her team, "I want each of you to search the personnel files in your area and come up with a list of likely candidates. The richer, the better. We'll recruit them, draft them, or kidnap them, if we have to, but I want a full squad of big-bucks bureaucrats assembled in the next three days. Okay, hop to it, people!"

THREE DAYS LATER, GLORIA, ALONG WITH PETRA and Althea, met with her new recruits in a small lounge area that was part of the OSI office complex. The eight wealthy bureaucrats were scattered among three couches, warily eyeing their new boss with a mixture of anticipation and dread.

Gloria stood before them, wearing a thin, tight, smart-fabric dress that featured a deep scoop neckline and diagonal stripes that cycled through every color in the spectrum, including clear. Since she wore nothing under it, the random motions of the clear stripe would have been the object of intense interest had her audience not had other matters on their minds.

Althea, a small, delicately beautiful woman with alabaster skin, long dark hair, and lively violet eyes, was wearing a sort of working-girl-in-a-harem outfit that left her breasts and belly mostly bare. Gloria was pleased to see that Petra, trying to be more of a Tiger, was in a shorter-than-usual Dexta-gray skirt and a gray shirt that she had left unbuttoned far enough to reveal the subtle undercurve of her pert breasts. Since there were rich men present, it was unlikely that even her mother would have disapproved.

"I'd like to welcome all of you to your temporary assignment with the Office of Strategic Intervention," Gloria began. "I know this was sudden and surprising, but I hope you'll accept the necessity for this move."

"I accept no such thing," declared a short, vaguely pear-shaped man named Barton Gates, who was the fourth son of a branch of an old and fabulously wealthy family. He rose to his feet and took a step toward Gloria. "I have been content in my present position in Sector 12 Administration for twenty-three years, Ms. VanDeen, and the only reason I am here at all is because it was made very clear to me that my future at Dexta depended upon my cooperation with this . . . this attempt to shanghai me. Nevertheless, I protest in the strongest possible terms."

Gloria nodded placidly. "Very well, Mr. Gates," she told him. "I accept your protest. You can return to Sector 12 Admin now, with my blessing. And I'll be sure to mention your protest to your superiors. Good-bye, Mr. Gates. Have a nice day."

Gates stared at her for a moment in shocked confusion. "But—"

"Good-bye, Mr. Gates," Gloria repeated, and nodded toward the door. Gates looked around for a moment, as if there had been some mistake, realized there hadn't, then walked stiffly toward the door and out of it.

"Now, then," Gloria said, turning back to the remaining recruits, "does anyone else wish to register a protest?"

No one did.

"Your assignment, which should last no more than about three months, will be to establish and maintain a Dexta office on Sylvania. You'll tend to the usual administrative chores, but your main task will be to enroll as many voters as possible from among the population of boomers. The goal is to reach a total of five thousand, at which point the Emperor will be able to appoint an Imperial Governor. When that is accomplished, we should be able to sustain a permanent office there and bring all of you back to Manhattan."

"Sounds delightful," said Jillian Clymer, a busty, apple-cheeked blonde who had volunteered for the assignment.

"Sounds dismal," countered Sintra Garbedian, a Level XI Corporate Coordinator from the Quadrant 4 staff. He was a swarthy, superior-looking bastard son of the Earl of Samarkand, and a draftee. "However," he added, "three months is hardly a lifetime, and I am willing to go wherever Dexta needs me. I am at your service, Ms. VanDeen."

Gloria nodded to him. The clear stripe in her dress momentarily revealed her most intimate regions, as if rewarding Garbedian for his loyalty.

"I'm a little hazy on the local governmental structure," said Palmer Ellison, an ambitious young Level XV, the lowest-ranking member of the team. Another volunteer, he evidently saw this assignment as a road to rapid advancement, and a way to impress upon the Dexta higher-ups that he was more than just the son of the richest man on New Cambridge, a fabulously prosperous world in Quadrant 4. "According to our briefing there's a local mayor, but no formal government structure. Can you shed a little more light on that?"

"Not much, I'm afraid," Gloria told him. "In the absence of regular reports from a resident Dexta staff, we're somewhat in the dark about conditions in and around the town of Greenlodge. The local power structure is centered in the Lodge, controlled by wealthy interests from Palmyra, and it seems that the mayor of the town is their handpicked deputy. His name is Kevin Grunfeld, and the word on him is that he's something of a strongman and enforcer. Apparently the Lodge uses him to keep the locals in line, but the influx of boomers has complicated the situation. We'll know more when we get there."

"Can we expect the cooperation of this Grunfeld?" Ellison asked.

"Unknown," Gloria said. "I wish I could tell you more, but, as I said, we're very short on local intelligence. Are there any other questions?"

There were none. Three of the remaining four recruits—Wilmer DeGrasse, Randolph Alexander, and Pearl Shuzuki, all draftees—sat silently in glum resignation. The fourth, Raul Tellemacher, a smooth, handsome Level XII from Sector 8 Finance, wore a thin, predatory smile as he watched the clear stripe in Gloria's dress perambulate across her anatomy.

"All right, then," said Gloria. "You all know Althea Dante. Althea will head up your party and tend to your immediate needs."

"I know you're all looking forward to our little adventure just as much as I am," Althea said, offering a waspish grin to her charges. "I'll do everything I can to see to it that we make Gloria, the Office of Strategic Intervention, and Dexta itself exceedingly proud."

"I know you will, Althea," Gloria said graciously. "I'm sure you all will. Now, as to our immediate plans, Petra and I will leave for Palmyra on a Dexta Flyer tomorrow. The rest of you will depart via a Dexta Cruiser in a few days. Hopefully, Petra and I will be able to lay the groundwork so that you can get straight to work as soon as we all meet again on Sylvania. Thank you for coming, and I'll see you soon."

With that, they all got to their feet and obediently followed Althea from the room. "Come, children," she said on their way out, "we must see to our packing. I think we can probably dispense with cocktail gowns and tuxedos." Petra followed them out, leaving Gloria alone with Raul Tellemacher, who had lingered.

Tellemacher approached Gloria, who already knew him better than she might have wished. Back in Sector 8, Tellemacher, a member of a powerful Swiss banking family, had made a predictable and, in Gloria's view, highly obnoxious run at her. She found him arrogant and boorish and had emphatically turned him down, resulting in a festering animosity that had added some unneeded spice to their lives in Sector 8.

"Raul," she said to him, "I'm not any happier to see you here than you are to be here. But you fit the profile as well as anyone we could find, so you're going to Sylvania, like it or not."

"Not," Tellemacher replied. "Seems like a stupid and trivial assignment. Still, I suppose it will be a chance to get out of the office and stretch my legs." He hardly needed the opportunity. Tellemacher was a famed and talented Martian skier, and routinely spent his weekends on the slopes of Olympus Mons.

"I hear there's snow on the mountains on Sylvania," Gloria said. "Maybe you should take your skis."

"I had a different sort of exercise in mind," Tellemacher told her. He stepped close to her, grinned, and softly tweaked her left nipple with his right thumb.

Gloria removed his thumb, getting him in a Qatsima grip. Qatsima was a combination of martial arts, ballet, and acrobatics that had been developed centuries earlier on the planet of Songchai. Gloria religiously practiced the discipline, leaving her fit, trim, and safe from all but the most skilled and determined of assaults. She applied a little torque to the grip and Tellemacher winced for a moment before she released him.

"Same old Gloria, I see."

"Believe it."

"I thought you might have changed, from what I've been seeing in the vids. Or is it just that you prefer debasing yourself with all those idiot jocks and low-class fame mongers?"

"I certainly prefer it to debasing myself with high-class oafs. Let me make one thing clear, Raul. If you think this assignment means you'll get another shot at me, you are sadly mistaken."

"No such thing," Tellemacher assured her. "I go in service to Dexta and the Empire. My motives are every bit as pure as yours are, Gloria. See you on Sylvania." Tellemacher allowed himself another few seconds to enjoy the permutations of the stripes on her dress, then left with a cheerful grin plastered on his face.

Gloria watched him go and felt a sudden stab of doubt. What had he meant by that, she wondered?

He couldn't possibly know anything, she told herself. The business about her motives was just Tellemacher being his usual boorish self. And her own moment of doubt was just another flash of the paranoia this mission was nourishing within her.

Paranoia, she figured, was natural enough, under the circumstances. What treasonous conspirator wouldn't feel it?

chapter 5

THE SHUTTLE FROM PALMYRA ORBITAL STATION
landed at the planet's main airfield in the midst of a driving rainstorm. Gloria and Petra, wearing raincoats and
hats, hustled into the waiting limo skimmer without being seen or recognized by anyone.

Their journey in the two-person Dexta Flyer had
taken them slightly more than five days. The Flyer,
which was little more than a hollow tube attached to a
fusion reactor and a Ferguson Distortion Generator,
was the fastest available means of interstellar transport
for human beings. A robotic courier could have made
the trip in less than two days, and a reusable messenger
vehicle in about two and a half. The Dexta Cruiser that
was to bring Althea and the rest of the team would make
the same 517-light-year journey in about seven days.
Getting to Sylvania, another thirty light-years distant,
would take a full day in a freighter.

The limo took them through the crowded afternoon
streets of Palmyra City to the Dexta offices in the heart
of the metropolis. Palmyra, with a population of 300

million, had been settled by humans three and a half centuries earlier. Its growth had been stalled by the proximity of the hostile Ch'gnth Confederacy, and the planet itself had come under attack during the war, some five decades earlier. After a period of recovery and rebuilding, Palmyra had become a crossroads for trade in this sector of the Empire, and was still riding a wave of postwar prosperity. The City was marked by soaring towers and graceful low-gravity (.89 G) architecture.

The limo parked in the basement of the Dexta building, and eager gofers shepherded Gloria and Petra up to the Imperial Secretary's offices. Since the creation of the OSI had been highly controversial—some Dexta offices had let it be known that any appearance by OSI personnel on their turf would be less than welcome— Gloria had decided to try for a first impression that would make the local staffers glad to see *her*, if not the OSI. That much was accomplished as soon as she removed her raincoat.

She wore only a flimsy, nearly transparent, pale yellow minidress with a wide V neckline that plunged to her navel and left her nipples only partially covered. No part of her golden body was fully hidden from view. She already had an Empire-wide reputation to live up to, and was determined not to fall short of anyone's expectations. Petra had settled for a standard Dexta-gray skirt and a loose white pullover, thin enough to make it obvious that she wasn't wearing anything under it. The ladies from OSI had arrived on Palmyra, and no one was disappointed by their appearance.

After an exchange of pleasantries, Sabaru Graff, the Level XII Imperial Secretary and head of the Dexta office on Palmyra, led them into a small conference room, where they met with the Undersecretary for Administration, Jennifer Astuni, and the Imperial Geologist for the sector, Stuart Eckstein. For historical reasons, Imperial Geologists were not under Dexta administration but reported directly to the Imperial Geological Survey and Parliament.

Graff had only been in his present position for a year, so he relied heavily on Astuni for information about Sylvania. She was an efficient, dark-haired woman of about fifty, and not nearly as impressed by Gloria as was Graff, but seemed eager to help. Eckstein, a tall, sandy-haired man in his forties, had little to say at first, but fixed his probing gaze on Gloria. They sat around a conference table and settled in while a couple of starry-eyed Level XV assistants served them coffee and sandwiches, as slowly as possible, until a frown from Graff finally sent them on their way. ·

Gloria briefly recapped the nature of their mission, on which the local staff had already received a briefing via messenger. Gloria's mention of Mingus and the Emperor caused Graff to straighten in his chair and sit at attention, but didn't seem to affect either Astuni or Eckstein. "What I need to know," Gloria told them, "is as much as possible about the current situation on the ground on Sylvania. Anything you can tell us would be of value, since we seem to be short of information about what's happening there."

"As are we," Graff admitted. "We pick up some news now and then from freighter crews, and, of course, we have contacts with the leaders of the Lodge and the corporate representatives, but we don't have anything like the detailed picture we would prefer. Jennifer was on Sylvania about two months ago, but we don't have any firsthand information more recent than that."

"I doubt that there have been significant changes in the interim," said Astuni, "but it's hard to be certain."

"I understand," said Gloria. "What can you tell me about your last visit?"

"Well," Astuni began, "the first thing I found there was an empty Dexta office and a note from the last staffer we had sent. It read, and I quote, 'I quit! I'm off to Californee with a banjo on my knee. Sincerely, Ben

Tomsczak.' Apparently, Ben went up into the hills to make his fortune. I don't know if he did or not."

Gloria nodded. "So, we still have an office there, I take it."

"We leased a couple of rooms in Elba's Emporium, and so we should still have a place for you to set up operations when you get there—assuming Elba hasn't converted them into more bedrooms."

"Who is Elba, and what is this Emporium?"

Astuni grinned. "Elba is Elba Larkspur, the local madam and entrepreneur. One of a kind, as you'll discover. Her Emporium is this amazing collection of wooden structures that just grew like Topsy in the past two years, one ramshackle addition after another. It started out as a brothel and bar, naturally; but Elba expanded her operation to include gambling tables, a dance hall, a restaurant, a general store, a number of offices, and for all I know, an amusement park. It's the center of practically everything that happens in Greenlodge. You have to see it to believe it."

"Dexta has offices in a bordello?" Petra asked in wonderment.

"We go where we must." Astuni laughed. "I gather that it was a bit of a distraction, but not exactly a hardship for Ben Tomsczak. But then, he got the get-rich-itch, same as practically everyone else on Sylvania."

"I would think that Elba must have the same problem as we do, keeping employees," Gloria said. "How does she manage to keep people working for her?"

"Good question," said Astuni. "For the most part, her employees are prostitutes and bar girls. The hookers probably make a fortune in bed, so they aren't tempted to leave until the right man comes along with a basketful of crowns. The bar girls make less, but they manage to snag their share of lonely boomers. Still, there's a pretty good turnover rate at the Emporium. As for the other workers, we're mainly talking about gamblers, grifters, and boomers who have gone bust and need a job."

"What about the preboom local population? What's become of them?"

"Still there, mostly. Some of them made their own strikes and either left the planet or invested in more mineral claims. But most of them have continued pretty much as before, working for the Lodge and trying to have a normal life in the midst of the chaos."

Gloria nibbled at a watercress-and-cucumber sandwich and thought for a moment. "Tell me about the Lodge," she said. "How do they cope with the labor situation?"

"As I said, they have quite a few locals who have remained loyal. But they've begun using Elba as a sort of employment agency. Bar girls take turns going up to the Lodge to act as serving girls and maids. Apparently it's a pretty profitable arrangement for them. And, of course, the prostitutes freelance at the Lodge on their own time."

"And who, exactly, is at the Lodge? Who runs it, who owns it?"

"The Lodge manager," Astuni answered, "is a no-nonsense character named Preston Thawley, who has been there since the beginning. The ownership consists of five prominent families from Palmyra, the foremost being that of Claude Rankus."

"Mr. Rankus," put in Graff, "is the patriarch of one of the founding families of Palmyra. I won't say that they run the planet, but even the Imperial Governor is careful to keep them happy."

"That would be Vincent DiGrazia," Gloria noted. "Political appointee, of course, and, according to my sources, something of a nonentity. Correct?"

Graff seemed a little annoyed by such a frank assessment, but could only nod in agreement. "He does as little as possible," Graff admitted. "Which, of course, is something of a blessing for Dexta. Spirit save us from activist ImpGovs, eh, Ms. VanDeen?"

"It's Gloria, and amen to that." Gloria had a brief,

unpleasant flashback to the last Imperial Governor she had worked with, the late Governor Rhinehart of Mynjhino. "Tell me more about Rankus."

"He's a reactionary pig," said Astuni, "but a very nice one."

"That's putting it a little harshly, Jen," Graff said. "And he is a very pleasant and engaging man, actually, as long as he gets his own way. He's over 140, and handed over the reins of the family interests on Palmyra to his sons a number of years ago. Spends most of his time now on Sylvania."

"He sees himself as essentially a feudal lord," said Astuni. "And many of the locals seem perfectly happy to be his serfs. But the boomers infuriate him."

"But he has this Grunfeld character to keep them in line," Gloria offered.

"Kevin Grunfeld," Astuni declared, "is the meanest, most thoroughly despicable son of a bitch I've ever met. The only good thing you can say about him is that he and his thugs manage to maintain some semblance of law and order on the planet, which is a necessity in the middle of a boom. Of course, the law is pretty much whatever Rankus says it is, or what Grunfeld decides it ought to be on any given day."

"I see," said Gloria. "Considering what you've said, I would assume that we could expect Rankus and Grunfeld to oppose our attempt to register voters?"

"Count on it," said Astuni. "As long as they can prevent the appointment of an Imperial Governor, Rankus stays in charge of his little fiefdom, and Grunfeld keeps his job."

"What about the other Lodge families? I would think that some of them would want to cash in on the boom and bring in the corporates."

"Some of them probably do," said Graff, "but even they tread lightly around Rankus. The profits from the small-scale mining going on now are probably not enough to tempt them into openly opposing him, but that could change when the Big Twelve arrive. From what I hear, some of them are apparently already looking for ways to circumvent him, but Rankus is rich, powerful, and highly respected. Even his partners at the Lodge would be reluctant to go against his wishes. For the moment, the most they've been able to do is invite representatives of some of the Big Twelve to stay at the Lodge and keep track of developments. Rankus allows this, but I gather that there is a lot of *sub rosa* politicking going on. We haven't been able to determine exactly what's happening, however."

"It would be nice if we could," Gloria said thoughtfully. She glanced at Petra, who had been industriously taking notes on her pad. Petra felt her gaze and looked up.

"What?" she said.

"Petra," Gloria said, "I think I have an assignment for you."

"Oh?" For some reason, Petra didn't seem to like the sound of that.

"We need to get a pair of eyes and ears into the Lodge. It occurs to me that if we could get you a job at the Emporium, you might be able to do a little spying up at the Lodge."

Petra gulped. Her eyes widened.

"Not *that* kind of job," Gloria quickly assured her. "I was thinking you could get a job as a bar girl and use that to worm your way into the Lodge as one of the maids or serving girls. What about that, Jennifer? Possible?"

Astuni grinned at Petra. "Elba would snap you up in a heartbeat, Petra. Of course, she'd try to get you to, uh, do the *other* work, but I think she'd be more than happy to have you working the bar."

Petra thought furiously. "But . . . well, I mean, I don't know how good a spy I'd make. I mean, I was on the vids for a while there during Mynjhino, Gloria. What if someone recognized me?"

"Your hair is a bit longer now," Gloria pointed out, "and anyway, all fame is fleeting. Tell you what, why don't you go blond or get some curls? Even a small change like that ought to be enough to keep you from being recognized. In the unlikely event that someone does connect you with me, you'd just be another Dexta staffer who quit to make her fortune in the boom. I think this will work, if you don't mind serving beer and mopping a few floors for a little while. After all, aren't you the woman who told me a week ago that she thought registering voters would be 'routine'? Being a spy ought to be anything but routine, wouldn't you say?"

Gloria sat there, grinning at her assistant, who could only take it in silence. Finally she said, "Okay, okay, I'll do it. I'll be your little Mata Petra. But I get to keep any tips I make, right?"

"You'll make plenty, then," Astuni assured her. "You'll remind all those lonely boomers of the girl they left behind them. Just be careful you don't let Elba push you into anything you don't want to do."

"No chance of that," Petra said firmly.

"I don't know," said Jennifer. "If I were a little younger and as pretty as you . . . it's not as if prostitution were still a crime, you know. And from what I hear, a lot of those girls have gotten rich."

"I'll pass," Petra said. "Anyway, if Elba wants to recruit some horizontal help, I know where she can find someone who wouldn't mind." She glared meaningfully at Gloria.

Gloria airily dismissed the notion, although it did intrigue her a little. "I'm too famous," she said. "It would disrupt the regular trade too much. Anyway, I expect to be busy with other matters."

She turned to the Imperial Geologist. "Dr. Eckstein," she said, "tell me about Fergusite."

"It's Stu," he said, "and I've prepared some material for you. If you'll look at the console, I'll take you through a quick course on Fergusite."

A series of images appeared on the console screen as Eckstein narrated. "Half a billion years ago," he began, as geologists often do, "a volcano erupted about a hundred kilometers inland from the present-day southern coastline. The flow of highly enriched silicate lava spread out in this fan-shaped pattern, to the south of the eruption site. The flow covered the existing terrain with a stratum that ranged from less than a meter to more than ten meters in depth. We don't have precise measurements because we've only had limited time and opportunity to take core samples, but the best guess is that the flow is about eighty kilometers from east to west, at maximum extent, where it reaches the modern coastline.

"Time passed," Eckstein continued, "lots of it. There were other eruptions, other flows, plus a lot of faulting, upthrusting, and erosion. In the process of all that activity, the initial flow was covered up and subjected to a great deal of heat and pressure. I won't bore you with the details, but the combination of factors was precisely what was necessary to turn that first flow into a natural layer of almost pure Fergusite. It's the only one we've ever found in the Empire, and—for all we know—it might be the only one in the entire galaxy. At best, it's exceedingly rare stuff."

"And it's pure enough to run a distortion generator?" Petra asked.

"The samples we've seen so far seem to be. Of course, the formation itself is not one hundred percent Fergusite because the crystals are embedded in a matrix of other minerals. But, again, I caution that we haven't seen very much of the formation. Here, let me bring up the map of the current landforms. As you see, the modern coastal plain is anywhere from ten to thirty kilometers wide, and the Fergusite layer underlies most of it. In the region of Greenlodge, it's at a depth of perhaps a hundred meters. The layer continues on up into the mountains, and there, erosion and faulting have brought it to the surface at some locations. But it's all one contiguous formation, all the way back to the volcano that created it."

"Does it continue out to sea?" Gloria asked.

"No more than a few kilometers. There's a pretty sharp drop-off to the continental shelf, and we don't think that the Fergusite continues beyond the shelf. Now, notice this inverted V in the coastline. That's formed by the Rankus River, which has eroded away a valley that extends inland about fifty kilometers. The river comes plunging out of the mountains at that point, forming a truly spectacular waterfall, which you really ought to take the time to see while you're there. Downstream, the river is fed by numerous creeks and streams coming out of the mountains on either side. It widens and becomes fairly placid here. It's quite deep in some spots, but there are shallows and a number of good fords."

"And Greenlodge is there, on the coast, on the east side of the river?"

"Right. And there's the Lodge, up on the slopes, about ten kilometers inland, to the northeast."

Eckstein hit a button on his pad, and a bright green stripe appeared on both flanks of the V formed by the Rankus River Valley. "That's the most accessible part of the Fergusite layer," he explained. "And that's where most of the mining claims have been established. However, over time, a lot of Fergusite has eroded away from the slopes and made its way down the streams and into the river. A good many of the boomers spend their time in the little creeks and the shallows of the river, panning for Fergusite. Most of the crystals they find are just a couple of millimeters in diameter, although I saw one that was as big as an apple."

"What good are the tiny crystals?" Petra asked. "I mean, you can't run a starship on something that small, can you?"

Eckstein shook his head. "All of the crystals have to be processed back on Palmyra before they can be used," he explained. "Impurities and bits of the country rock that cling to the crystals have to be removed, then the crystals themselves are run through a hyperpressure amalgamator that turns them into slabs appropriate for distortion generators. But it all adds up, so even the millimeter-sized crystals have value."

"So all of the Fergusite comes from the creeks?" Gloria asked.

"Not exactly. That's where the first discoveries were made, and it's still where most of the production comes from. But there's more of it up on the slopes, although it's harder and more expensive to get at. You see, the miners are limited in their use of plasma drills. A lot of the work is plain old pick-and-shovel digging."

"I couldn't believe it when I saw it for the first time," Jennifer Astuni added. "It's like looking at a vid of the California Gold Rush in the eighteenth century—"

"Nineteenth," Eckstein corrected.

"Whatever," Jennifer said. "But you see all these characters straight out of a history vid, banging away with hand tools and nothing but their own muscle power. Amazing."

"That's mainly, but not entirely, a consequence of the nature of Fergusite," Eckstein said. "It's also a consequence of the way Rankus and Grunfeld run their little realm, but we can talk about that later." He glanced at Gloria, who nodded.

"Why can't the miners use plasma drills?" Petra wondered.

"They can," Eckstein replied, "but only with the greatest of care. What makes Fergusite so valuable is the way its unique crystal structure focuses energy. In a distortion generator, it's used in the form of small rectangular slabs, about a centimeter thick, five centimeters wide, and ten long. The slabs slide through the locus of the generator as a thin plasma stream from the fusion reactor plays back and forth across it, at a precisely controlled rate. The infusion of all that energy, as focused by the latticework in the Fergusite, warps space-time and forms the Yao-space membrane that lets starships slide through normal space at superluminal velocities. At least, that's what they tell me—I'm a geologist, not a physicist."

"We aren't even geologists," Gloria said. "Assume, for the moment, that we are, in fact, complete idiots."

Eckstein smiled at her. "I don't believe that for an instant," he said, "but I'll try to make this as clear as possible. When the plasma beam strikes the Fergusite, the crystal latticework quickly breaks down, making it unusable, which is why the beam must keep in motion continuously as fresh slabs slide through the locus. Now, if you input too much energy at any one spot, not only does the lattice decay, but the excess energy is transmitted to the adjoining Fergusite, destroying it, as well. If that happened in a starship, you'd collapse the Yao bubble, rupture the fusion reactors, and get a helluva big explosion."

Petra and Gloria looked at each other. On Mynjhino, they had witnessed—from a safe distance—precisely such an event, when the FDGs on an Imperial Marine vessel suffered an apparent energy overload as it attempted to perform a task for which it had never been designed. The ship disappeared in a nanosecond of thermonuclear fury.

"So if the miners used a plasma drill, they'd cause an explosion?" Petra asked.

Eckstein shook his head. "No, but what would happen is that the energy overload from the drill would flow outward from the spot of impact and destroy the crystal structure of the surrounding Fergusite, making it completely worthless. You'd wind up destroying the very stuff you were trying to get. So the miners can only use the plasma drills to cut into the overlying rock layers, enabling them to get at the Fergusite with pick and shovel. Even then, it's a tricky business. If their aim is off by only a little, and they hit any part of the Fergusite deposit, they can ruin an entire outcrop." He glanced quickly at Gloria, who gave him a subtle nod.

"Well," Gloria said, "thank you very much for the primer. I have some more questions for you about the mining operations on Palmyra, but I don't want to burden everyone else with that. What I suggest, instead, is that you show me the best restaurant on Palmyra, my treat, and we can discuss this further. Meanwhile, Petra, why don't you coordinate details with Sabaru and Jennifer concerning the arrival of Althea's team? Also, make sure our own transport to Sylvania is set. Okay?"

Petra nodded obediently. Petra was Gloria's friend, but she was also her assistant. And sometimes, the boss got to go off to an expensive dinner with a handsome guy, while the loyal assistant did the drudge work. Gloria wasted no time feeling guilty about it.

THE BEST RESTAURANT ON PALMYRA WELCOMED Gloria as if she were visiting royalty. She and Eckstein chatted idly over an excellent dinner and some passable wine while other diners gawked. Inevitably, some local media reps showed up, and Gloria gave them a few minutes to ask stupid questions and image her famous face and nearly nude body. Then she sent them on their way and returned to her table to share coffee and brandy with Eckstein.

"They'll give us some privacy now," she explained. "It's sort of an unspoken deal I have with the media. Seems to work."

"Do you think it's a good idea to bring so much attention to yourself, all things considered?" Eckstein asked dubiously.

"All things considered," she replied, "it's the perfect cover. I make something of a splash wherever I go, so it's better to play to it than try to hide from it—that would only make them suspicious."

"And we don't want that."

"We're just a couple out for dinner—there's certainly nothing suspicious about that, is there?"

"Spirit, I hope not," Eckstein agreed. "All things considered."

STUART ECKSTEIN LAY BACK ON THE PILLOW and tried to catch his breath, following the best sex of his life. Gloria, still panting a little, cuddled up next to him and played with the hairs on his chest.

"I didn't expect this," Eckstein admitted.

"Well," Gloria said, "I figured that if we were going to be plotting treason together, we should have a close working relationship." Her hand moved downward over his torso. "I mean, consider my position. Here I am, caught between a rock and a hard geologist!"

Eckstein laughed and gave her a kiss. "I'll try not to give you as much trouble as the rock," he said. "Goddamn Fergusite! I wish I'd never found the stuff."

"You made the discovery? I didn't know that!"

"Not personally. Someone brought me a sample on Palmyra and asked me what the hell it was. When I realized what I had . . . well, I was dumb enough to report it to the Imperial Geological Survey. So this whole mess is my fault, in a way."

"Is that why you're doing this?"

Eckstein shook his head. "I'm doing it because when I was on Earth last month, Mingus confronted me with the logic of my own position and used that to beat me into submission. So I found myself enlisting in his little scheme. Until tonight, I was still tempted to desert. Is that why Mingus sent you here?"

Gloria looked at Eckstein's tanned, weather-beaten face and saw that his question was sincere. "If it was," Gloria told him honestly, "he didn't tell me. But knowing Norman, I suppose he had this in mind all along. He would never ask me to sleep with someone—I think—but he probably counted on it happening. He knows me pretty well, too."

"I'm getting to know you a little myself," Eckstein

said, and began to massage her left nipple between his thumb and forefinger. "You are every bit as remarkable as I've heard."

"If you keep that up," Gloria assured him, "you'll see just how remarkable I can be. And *you*, Mr. Imperial Geologist, are pretty remarkable yourself. How come some smart woman hasn't already grabbed you?"

"One did, but she thought I spent too much time with rocks and not enough with her, so she dumped me. A good move for both of us."

"Speaking of rocks," Gloria said, trying to keep focused as Eckstein shifted his attentions to her other nipple, "can we really do this? Will it work?"

Eckstein shook his head indecisively. "It should, but it's only theory. Spirit only knows what will happen in the end. The computer models indicate that it ought to work, but the real problem will be getting the equipment in place, finding the right spot, and keeping it all under wraps. I still don't see how the hell we're going to do that."

"Couldn't we just use a plasma drill? From what you said earlier, it sounds like that ought to do the job."

"Not enough power," Eckstein said. "Plasma drills just damage the crystals in the immediate vicinity. To destroy the entire Fergusite layer, we'll need a fusion reactor. The energy input has to be constant and precisely regulated. Too much power, and we'd destroy the crystal structure and ruin the energy-transfer properties of the Fergusite, which would prevent us from getting at the rest of the layer. Too little, and the energy never reaches the rest of the layer. A fusion reactor is the only option, and we have to find a spot where we can let it run for more than a month."

"Couldn't we go way up into the hills or mountains where no one would see it?"

"I don't think that would work. There are prospectors wandering around all over the place, even a hundred kilometers inland. Wherever we set it up, someone would spot it sooner or later. And if anyone ever finds out what we're up to, you and I will spend the rest of our lives on a prison world . . . assuming the boomers don't just lynch us on the spot."

"Well, we'll think of something when we get to Sylvania. I hope." Gloria drew her breath in sharply and managed to stave off a miniorgasm. Her hypersensitive nipples—and navel, as Eckstein was now discovering—were undoubtedly a blessing, but also a powerful distraction.

"Maybe we should just tell Mingus that we couldn't find a way to do it and call off the whole thing," Eckstein suggested.

"You know we can't do that," Gloria responded sharply.

Eckstein sighed audibly. "No," he agreed, "I suppose we can't. In for a penny, in for a crown. Considering what's at stake, we'll have to give it our best shot, no matter what."

"Give *me* your best shot!" Gloria abruptly insisted. Eckstein had driven all thoughts of Fergusite and treasonous conspiracy from her mind. For the moment.

But the moment went on for quite some time.

chapter 6

THE TRAMP FREIGHTER MADE A SMOOTH LAND-
ing in the sea south of Greenlodge and cruised to the
dock at the mouth of the river. The journey from
Palmyra had taken a little more than a day, and Gloria
and Eckstein had spent most of that time in their tiny
private stateroom; back home, Gloria had closets that
were bigger. Petra, meanwhile, after a hurried shopping
expedition to acquire a kit more suitable to her new station in life, had spent the trip in the hold, competing for
hammock space with other low-budget travelers. Most
of them were boomers, who paid her little attention;
their minds were fixed on the fortunes they were about
to make.

Gloria and Eckstein debarked, and were quickly ac-
costed on the pier by two skinny teenage boys who offered to carry their baggage for ten crowns apiece. The
deal made, they followed closely behind Gloria, snicker-
ing to each other about the view. Gloria was wearing a
sheer white shirt, knotted at the waist and unbuttoned,
and a pair of jeans slung perilously low on her hips.

"How do you keep them from falling off?" Eckstein asked as he surveyed the expanse of bared belly and buttocks.

"I only wear them on low-gravity worlds," Gloria explained with a smile.

Sylvania's gravity was only .93 G, putting a spring into the step of new arrivals. Perhaps it also accounted for the air of bustling energy that permeated the dockside. Stevedores were already busy unloading the freighter and transferring its contents to the row of warehouses that fronted the pier. Hustlers of every description were loudly hawking wares ranging from maps to mining equipment, while the newly arrived boomers made their way through the confusion with feigned confidence and brisk strides. Among them, a newly blond and curly-haired Petra lugged a duffel bag over her shoulder and successfully blended into the scene.

Gloria paused at the end of the pier and looked around. Ahead of her, she saw the town of Greenlodge, in all its seedy splendor. Everything seemed to be made of wood, the only available local building material. Looking upriver, she noticed a sawmill and a large float of logs bobbing in the tidewater. Utility skimmers were hauling fresh-cut boards directly to a half dozen building sites that punctuated what passed for the town's main street. It was unpaved and muddy, with dozens of unconcerned boomers sloshing along on their errands. Everyone seemed to have someplace to go, something important to do.

She spotted Elba's Emporium almost immediately. It looked like an old wooden barn that had started to explode but changed its mind. In places, it was as much as three stories high, with various extensions that seemed to have been added as hasty afterthoughts. Wings stuck out at odd angles, and here and there a door or window interrupted the siding. Some of the structure was painted a luminous green, some of it had been sloppily whitewashed, and large sections of it consisted of raw, unpainted wood. A red-paint sign on one side declared:

ELBA'S EMPORIUM! GIRLS! BEER! ROOMS! GIRLS! GEAR! FOOD! EATS! GIRLS!

THE EMPORIUM DOMINATED THE CENTER OF THE town, with other, less ambitious structures strung out to its flanks, on both sides of the street. These included such establishments as boardinghouses, metalsmiths, equipment rentals, a Vid Palace, some small bars and restaurants, a place that offered hot showers, a hardware store or two, and unidentifiable hovels that already seemed to be sinking back into the mud. Beyond the permanent or semipermanent structures, Gloria noticed several acres of tents, large and small, canvas and synthetic, in a rainbow of hues; it looked like the bivouac grounds of a defeated army of color-blind circus clowns.

To the left of the Emporium, she saw a white, two-story building with a sign on it that said, GREENLODGE CITY HALL. KEVIN A. GRUNFELD, MAYOR. No one was going in or out of the front entrance at the moment, but in the alley to the right, there was a long queue of boomers waiting to gain access to a side door. Two large men with plasma pistols holstered on their hips stood leaning against the wall, keeping watch.

"That's the assay office," Eckstein explained. "It's where the miners bring their crystals and exchange them for crowns. Grunfeld runs it, of course, and takes 20 percent off the top."

"How much would that amount to?" Gloria wondered.

"By now, millions. Grunfeld has expenses of his own, and probably has to pay a cut to the Lodge, but he's already a wealthy man. See those little knapsacks the miners are clutching? Every one of them is probably worth tens of thousands of crowns."

"That much?" Gloria gave a low, impressed whistle. "I had no idea."

Eckstein nodded. "A kilo of pure artificial Fergusite is worth about a hundred thousand crowns. The same amount of processed Sylvania Fergusite is worth about ten thousand, back on Palmyra. The raw stuff is worth about half that, here, and the miners only get about thirty-five hundred or four thousand for it from Grunfeld. Still, somebody with ten kilos of it in his pack could walk away with forty thousand crowns."

"So people really are getting rich here?"

"Momentarily, at least," said Eckstein. "See those boomrats waiting in line? Most of them will spend a week in town, whooping it up and blowing off steam. By the time they go back to their diggings, half of them will be as broke as they were when they got here. A steak dinner, a few beers, and a room for the night at Elba's will cost them about five hundred crowns, not including a girl. Then there are the gamblers, the inflated charges for everything from shovels to toilet paper, and various bad guys who will try to separate them from their money."

"Isn't there a local police force?" Gloria asked.

Eckstein pointed toward the two men with plasma pistols at City Hall. "Grunfeld's thugs," he said. "Of course, they also steal, as well as protect and serve. And sometimes, they just dispose of anyone who gives them trouble."

"Why doesn't the Imperial Marshal's Office on Palmyra send someone?"

"Oh, every few months, they'll send a couple of deputies, who look around for a day or two, then leave. I suspect that the Marshal's Office is worried about its personnel here the same way Dexta is."

"Well, there must be some way for those miners to hang on to their money. Isn't there a bank?"

"Sure. Grunfeld. He's got the only vault on the

planet, along with his other enterprises. He only charges 10 percent a month for its use."

"Wait a minute. He doesn't *pay* interest, he *charges* it?"

Eckstein nodded. "It's either that or sleep on your crowns and hope they're still there when you wake up. *If* you wake up."

Gloria shook her head in amazement. "Doesn't *anyone* get off Sylvania with their money?"

"Some do," said Eckstein. "Look there." He pointed toward the end of the dock, where a black-bearded man, resplendent in brand-new store-bought duds, was making his way toward the freighter, his gaudy new bride at his side. He was smoking a big cigar and tossing crowns to a bunch of kids, laughing expansively.

"Of course," Eckstein pointed out, "when he gets to Palmyra, the locals *there* will try to strip him just as clean as the locals here. They'll just do it in a more civilized manner."

"Whew," said Gloria. "Quite a place!"

"Just a typical boomworld," Eckstein said. "Not much different from the thorium strike on Mirabelle Four a century ago or, for that matter, the California gold fields or the Klondike, fourteen centuries ago. What everyone wants is in the ground. What everyone *needs* has to come from somewhere else, at great expense. For every miner who makes a fortune, there are ten merchants, hustlers, and thieves who make a bigger one."

"What we need now, I think," Gloria said, looking around, "is a taxi—unless we want to walk through the mud all the way to the Emporium. Are there any?"

"Best just to rent a skimmer." Eckstein pointed to a rental lot a few meters from the end of the pier. "They're expensive as hell, naturally, but we'll need one to get up to the diggings. Not that you can use them all the way up into the slopes. Skimmers don't work well in broken ground, you know. In terrain like this, the mass repulsion unit will flip you over if you aren't careful."

They approached the rental agent and found a serviceable utility skimmer at a price so low that Gloria managed not to gasp out loud. But when she attempted to pay with her pad, the agent insisted on cash. "This ain't no city, lady," the agent told her. "Don't matter how pretty you are, it's crowns on the barrelhead for everyone."

"But it's a Dexta account," Gloria explained. "And I'm—"

"Shitfire!" cried the rental agent. "I know who you are! You're that Gloria gal, ain't you?"

Gloria grinned at him and hooked her thumbs in her jeans, tugging them downward another centimeter. "I sure am," she said, "and I just know you aren't going to let me down, Mr. . . . uh . . . ?"

"Tom Greeley, ma'am! Mighty pleased to make your acquaintance, damned if I'm not! And you say it's a Dexta account? Well, I guess I can make an exception in your case."

"Thank you so much, Mr. Greeley." Gloria gave him her Grade-A smile. "I knew I could count on you. I hope I'll see you around town while I'm here."

"Ain't no doubt about *that*, ma'am!"

As they got into the utility skimmer, the boys with the bags piling into the back, Eckstein looked at Gloria and shook his head. "You could own the entire planet in about a week if you put your mind to it."

Gloria simply shrugged. "I use what I've got," she said. "Life's a little easier that way."

THE INTERIOR OF ELBA'S EMPORIUM WAS AS helter-skelter as its exterior. They entered through the front door, dodging a rowdy drunk who was busy being ejected by a bouncer the size of a small mountain, and found themselves in a sort of anteroom with a front desk, as in a hotel. At the desk, a sleepy-looking old man roused himself, did a double take at the sight of Gloria, then quickly resumed his somnolent demeanor.

"What'll it be? Room? Meal? Drinks? Through the door to your right. General store's to your left."

"We'd like to talk to Ms. Larkspur," Gloria told him. "I'm from Dexta, and we want to see about our offices."

The old man took new interest. "Dexta, eh? Figured you'd be back. I'll get Elba." He hit a button on the desk, then sat back on his stool.

While they were waiting, a grime-covered boomrat strolled over to them and carefully inspected Gloria. "You the new whore?" he asked. "Sure hope so. Just lost that pretty little Della. Up and married Jim the Jumper. Ol' Jim's takin' her off to Palmyra with him. Like she ain't gonna grab his wallet and hightail it, soon as she can. Sure will miss that gal. But I'd pay double for you, missy, damn sure I would."

"Out of curiosity," Gloria asked, "how much would that be?"

"Two thousand a night for you." The boomrat took a closer look, taking particular note of Gloria's jutting nipples, barely contained and not at all concealed by her shirt. "Shit, make that three. Spirit's holy tits, make it five!"

"And you could afford that?"

"Damn straight, I can! Lookit here, missy!" The boomrat turned his pockets inside out, and hundred-crown coins rattled onto the floor.

"Oh, stop showing off, Willie," said a scratchy voice coming up from behind them. "Pick up your money and go find another one of the girls. This here lady ain't for sale anywise. She ain't no whore, she's Gloria VanDeen from Dexta, ain't you?"

"That's who I am," Gloria said, turning to meet Elba Larkspur with a smile. "Pleased to meet you, Ms. Larkspur." She extended her hand.

"The name's Elba," replied the massive woman approaching her. They shook hands and stepped back to take each other's measure.

Elba Larkspur might once have been a beautiful woman, a century earlier. Now, she was merely impressive, the way old cathedrals, ancient ruins, and extinct volcanoes are. She was tall but slightly stooped, well rounded but not quite fat, and overflowed from a black-and-scarlet bustier in a manner that was equally sexual and slovenly. Her face was lined and craggy, with the red nose of a longtime drinker and watery blue eyes that had seen more than they should have. Her hair was a strange mix of gold and silver, in extravagant disarray, like a battle plan with sound strategy but faulty tactics. She gave the impression of a woman who had once cared a great deal about the way she looked but no longer did, while still remembering that she once had.

She turned toward Eckstein and gave him a yellow-toothed smile. "Good to see ya back, Stu. Tell me . . . ya fucked her yet?"

Eckstein didn't quite blush, but found himself tongue-tied for a moment, so Gloria answered for him. "Indeed, he has," she said.

"And is she all she's cracked up to be?"

"More," Eckstein managed, with a crooked smile and a glance toward Gloria.

"Pity you're already rich, hon," Elba said to Gloria. "Don't suppose I can talk ya into takin' a turn in the rooms? Might be interestin' for ya. Educational, mebbe."

"Business before pleasure, Elba," Gloria said.

"You've come about the office, then. Knew somebody would, so I kept 'em for ya. Damn near broke my heart to leave those rooms empty, but I made a deal, and I always keep my word. In a business like mine, sometimes my word is all I've got to fall back on. Okay, I'll show 'em to ya."

Elba laboriously led them up a creaky wooden staircase to the second floor and pushed open a door. Inside, they found nothing but a broken chair and a few files scattered on the floor.

"What happened to the computers that were here?" Eckstein asked her.

"Said I'd keep the rooms for ya. Didn't say I'd guard 'em night and day."

"It doesn't matter," Gloria said. "We'll be bringing in new equipment and a new staff in about a week. I'll also need to find lodging for eight people."

"Can't spare that many rooms," Elba said. "But I'll talk to Mort Newsome and see if he can accommodate ya over to his roomin' house. What about you two? Got a room?"

"Not yet," Gloria told her. "Can you do something about that?"

"Glad to. Even give ya a rate. I figure it'll increase trade 20 percent, just havin' ya here. People are gonna walk a long way just to get a look at you, hon. But ya gotta promise to have dinner with me downstairs tonight. I wanna show off my high-class clientele, ya know what I mean?"

"It will be a pleasure," Gloria told her, grinning. "I'll try to give them something worth seeing."

GLORIA AND ECKSTEIN WENT OFF TO TAKE A stroll around the town. Elba went back down to the bar and found a young woman waiting to speak with her. She was short, with curly, medium blond hair, a pretty face, and a cute little body.

"My name's Petra," she said. "They told me I might find work here."

"They told you right, hon," Elba said. "You got any experience?"

"Well, I waited tables for a while when I was in school."

"Tables? Shit, that ain't what I meant. You mean to tell me, you ain't fixin' to work the rooms?"

"The rooms? You mean . . . oh . . . the *rooms*. No, no, I just wanted to get a job as one of your bar girls, that's all."

"You sure? You could make a pretty penny in the rooms, hon. You ain't what I'd call gorgeous, but ya got that 'girl next door' look that a lotta men get all mushy for. And I'd treat ya right, just ask any of my girls. No more'n ten men a night, no kinky stuff unless they pay extra and you agree, and I only take half. Ya won't find a better deal anywhere."

"No . . . no, I mean, I know you would . . . that is, if I were . . . uh . . . please, I just want to work the bar."

"Well," said Elba, "if that's what ya want. But if ya change your mind, let me know. Okay, let's see your stuff, kid."

"My stuff? It's all in my duffel bag, but—"

"No, no, hon—*your* stuff. Take off those duds and let me see what ya got."

"What? *Here?*"

"Well where did ya think I meant? Take a look around, hon. This here's Elba's Emporium, not some hoity-toity tearoom."

PETRA DID LOOK AROUND FOR THE FIRST TIME, and her mouth dropped open at what she saw. At a nearby table, a round of beers was being served by a frizzy-haired redhead, wearing nothing but a tiny G-string and a smile. Petra groaned, and silently cursed Gloria. And Jennifer Astuni, too—she might at least have mentioned this minor detail about Elba's bar girls.

"C'mon, hon. Ain't got all day. Ya want the job or not?"

Not, thought Petra, but she knew that she couldn't back out now. Gloria trusted her to get the job done, and if she let her down, that trust might never fully return.

Petra closed her eyes for a second, then got to work unbuttoning her shirt. She hesitated, then unfastened her skirt and let her garments drop to the floor. She was left wearing only the tiniest pair of pale blue bikini panties that she owned. She mentally kicked herself for having chosen *them* this morning.

"Not bad at all," Elba declared. "Great little ass, hon, very sexy twat, and those cute little tits will get you a lot of tips. Those shoes won't do, but I'll have one of the girls get you some high heels. The panties will be okay until we can get you a G-string, unless you'd rather go without. Bigger tips that way. No? Okay, hon, bar's right over there. Get to work."

"Now?"

"Why the hell not?"

"But . . . but . . . uh, I mean, what do I get paid?"

"Room and board, of course. What did ya expect? I split the tips fifty-fifty, and don't try holdin' out on me. Look, hon, I can see you're new at this, but you'll get used to it quick enough. And when ya work for Elba, ya got nothin' to worry about. Oh, the men can give ya a little squeeze or a pinch, long as they don't bruise the merchandise. That just gets them primed for the rooms, ya see. But anyone gives ya real trouble, just call for Ernie, over there." Elba pointed toward the bouncer, standing near the bar. "I don't stand for no one givin' my girls a hard time. The boys know that, and they'll behave themselves proper, or Ernie'll show 'em the door good and quick. You'll do just fine, hon. So get to work now. I can't stand here all day yappin'!"

Petra nodded obediently and got to work, reminding herself that she was—thank the Spirit—542 light-years from Weehawken.

GLORIA AND ECKSTEIN EMERGED FROM THEIR room on the second floor, then paused for a moment at the top of the staircase that led down from the encircling balcony to the big, main room, where scores of boomers were eating, drinking, gambling, and ogling the bar girls. The hubbub in the Emporium gradually died away to dead silence as people noticed her.

She was wearing a deep purple dress that displayed rather than concealed her legs, breasts, belly, and blondness; it was held together by a diamond brooch at her navel, and was as revealing in back as in front. Gloria loved moments like this, when she was undressed to the nines and every eye was on her. Beyond the intense sexual thrill, she felt as if she had just taken a big, juicy bite out of the apple of life. She was Gloria VanDeen, Sweetheart of the Empire, dammit—every man's dream, every woman's envy. That was what they said about her, at least, and she had long since decided that she would be a fool not to revel in it.

At the same time, there was calculation behind her exhibitionism. As she had discovered on Mynjhino, she had the power to attract the loyalty and devotion of practically everyone who saw her, and she could use that power to achieve her ends. The boomers of Sylvania would rally to her and help her succeed in her mission, just for the sake of a close look at her body and the sight of her smile.

She gave them the smile now, and a friendly wave.

The place went crazy.

Gloria and Eckstein slowly made their way down the staircase as the boomrats roared, whooped, shouted, and stomped.

"You certainly know how to make an entrance," Eckstein said to her.

"It's the exits the matter the most," she replied. "But a good entrance certainly helps."

In due course, they arrived at the small table where Elba was waiting for them and took their seats. The noise level in the Emporium gradually died down to something near normal. "Hon," Elba said in honest admiration, "I never seen the like. But let me tell ya somethin'. I ain't sayin' I was ever as gorgeous as you, but a hundred years back, if a man was to have to choose between the two of us, he might've had to take a couple of minutes to make up his mind."

"I believe you, Elba," Gloria said.

ELBA ORDERED BEERS AND DINNER DIRECTLY from the kitchen on her wristcom. The beers promptly arrived, carried by a pretty young woman with a cute little body and a forced smile on her face. She was wearing only a tiny, nearly transparent white G-string that didn't quite cover her most intimate region. A hint of reddish blush spread across her cheeks and throat, and her pert, pink nipples were fully erect. Gloria suppressed a grin while Eckstein looked away, trying not to embarrass Petra.

"Off to a good start, hon," Elba told her. "The boys been talkin' 'bout you a lot. Sure ya won't change your mind about workin' the rooms? You could make a fortune."

"No thank you," Petra said primly.

"You don't wanna get rich? Why the hell ya come here, then?"

"It was to get away from someone."

"Ah," Elba nodded. "A man."

"No," Petra told her, "a woman. I worked for a horrible, evil woman who kept making me do all these terrible things." She glanced at Gloria and added, "But I'll get even with her someday, if it's the last thing I do."

While Gloria put her hand over her mouth and tried not to laugh out loud, Elba offered Petra counsel. "Child, ya can't spend your life studyin' revenge. Shit, if I carried all my old grudges around with me, I'd need a Trans-Empire freighter just to tote 'em. Now you just go back to work and think happy thoughts."

Petra did as she was told, but didn't look as if her thoughts were very happy.

"Now then," Elba said, wiping some beer suds from her mouth with the back of her wrist, "let's get to the conversation. First thing you're gonna ask me is what's a nice girl like me doin' runnin' a place like this, right?"

"Absolutely," Gloria agreed.

"Well, it's like this," Elba began. "I was born out on the Frontier in Sector 4 on Hitchen's Haven, back durin' the Troubles. One war after another in those days, and half the time we were cut off from the rest of the Empire.

So I never got much education, but I bet I've read more books than you have, hon. I could talk just as formal and refined as you, had I a mind to, but the places I've been, it's best to be as folksy as the clientele."

"And what places are those?" Gloria asked.

"Places like this one, mainly. Every damn boom-world for the last century, I'd guess, half the hellholes, and one side o' the Frontier to th' other. You ask 'em about me the next time ya get to Jensen's Reef or Bagosian Five. They'll tell ya, all right. Been runnin' bawdy houses since the time of Edward III, and no one ever said Elba gave 'em anything but the best, circumstances allowin'. But I'll tell ya, hon, this here's my last go-round. I'm old and tired and used up, and Sylvania's gonna be my swan song. Gonna go live with my great-granddaughter on Flavin Three. Gal's got the best house in that whole damn sector, or so they say. Twenty girls, silk sheets, the works. I guess the talent sorta runs in the family."

Their meals arrived, interrupting Elba's flow. Everyone got beef stew. Between bites, Elba explained that nearly all the food on the planet had to be imported, except for what was produced exclusively for the Lodge by their own small truck farm and cattle ranch. There were a few shepherds up in the hills, so lamb and mutton were sometimes available, and a handful of fishermen trawled for Sylvania's native fish, some of which were edible, if bony. But for the most part, people had to get by on expensive frozen imports from Palmyra.

"Got a cook who knows how to make a passable meal from what we get," Elba said. "It ain't no filly-mignone, but it sticks to your ribs and there's plenty of it."

"It's excellent," Gloria said, meaning it.

"Thankee," said Elba. "Now, where was I? Oh, I was leavin', that's where I was. Yep, I'd leave tomorrow if I could find someone to take this place off my hands and take care of my girls. But the only one around here who wants it and can afford it is that goddamn Grunfeld, and

I'd hate like Hades to hafta sell it to him. He's been tryin' to pressure me ever since the beginning, but I just won't give him the satisfaction, ya see? Bastard already has his hooks in everything around here, and if he got the Emporium . . . well, folks would have a worse time of it than they already do. So I'm real glad to see you Dexta folks come back, hon, I truly am. Mebbe if ya put Grunfeld in his place, a respectable buyer will show up and let me retire. That's what you're gonna do, ain't ya?" She looked hopefully at Gloria.

"Well," Gloria admitted, "not exactly. We're just here to register voters, Elba, not to replace Grunfeld or the Lodge or anyone else. Eventually, when we register enough of them, the Emperor will appoint an Imperial Governor, then—well, I suppose things will change around here. But maybe not in the way you want. I'm sorry, Elba, but I can't promise you anything."

"That's disappointin', I don't mind tellin' ya. And— shit, speak o' the devil!" A big, swaggering man with a full black beard and a plasma pistol on his hip entered the main room and started toward their table.

"That's Grunfeld?" Gloria asked.

"No, just one of his pukes. Name o' Karl Cleveland. Don't come no worse."

Cleveland sauntered up to their table, ignored Elba and Eckstein, and stared down at Gloria's bare breasts for several seconds before speaking. "You VanDeen?"

"I am."

"Boss wants to see you."

"You mean Mayor Grunfeld?"

"I mean the boss."

"Tell him I'll see him in the morning."

"Boss says now."

"I'm busy. I'll see him in the morning. I assume I can find him in City Hall?"

Cleveland offered a sneer from behind his beard. "You don't find him, he'll sure as shit find you." He stared at her another moment, then casually turned away and left.

"Charming," said Gloria.

"Not a man here ain't afraid of him—and the rest of Grunfeld's pukes. Oh, some of 'em talk tough about what they'd like to do to 'em, but nobody ever lifts a finger to *do* nothin'."

"Well," said Gloria thoughtfully, "maybe that can change. I think I'll take a little walk around the room and meet some of the boys. Don't get up, Stu, I'll be fine."

GLORIA GOT TO HER FEET, AND THE BIG ROOM was momentarily filled with the sound of clicking eyeballs. She sauntered off to the next table, bare bottom swaying, and said, "Hi boys! How's it going?"

Eckstein watched her progress around the room, and Elba watched Eckstein.

"You ain't gonna let yourself get stuck on her, are ya, Stu?" Elba asked solicitously. "She's too much woman for any one man, ya know."

"I know," Eckstein said, sounding more philosophical than he felt as he watched the boomers exchanging greetings with Gloria. "She's just one of those incredible things that happen sometimes, like a big comet sweeping across the sky. I know I can't keep her, but I can enjoy her while she's here."

"You do more than that, Stu," Elba told him. "You take care of her, ya hear me?"

"From what I hear, she's pretty good at taking care of herself."

"You take care of her anyway. Dammit, Stu, she may think she can handle Grunfeld, but she don't know what she's up against. You take care of her."

"I'll try," said Eckstein. "Spirit knows, I'll try."

chapter 7

"I'M SEEING HIM ALONE, STU, AND THAT'S ALL there is to it."

"You are *not* going in there alone, Gloria. I know you think you can handle him, but he's got five big goons to help him."

"He won't start anything. Not now, anyway. He'll try to scare me and intimidate me, but his main purpose for the moment will be to find out as much as he can about what Dexta intends to do. Stop worrying; I'll be fine."

They were standing together outside Elba's and had begun to attract attention—and not simply because they were arguing. Gloria was wearing an electric-blue, molecules-thick bodysuit that clung to her like wet tissue paper. She had left the pressure seam in front open to her navel, and had set the transparency at 70 percent. Early-morning passersby stopped and gawked.

Gloria leaned over to Eckstein and gave him a quick kiss on the cheek. "Now go get the skimmer ready. I should be back in no more than half an hour. If I'm not . . . well, then you can come in after me and be a big, hairy-chested hero. But not before, okay?"

Eckstein clearly didn't like it, but had already learned that it was useless to argue with Gloria once she had made up her mind. "Okay," he said grudgingly. He gave her a firm kiss on the lips, then trudged off toward the skimmer, mumbling to himself.

Gloria watched him go, then set out for City Hall. She didn't mind that Eckstein wanted to be her protector—that much was a given. What she minded was that he might get himself hurt in the process, and that was something she couldn't afford to let happen. Without Eckstein, her mission would be a failure.

She paused at the front steps of City Hall and opened the pressure seam of her bodysuit all the way down to her crotch and reset the garment's transparency to 90 percent. She wanted Grunfeld to see everything she had, not simply as a sexual ploy, but as a frank display of her own weapons. Grunfeld expected her to be cowed by the muscle at his command, but she had powers of a different sort and wanted him to realize it. Men responded to many forces, and some of them were more powerful than fear.

Making her way around the tables at Elba's last night, she had let the men know why she had come to Sylvania. Most of them would never have dreamed of registering to vote, even if Grunfeld hadn't actively discouraged it. But Gloria had given them an entirely new perspective on the matter, and suddenly, it seemed like a pretty good idea. Their newly discovered interest in democracy had been enhanced even more by Gloria's promise of a kiss and a hug for every man who registered. She could have signed up a couple of hundred men on the spot if she'd had the registration paraphernalia handy. By now, Grunfeld had to be aware of this.

As she made her way up the front steps of City Hall, she noticed that a crowd had begun to collect in the streets. She pushed open the doors and found two tall, muscular, and rather hairy men lounging in the hallway. "Where's the Mayor's office?" she asked them.

They took their time to stare at her before one of them indicated an office to Gloria's right with a jerk of his thumb. Gloria nodded her thanks, the men smirked, and she went in to meet the local power structure.

Two even bigger, hairier men stood just inside the door. One of them was Karl Cleveland. It was a fairly small room for a mayor's office, and the two men took up a good percentage of the floor space. A massive wooden desk took up most of the rest. At the moment, there was no one behind it, but a few seconds later, to the sound of a toilet flushing, Kevin Grunfeld emerged from a doorway, wiping his hands on his rough brown trousers. He looked up, saw Gloria, and stopped in his tracks.

He was a hulk of a man, a good six and a half feet tall, with a big walrus mustache, stubble on his chin, longish brown hair pushed to one side of a high forehead, and dark, deep-set eyes that would have done credit to a pit viper. He might have been close to fifty, and despite his obvious muscles, there was a hint of flab about him, like an athlete who had gone to seed. He stared at Gloria for a few moments, slowly taking her in from head to toe and back again, and a surly smile formed beneath the mustache.

"Gloria VanDeen," he said. "Welcome to my town. And to my planet."

"Thank you, Mr. Mayor. You won't need your bodyguards," she said, indicating the two men with a short motion of her head. "I probably won't hurt you."

Grunfeld snickered at that. It was a sound similar to that made by a pig rooting through slop. "That's just Karl and Hank. They won't hurt you none, neither, 'less I tell 'em to."

"That would be an exceptionally stupid thing to tell them, even for a small-town oaf like you, Grunfeld." The Mayor's eyes widened a fraction at her words. "I'm a representative of the Department of Extraterrestrial

Affairs, here on official business. Any attempt by you or anyone else to impede, obstruct, harass, or hinder me in the lawful performance of my duties would constitute a violation of the *Dexta Code*."

"No shit," said Grunfeld, who was seldom at a loss for snappy comebacks.

"Have you ever heard of a man named Randall Sweet or a planet called Grisham Three?" Gloria asked him.

"No," Grunfeld said after a moment's thought. "Why? Any reason I should have?"

"Grisham Three," Gloria informed him, "is a prison world with gravity of 1.4 G, a mean surface temperature hot enough to fry eggs, and an atmospheric sulfur-dioxide content that smells even worse than your two friends. Randall Sweet is the last man who attempted to impede, obstruct, harass, and hinder me, and he's spending the rest of his life there."

"No shit," Grunfeld responded again.

"Let me make this as clear as possible, Grunfeld. You may be the biggest fish in your little puddle here, but the tide is coming in and you are about to be swamped by the Empire. My team will arrive in a week, and we will begin registering voters. If you get in our way, a shipload of Dexta Internal Security forces will follow us shortly to make travel arrangements for you and your Neanderthals. Be sure to say hello to Randy Sweet for me."

"Well, ain't you somethin'!" Grunfeld declared. A full-scale smile, or something like one, spread across his face. "Heard about you, but I never quite believed it. Emperor's ex-wife, they say. You sure sound like it, and ain't no doubt you look like it, but, ya know, this ain't no Imperial Palace you're in now. You're in Greenlodge, Territory of Sylvania, and we got our own law around here. In fact, you're lookin' at it. What I say goes, and that's all there is to it. So don't think you can scare me with all this *Dexta Code* shit. See, I know a little about that particular bullshit, and I know there's somethin' called *habeas corpus*, which means ya gotta *have the body* before you can arrest someone. If I decide to get rid of you, Miz Gloria, there won't be no body for no one to find."

"A hundred people saw me walk in here," Gloria said, unperturbed. "They'll expect to see me walk out again."

"You keep givin' me that smart mouth o' yours, could be they'll see you carried out." Grunfeld took two steps forward, closing the distance between them. Still smiling, he took a closer look at her. "So," he said at last, staring at her exposed crotch, "that's where the Emperor sticks his scepter, huh?" He laughed at his wit.

"Not anymore," Gloria told him. "I just wanted you to see the only thing on this planet that you don't control. And never will."

"Thatta fact? Well, mebbe we should just see about that."

Grunfeld reached for her with his right hand, palmed her belly for a moment, then moved downward. Gloria made no move to stop him, and as Hank and Karl snickered behind her, Grunfeld moved his fingers through the tangle of her pubic hair. He soon found what he was after and began stroking and probing deeper into her.

Gloria let him continue to manipulate her for a few moments, then reached down and expertly broke his middle finger. The sharp crack of snapping bone was followed by a bellow of pain and outrage. Hank and Karl were frozen in surprise.

"You fucking cunt!" Grunfeld screamed as he examined his damaged digit.

"Just imagine what I'd do to your cock," Gloria said calmly.

"You crazy bitch, ya think I'm gonna let you get away with that?" Grunfeld reared back with his left hand to slap her. Gloria saw it coming with plenty of time to spare, adroitly ducked under his hand, snagged it on the way by, and broke his remaining middle finger.

Grunfeld doubled over in pain, screaming incoherently. Karl and Hank reacted this time. Karl was closer and grabbed for her arms, but Gloria's bodysuit was too slick for him to get a grip; that was one reason why she had worn it. As he tried for another hold, Gloria twisted around in a lightning Qatsima move and got a handful of his thick beard, just beneath his chin. Using full leverage from her legs as she fell forward, she pulled on the beard and set Karl into irreversible motion.

Outside on the street, people were startled by the sound of breaking wood and glass and astonished to see Karl Cleveland come flying headfirst out of a window. He landed in a mud puddle with a resounding splat, and lay still.

Gloria had already calculated time, distance, and motion, and didn't have to look to know where Hank would be by now. She simply balanced on her left foot, bent her knee slightly, and thrust out to the rear with her right foot, hitting the precise spot she had intended to hit—Hank's right knee. He screamed, even louder than Grunfeld had, and crumpled to the floor.

Not quite finished, she gave Grunfeld a right-foot kick to his groin, spun left, and kicked the plasma pistol out of Hank's fumbling grip. Hank seemed to know what was coming next as he stared at her, wide-eyed. Gloria spun left again, right, left once more, and unleashed a sidewheeling kick from the left that caught Hank flush in the temple and removed him from further participation in events.

Gloria quickly retrieved the plasma pistol and was sticking the barrel up Grunfeld's left nostril by the time the two men in the hall came in to see what the commotion was all about. "Move another millimeter," she told them, "and I'll part your boss's hair from the inside."

The two men froze in position, and Gloria turned her attention back to Grunfeld. "Now, then, Kevin, I have just one more thing to tell you. *Don't fuck with me!* Don't even *think* about it. Got it?" She shoved the barrel a little farther up his nose, for emphasis. Grunfeld could only gasp, and nod.

A few moments later, Gloria emerged from the front entrance of City Hall. After an appropriate period of stunned silence, the crowd began to cheer and holler. Gloria smiled and waved to them, then got into the skimmer parked in front.

Eckstein was as stunned as everyone else, but finally put the skimmer into motion. He turned to look at her, slowly shaking his head from side to side.

"I thought you said Grunfeld wouldn't start anything," he said.

"Grunfeld didn't," Gloria told him, smiling in satisfaction. "*I* did."

THE SKIMMER FLEW UPRIVER A FEW METERS above the water. Eckstein pointed out various sites of interest as Gloria took in the scene with a growing sense of wonder. She had seen many planets during her Empire-cruising days with Charles, but Sylvania may have been the most beautiful of them all. It was not a spectacular, jaw-dropping beauty of the kind one found on the big tourist worlds like Glendower or Nehru, but a quiet, tranquil, and beguiling beauty that whispered of serenity and peace of mind. The high, snowcapped mountains in the distance—comparable to the Andes, Eckstein told her—framed the scene in purple and lavender, while the green slopes of the nearer peaks enclosed the V of the river valley in a calm embrace. After they passed the sawmill and the logging camps along the riverside, all signs of human presence faded away, leaving Gloria with a quiet sense of grace. She felt the land and the river offering her a silent welcome.

Farther upriver, the trees were huge, towering a hundred leafy meters into the deep blue skies. They reminded Gloria of the great sequoias and redwoods that had once grown in California, but which she had never seen—nor had anyone else in many centuries. Unlike so many worlds, Sylvania's native biosystem was hauntingly terrestrial, with no jarring alien intrusions. She saw birds that might have been hawks or eagles soaring on the thermals above the valley, and animals that only a trained exozoologist could distinguish from deer and elk browsing placidly in the deep grasses at the river's edge.

"When they established the Lodge," Eckstein told her, "they thought they would spend a lot of time hunting. But the native fauna had absolutely no fear of humans, and it wasn't much sport shooting animals that only wanted to lick your hand. So they gave up on the hunting angle pretty quickly. Oh, there are a few bearlike critters that are worth tracking, but they've learned to steer clear of humans, and you have to go way up into the mountains to find them nowadays. The other animals tend to avoid the town and mining camps now, since the boomrats are always hungry, but for the most part, people have had remarkably little impact on the existing ecosystem."

"How long can that last?" Gloria wondered.

"It will all be gone in the blink of an eye as soon as you get those voters registered," Eckstein told her.

Gloria nodded and said nothing more.

SOME THIRTY KILOMETERS UPSTREAM FROM Greenlodge, they came upon a mining camp littering the east bank of the river, where a plunging, rushing stream disgorged into the Rankus. Eckstein brought the skimmer to rest on the gravel bank, and they got out to meet the boomrats in their native element.

There were a dozen or so tents and a couple of wooden shacks scattered randomly along the shore, and Gloria saw thirty of forty men—and a couple of women—engaged in various tasks. Some were chopping wood, a handful were gathered around what seemed to be a cookfire, but most were busy with the endless chores of Fergusite mining. A long, black flume descended from the narrow stream, providing a gushing torrent that was diverted into three wooden sluice boxes that had been set up along the edge of the river. Several men were busy dumping sand into the boxes, while others were squatting in the river itself, concentrating on their solitary efforts with shallow metal pans. Most everyone wore slick black waders held up by colorful suspenders, ragged flannel shirts, and go-to-hell hats.

"Lookit here," called one of them. "It's Stu Eckstein— and just look what he brought us!"

Work suspended as abruptly as if someone had sounded an air horn. The boomrats gathered around them on the gravel shore, shoving one another out of the way as they fought to get a better view of Gloria. Eckstein, grinning, greeted many of them by name and shook hands with some. He threw his arm around the shoulders of one of them and ushered him over to where Gloria was standing.

"Gloria," he said, "I want you to meet Gus Thornton, the King of Pizen Flats."

Gloria bowed her head and said, "Your Highness."

"Highness, nothin'," the king declared. "C'mere, gal, and give a man a proper greetin'!" Thornton embraced Gloria in a bear hug and gave her a whiskery, tobacco-flavored kiss, which she returned with enthusiasm.

Thornton released her, stepped back, and said, "So you're the little gal who tossed Karl Cleveland outta the Mayor's front window, eh?"

Gloria wondered how he had heard the news so quickly, but then noticed that Thornton was wearing a wristcom. It was easy to think that it was still the nineteenth century out here, but little touches of the thirty-third did intrude.

"I'm the gal," Gloria told him, returning his grin. "And tell me, Your Highness, how do you come by your title? I didn't realize there was a branch of the royal family in these parts."

"I come by it 'cause I was the first one here, 'cept for Old Abel. I ain't really no king, but folks figgered if they could have a Mayor down in Greenlodge, why, we needed ourselves a king up here. C'mon, Gloria, let's go get us some coffee. And the rest o' you bastards can just clear a path for us and keep your grubby paws to yourselves, ya hear? I won't have no damn shitstompers molestin' as fine a lady as this!"

Thornton took Gloria's arm and they made their way from the gravel embankment up to the cookfire through the swarm of grinning boomrats. He gestured to a handmade wooden chair in front of the fire. "This here's my throne," he said. "But it's yours, milady, since you are Queen Gloria the First for as long as you're here."

Gloria sat down, Thornton and Eckstein pulled up other makeshift chairs next to her, and everyone else squatted on their haunches or stood around the fire in a semicircle. Someone handed her a metal cup of coffee, and she took an experimental sip. It didn't quite scorch her tongue or dissolve her teeth, but it was close.

"Here," said Thornton, "lemme sweeten that up for ya." He poured some brown fluid from a flask into the cup, then did the same for Eckstein and himself. "Bottoms up, and confusion to Grunfeld and his pukes!" There were cries of "Hear, hear!" and Gloria took another sip, which made her eyes water.

"How's the digging, Gus?" Eckstein asked him.

"Goin' strong, goin' strong," Thornton assured him. "Found a crystal the size of a walnut just the other day. O' course, mostly we're just pannin' and sluicin' for the little stuff, but there's plenty of that, and plenty more where it came from." He gestured upstream toward the slopes.

"And what about the highboys?" Eckstein asked, referring to the miners who worked the outcrops on the cliff faces and mountainsides.

Thornton shook his head. "Still tough sleddin' up there, but some of those bastards are hauling down crystal by the ton, or so they claim. But they still ruin more than they get, what with all that goddamn sloppy drillwork most of 'em do. O' course, the only ones who can use the drills anymore are the ones who already sold their claims to Grunfeld, so they can zap every damn outcrop they find, for all o' me." Several of the boomrats grunted and nodded in agreement.

Gloria, a puzzled look on her face, turned to Eckstein for an explanation. Eckstein took another sip from his cup, then said, "You see, Gloria, there are what you might call philosophical differences among the miners. These boys here work the streambeds and rivers, panning for crystals that have eroded from the slopes. They make a pretty steady return, but stand little chance of making a really big score. Then, you have the highboys, who work the outcrops up on the slopes. Some of them have made fortunes, but more of them have destroyed fortunes by using their plasma drills a little too carelessly. It's harder work with bigger risks, bigger returns. The riverrats down here tend to sneer at the highboys—"

"Damn right we do!" cried someone, to general approval.

"—while the highboys think the riverrats are just, well . . ."

"They think we're milksops and cream puffs," put in Thornton. "But some of us have been here two years, and them fuckin' highboys, beggin' your pardon, ma'am, come and go like the mornin' dew. Some of 'em make their strike and leave, some of 'em quit the first sign o' trouble, and some of 'em wind up dead when they run afoul o' Grunfeld and his pukes."

"And some of them hear the Voice," someone said. Silence followed his words.

Gus Thornton spat into the fire. "Pasco Zuckerman heard it just the other day," he said.

"Pasco?" asked Eckstein. "Damn, he's been here forever!"

"Ain't here no more," Thornton said. "Never put much stock in the Voice, did ol' Pasco. But he finally heard it. Told him to git, and he got."

"What voice?" Gloria asked.

"Didn't Stu tell ya about the Voice?"

Gloria turned to Eckstein, frowning. "No," she said, "he didn't."

Eckstein looked mildly embarrassed. "Well," he said, "it's just this local superstition—"

"Ain't no fuckin' superstition!" roared one of the boomrats. "Heard it myself, and so did half the boys here." A rumble of emphatic agreement and milder dissent spread around the cookfire for a minute or two.

Finally, Thornton raised a hand and the hubbub died away. He turned to Gloria and said, "Missy, the thing of it is, is that sometimes when a man's alone out here, he gets to hearin' things. 'Zackly *what* he hears is . . . well, it's like this voice. Sorta comes outta everywhere and nowhere. Ya look around, but no one's there. Ya hear it, then ya don't hear it, and ya wonder if ya ever really heard it at all. Some of the boys swear it's real, and some think it's just a bunch o' hooey. And some of us don't quite know *what* to think."

"And what does this Voice say?"

"Says different things to different people. Mostly, it tells the highboys to get the hell out, and mostly they do. And mostly it just tells us riverrats, 'Don't hurt me.'"

"Only that?"

"That's about it," Thornton said. "The Voice ain't much for makin' speeches."

"What do you think it means?"

"I think it means just what it says. So down here, we try to be a little more considerate than them damn highboys. We take better care o' things. The highboys just rip and zap and let the splinters fall where they may. Take a look up thataway." Thornton twisted around in his chair and pointed toward a brown scar on the mountainside. "That's what the highboys do. Clear the trees outta their way, spill tailings all over the place, and leave a mess behind. Now, down here, we take what we need and do what we gotta do to get the crystals, but we don't just smash up the place. We gotta live here, ya see."

Gloria nodded and said nothing.

One of the boomrats stepped forward and removed his hat as he looked at her. "Miz Gloria," he said, "you probably think we're just a bunch of crazy old boomrats, and some of us may be, but what we're tellin' you about the Voice is the Spirit's own truth. If you was to spend some time out here, might be you'd hear it yourself. The Voice might just talk to someone like you."

There was general agreement with this sentiment. Gloria suspected that they were just trying to get her to stay for a while, but she couldn't ignore the evident sincerity in their voices and faces. "Who knows the most about the Voice?" she asked.

"Old Abel," said the boomrat. " 'cept he won't talk about it none. Mebbe he'd talk to *you*, though."

"Mebbe he would at that," Thornton agreed.

"And just who is Old Abel, and where can I find him?"

"You don't find him. He finds you, ma'am. If he wants to," Thornton explained. "But even Old Abel ain't so crazy that he wouldn't want to talk to a gal like you. As to who he is, well, all anyone knows is that he was already here when the rest of us arrived. Some say he helped build the Lodge, way back in the beginning, and just stayed on. He lives in the forests upstream from here, somewhere, no one can say, prezackly. Kinda like the Voice, himself, is Old Abel. If anyone knows what it is, it'd be him. But he won't say."

Another boomer stepped forward. This one was younger than most of them, and a little better groomed. "Miss VanDeen," he said, "my name's Ted Oberlin, and unlike most of these riverrats, I've had some education and can speak the Emperor's English."

That produced a round of jeers and laughs, but Oberlin ignored it. "We've heard that you are here to register voters so that the Emperor can appoint an Imperial Governor. Is that true?"

"It is," Gloria said. "A team from Dexta will be here in about a week to start enrolling voters. And, yes, the Emperor does intend to appoint an Imperial Governor."

"And what will happen then?" Oberlin asked her.

"I can't tell you that with any certainty. But one thing that definitely will happen is that all of your rights will be respected. You won't be at Grunfeld's mercy any longer, that's one thing I can promise you."

The boomrats cheered at that, but Oberlin continued standing there, a look of deep concern on his face. "Whose mercy will we be at?" he asked her. "Imperium's? Excelsior's? Prizm's? I studied a little law once, Miss VanDeen, and I know that when this territory is incorporated, the Emperor can grant a concession to any or all of the Big Twelve. Where will that leave us?"

"Under the protection of the Homestead Acts."

"We're supposed to be under the protection of the Homestead Acts right now—for all the good that's done us. But we'll also come under the aegis of the Eminent Domain Statutes, isn't that true?"

"Eminent Fuckin' Domain!" roared another boomrat. "You know what they can do with that!" The boomers joined in a nearly unanimous and profane condemnation of the Eminent Domain Statutes.

When the outcry had subsided, Gloria got to her feet and slowly turned to look each one of the boomers in the eyes. "Men," she said, "I know that you're concerned about what the Eminent Domain Statutes could mean for you. And you're right to be concerned. A lot of things will change once the territory is incorporated, and I won't try to stand here and tell you that all of the changes will be to your liking. But there's one thing that I can tell you. Until you have an Imperial Governor who can protect your rights, absolutely *nothing* will change.

The law on Sylvania will still be whatever Grunfeld and the Lodge say it is. So, if you like things the way they are and don't mind being terrorized by Grunfeld and his pukes, then, by all means, don't register. But if you are willing to take a chance on a better future—uncertain as it may be—then my people will be here in a week or so to sign you up. I hope you'll be as kind to them as you have been to me. And now, I think Stu and I have to be leaving if we're going to see the high country today. Thank you for your hospitality, Your Highness, and thanks to all of you. I'll be seeing you again real soon."

As quickly as they could, Eckstein and Gloria made their way back to the skimmer, rose into the air, and turned up the valley of the rushing stream, cautiously ascending toward the slopes.

"I hated that," Gloria said, more to herself than to Eckstein.

"You didn't lie to them," Eckstein reassured her. "And if what we're trying to do works—"

"What if it doesn't?" Gloria demanded. "What happens to those men *then*? What happens to this valley?"

"Then," Eckstein told her, "the corporates will peel this valley like an apple, and core it. Everything you've seen today will be gone. Forever."

chapter 8

AFTER SPENDING MOST OF THE MIDDAY WITH A small group of highboys on the slopes, Gloria and Eckstein carefully picked out a circuitous route that was accessible for a skimmer, leading up to an alpine meadow at the summit of one of the peaks rimming the valley. They got out, and Gloria drank in the magnificent view, south toward the river and the sea and north toward the jagged range of mountains. Perhaps it was just the thin air, but she felt light-headed, giddy, and intensely alive.

Eckstein stood close behind her, wrapping his arms around her waist. He began stroking and massaging her navel, sending shivers of warm sensation coursing through her. Finally, she shuddered in uncontrolled ecstasy, gasping in the thin air as the orgasm overtook her.

She twisted around and kissed Eckstein on his throat and neck. "I shouldn't have told you about that," she said.

"But I notice you always dress in a way that lets me get at it."

"You noticed that, did you?" Gloria began snaking

herself out of the bodysuit. "Show me what else you've noticed about me."

THEY LAY DOWN IN THE SOFT GRASSES, AND Eckstein proceeded to offer a detailed inventory of all the things he had noticed about her. The thin, firm lips that curved upward at the corners in a smile that never quite went away. The delicate chin and throat where her veins visibly pulsed in urgent throbs. The soft globular mounds of her breasts and the dark conical protrusions that rose to stiff, swollen, cylindrical nipples standing like silos on hilltops. The exquisitely whorled cavity of her magical umbilicus. The smooth, brown expanse of her belly and the rising counterpoint of her pubic mound, with its wispy, honey-colored curls. The engorged, pink bud of clitoris, where even the slightest pressure of finger or tongue brought spasms of electric pleasure.

He slid into her as one might enter a cathedral, with awe and respect, but as eagerly as if plunging into a hot, soapy bath on a cold night. Her genetically enhanced vaginal muscles clutched at him, and he could feel the explosions rippling through the interior nerve clusters that the genetic sculptors of long ago had bequeathed her. Gloria, Gloria, he wondered, what *are* you? And how did I come to be here, inside you?

Too soon, he surged in ecstatic release, and Gloria twisted and writhed beneath him, timing her own seismic convulsions to match his own. Her orgasms continued long after his had run its course, and even after he had finally withdrawn from her and rolled away, she shuddered in rhythmic gasps until, at last, she lay still.

THEY LAY IN SILENCE BENEATH THE COOL SUN of Sylvania for a long while, until Gloria said, "I'll always remember this. Especially if . . . if all of this is gone someday."

"And it will be," Eckstein answered softly, "unless we can come up with something soon. You saw for yourself, the cliff faces are just too exposed for our purposes."

"Maybe a cave?"

"Any caves along the outcrop layer have already been found by the miners. We need something else."

Gloria turned onto her side and threw her arm across Eckstein's chest. "Dammit," she said, pulling herself close to him, "I just hate this. Everything in my heart is telling me that we can't let them destroy this valley and the lives of those good men we met today. And everything in my head is telling me that if we don't register those voters, Charles will throw Norman Mingus to the wolves. Without him, Dexta and the Empire itself might fall apart, Fergusite or no Fergusite. I can't imagine what will become of the Empire after he's gone and there's no one left to stand in Charles's way. Dammit, Stu, what can we do?"

"I wish I knew."

"I always think better after a good fuck," she told him, giving his earlobe a quick kiss. "So I ought to come up with the best idea in the whole history of good ideas, now. What was that they said, about how only some of the highboys can use their plasma drills?"

"Only the ones who have sold their claims to Grunfeld," Eckstein said. "They can continue working them, but Grunfeld gets a cut, and will control the claim when it comes time for the Eminent Domain vote."

"How come?"

"Grunfeld has the only plasma recharger on the planet," Eckstein explained. "The only alternative would be to take their drills back to Palmyra after every twenty shots, and that would just be too expensive. So if they want to use plasma drills, they have to play ball with Grunfeld. In a way, that's good, because it slows down the work and limits the amount of incidental damage that's done to the outcrops. But, of course, it also means that the miners will get royally screwed by Eminent Domain."

"Because Grunfeld owns the claims."

"It's more than that. You saw the difference between the riverrats' camp and the highboys' camp, didn't you? The claims on the slopes are worked by only a few men at any one site, sometimes by just a single man. But the camp on the river belongs to forty or fifty people. So there are lots of claims held by just a few people on the ridges, but only a few claims on the rivers, held by many people. But each claim just counts for one vote in an Eminent Domain poll."

"I see," said Gloria. "So if there were another plasma recharger around, one not controlled by Grunfeld, that would make for a lot more claims on the slopes."

"True, but that wouldn't help the riverrats."

"No, but it might make the Eminent Domain vote more interesting. Just exactly what is a plasma recharger, anyway?"

"Well, you know that plasma weapons have to be recharged after a few shots, right? Same thing with a drill, which typically gets about twenty shots before it needs to be recharged."

"Yes, but what does it *do?*"

"It recharges the plasma, simple as that."

"Remember that you're talking to a technological moron, Mr. Imperial Geologist," Gloria reminded him. "Spell it out for me."

Eckstein chuckled, then turned to face her. "All right, Ms. Moron, it's like this. Plasma is the fourth state of matter, atoms stripped of electrons, but really, it's more like concentrated energy. You can only store the stuff in a magnetic containment vessel. That's the replaceable cylindrical thing you see in plasma pistols. When you've discharged all your plasma, you need to get more. To get it, you need a fusion reactor, but you can't carry one of those around with you. So you go find a plasma recharger. The Imperial Marines have small, portable ones, specifically designed for their weapons. But to recharge a drill, you need a big, industrial-sized recharger, which is basically just a fusion reactor with a few refinements for storing and releasing the plasma it creates."

"Thank you. I think I get it now. The fusion reactor can just keep turning out more plasma, more energy?"

"Continuously, if necessary. Of course, a recharger doesn't generally need that much, so you only turn it on when you need it."

"But it could just keep going, couldn't it? If you wanted it to, right?"

Eckstein caught on, but shook his head. "I see where you want to go with this, and yes, a suitably modified plasma recharger could do the job for us. It's not what I had in mind originally, but yes, it would work. But we'd still need a place to put it, and anywhere we put it on the slopes would be discovered."

"On the *slopes*, yes," Gloria declared, a big grin slowly spreading across her face. "But what if we had another place to put it where it *wouldn't* be discovered? Or rather, where it would be seen by everyone, but no one would know what we were really doing with it?"

"You have someplace in mind?"

Gloria sprang to her feet and spun around, raising her right fist in triumph. "Oh, yes," she cried. "I know the very place!"

"Tell me," insisted Eckstein.

So Gloria told him, and soon the mountainside echoed with the sound of their laughter.

PETRA HAD SPENT THE NIGHT—OR RATHER, THE morning—sharing a room with three other bar girls. They were friendly and informative, glad to fill her in on details of life at Elba's. Debbie Hansen, the frizzy red-head she had seen earlier, had been there six months. She had come to Sylvania with her boyfriend, who was off on the slopes hoping to strike it rich. He didn't want her working the rooms, and wasn't crazy about her being a bar girl, either, so she was the only one of the three who wore a G-string. Myra Gazivoda and Lynisha Moses had been there about four months; they shared a bed, making it clear why they chose not to work the rooms.

The men, they agreed, were generous, lovable, and mostly harmless. None of them had ever had any real trouble with the boomers, possibly due to the presence of Ernie the Bouncer, but also because there was no need for them to accost unwilling bar girls when the hookers were so readily available. Grunfeld's thugs, on the other hand, could be a problem both in and out of Elba's. Even Ernie refrained from tangling with them, but an informal truce between Grunfeld and Elba offered them a degree of protection while they were in the Emporium. Out on the streets, it was another story. Hank Frezzo, whose knee Gloria had bashed that morning, had once raped Lynisha. She seemed to take it philosophically, reckoning it as just another hazard of her occupation, but Myra swore she was going to cut off Frezzo's balls for him one day. She showed Petra the knife she intended to use for the operation. All three girls advised Petra to get a knife of her own for when she was outside.

"What about the Lodge?" she asked them. "I hear the bar girls can pick up some extra tips doing work up there."

"Myra and I do," Lynisha said, "but Debbie won't go near the place."

"Weird stuff happens up there," said Debbie. "I heard there was a girl here about a year ago who went up to the Lodge and never came back."

"What kind of weird stuff?"

"I don't know, and I don't want to know."

"Oh, Debbie's just jumping at shadows," Myra said. "We've never had much trouble up there. It kind of depends on who's there. Old Man Rankus is just as sweet as he can be, as long as you don't break any dishes or sweep stuff under the beds. But sometimes they have guests who don't really know or care that there's a difference between us bar girls and the hookers. We're just there to look pretty and do the chores, and the girls from the rooms are supposed to handle the sex part."

"How do you get along with the girls in the rooms?" Petra wondered.

"About like Cinderella got along with her stepsisters." Lynisha sniffed. "They think they are Spirit's gift to the galaxy, and we're just dipshit little serving girls. Every now and then, one of us gets into a fight with one of them, which the boomrats all love, of course. But mostly, we get along okay." Lynisha took a closer look at Petra and added, "I'm surprised Elba doesn't have you working the rooms. You'd make a fortune with a face and body like yours."

"Everyone keeps telling me that." Petra sighed.

"Then why not? Shit, I'd do it myself, except for the fact that I just don't like having sex with men. You feel that way too?"

"Uh, no . . . no, I like it fine. Just not ten in one night."

"One, ten, what difference does it make?" Lynisha asked. "If you're gonna let 'em do it at all, you might as well let 'em do it a lot. There's big money to be made in those rooms, Petra."

"Yes, well, maybe after I've been here a while."

"Speaking of money," Myra advised, "ditch that G-string. Your tips'll go up 50, 60 percent. Ours did."

"Or are you saving it for someone special?" Lynisha giggled. "Mr. Right, maybe?"

"Not exactly," Petra said. "I'm just a little shy, I guess."

"Get over it, honey," Myra said.

"Oh, just ignore them, Petra," Debbie said. "They only want to see *yours*. Honestly, you'd think a woman could have a *little* privacy!"

• • •

THAT AFTERNOON, WHILE ON A BREAK, PETRA
hesitantly entered the little alcove that served as Elba's
first-floor office. Elba looked up from her desk, smiled,
and bade Petra to come take a load off. Petra was glad
for the chance to sit down; aside from the occasional
tweaks of her ass and tits, being a bar girl was hardest on
the feet. High heels took some getting used to.

"So, how ya gettin' along, hon?" Elba asked her.

"I'm doing okay," Petra told her, and honestly, she
was. Already, being nearly naked in front of so many
people didn't bother her as much as she had expected it
would. It wasn't so different, really, from Visitation Day
in Central Park. It was surprising how quickly you could
get used to something like that.

"Lotta talk 'bout you, girl," Elba said. "One o' the
boys offered me two thousand for an all-nighter with
you. That's twice the goin' rate, ya know, and half of it's
yours, just one man."

Two thousand! Petra was impressed, in spite of herself.

"Uh . . ."

"Just don't like the idea of sellin' it, huh?"

"Well . . ."

"Shitfire, hon, it ain't like you'd be sellin' your soul,
or even your body. Just rentin' it."

"I know. But, I guess I just don't like the idea of being . . . a *commodity* . . . like a . . . a . . ."

"Piece o' meat?" Elba laughed. "Heard that one
plenty o' times. Hell, girl, ya know what a side o' beef
costs around here? Look, I been a businesswoman all
my life, and lemme tell ya, it's all about supply and demand. If supply is short, demand is high. And the supply
o' pretty girls is pretty damn short around Sylvania. And
it ain't got nothin' to do with bein' a vulnerable, op-
pressed woman. 'Bout eighty years ago, I ran a place just
like this on Beta Nakashima. Was just after one o' the

Frontier Wars, and those bastard Skoonzi reptiles used a biological weapon that killed 90 percent of the males on Beta N. So then, it was men who was in short supply. So I didn't have girls workin' the rooms, I had *men!* Did a pretty brisk business, lemme tell ya, although the profit margin was kinda low. Women can handle ten in a night, but those boys got all tuckered out after three or four." Elba erupted into mirthful laughter at the memory.

"I understand what you're saying," Petra said, "but, still . . ."

"Come on, hon, you can't tell me you never thought about doin' it."

"Well, sure," Petra admitted, blushing a little, "I suppose every woman has *thought* about it . . ."

"Then why not *do* it, this one time in your life? Shit, you're a zillion miles from wherever ya came from, so who's gonna know? Who's gonna care?"

"*I'll* know," Petra responded quickly. "*I'll* care."

"And you think you'll feel worse about yourself 'cause ya did it? Feel all lowly and degraded?"

"Sort of."

"Ya think *I'm* lowly and degraded?"

"No," Petra protested. "No, not at all! Elba, I swear, you are one of the most amazing women I've ever met. I have a tremendous amount of respect for you, I truly do!"

"But ya couldn't respect yourself if ya did what I've done?"

"I . . . I just don't know. I'm not sure."

"Well, then," Elba said, "let's just leave it be for now. I don't want to push ya into nothin' ya really don't want to do. But do us both a favor, and think about it, at least."

"I will, Elba, I promise."

"So," said Elba, "what did ya wanta see me 'bout, then?"

"I wanted to ask if I could get on the list to work up at the Lodge," Petra told her.

"The Lodge!" Elba flung herself back into her chair and looked up at the ceiling for a moment. "O' course, I shoulda known. I couldn't understand why Dexta would send someone here just to spy on *me*. But you wanta spy on the *Lodge*!"

Petra was aghast. "You *knew*?"

"Not right away," Elba said. "But when I saw you and Gloria together last night, somethin' clicked in my old brain. We get the news here, ya know. Late, but we get it."

"Spirit! Does anyone else know?"

Elba shook her head emphatically. "Hell, no. I'm about the only one who bothers to watch the news vids. Remembered you from that Mynjeeno business, few months back. You lost your man there, didn't ya, hon?"

Petra nodded.

"Damn sorry about that. I know how ya feel, dear, and I offer my sincerest sympathies, but you'll get over it. Truly, you will. I'll tell ya, I've lost more men than you've probably ever had. Wars, brawls, accidents. Hell, I killed one o' them myself. Hated to do it, but he was cheatin' on me—not just with other women, but on my *accounts*. Couldn't let him do *that*, now could I? Anyway, I was younger then. Man did that to me today, I'd probably just hire someone to stomp the shit outta him, then send him on his way. Gettin' mellow in my old age, I guess."

"Elba," Petra said, "this is very important. No one else can know why I'm here."

"Don't worry, darlin', your secret is safe with me. And you want to get into the Lodge, consider it done. I'll send ya up in the next batch, and good luck to ya. But you be careful up there, hear me? It ain't no picnic up there, and if they catch ya doin' somethin' they don't like, it could go rough on ya. Very rough. That old Rankus may seem friendly, but he's as tough and mean a bastard as you'll ever come across. And he ain't stupid, like Grunfeld. Grunfeld works for *him*, ya know. And it ain't just Rankus ya gotta worry about. He has some very peculiar people up there, sometimes, like those corporate reps he's got up there now."

"Do you know anything about them?"

"Not much. They don't come down here and mingle with the masses, but I hear things now and then. I hear somethin' interestin', I'll be sure to let ya know. I don't know what you Dexta people are up to, but I think I'd trust you and your friend Gloria before I'd trust them bastards up at the Lodge."

"Thank you, Elba," Petra said. "It means a lot."

"But ya gotta do me a favor in return, hon. Eighty-six that G-string, okay?"

"What?" Petra was shocked. "Why? Does the extra tip money mean that much to you?"

"Don't mean a thing," Elba said, smiling.

"Then why?"

"Ain't askin' for myself, hon. I want ya to do it for *you*. And if ya wanta know why, ask your friend Gloria. She'll understand. Hell, I think you'll understand it for yourself pretty quick if you're as smart as I think you are. Just do it, hon."

Reluctant and mystified, Petra nevertheless got to her feet, peeled off the G-string, and tossed it to Elba, who caught it and smiled.

"Have fun," Elba told her.

Petra walked back out to the main room, naked as the Spirit made her, feeling very strange.

KEVIN GRUNFELD DIDN'T SEE WHAT WAS SO fucking funny about it. Even Doc Harkins snickered a little as he was bandaging the fingers, until Grunfeld shut him up with a threatening look. The doc had given him an injection of Quik-Knit, which hurt like a son of a bitch, but would heal the breaks in a week or two.

But it wasn't just the doc. In the streets, he thought he could hear the guarded laughter of people he passed, and everyone seemed to sneak a peak at the white bandages on his fingers and look away before Grunfeld could meet their eyes. And that old bastard Rankus didn't even try to hide the fact that he thought it was just one big hoot.

Rankus had summoned him up to the Lodge after he got word that the Dexta bitch was in town. Grunfeld had grown to hate these trips up the slope to wait on the pleasure of the man who had hired him a dozen years ago. It had been easy, then—just a matter of keeping the locals in line with tough looks and the occasional stomping. Kind of dull, really. But then came the boom, and life had gotten very interesting and very busy. And aside from keeping Rankus and the Lodge happy, there had been a lot of opportunities for a clever man to make some serious money. Grunfeld had difficulty keeping track of everything he had going these days, but he knew he had several million crowns salted away in a bank on Palmyra. He had enough money to buy himself a spot at the Lodge, if he wanted to, but Rankus would never let that happen.

To Rankus and the barons of the Lodge, Grunfeld was just hired help, and that was all he would ever be. He ran this planet for them, but that didn't keep them from looking down on him. They got a cut of everything he made—or they thought they did, at least—and if it hadn't been for him, they would already have lost control of their little paradise. Some of the corpos had even made him offers on the sly, but Grunfeld turned them down—for the moment. He had too sweet a deal to risk it for the word of some Big Twelve slicker. Still, it could be even sweeter.

Elba had been a thorn in his side ever since she got here and set up the Emporium. That old bitch wasn't afraid of him at all, and she was too popular for him to take a chance on simply shutting her down or forcing her out. But if he could finally get his hands on the Emporium, his control of Greenlodge and the valley would be absolute. He had been willing to wait her out, knowing that she was old and tired and wanted to leave anyway, but now, with Dexta back in town, things had changed.

That VanDeen bitch wanted to register enough voters to get the territory incorporated, and he wasn't fool enough to think that she could be stopped. She was right; if the Emperor and Mingus and the Big Twelve wanted to take control of Sylvania, they would—and nothing Grunfeld or even Rankus could do would prevent that from happening. He could do things that would make it later rather than sooner, but he had to be careful. He had heard about what the Dexta IntSec people had done on some other planets, and he didn't want to tangle with the Bugs if it could be avoided.

So, the end was in sight, and Grunfeld knew it. He supposed he could just walk away from it all, take his money, and set himself up in style on some other planet, like maybe Vegas Two. He had been there on vacation a few years back, and it was the kind of place where a man could have a real nice life if he had the crowns to swing it.

But the problem was, he didn't want to leave. He liked it on Sylvania, liked being the top dog. He knew he couldn't compete with an Imperial Governor and the Big Twelve, but it might at least be possible for him to stay and maintain his position in Greenlodge, no matter what changes were coming. What he needed, he realized, was a solid base—something that would be his to have and hold even after the day came when he was no longer Mayor. What he needed, in short, was Elba's Emporium.

He gave the matter some thought as he sat in the back of the skimmer on his way down from the Lodge. Rankus had told him to be careful with the Dexta people, and Grunfeld had nodded and yessirred as usual, although he hadn't made any promises as far as VanDeen was concerned. He had a score to settle with her, and not even Rankus was going to keep him from doing it. But as for Elba, the time had come—before Dexta and that VanDeen bitch could find a way to fuck it all up for him.

Grunfeld signaled to Karl and Hank in the front seat of the skimmer. "Take me to the Emporium," he told them. "We got some business to settle there."

They walked into the main room with their usual swagger—except for Hank, whose usual swagger was slowed by a limp—and paused to look around. The noise from the gambling tables and the bar faded slowly as people noticed them. All was as normal—except that, tonight, somehow, it wasn't *quite* normal.

It slowly dawned on Grunfeld that people were laughing at him. Not quite laughing out loud, not quite openly defying him, but he saw the hidden smiles and mocking grins of the boomers. He saw them staring at Hank's limp, and the bandages on Karl's face where the glass had cut him on his way through the window, and the white splints on his two middle fingers, where that VanDeen bitch had snapped them.

Grunfeld had probably not felt embarrassment since he was twelve years old, but he felt it now, and the realization brought a sense of outrage and anger that outdid anything he had ever felt in his life. He wanted to grab the nearest boomer and smash the grin right off his face—except that he couldn't grab or smash anyone with his fingers in these fucking splints!

He forced himself to calm down. He had business there tonight. Once that was taken care of, there would be plenty of time to make the goddamn boomers rue the day they had laughed at him. Grunfeld even paused to congratulate himself for his growing sense of maturity. Time was, he'd have tried to set everything straight right there, now, tonight—starting with that VanDeen bitch, who was sitting at a table along with Elba and Eckstein, looking at him with that superior smile of hers.

Grunfeld walked over to the table. He carefully avoided looking at VanDeen, even though her tits were all but bare and she was taunting him with those blue eyes, and concentrated on Elba. He gave her his best sneer and said, "I'm tired of waitin' on you, Elba. We got business to do, and we're gonna get it done right now."

"What business you think we got, Kevin?" Elba asked him.

"I'm buyin' the Emporium from you. I'll give ya a fair price, like we already talked about. Ain't gonna try and cheat ya none. But I'm buyin' and you're sellin'— tonight—and that's all there is to it."

"Really?" Elba asked sweetly.

"Really," he said. He turned to Cleveland and said, "Got a seegar, Karl?"

"Sure do, Boss," Cleveland said eagerly. He took one from a pocket and handed it to Grunfeld, who bit the tip off, spat it out, and stuck the cigar in the corner of his mouth.

"Ya see, Elba," he said, sounding like the Voice of Reason itself, "if you don't sell me the Emporium tonight, it might just be that by tomorrow, you won't have nothin' left to sell."

Grunfeld pulled a matchbox out of his vest pocket, extracted a match, and tried to strike it. But with his splinted fingers, he couldn't quite manage it. He dropped the first match unlit, which pretty well spoiled the dramatic demonstration he had planned. The idea was to drop a *lit* match on the wooden floor, so everyone could imagine what might happen to the Emporium if Elba refused to sell it. He tried again, but just couldn't get the fucking match *lit* . . .

"Poor boy," Elba cooed. Before he could stop her, Elba scooped up the dropped match, lit it, and ignited the cigar for him. "That better, hon?"

"Listen, you old bitch, I ain't playin' games here. You're sellin' the fuckin' Emporium, and you're sellin' it tonight!"

"That's right, Kevin, I surely am. In fact, I already sold it. So if *you* wanta buy it, you're gonna hafta make a deal with the *new* owner."

Gloria got to her feet and smiled.

Grunfeld's jaw dropped, and the cigar fell to the floor. Gloria carefully stepped on it, crushing it out.

"In the future," she said, "I'd appreciate it if you'd use the ashtrays, Kevin. I intend to run a tidy establishment."

chapter 9

GLORIA AND ECKSTEIN FINISHED THEIR LATE
breakfast in the nearly deserted main room of the Emporium. No one was around except for Petra and another bar girl, who were sweeping up the place; a few
scattered, hungover boomers; and one of the professional gamblers who leased tables from Elba. Slim Jim
Zuni was sitting alone at his table, knocking back bour-
bons and dealing himself solitaire hands.

"I hate like hell to leave you here alone," Eckstein
said.

"I won't be alone. Petra's here, and Elba will stay
until Althea and the team arrive."

"Let me rephrase that, then. I hate like hell to
leave *you*."

Gloria reached for him and squeezed his hand. "I
know," she said. "I hate it too. But you've got to get the
technical team and the equipment lined up on Palmyra,
and you'll only have a week to do it."

Eckstein nodded. "That will be enough time, I think.
I already have the people in mind, and I know where we

can get a recharger. The modifications shouldn't take more than a couple of days. I guess what really bothers me is that I won't be coming back with the Dexta team."

"We already discussed that, Stu. You know you can't be seen around here until after we're up and running. If anyone connects you with what's supposed to happen here—"

"I know. I can't come back until we're ready to do the survey. And I have to delay that as long as I decently can in order to give you the time that you need. It could be two or three months before I see you again. *That's* what bothers me."

"Do you think that doesn't bother me, too?" Gloria gave him a sad smile.

"Oh, I flatter myself that you'll miss me . . . for maybe fifteen or twenty minutes."

"Nonsense!" She laughed. "It'll be at least an hour." She leaned over and kissed him on the lips. "Maybe two," she added.

"Well," he said, "just do me a favor and don't take the next guy up to that spot on the mountain. I want that to be exclusively ours."

"I want that, too," she said in a soft whisper.

Petra came up behind them and politely cleared her throat. "Will there be anything else today? More coffee?"

"No, I think we're all set, Miss . . . Petra, isn't it?" Gloria grinned at her, not failing to note that Petra's body was now entirely uncovered.

"That's right, ma'am," Petra said as she bent over the table to clear the dishes. "I'm looking forward to being in your employ, Ms. VanDeen." As she worked, she added in a harsh whisper, "I'm also looking forward to seeing how in the world you are going to explain to the Comptroller's Office that Dexta has just bought itself a bawdy house!"

"Oh, they won't mind," Gloria airily assured her. "We'll probably even turn a profit. Of course, it would probably help the cash flow if I could get you to work the rooms. I hear you're quite an attraction around here. What happened to the fig leaf?"

"As a matter of fact, I want to talk to you about that. But not now. I should get moving, but I just wanted to let you know that I'm on the list for the Lodge."

"Elba told me. Be careful up there. Oh, and Stu, this reminds me. Make sure you tell Althea and the others not to let on that they know Petra. Tell them that she's here working undercover—figuratively, at least."

Petra stuck her tongue out at Gloria, then gathered up the tray. She started to leave, but Gloria grabbed her elbow to stop her. She reached into her purse and tossed some coins onto the tray. "You're doing a great job, Petra. Thanks!"

"My pleasure, ma'am," Petra answered, then walked off toward the kitchen, her bare behind swaying freely.

Eckstein watched her go, then turned back to Gloria. "You know, she raised a good point. Just how in hell *are* you going to explain this to Dexta?"

"It's all in the *Code*," Gloria assured him. "Look it up sometime. Chapter Forty-two, Paragraph Three, Subsection B. It authorizes Level XII personnel and above—that's me—to purchase, lease, rent, or otherwise acquire on an emergency basis such businesses, enterprises, or other facilities, the continued operation of which is deemed necessary to assure the economic well-being of a region within their jurisdiction. It further authorizes said personnel to operate such enterprises on an ad hoc basis until a suitable disposition of them can be arranged."

"Whew," Eckstein whistled. "That's some *Code*, that *Dexta Code*."

"Sure is," Gloria agreed.

GLORIA DROVE THE SKIMMER OVER TO THE PIER and helped Eckstein with his bags. The freighter in the slip was already clearing its throat, in anticipation of the daylong journey back to Palmyra.

"Listen," Eckstein said, "I know you think you can take care of yourself, and I know you think Grunfeld won't want to risk the wrath of Dexta, but you embarrassed him yesterday and made it personal. He's bound to try something."

"I know. But I think I'll be safe precisely because I *did* make it personal. He won't just have someone sneak up from behind me and burn my head off. Whatever he does, he'll try to fuck me first. His ego will demand that."

"That doesn't exactly make you any safer."

"But it will give me time and opportunity. Relax, Stu. I'll be fine."

A blast from the freighter's air horn prevented Eckstein from registering any further protests. They had time for one last, urgent kiss, then he was running down the pier toward the freighter's hatch.

Gloria stayed to watch the freighter back out of the slip, maneuver out into the river, and make its noisy ascent into the deep blue skies of Sylvania. Then she got back into the skimmer and headed upriver.

She spent the day visiting the camps of the riverrats along both banks of the Rankus and its tributaries. Everyone had heard about her by then, and she received a warm and enthusiastic welcome wherever she went. The news that she had acquired Elba's had traveled fast, and her new status earned her the nearly reverent devotion of everyone she met. She might have been the Emperor's ex-wife, a Dexta big shot, and the darling of the Empire's media, but what really mattered to the boomers was that she was now the proprietor of the Emporium.

It didn't hurt that she had stripped off her red flannel shirt on this sunny day and was wearing nothing but her low-cut jeans. She was completely on her own, on a strange and dangerous world, and that somehow made her feel recklessly alive.

Everyone wanted to know if she was going to work the rooms herself, and her answer was always ambiguous. In fact, she hadn't really decided about that. Every man on the planet wanted to fuck her, and she didn't object to the idea in principle. Still, she had an entirely different job to occupy her time and attention, and she couldn't let sex get in the way of that. However, the *idea* of sex never left her mind, and she made certain that it assumed a central position in the minds of everyone she met. In the battle to come, her personal appeal to the boomers would be the most powerful weapon she would have.

She stopped for lunch in Pizen Flats, sharing a fish fry with King Gus Thornton and some of the other riverrats, including Ted Oberlin, the law-student-turned-prospector. He wanted to raise more questions about the voter registration drive, the Homestead Acts, the Eminent Domain Statutes, and the Big Twelve. In fact, he raised entirely too many questions for Gloria's comfort or the patience of the other riverrats, who were much more interested in what Gloria intended to do with the Emporium. She told them that she had a few changes in mind, and maybe a couple of surprises, but that her main goal was to keep it running as well as Elba had. That produced a lot of happy smiles.

As she was returning to her skimmer, she buttonholed Ted Oberlin and told him, quietly, "I'm planning to camp tonight upstream near the waterfall. If you can find the time to drop by, maybe we can discuss some of those questions you raised in a little more detail." He smiled in surprise, then nodded. Gloria got back into the skimmer and flew onward toward the next camp, feeling pleased with herself. After all, it had been at least three hours since Stu Eckstein had departed.

• • •

AS SHE CONTINUED HER JOURNEY, THE RIVER narrowed and became swifter, rowdier. The deep forests lining the river gave way to steep inclines and sheer cliffs, as the enclosing mountains tightened their embrace. The skimmer negotiated a passage through a towering canyon and brought her to a place that simply took her breath away.

It was like a deep bowl, almost circular, bisected by the river. Forests on each side framed the scene and offered a tranquil respite from the furious activity of the river itself. Foam boiled and spumed everywhere in the shadow of the most dramatic waterfall Gloria had ever seen or imagined. She had to tilt her head all the way back just to get a glimpse of the top through the swirling mists that floated through the little valley. The falls must have dropped a thousand meters or more in three stages, with a final plunge of five hundred meters straight down. The roar of falling water was almost deafening, and Gloria's heart was in her throat as she tried to take in the magnificence of what she was seeing.

"Spirit," she whispered.

She halted the skimmer a few meters above the rushing waters, perhaps a kilometer away from the base of the falls, and just sat there and stared in awe and wonder. Stu had said the falls were spectacular, but his vocabulary was simply too limited to fully describe what she was seeing. There were no words adequate to the task in any language. Gloria didn't even try to think. She let nature engulf her and lost herself in the majesty of it all.

After some unmarked passage of time, she forced herself to run the skimmer over to the east bank of the river, where a calm and sedate pool had formed in the lee of the falls. She parked on a little bluff several meters above the pool and got out. It had been easy to think that she had been witnessing some scene from the beginning of time, but she was quickly brought back to her own era by the sight of the ashes of an old campfire and some thoughtlessly discarded trash. It looked obscene.

Even before she set up her own campsite, she collected all the trash and stuffed it into the back of her skimmer. Satisfied with her efforts, she set about arranging her own equipment. She found a level spot, laid out her tent, pushed a button on it, then stepped back to watch as the tent erected itself. Carbon dioxide charges thrust the pegs into the soil to provide a firm anchor, then the smart composites in the poles remembered their proper shape and assumed it. The smart fabrics of the tent top and sides unrolled themselves from the poles, latched onto the appropriate tabs, and the operation was complete in less than fifteen seconds. Gloria suspected that Lewis and Clark had not done it quite this way, but she was content with the result.

She unpacked her remaining gear, then walked over to the edge of the bluff to stare some more at the waterfall. The water would be cold, but the day was warm, and she could not resist. She kicked off her boots, slipped out of her jeans, got a running start, and dived into the pool, ten meters below.

Gasping as she returned to the surface, the shock of the icy water driving the breath from her lungs, she struggled for a moment before finding her equilibrium. Then she began to swim, cutting through the water like some aquatic mammal, heedless of the cold. She rolled over onto her back and floated for a while, gazing upward at the incredible waterfall, feeling the warmth of the sun on her face. The pool, she decided, was too calm, and willed herself to challenge the riotous river and all its power. She fought against the current, battling it with every atom of strength in her body, until finally she was nearly under the waterfall itself. The plummeting water would probably knock her unconscious, so she dived deep and surfaced behind it, deafened by the roar, veiled by the swirling mists. She lingered there, simply treading water and marveling that she was in such a place. At last, cold and exhaustion drove her back to the bank, where she dragged herself onto the smooth rocks and picked out a route up to the top of the bluff. There, she simply sprawled on her back and lay still and drained in the cool grasses and soft, warm sunlight.

At length, some primal instinct told her that she was not alone. She sprang to her feet, whirled around, and saw a small, wizened, stoop-shouldered man standing at the edge of the forest. They stared at each other wordlessly for several moments. Then he stepped forward a few paces and said, "Never seen that before."

Gloria took a few steps toward him. He had long, untamed white hair, a scraggly beard, and wore unclassifiable garments that might have been made of animal hides. His face was pinched and forbidding, but his blue-gray eyes seemed to sparkle.

"Never seen what?" Gloria asked him.

"Someone swimming out that far in the river. You swim well."

"Thank you. Are you Old Abel?"

"That's what they call me," he said. His voice sounded like a piece of sandpaper being ripped apart.

"My name's Gloria."

"Knew that. Glad to meet ya."

"The pleasure's all mine."

"Not from where I'm standin'," he said, a hint of a smile forming beneath his tangled whiskers.

Gloria smiled back at him. "I was going to make some coffee," she said. "Will you join me?"

He shook his head. "Not just now, thankee. We'll talk some other time, mebbe. Just wanted to meet ya, and compliment you on your swimming . . . and everything else."

Abel turned to go, but Gloria called to him. "Wait, please," she begged him. "I wanted to ask you about the Voice."

He cocked his head to one side. "You heard it yet?"

"No."

He nodded. "When you do, then mebbe we'll talk about it."

"What if I don't hear it?"

Abel offered her another smile. "I 'spect mebbe you will." He nodded politely, then turned and walked away into the forest. Gloria stood there for a moment, then started after him, but by the time she reached the edge of the forest, he had completely vanished from view.

Nude and shivering a little, Gloria hesitated, then continued into the forest. The trees seemed to muffle the sound of the waterfall, and by the time she had gone a few meters into the woods, it was as if she had entered a completely different world. Here, the dashing waters and blunt, shiny boulders were gone; soft leaves and mosses on the forest floor made each step easy and sensual, and each massive tree trunk seemed to beckon her onward to the next. She walked for uncounted minutes, realizing somewhere deep in her mind that she had no idea where she was, or what might be waiting ahead of her in the darkening woods. Somehow, it didn't seem to matter. She kept walking . . .

Who are you?

Gloria stopped in her tracks, whirled around—but no one was there. Had she heard something? She couldn't be sure . . .

Who are you?

Again, she whirled, and again, saw no one. She was completely alone, yet she was certain she had heard . . . the Voice?

"I'm Gloria," she said, barely whispering.

Gloria.

"Yes! I'm Gloria! And—"

You are not like the others.

Gloria wasn't sure what the Voice had meant at first, but then figured it out. "I'm a woman," she said. "A female."

Yes.

"And who are you? Are you the Voice that I've heard about?"

I am . . . here.

"Yes, I know, but—"

You must not let them hurt me.

"What? What do you mean?"

Don't . . . let them hurt . . . me . . .

"But . . ." Gloria didn't know how to respond, and in her moment of hesitation, she suddenly—somehow—became aware that the Voice was gone. She called to it for several minutes, but hers was the only voice in the forest.

Alone, she walked slowly back to the river.

WITH THE SUN LOWERING BEHIND THE MOUN-tains, the air had turned cool. There was something indescribably sensual about being nude in the great forest, so she compromised and donned only her shirt. She tossed an artificial log from her kit into the ashes of the old campfire, started it, and squatted down in front of it for a few minutes to warm up. Then she went down to the river for water, set up a kettle over the fire, and waited for it to boil. She had some freeze-dried glop she could prepare for dinner, but decided to wait to see if she would be cooking for two.

The answer soon came in the form of a battered old utility skimmer that materialized from the mists on the river and came to rest on the bluff next to her own skimmer. Ted Oberlin got out, looking as if he had perhaps taken a bath and done his laundry since the last time she had seen him. Gloria unbuttoned her shirt and walked over to meet him.

His eyes popped out a bit as he stared at her. "Hi," he said, "I—"

Gloria raised a finger to her lips and shushed him. She leaned forward on tiptoes and kissed him on the lips, hungrily, expertly, then slowly moved downward.

Later, lying nude on the grasses by the fire as the sun went down, Oberlin returned the favor. Gloria simply lay back and let him take her from one rippling orgasm to the next, until he thrust into her and kept on thrusting for a long, liquid time, at last bringing them both to a climax that was as dramatic, in its own way, as the roaring waterfall above them.

They cooked dinner and made coffee, enjoying it along with a bottle of cheap but effective whisky that Oberlin had brought with him. Warmed inside and out, Gloria left her clothes off, but Oberlin decided to get back into his trousers and shirt. They talked a little, and Oberlin told her something of his past—college, law school, family conflicts, angry departure, determination to make it on his own, arrival on Sylvania—but mostly they were content to stare at each other and listen to the rushing waters.

He was a good-looking man, now that he had cleaned himself up a bit, with long dark hair, a newly trimmed beard, and intelligent brown eyes. He was the same age as Gloria—the first time she had been with someone that young in quite a while. Older, more confident and powerful men generally got there ahead of the young ones, but Gloria was pleased to have had this opportunity. Benjamin Franklin had once said something famous about older women being grateful, but Gloria had found that this was also true of younger men.

"You don't give a man much chance to make conversation," Oberlin said. He took a swig from the whisky bottle and passed it to Gloria, who took a long pull at it.

"Sometimes words just get in the way."

"Sometimes they do," Oberlin agreed, "but there are some things I wanted to talk about with you."

"So talk, while I get us a treat." Gloria began rummaging around in her backpack.

"Well, there are a lot of things. You do a good job of selling this voter registration drive of yours to the river-rats, Gloria, I admit. But you know as well as I do what's going to happen once this territory becomes incorporated. The Empire will strike a deal with the corporates, and they'll come in here and rip up the valley and drive all the boomers off their claims."

"You're forgetting about Eminent Domain," Gloria said. She fished a long, fat cigarette out of her pack. "The corporates will need to get the proxies for 60 percent of the registered claims before they can drive *anyone* off the land." She held the cigarette close to the fire to get it started, then took a long drag at it, coughing slightly. She handed it to Oberlin.

"What's this? Marijuana?"

Gloria noisily exhaled, shaking her head. "Better," she explained. "It's called jigli, and it comes from Mynjhino. I brought some back with me."

Oberlin took an experimental puff, then another, deeper one. He tried to say something, but exploded in spasms of coughs. Gloria handed him the whisky bottle, while she retrieved the jigli and took another pull at it.

Between smoke and drink, it was a while before Oberlin was able to respond to Gloria's point about Eminent Domain. "Look," he finally insisted, "between the claims Grunfeld and the Lodge already control, and the claims of the highboys who will want to get what they can for their work, it'll be no problem for them to get that 60 percent. And once they have it, the riverrats and anyone else who wants to hang on will be removed, by force, if necessary. Say, what the hell *is* this stuff, anyway?"

"It is," Gloria declared, "the most powerful natural aphrodisiac in the Empire, and you and I are consuming heroic quantities of a specially refined and potent version of it."

Oberlin's eyebrows went up as he examined the stub of the cigarette in his hand. "No kidding," he said, and took another drag, ending up burning his fingertips. He stuck them in his mouth, while Gloria poured more whisky into hers.

"Anyway . . . where was I? Yes, the Eminent Domain

Statutes. They'll get their 60 percent, Gloria. You know it and I know it."

"Maybe they will," she said, "and maybe they won't. And maybe even if they do get it, they won't want it once they have it."

"What do you mean by that?"

"I mean, Ted, my dear, that there is more going on here than meets the eye. So don't get in the way of what I have to do, okay?"

"I knew it!" Oberlin said, a hint of anger in his voice. "You've been busy distracting me all night, trying to keep me from having my say."

Gloria shrugged. "You've had it, haven't you?"

"Not really. There were a lot of things—"

"That you spent all afternoon rehearsing," Gloria interrupted. "Lots of fine, legal-mind kind of points that would have gotten you a good grade in law school. Look, Ted, just consider them said, okay? And let me explain something to you. The Empire is coming to Sylvania, and it's coming in with both feet. If you try to lead some heroic opposition to voter registration, you're just going to fail in the end, and maybe even get yourself hurt in the process."

Oberlin started to protest at what sounded like a threat, but Gloria shushed him again.

"Think about it, Ted," she said. "If you try to organize opposition to voter registration, that's going to put you on the same side as Grunfeld—for the moment, at least. Do you really want to be there? Is he the kind of ally you can trust? Besides, he'll sell you out in the end. Right now, he wants to keep his little dictatorship-of-the-pukes, but sooner or later he'll see the light and decide to cash in his claims. And meanwhile, you'll be opposing some very powerful corporate interests, who will squash both you and Grunfeld like bugs, if it suits their purposes."

"Yes, but—"

"Listen to me, Ted. You can't stop what's going to

happen, and you could get hurt if you try. Don't fight me on this."

"And what about all the boomers? What will happen to them? What will happen to all of"—he flung his arm out to encompass the valley—"*this?*"

Gloria leaned over to kiss him. Then she started unbuttoning his shirt.

"Ted," she said, "your heart is in the right place." She put her palm on his bare chest and smiled. "Right there, in fact. I can feel it. Now, feel mine." She took his hand and guided it to her own chest. "See? Mine's in the right place too."

Oberlin felt her heart, seized the moment, and moved on to feel her breasts and swollen, erect nipples.

"Wait a minute!" he snarled abruptly. "You're doing it again. You've seduced me, plied me with drugs and whisky—"

"You brought the whisky," she reminded him.

"Oh. Yeah."

"I'm half-drunk already," she said. "Consider me successfully plied. I am officially at your mercy." She opened his trousers and took his cock in her hand, making it unclear just who was actually at whose mercy at the moment. Gloria took his lengthening member into her mouth and moved up and down on it a few times.

"Wait a minute!" he cried with the last of his resistance.

She paused and looked up at him. "Ted, please," she said primly, "I can't do this and talk at the same time. So just shut up and listen to me for a minute, and then we'll get down to the real reason you're here. Listen to me, Ted—I heard the Voice!"

"What? Spirit, not you too!"

"Ted, it's not just superstition, it's real! I heard it as clearly as I can hear you. And that was before the whisky and jigli. It's real, Ted. Please accept that."

Oberlin stared at her dubiously, then blew out some air and said, "Okay, you heard the Voice. So what did it say?"

"It said, 'Don't let them hurt me.' And Ted, I'm not going to."

"What do you mean? Hurt whom?"

"The *planet*, Ted! This place."

"But—"

"I think the Voice is . . . well, never mind what I think it is. All that matters is that you believe me when I tell you that I am *not* going to let this place be destroyed. Not the place, or the people who live in it. Do you understand me? Do you belive me?"

Oberlin looked down at her and met her blue, intense eyes. He had a million questions, and 10 million concerns, but somehow, he found it impossible to doubt her.

"I believe you, Gloria," he said at last.

"Good," she said. "Now, please, stop interrupting me."

Gloria resumed what she had been doing, and Oberlin decided that he had said enough for one night.

chapter **10**

GLORIA SPENT THE NEXT THREE DAYS MEETING
with the highboys, spreading her gospel of voter registration. That entailed a great deal of hiking and climbing, since the skimmer could not safely negotiate the
steeper slopes, but by the time she returned to her
campsite on the third night, she calculated that she had
personally met with more than half of the boomers on
the planet. Their enthusiasm for Gloria was undoubted,
but whether she had sold them on registration remained
an open question.

In the late afternoons and evenings, she had gone
for a swim and wandered again through the forest, nude
and questing. But she did not hear the Voice again, and
was beginning to wonder if she had ever really heard it
at all. Nor did she see Old Abel, although there were
moments when she sensed that he was out there somewhere, watching her.

She had time for a lot of serious thinking each night as
she sat before her campfire or curled up in her sleeping
bag. Gloria was not, by nature, philosophically inclined.

She tended to take what came, and generally ignored the deeper meaning of it all—if, indeed, there was any. But it was hard to ignore the Voice, and she puzzled over what it meant and what it was.

Ted Oberlin managed to borrow the skimmer again and joined her on the third night, bringing with him some fresh antelope steaks and another bottle of whisky. Gloria provided some wild onionlike vegetables she had found, a freeze-dried potato concoction, and some more jigli. They made love to the point of mutual exhaustion, and by the time a steady rain began to fall, they were ready to retreat inside the tent and talk of immediate prospects and eternal questions.

"I have a theory about the Voice," she told him.

"Everybody has a theory about the Voice," Oberlin replied. "Okay, what's yours?"

"Well . . . it's just a theory, but I think it might be like the Spirit. Maybe it's Sylvania's version of the Spirit, only not as articulate because until humans got here, this planet never had any intelligent life. Maybe every planet has such a . . . a being, a presence. A lot of alien races have similar stories and legends."

"It's a theory," Oberlin agreed.

"But you don't like it."

"I don't even think the Spirit was real, Gloria. Do you mean to tell me that you do?"

Gloria shrugged. "I never quite made up my mind about that," she said. "But if the Spirit is real, then maybe the Voice is the same sort of thing."

"You're welcome to your theory. But I prefer to deal in facts. I mean, look at what the Voice actually says. It tells the highboys to leave it alone and go away, presumably because they do the most damage to the planet. It tells the riverrats, 'Don't hurt me.' But what did it say to you?"

"It said, 'Don't let them hurt me.' "

Oberlin nodded. "Right. Very different. But what did it say to you first? It asked who you were, didn't it?"

"Yes."

"Which implies that it didn't know anything about you. Not even that you were a woman, because it mentioned that you were different from the others."

"Okay. So?"

"So, if it didn't know anything about you, how did it know that you were in a position where you could prevent anyone from hurting it?"

Gloria frowned, her brow wrinkled. She didn't like Oberlin's point, but she got it. After a moment, she said, "That's just your legal-beagle mind, Ted. Law school makes you cynical."

"Undoubtedly. But the question remains. What we have here is a logical inconsistency in what the Voice said. Would some sort of mystical planetary spirit make a mistake like that? Sounds like a pretty human mistake to me."

"But there was no one else around! There never is."

"Convenient, isn't it?"

Gloria punched him in the ribs. "Cynic!"

"Pushover," Oberlin parried.

"I am not a pushover! I'm just . . . receptive . . . to different possibilities."

Oberlin grinned at her. "You're certainly receptive," he agreed. "As to those different possibilities . . ."

"Careful! You're going to knock over the tent poles."

As it turned out, he did. But Gloria didn't mind.

PETRA RODE UP TO THE LODGE IN THE BACK OF a utility skimmer along with another bar girl named Rana Mohr and two of the hookers, Eva Shields and Lulu Villegas. The skimmer followed a grassy path, not really a road, up a series of switchbacks along the side of a mountain that overlooked Greenlodge and the river. After half an hour, they came within sight of the Lodge, which was really a series of connected wooden cabins surrounding a large, circular central building with a broad veranda and big plate-glass windows.

It was the first time Petra had even been outside in days, and she luxuriated in the fresh air and the magnificent scenery. She was also relieved to be wearing clothing again, even the ridiculous costume that had been provided for her. Someone at the Lodge had evidently seen too many millennium-old French bedroom farces and decided to clothe the help in upstairs-maid outfits— very short black dresses with white lace trim around their plunging necklines. Petra's was too large for her, which meant that her crotch and fanny were covered but that her breasts were all but completely exposed. She couldn't bend over without flashing her nipples, which somehow seemed a lot more risqué than simply baring it all at Elba's.

Rana, a thin, dark-haired, dark-skinned beauty, had worked the Lodge before and assured Petra that the work was usually routine and perfunctory—beds to be made, silver to be polished, meals to be served. Eva and Lulu looked down their noses at such labors and teased Rana and Petra about being too scared to work the rooms. They wore fancy, revealing, and slightly outlandish dresses, and spent a lot of time checking their hair and makeup.

When the skimmer had parked next to the central part of the Lodge, they got out and were led inside to a basement workroom, where they were inspected by Preston Thawley, the Lodge Manager. He was a fit, wiry, silver-haired man of about sixty, who had all the charm and subtlety of an Imperial Marine drill sergeant. "Lulu, Eva, you know what's expected of you," he barked. "Mr. Rankus will give you your assignments later. In the meantime, just go to your rooms and keep out of the way. Rana, you'll perform the usual tasks, under the direction of Mrs. Thawley. And your name is Petra?"

"Yessir," Petra said.

"Welcome to the Lodge. You'll find the work easy

enough if you do as you're told, and the payment will be more than what you're accustomed to down at the Emporium. If you do a good job, you'll be asked back. I'll be checking on you periodically. We have guests coming for dinner tonight, so I expect you to be efficient and accommodating in every respect. Understood?"

Petra wanted to ask what he meant by "accommodating," but decided against it. She figured she would find out soon enough.

Mrs. Thawley was as robust and healthy as her husband, but softer spoken and a bit motherly. She showed Petra around the main part of the Lodge, acquainted her with the kitchen and closets, then sent her off to begin tidying up the cabins. There were a dozen of them, all told, but only three of them were currently occupied by guests. Claude Rankus and the other barons from Palmyra had their own permanent quarters on the upper floors of the central building.

On her way to the cabins, Petra got a good look at the land on the other side of the peak, away from Greenlodge and the coast. In the small valley below, she saw a farm and cattle ranch, stables, an orchard, a nine-hole golf course, bridle paths, and a lake with boathouses for canoes and sailboats. Scattered around the valley were small homes for the Lodge's permanent workers, who tended the animals, raised the crops, and trimmed the fairways. The valley was known as Overhill, and its denizens rarely ventured into Greenlodge.

Two of the workers from Overhill were eager to make her acquaintance. Ed Watson and Ramdath Knipper ogled her from a polite distance and offered to show her around the establishment. Petra declined the offer, but the two young men said that they'd be seeing her again.

Petra told herself that she wasn't really changing linen, sweeping floors, and scrubbing toilets; rather, she was embarking on her new career as a spy. She dutifully searched for evidence of conspiracies and plots, but found nothing that qualified. In the occupied cabins she did find some unlocked suitcases, but a quick check of them revealed nothing more incriminating than a bottle of hair dye and some antigerontological drugs. If there were any hidden microphones or clandestine comm units around, they eluded her. The only conversation of any note that she overheard was between the chef and Mrs. Thawley, who disagreed about the relative ripeness of some blueberries. Mrs. Thawley's point of view prevailed. Meanwhile, there were more toilets to clean.

GLORIA WAS HAVING AN EQUALLY TEDIOUS DAY at the Emporium. Upon her return from her campsite, she huddled with Elba to get a quick course in brothel management, but found the course neither quick nor easy. There was more to the business than she had ever imagined.

The care and maintenance of whores was a major topic, as was the proper tone to strike when dealing with menials, bartenders, bar girls, and general store clerks. She learned about the ins and outs of the deals Elba had struck with the professional gamblers who leased tables, the importance of clean sheets, clean dishes, and clean floors, and the necessity of paying carefully negotiated kickbacks to the frieghter captains who delivered goods from Palmyra, the jobbers who provided needed merchandise, the liquor suppliers, and even Mayor Grunfeld. The last one was for "municipal services," which Gloria decided she would do without.

Elba showed her the books, which were actual books written in longhand, and required translation by Elba, who employed a complex system of abbreviations and codes. Gloria inwardly groaned when she realized that she was going to have to transfer the whole nearly illegible mess into the Dexta computers when they arrived; the Comptroller's Office would insist upon it.

She had planned to spend the evening in her room, familiarizing herself with the books, but was rescued by the delivery of an invitation, in beautiful calligraphy, asking her to dine tonight at the Lodge. Dress was formal, and a limo skimmer would pick her up at eight. She had been expecting some overture from the Lodge—in fact, she thought it overdue—and welcomed the opportunity to enjoy a dinner that was not freeze-dried.

The limo arrived punctually, and the driver, an Overhill man named Gonzales, solicitously opened the door for her. During the trip up the mountain, he kept glancing back at Gloria, but managed to get them safely to the Lodge in spite of the distraction.

Gloria was welcomed at the main entrance to the central building by Mr. and Mrs. Thawley, who introduced themselves and graciously ushered her into a reception area where plush divans overlooked the big windows and a darkening view of the distant, faintly glimmering sea. Six men quickly rose to greet her, and the oldest of them stepped forward and bowed very formally.

"Ms. VanDeen," he said, "we are honored that you have chosen to grace our humble Lodge with your presence this evening. I am Claude Rankus."

"A pleasure, Mr. Rankus," Gloria said, tilting her head forward slightly, as she had learned to do during her years at Court. Rankus was a medium-sized man with a bit of a pot belly, but looked in excellent shape for 140. His hair was white and very thin and his nose was something of a beak, but his eyes were a clear, unwavering blue, and there was an air of confidence about him. He wore a black tie and dinner jacket with a cummerbund that seemed to be some sort of tartan.

"Allow me to introduce my associates and guests, Ms. VanDeen. Myron Vigo is my oldest friend and helped me to found the Lodge some twenty years ago. And Rahim Ogunbayo is a mere parvenu, who joined us just seventeen years back. My guests this evening are men of power and substance, as befits their mission here. May I present

Mr. Thomas Shoop of Imperium, Mr. Sherwin Lund of Excelsior, and Mr. Gaspar Norfleet of Servitor?"

Each man, in turn, bowed to Gloria, who repeated her aristocratic head tilt to them. They tried to meet her eyes, but found it difficult in light of what she was wearing. Realizing that Rankus was a conservative and formal sort of man, she wore a frilly white dress that covered her from neck to knees, although it dipped deep enough in back to reveal most of her derriere. Also remembering the Lodge's notorious reputation, she had set the transparency of the smart fabric of her dress at 80 percent, making her look as if she were clothed in nothing but a thin white mist.

Vigo and Ogunbayo also looked to be centenarians, although somewhat younger and better preserved than Rankus; both of them wore the same tartan cummerbund, apparently a symbol of the Lodge. The corporate reps were men in their fifties or sixties, their prime, and each gave her a wary but probing stare. Everyone in the room, including Gloria, was well aware that this small group would be determining the future of Sylvania.

She sat on a divan next to Rankus and made inconsequential small-talk compliments about the beauty of the Lodge and its surroundings. Then Petra and Rana served them champagne and canapés. Since the two women already worked for her at the Emporium, she greeted them by name, making no attempt to pretend that she didn't know Petra. Both women curtsied to her, then left.

"I hope you intend to continue Elba's arrangement with us, Ms. VanDeen. We could find serving girls in Overhill, I suppose, but yours have an undeniable charm."

"By all means, Mr. Rankus. I'll be making a few changes at the Emporium, but that won't be one of them. I hope you've found their work to be satisfactory."

"Very much so. Rana is well known to us, and Petra promises to be a fine addition to our staff."

"Ms. VanDeen," said Sherwin Lund, the Excelsior rep, "I understand that the rest of your Dexta team will be arriving in a few days to begin voter registration." Lund was a thin man with very white skin and very dark, slicked-back hair.

"Oh, please, Sherwin," Rankus interjected, "we have plenty of time for that. I prefer to get to know Ms. VanDeen as a person, and she us, before we plunge into the inevitable. Tell me, Ms. VanDeen, have you enjoyed your stay thus far on Sylvania?"

"Immensely, Mr. Rankus—and please, call me Gloria. I've spent some time upriver and I camped out near the waterfall for several nights. I don't believe I've ever seen such a beautiful place."

Rankus smiled and nodded. "Thank you, Gloria," he said. "We are very proud of it."

"Does it have a name?" Gloria wondered.

"Rankus Falls, of course," said Myron Vigo. "There is also a Mt. Vigo around here somewhere, and even a Lake Ogunbayo—a small one. We're very modest men, you see."

"We shall have to name a mountain after you, Gloria. I know the very one." Ogunbayo laughed and exchanged a sly look with Vigo.

"Oh?" asked Gloria.

The two men snickered like teenagers, but Rankus put a quick end to that with a stern look. Then he turned to Gloria and said, "Forgive my friends' rather low sense of humor, my dear. They were, I believe, referring to the twin prominences to the southwest of the falls."

"I apologize most humbly, Gloria," said Ogunbayo.

"No offense taken, Mr. Ogunbayo," Gloria assured him. "Tell me, Mr. Rankus, how have you managed to keep such a large and loyal staff at the Lodge since the boom began? I would think many of the people in Overhill must have been very tempted to leave the Lodge and try their luck at mining."

"Some few gave in to temptation," Rankus admitted, a

sour look on his face. "But we are a unique community here—more of an extended family, really. Everyone knows his place and performs his duties. We have little truck with the boomers and have preserved our way of life in spite of the distractions." He glanced at the corporate reps, who looked a little uncomfortable.

"We shall hold out to the bitter end," Vigo said, "and the last man standing will die on the ramparts cloaked in our sacred tartan. At least, Claude insists that we shall, and Claude always gets his way."

"If that were true"—Rankus sniffed—"none of you would be here tonight—except, of course, for our lovely guest. My dear, may I take you on a little tour of the Lodge?" Rankus rose, held out his arm, and escorted Gloria to the stairway.

They paused briefly on the next floor and the one above it to see some of the quarters of the other Lodge trustees, then continued to the top floor, which belonged to Rankus. The view from the circular balcony was spectacular even at night, and the rooms Rankus occupied were self-indulgently luxurious without being flashy. Rankus took notable pride in showing Gloria some old golfing trophies and his gun collection. In a display case along one wall there were some early-model plasma weapons, a few lasers, and a number of gunpowder-and-lead antiques, ranging from rifles and shotguns to Colt revolvers, a Kentucky long rifle, a Brown Bess musket, and even an arquebus. Gloria made note of the layout of the apartment, paying particular attention to the location of the private office. The information might be useful for Petra.

At dinner, Rankus sat at the head of the table, with Gloria next to him. The wine was first-rate, and they dined on a native-Sylvanian version of salmon and imported game hens. The conversation remained general, with Ogunbayo pressing her for details about her adventures on Mynjhino. That topic seemed to discomfit Gaspar Norfleet; Gloria's actions had cost his company, Servitor,

potential billions. Thomas Shoop, of Imperium, Ltd.—
the ultimate beneficiary of the outcome on Mynjhino—
didn't seem to mind.

By the time they reached coffee and brandy, the inevitable could no longer be ignored. Sherwin Lund, of
Excelsior, repeated his earlier question about voter registration and wanted to know how long it would take.

"As soon as the team is in place, in a few days, we
should be ready to start registering voters," Gloria told
him. "I've been doing some groundwork in the last few
days, talking up the idea to the boomers, so I expect we
could get a fairly good response immediately. But as to
how long it will take to reach five thousand, I couldn't
say. At least a month, possibly two—I hope no more
than that. But there will be opposition to the drive."

"Some of it right here in this room," Lund said with
a nod toward Rankus.

"You may rely on it, Ms. VanDeen," Rankus said. "I
have no intention of turning this world into an incorporated territory, subject to the whims of Dexta and an Imperial Governor, and the none-too-tender mercies of
our corporate friends. Do you know what they will do to
Sylvania if they have their way?"

"I have a pretty good idea," said Gloria.

"They will destroy it," Rankus said, with some heat.
"Destroy it utterly!"

"Oh, now, Claude," Vigo soothed, "it may not be
that bad. You know that all of the interested parties have
assured us that they won't touch the Lodge or Overhill.
Isn't that right, gentlemen?"

"Absolutely," said Norfleet.

"Nonsense," snarled Rankus. "You'll rip up the
ranges on both sides of the river all the way up to the falls.
Whether you despoil the Lodge directly or indirectly is
of no moment. You'll turn this place into a goddamn in-
dustrial wasteland."

"You can't fight it forever, Claude," said Ogunbayo. "I
regret the necessity as deeply as you, and I shall certainly

miss all that we have come to enjoy here, but you know as
well as I do that we cannot go on battling the tide."

"I know no such thing! If you two and the other
trustees would show a little spine, we could keep these
corporate jackals at arm's length indefinitely."

"We are not jackals, Mr. Rankus," said Lund, a little
stiffly. "We are businessmen, and we do what we must
for the benefit of our stockholders and, ultimately, the
Empire itself."

"Bushwah!" Rankus snorted. "I try to be tolerant,
but I'd throw the three of you out of here right now if
my . . . *colleagues* . . . didn't insist on making you welcome."

"It's to our ultimate advantage, Claude," insisted
Vigo. "Whatever happens, we need the goodwill and understanding of these gentlemen and their corporations.
I apologize to you, gentlemen, on behalf of the Lodge
and its sometimes cantankerous and disagreeable
founder."

Rankus snorted again, then turned to Gloria. "As for
you, my dear," he said, "charming as you are, I hope you
realize that I will use every means in my power to oppose you."

"Every *legal* means, Claude," Vigo quickly interjected. "I'm a lawyer by trade, Gloria, and I have to tell
you that there are some legal cards we can play that will
make your job more difficult."

"Play them as you will, Mr. Vigo," Gloria said pleasantly. "Dexta has no shortage of lawyers. But speaking of
legal matters, let me caution *you*, Mr. Rankus, that your
Mayor Grunfeld is treading on very thin ice. You might
mention to him that any strong-arm tactics employed
against Dexta personnel will be met with swift and se-
vere reprisals."

"Ah, Mayor Grunfeld," said Rankus. "He is, I admit,
a bit crude, as are some of his methods. Nevertheless, he
has proven useful in the past, and may in the future, as
well. I heard about your little meeting with him the other

day." Rankus grinned. "Very creative, very enterprising, and very courageous of you, Gloria. And it doesn't hurt to give Mayor Grunfeld a little comeuppance now and then. Reminds him of his place in the grand scheme of things. Still, he *is* the existing legal authority in Greenlodge at the moment, and I would advise you and your people not to overstep *your* legal bounds."

"I might say the same thing to you, Mr. Rankus," Gloria replied. "With all due respect. The boomers have rights, and Dexta will protect them. You may have founded the Lodge and brought humans to Sylvania in the first place, but this is not a proprietary colony. It's not your feudal fiefdom."

"More's the pity," grumbled Rankus. "You know, I tried to get a grant from old Darius, but he wouldn't even accept my petition. Seems my blood isn't blue enough. And now that young rascal Charles is in league with these corporate hooligans. I wonder, sometimes, what is to become of the Empire in this age."

"Whatever you or I may think of Charles, Mr. Rankus," Gloria said, "he *is* the Emperor, and he has a strong interest in this matter. He expressed his wishes directly to Norman Mingus, who personally gave me my orders. I have every intention of carrying them out."

"Spirit be praised!" Sherwin Lund sighed. "We'll do everything we can to assist you, Ms. VanDeen. The sooner we get those voters registered, the sooner things can proceed."

"Thank you, Mr. Lund, but I would advise you to stay out of it as well. Dexta is perfectly capable of handling its mission, and interference from the corporates or any other source"—she glanced at Rankus—"would not be welcome."

Rankus abruptly got to his feet. "Very well, then. The gauntlet is down. The challenge is clear. Do what you think you must, Ms. VanDeen. As I shall."

Rankus walked from the room and up the stairs to his private apartment. The others watched him go in silence.

Finally, Vigo said, "Forgive him, Gloria, gentlemen. Claude is not a well man these days, and this business is taking a toll on him. But don't underestimate him just because he is old and tired. Claude Rankus will not go down without a fight."

chapter 11

THE SMALL, SLEEK DEXTA CRUISER GURGLED into the pier, and Gloria was waiting there to greet her team as they disembarked. They emerged into the sunlight, toting their bags and looking around dubiously, as if unsure whether they had landed on the right planet. Althea Dante was wearing khaki shirt and shorts and a pith helmet, as if she were planning to go off with Stanley, in search of Livingston.

"Gloria, darling, how grand to see you again!" Althea called to her. Gloria walked over to her and gave her a hand with one of her bags.

"Is this *it*?" Althea wondered as she gave the small town a once-over.

"What were you expecting? Paris?"

"If only!"

"How was the trip? Any problems?"

"None that led to bloodshed. Where's the hotel?"

Gloria turned and pointed to the Emporium.

"Seriously, Gloria. I'm sure everyone is looking forward to getting settled in their rooms."

"Then they should be happy with the Emporium. Did you meet Stu Eckstein on Palmyra?"

"He came up to the Palmyra Orbital Station during our layover," Althea confirmed. "He was distressingly vague about details, although he did mention that our dear little Petra is now some sort of spy. Was he serious?"

Gloria nodded. "Entirely. You and the team are not to acknowledge knowing her. Is that clear to everyone?" The team had gathered around them by that time, so Gloria looked at each one in turn. Everyone nodded in the affirmative.

"Good," Gloria said. "Now, as to the immediate future, we have temporary rooms for you in the Emporium, over there."

"And then we transfer to a hotel?" asked Sintra Garbedian.

"Not exactly. Tomorrow, you'll be taking up residence in a local boardinghouse. The nearest hotel is back on Palmyra. You'll be roughing it here, but it's really not as bad as it looks at first sight."

"How could it be?" wondered Wilmer DeGrasse.

"Oh, don't be a snob, Wilmer," piped Jillian Clymer. "I think this is going to be fun!"

"Fun, I can't guarantee," said Gloria. "But it will definitely be interesting. For one thing, we've had a slight change of plans. Althea, I have another assignment for you."

"On Palmyra?" Althea asked hopefully.

"No such luck," Gloria told her. "I'll give you the details in a moment. But this means that we need to appoint someone to lead the registration team in your place." She turned to Raul Tellemacher. "Raul, you're senior, so you get the job."

"My pleasure."

"I'll give you your marching orders later, but for now, get things organized and take everyone down to that black utility skimmer at the end of the pier. I think we should be able to crowd everyone in."

"After a week in a Cruiser, it will seem downright roomy," Garbedian assured her as he hefted his bags. Tellemacher led the team toward the skimmer, amid an undertone of grumbles.

"Now, then, Althea," Gloria said, grinning, "let me tell you about your new job."

Althea frowned skeptically. "Am I going to like it?"

Gloria laughed. "You know," she said, "I think you just might."

"SO," PETRA ASKED LATER, IN GLORIA'S OFFICE, "how did Althea take the news that she's going to be the new madam at Elba's?"

"Not as badly as you might expect." Gloria shrugged. "I mean, I don't think that Althea actually knows a Vassilian hit man. Anyway, I'm sure I saw that wicked little gleam in her eye once she calmed down. Trust me, she'll take to it like a duck to water. And how goes it with you, kiddo? You seemed to be doing fine the other night at the Lodge."

"I've gotten to be very proficient at scrubbing toilets. They've asked me back, so I guess that means that I'm doing something right. I never realized the spy business could be so glamorous."

"You want glamour, go ask Althea if you can work the rooms. As to the spy business, I've got something for you."

"Really?" Petra seemed positively giddy at the news.

"I need you to find out everything you can about someone who may have been involved in building the Lodge, twenty years ago. Do you think you can get upstairs to Rankus's quarters and tap into his computer?"

"No chance," Petra said, shaking her head. "Mrs. Thawley handles everything above the main floor herself. If they even saw me trying to go upstairs, they'd kick me out—at a minimum."

"Damn."

"However," Petra added, "if it's employment records you need checked, I think I might be able to manage that."

Gloria smiled. "I knew you'd make a great spy. How will you work it?"

"Mr. Thawley has a console in the workroom in the basement. I think he uses it to keep track of all the work assignments, payments, and general personnel records. I don't know if the database goes back twenty years, but I don't see why it wouldn't."

"Great. And can you get at it safely?"

"I think so. He seems to be elsewhere a lot of the time, and I have to go back and forth to the workroom a lot for tools and mops and such. If I can stick my pad somewhere within a few feet of the console, it ought to be able to get at anything that's stored there."

Petra's pad was not the standard-issue Dexta utility. It had been a gift from Gloria to celebrate Petra's promotion to a Thirteen, and it was the fanciest device on the market. It had thousands of functions, most of which Petra had never tried, but one of them was a decryption algorithm that allowed it to tap into most standard computers, even from a distance.

"What I need," Gloria said, "is anything you can find on a man named Abel. I don't know if that's his first name or last. He's been here forever, and people seem to think that he was on the crew that built the Lodge." Gloria decided not to mention her encounter with the Voice, or the reason for her curiosity about Abel.

"If anything's there," Petra promised, "I'll find it."

"Great. Now, about the Dexta team. They all know you're working undercover, so they'll pretend they don't know you and you'll pretend you don't know them. You'll undoubtedly have to deal with them in your role as a bar girl, and I'm sorry, Petra, but there's nothing I can do about that. If I started putting clothes on the bar girls, the boomers would riot."

"No problem. I'm getting used to it, anyway."

"Is that why you got rid of the G-string?" Gloria asked.

Petra shook her head. "It was a favor to Elba," she said. "Although Elba seemed to think it was a favor to me. She said if I wondered why, I should ask you." Petra looked at her expectantly.

"I see," said Gloria. "To tell you the truth, I think she just wanted to boost your confidence. I mean, if you can handle being naked in a roomful of lonely boomrats, what *can't* you handle?"

Petra grinned. "I see what you mean."

"Maybe you *should* try working the rooms."

Petra thought about it for a moment, then said, "I will if you will."

"Hmmm. I'm tempted, but it would get in the way of too many other things I have to get done. Maybe before we leave."

"Scaredy cat!" Petra made a face at Gloria, then left the office, smiling happily.

AN HOUR LATER, THE DEXTA TEAM CROWDED into Gloria's unfurnished office and stood waiting, some of them as if they were expecting a firing squad. It was already apparent that the volunteers, Jillian Clymer and Palmer Ellison, were champing at the bit and ready to plunge into their assignment with gusto; and that the draftees—Sintra Garbedian, Wilmer DeGrasse, Randolph Alexander, Pearl Shuzuki, and Raul Tellemacher—were, in varying degrees, dreading every moment of their time on Sylvania. Tellemacher's presence still bothered Gloria, but if he had a brain in his head—and he did—he should have realized that he had absolutely no chance of bedding her. Personal matters aside, he had the necessary qualities of intelligence and leadership for his new position, and she was reasonably confident that he would perform well.

"Here's the plan," Gloria told her troops. "Tomorrow, we'll get you settled in at the boardinghouse. Then Raul will assign you to two-person teams; we've leased three skimmers for your use, although you may end up doing a lot of hiking. Skimmers can be dangerous in mountainous country because of the mass-repulsion unit. If the ground beneath you rises or falls away suddenly, the skimmer can flip over—so be very careful with them, and if you're in any doubt, get out and walk. Some of you look as if you can use the exercise.

"I'll have maps available for you, but they aren't great and the precise location of the miners and their camps is not known. I want you to be as thorough as reasonably possible and get to everyone you can. The situation is different along the rivers, and you'll have no trouble spotting the major concentrations of boomers in that area."

"Gloria?" Palmer Ellison started to raise his hand as if he were still in school, but managed to stop himself. "What about all the people in town? Shouldn't we start with them? There must be a couple of thousand of them, from what I've seen."

"They'll come to us," Gloria replied, "or I hope they will. While the mobile teams are off tracking down miners, the seventh person will stay here and register voters at the front desk of the Emporium. Depending on how things go, later on we may have to do a house-to-house, tent-to-tent canvass. There are also several hundred people in a place called Overhill in a valley beyond the Lodge. We'll leave them alone for the present, but eventually we'll try to get them registered, as well.

"By the way, we'll use wristcoms to keep in touch, but be advised that there are no comsats here, so communication will be short-range and unscrambled. So if you have anything to say that you don't want overheard, don't say it over the comm. I assume you all have your registration pads?"

They all held up their pads, which were a little larger than ordinary models.

"Take good care of them, and download everything

you get each night into the office computer." She looked around the bare office and added, "I promise you, we'll have one soon. And when you are registering people, make damn good and sure that you get the retinal scan, because every registration we record is likely to be challenged. Don't take no for an answer. That's important, because a lot of boomers would rather not become part of any official nose count. You'll find an astonishing number of people up in the hills named Smith or Jones. Just assure everyone that the registration scans are inviolate and will be used for no other purpose. If they want to be Smith or Jones, that's fine with us."

"And what about this Grunfeld character?" asked Garbedian. "I've already heard that he's going to try to prevent the registration drive."

"The boomers themselves may have some worries about Grunfeld and his thugs," Gloria told him, "but I've already made it very clear that any attempt to interfere with Dexta personnel will get them a trip to Grisham Three. I think they got the message. Nevertheless, I want every team to carry at least one plasma pistol. I doubt that Grunfeld will try anything, but I don't want to underestimate his stupidity."

"And what of Rankus and the people at the Lodge?" Jill Clymer asked. "Where do they stand in all of this?"

"Mr. Rankus," Gloria said, "is determined to resist us, but he has a smart lawyer named Myron Vigo who will probably be his point man. If necessary, we'll import some legal talent of our own from the Dexta office on Palmyra. Just do your jobs and don't worry about that aspect of things. I think some of the Lodge trustees would just as soon go along with us anyway, if they could find a way around Rankus. Also, there are some corporate reps in temporary residence at the Lodge. They, of course, want registration to go as quickly as possible, and may attempt to speed things along. Ignore them, too. This is our job, and we don't want or need assistance from anyone else. Does anyone have any questions?"

Wilmer DeGrasse stepped forward. He was a lumpy, middle-aged man who had been a Level XIII for thirty years; he was also heir apparent to a vast fortune, and had been unhappily marking time at Dexta while waiting for nature to take its course.

"Ms. VanDeen," DeGrasse began, "is what I hear about this place true?"

"It depends, Mr. DeGrasse. Just what have you heard?" Gloria gave him a patient smile.

"I have heard," he said, "that Dexta has acquired— or rather, that *you* have acquired on Dexta's behalf— this . . . this *bawdy house* we find ourselves occupying. Is that correct?"

Gloria nodded. "Indeed I have. We needed a base of operations, and this is it. In addition, it seemed necessary to acquire the Emporium to keep it from falling into the hands of Grunfeld. If he had it, he would gain complete control over virtually every aspect of life on Sylvania. Not only would that be disastrous for the boomers, it would also make our job nearly impossible."

"And you intend to keep this house of ill fame in operation, as before?"

"Better than ever, in fact."

"That," DeGrasse declared, "is nothing short of an outrage, Ms. VanDeen! When I was dragooned into this venture, I had assumed that it would at least be a reputable and honorable undertaking. I was willing to go along with that for the sake of Dexta—"

"For the sake of your job, you mean," Jillian Clymer snorted.

"Be that as it may," DeGrasse continued, "I have no intention of working or dwelling in this bordello! I am a Christian, Ms. VanDeen, not one of your anything-goes Spiritists, and morality and decency still have some meaning for me. I am not surprised that *you* feel at home in such a place—indeed, it is exactly where you belong! But I shall have nothing whatsoever to do with this project under the circumstances. Do you hear me? Nothing!"

Gloria ignored the personal insult; she'd heard far worse. But for a long, silent moment she gave him her most officious stare while the other members of the team waited in suspense.

"Mr. DeGrasse," she said at last, "Dexta has just brought you, at considerable expense, some 540 light-years on a field assignment you accepted before departure. Am I to understand that you are now refusing to carry out your duties? Before you answer, let me remind you of the sections of the *Dexta Code* relating to willful misconduct, disobedience, and neglect of responsibilities during the course of a field assignment. Let me further remind you of Chapter Thirty-seven, Paragraph Nine, Subsection G, which specifically prohibits Dexta personnel from making derogatory or prejudicial statements or comments concerning the racial, ethnic, linguistic, sexual, or religious orientation of other Dexta personnel. Now . . . would you care to answer my question? Or would you prefer to apologize to your colleagues and get on with your assignment?"

DeGrasse needed only a few seconds to think it over. He turned to the others and mumbled, "I offer my most sincere apologies if I have inadvertently offended anyone. And to you, as well, Ms. VanDeen. I shall, of course, carry out my assignment as lawfully directed by superior authority."

"Nice save, Wilmer," said Palmer Ellison with a smirk.

"Oh," said Gloria, glad to be past the awkward moment, "I forgot to mention one thing. The fact is, the other night I promised the boomers that anyone who registered would get a hug and a kiss from me. Tell them that they can collect on that right here at the Emporium, any night."

"What about us?" asked Tellemacher. "Fair's fair.

Shouldn't *we* get a hug and a kiss for every boomer we register?"

"Absolutely, Raul. But not from me. On that one, you're on your own. That, I think, covers our immediate business. But let me invite you all to join in the party tonight. We're giving Elba a big, bawdy send-off, and hugs and kisses should be freely available for all. If you want more than that—well, I think we can offer a discount for Dexta people. But you'll have to check with Althea about that."

FIVE HUNDRED BOOMERS CROWDED INTO THE main room of Elba's Emporium, threatening to burst the structure at its rickety seams. Scores more in the street outside wanted to get in, but Ernie the Bouncer stood squarely in the middle of the doorway, preventing further access. A big banner hung from the second-floor balcony, shouting, "Good-bye Elba! We'll Miss You!" in meter-high red letters. There were far more boomers than chairs and tables to accommodate them, so the mass of ragged, odoriferous humanity swirled around the wooden floor like a school of fish drifting in a tidal current.

When Gloria emerged from her room and stood at the balcony like a dictator about to address her subjects, there was a sustained roar of approval for the new mistress of the Emporium. Her approval rating was undoubtedly boosted by the fact that she was entirely nude. She raised her arms and slowly quelled the vocal enthusiasm of the mob below her, eventually gaining enough silence to permit her to speak.

"Ladies and gentlemen!" she shouted, "My name is Gloria, and I'll be your server this evening!"

That produced another round of roaring, whooping, and foot-stomping. The entire Emporium shuddered and creaked ominously.

When she could speak again, Gloria proclaimed,

"For tonight only, I'll be working the bar and the tables!" More huzzahs.

"And since I'm new at this," she went on after a minute, "just to make things easy for myself . . . *drinks are on the house!*"

Sylvania was a geologically quiescent world, but if Stu Eckstein had bothered to set up any seismometers in the region, they would have gone off the scale.

After more sustained celebration, Gloria raised her arms again and was finally able to continue. "Now," she said, "I have an announcement that concerns all of you, customers and staff alike. Tomorrow morning, a freighter is scheduled to arrive here, bringing a work crew and a lot of new amenities for the Emporium—including a few surprises. We will need time to install the new equipment, and it will also be necessary to shore up the foundations of this building. It was built in a hurry, but we'd like it to be around for a while—assuming it doesn't fall down tonight! But this means that beginning tomorrow, and for the next week, the Emporium will be closed for renovations."

The boomers didn't like that at all, and let Gloria know it. She waited until their protests had subsided, then continued. "I'm sorry, but there's just no other way to do this. All the resident staff will be transferred to boardinghouses and tents for the duration. Just think of this as a vacation with pay. For the rest of you, I apologize for the inconvenience, but I think that after tonight, most of you will be nursing hangovers for the next week, anyway!" The boomers roared their agreement.

"And before we get on with the party, I just want to introduce the members of our Dexta team. You all know why they're here, but for tonight, we won't be registering anyone. I know you'll all be as kind to them as you have been to me. Stand up and let everyone see you."

The Dexta people, sharing a large table at one end of the main room, reluctantly got to their feet. The boomers seemed unsure how to react at first, but finally greeted them with a round of tepid applause. The bureaucrats quickly sat down again.

"Finally," Gloria said, "I want to reassure all of you that we're going to continue business as usual here—in fact, better than usual, as you'll discover at our grand reopening in a week. But this is *not* going to become Gloria's Emporium. It will always be what it has always been—*Elba's Emporium*!"

More cheers and huzzahs followed that announcement, and when she judged the time was right, Gloria launched into her finale. "We are all here tonight to say a fond farewell to the magnificent lady who created the Emporium and made Greenlodge the town that it is today. We'll follow in her footsteps, but we can never fill her shoes. So let's hear everything you've got for the grandest old broad in the Empire—Miss Elba Larkspur!"

With that, Elba emerged from a room and stood next to Gloria on the balcony, while the boomrats went crazy. She basked in the reception, put her arm around Gloria, and gave her a kiss on the cheek, as if performing a rite of succession.

When the uproar had finally died away, Elba looked down at the swarm of boomrats and said, "I wanna thank ya for your bein' here tonight, even though I see some o' ya ain't bothered to wipe the mud off your boots. Don't matter none to me now, but Gloria's a goddamn lady, an' ya oughta treat her right."

She looked around the big room for a few moments, then sniffled for a second, but neatly covered the lapse into sentimentality by wiping her nose with the back of her wrist.

"Sign there says you'll miss me. Well, I gotta tell ya, I ain't gonna miss none o' you bastards for a second. Oh, I guess I'll think about ya some. Every time I see some poor drunk galoot pukin' his guts out on a street corner, every time I see some fool bettin' his last crown on double zero, every time I see a pretty gal with muddy fingerprints all over her . . . well, I guess I'll think about the ol'

Emporium for a second or two. Shit, maybe I'll even miss it. You bastards do kinda grow on a gal. But enough o' this slop . . . let's get them free drinks!"

Elba and Gloria descended the stairway arm in arm, to the heartfelt cheers of the boomers. They made way as Gloria escorted Elba to a table at the center of the room. Someone started singing "Auld Lang Syne," everyone picked it up, and the Emporium resounded with bad harmony and the sound of tough, flinty boom-rats choking back sobs. As soon as the song ended, the bar girls and hookers arrived at the tables with the first round of free drinks, and unrestrained merriment en-sued. Gloria, grinning from ear to ear, reflected that there might be worse ways to spend one's life than as the madam of a boomworld bawdy house.

As the evening unfolded, Gloria found that being a bar girl was not quite as easy as it looked. She was soon glistening from head to toe with spilled beer and the slobbering kisses of boomrats. However, the boomers, remembering what she had done to Grunfeld, treated her with a measure of caution and respect. She'd been handled less gently in some Manhattan nightclubs.

She and Petra brought several pitchers of beer to the Dexta table, where everyone seemed to be having a good time. Jillian Clymer was wearing a skimpy red dress that showed off most of her ample bosom, and Sintra Garbedian was demonstrating some ethnic folk dance to Carmela Evanueli, one of the hookers. Raul Tellemacher was off somewhere, possibly with one of the whores. Young Palmer Ellison was happily watching every motion of both Gloria and Petra, while the nor-mally stuffy Randolph Alexander and the normally re-served Pearl Shuzuki were exchanging hungry glances. Wilmer DeGrasse had attracted the attention of Lulu Villegas, who had wormed her way into his lap. DeGrasse looked a little at odds with himself over it.

"Lulu can smell money," Petra explained to Gloria. Althea Dante, wearing only a flimsy piece of black lace tied low on her hips, was circulating throughout the throng, playing the role of charming hostess to the absolute hilt. She approached the Dexta table and laughed lasciviously at what she found there.

"Ah, my children," she cooed, "I'm glad to see that you're blending in with the surroundings. Wilmer, the drinks are free, but Lulu isn't. But I'll give you a rate, for tonight only."

"That won't be necessary, Ms. Dante," DeGrasse replied. Althea simply laughed and moved on through the crowd, her hips swaying.

Eventually, Gloria found time to take a break and joined Elba at her table. Elba was in her cups by then, but still coherent. Gloria leaned close to make herself heard above the continuing uproar.

"Elba," she said, "I wanted to ask you about Old Abel. What can you tell me about him?"

Elba gamely focused on Gloria, gathered her thoughts, then said, "I can tell ya he's the smelliest ol' varmint on the planet. But he ain't so bad. Why?"

"I was just curious. They say you give him free meals and drinks, so I guess I should do the same."

"Free?" Elba laughed. "Hell, no! Do I look like a goddamn charity? He pays, same as everyone else. Runs a tab, in fact."

"He does?"

"Sure. Right there in the books. You'll see it."

"But how does he pay? He doesn't seem to have any visible means of support."

"Got a bank account on Palmyra. Never had any trouble with the payments."

Gloria's brow creased. "That's a bit of a surprise. Do you know where he got his money?"

"I never pry, hon. You oughta make that a rule o' your own. But Old Abel has what he needs. He even gets packages shipped to him here."

"Really? Do you know what's in them?"

"Told ya, I never pry. Stuff he needs, I guess. Can't

imagine what that would be, what with him livin' out in the woods like an animal. Probably just girlie magazines or some shit like that. Why all the curiosity?"

"Well," Gloria said, "I met him once, up near the falls. And I wanted to ask him about—"

"The Voice?" Elba asked. "You heard it, hon?"

"As a matter of fact, I did. Have you?"

Elba shook her head. "Hell, no. I don't get out in the woods much, and that damn Voice is just for lonely ol' boomrats and crazy people." Elba paused, then leaned closer to Gloria. "Although there was one time, late at night when I was closin' up and I was all alone here. I coulda sworn . . ."

"What?"

Elba shook her head again, but she had a wistful look in her eyes. "Just the delusion of a drunk ol' woman, hon. Nothin' more'n that."

"But what did you think you heard?"

"I thought I heard this voice—I don't know, maybe it was *the* Voice—sayin' 'Thank you.' Didn't say nothin' more, and I was probably imaginin' the whole thing. Still, makes ya wonder a bit, don't it?"

Gloria nodded. "It does, indeed. Thanks, Elba."

The noise level in the Emporium suddenly dropped sharply, and Gloria got up to look around. At the main entrance, she saw Mayor Grunfeld and four of his thugs advancing into the room. Grunfeld stopped and waited until the noise had died to zero. He looked around, sneering, cleared his throat, then spat on the floor.

"Listen up, all you assholes!" he bellowed. "I see you're havin' yourselves a high old time tonight. Well, that's just fine with me. Drink yourselves sick. But just remember come tomorrow mornin' that nothin' has changed around here. And ain't nothin' *gonna* change! You keep that in mind when these Dexta people start tryin' to sign you up. I'm still the law around here, and I will be long after these fuckin' bureaucrats have gone.

You boys keep that in mind. Whatever happens, you're still gonna have to answer to *me*!"

Grunfeld regarded the boomers with a satisfied sneer. When he was certain the message had sunk in, he started to turn to leave, but was stopped in his tracks by an anonymous boomrat in the middle of the crowd, who stood up and called, "Hey, Grunfeld!"

Grunfeld stared at him. "What?" he demanded.

"How's your finger?" The boomer held his right hand high, middle finger extended.

The boomers roared, and within seconds, Grunfeld found himself staring at five hundred defiant digits. He took in the sight for several seconds, then spat on the floor again and stomped out of the Emporium.

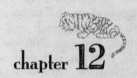

chapter 12

GLORIA MET THE FREIGHTER AT THE DOCK, boarded it, and huddled with Samuel Roosa, the head of the work crew, as the stevedores began unloading the cargo. Roosa was a small, florid man, with curly red hair and a pug nose. He led Gloria into his tiny stateroom, closed the door, and offered her a seat on his bed, which she declined.

"Eckstein told me to look for you, Ms. VanDeen," said Roosa, "but I don't think there's much chance I would have missed you. A pleasure to be working with you." Gloria, in her jeans and a nearly transparent tee shirt, smiled at Roosa and shook hands.

"I assume Stu gave you all the particulars."

Roosa nodded. "We know what's involved here. I told the five men in my crew everything they need to know to get the job done."

"Can they be trusted?"

"For what they're being paid, they can be trusted about as far as anyone can be, I suppose."

That didn't entirely satisfy Gloria. "Sometimes money isn't enough," she said.

"If it isn't," said Roosa, "then protecting their own backsides ought to do it."

"So they know what's really going on here?"

"They do. And they know that if anyone finds out about it, they'll be in just as much trouble as you and Eckstein. What about your Dexta people? Do they know?"

"No, and I want to keep it that way. The Emporium will be off-limits to everyone but you and your crew for the next week. The cover story is that we want to make sure nobody finds out about our surprises until the grand opening. But don't take any chances. Seal off all the doors and windows, and don't let anyone get inside or see the equipment you're bringing in. Ernie the Bouncer will help you guard the door, but don't let him inside, either."

"Understood."

"Now, can you really get this done in a week? The way Stu described it, there will be an awful lot of digging to do."

"Not digging, exactly. Plasma drills will do the job, and there won't be any dirt or rocks to dispose of. A lot depends on how accurate Eckstein's estimate is. Here," said Roosa, "let me show you a schematic of what we have in mind. Of course, it's based on the sketches Eckstein showed us, and we may have to make a few changes once we see the actual layout, but I think we can do this in a week."

Roosa pulled a piece of paper from his pocket, unfolded it, and spread it out on the bed. Gloria studied it for a few moments and nodded. The plasma recharger would be set up in the anteroom, in full view of everyone. While boomers recharged their drills, the device's fusion reactor would be quietly pumping a fatal overdose of energy into the Fergusite layer below. That was the plan, anyway.

"That's Room 9," she said, pointing to a small box in the schematic. "That's normally one of the hookers' rooms, but I'll instruct Althea Dante to reserve it for you. No one else will be allowed in, and you'll stay in it for as long as you're here."

"Me and one other guy, Ms. VanDeen. His name's Dwayne Cherry. It'll take two of us to keep this up and running. The rest of the crew will leave next week, as soon as we complete the installation."

"Good. And it might be helpful if you could tell them all to scatter as soon as they get back to Palmyra. I don't want to take a chance on them talking about it and being overheard."

"Already done," said Roosa. "And I'm glad to see you've thought this thing through so well, Ms. VanDeen."

"It's Gloria. And you're Sam?"

"Right."

"Well, Sam, I *hope* I've thought it through completely. But if you think of anything I've missed, don't hesitate to tell me. We've all got a lot at stake here."

"No doubt of that," Roosa said, grinning. "I mean, I've done a lot of things in my life, but this will be the first time I've committed treason."

"That makes two of us," Gloria told him.

AS THE WORK BEGAN, IT ATTRACTED THE ATTEN-tion of crowds of idle boomers, who collected in the streets outside the Emporium and tried to converse with the workers. Roosa's crew simply ignored them and focused on the job. Their covered freight skimmer backed up to the front door of the Emporium and tarpaulins were quickly spread over the entrance and all the windows.

Gloria offered herself as a distraction while the unloading continued. Dispensing with her tee shirt, she strolled among the boomers in her low-slung jeans, giving them a good look as she engaged them in idle conversation. The boomrats quickly decided that Gloria was a lot more interesting than a bunch of workers, and she became the center of attention.

"You gonna be workin' the tables again, Miz VanDeen?" one of them asked eagerly.

"You never know, boys," she said. "I had fun doing it last night, and I might just make a habit of it, if I have the time."

"And what about the rooms? You gonna be in the rooms?" asked another.

Gloria just smiled enigmatically. "We'll have to see about that," she said.

"Well, that Miz Althea said you might. Said she might just work the rooms herself, too. Might pretty lady, that Althea."

"Althea will do whatever she feels like doing, as usual," Gloria assured them. "Tell me, how do you men feel about registering?"

That produced some foot shuffling and throat clearing. After a few seconds, one of the older boomrats said, "Hard to see how that'd do a man any good, Miz Gloria. They say if enough of us sign up, they'll bring in an Imperial Gov'nor. That don't sound too good to me."

"It might put Grunfeld outta business, though," said someone else. "Can't tell me *that* wouldn't be a good thing."

"Yeah, but what about the corporates comin' in and takin' over all the claims?" one boomrat demanded.

"They won't just take 'em over, ya thimblewit," someone responded. "The way I hear it, this Eminent Domain stuff means they gotta pay everyone for what they take. Shit, the luck I've had up in those hills, they can have my claim for the price of a ticket back to Palmyra."

That statement brought a small storm of comments, with highboys generally agreeing with the opinion and riverrats generally disputing it. Distinguishing between the two was easy enough even without their comments; the riverrats were streaked with dried river mud, while the highboys were dustier and wore hiking boots instead of slick waders.

The split between highboys and riverrats was not something Gloria had anticipated. She wasn't sure whether it represented an opportunity or a possible problem. In terms of absolute numbers, she estimated that the two groups were about equal in size. However, the highboys held far more individual claims, which would give them greater weight in the Eminent Domain battle. Based on her limited sampling of opinion, it seemed likely that the highboys would be more willing to give their proxies to the corporates. Although some of the highboys had already made genuine fortunes in the hills, the majority of them probably would have been happy to get what they could for their claims and call it quits.

As the debate continued in the streets, Gloria saw Karl Cleveland and another of Grunfeld's men, "Noz" Gnozdziewicz, emerge from City Hall and saunter over toward the crowd in front of the Emporium. They casually shoved a few people out of their way and pushed in close to Gloria. The boomers stepped back to stare at them, but said nothing. Grunfeld's men wore their usual self-satisfied sneers.

"Mornin', Miz VanDeen," said Cleveland. "You're lookin' real good today."

"Anything I can do for you boys?" Gloria asked them.

Both men thought that was funny and allowed themselves a few snickers.

"You can do 'bout any damn thing ya want for us, Miz VanDeen," said Noz. "Mebbe we'll give ya the 'zact particulars sometime."

"I'll look forward to it," Gloria told them. "But maybe you ought to shave first, Karl—remember what happened the last time."

Now it was the boomers' turn to snicker. Cleveland gave them a menacing glare, which more or less shut them up. He looked back at Gloria.

"Hear ya sent those Dexta people o' yours out today," he said.

"That's right. And if you or any of your pals get in their way—"

"Shit, no, Miz VanDeen! We ain't gonna do nothin'—not to *them*, anyhow. But it can be kinda dangerous up in them hills, ya know. Never can tell what might happen to a body, 'specially someone who don't know their way 'round. People get lost up there and never get themselves found. Know what I mean?"

"I know exactly what you mean, Karl. That's why all of our people have wristcoms with locational transponders. You might mention that to your boss, just in case he's having another attack of acute stupidity."

The boomers laughed, and Cleveland decided that he'd endured enough of that for one morning. He and Noz turned to leave, but Cleveland paused and looked back at Gloria.

"The Mayor ain't done with you, Miz VanDeen. Ain't done at all."

"And I'm not done with him, Karl. He's still got eight fingers I haven't broken yet."

Cleveland couldn't seem to think of a comeback to that, so he just pushed his way through the crowd and headed back to City Hall.

"Miz VanDeen?" one of the boomrats said. "We sure do like the way ya handle Grunfeld and his pukes. But that don't mean we ain't worried about ya. That Grunfeld, he's one mean man. Don't go pushin' him too hard. We'd hate like the devil to see you get hurt."

"Never happen," Gloria told them, smiling. "I've got too many friends here."

"You got that, for sure, ma'am. But you be careful, just the same."

"You boys be careful, too. For now, Grunfeld and his pukes are still a force around here. But once we get enough of you registered, all of that will change. You have my word on it."

• • •

REGISTRATION WORK WENT SLOWLY AT FIRST.
On the first day, two teams went up into the hills on each
side of the river, and the third team went along the river
itself to the camps of the riverrats. Tellemacher, not
needed for the moment at the Emporium, accompanied
the river team, which consisted of Palmer Ellison and
Jillian Clymer. Each team found varying degrees of resistance.

The highboys on the slopes were harder to find but
easier to convince. Those who had already sold their
claims to Grunfeld had nothing to gain from the arrival of
the corporates and were reluctant to register, but many
independents, discouraged by months of hard labor with
little to show for it, saw the eventual sale of their claims
as their surest road to a profit; accordingly, they had their
retinas scanned and signed their names on the registration pads. Down on the river, there were many different
opinions and much discussion, but few actual registrations. Jillian Clymer quickly adopted Gloria's strategy of
a hug and a kiss for a signing, and got quite a few takers.
Ellison doggedly pursued any riverrat who seemed re-
motely sympathetic, while Tellemacher wandered
around the camps and spoke in very general terms of the
inevitability of what was coming. He didn't seem to impress many of the boomers, and didn't seem to care
whether he did or not.

The first day's harvest amounted to seventy-four
registrations. The next day, they got eighty-one. The day
after that, only fifty-four. Each night, the Dexta teams
returned to their boardinghouse, compared notes, and
sighed wearily. It looked as if it was going to be a long,
hard job.

PETRA, FOR HER PART, RETURNED TO THE LODGE
for another session of scrubbing toilets. She carried her

pad with her in a pocket of her French-maid outfit, worrying that the slight bulge it made might give her away. But she soon realized that she had already become more or less invisible at the Lodge, except to the young men who worked there. She was simply hired help. So she turned to her chores and waited for an opportunity to begin her career as an operational spy.

She spotted her chance about midmorning, when she returned to the basement workroom to get some more cleaning fluid. The place was empty, and she hadn't seen Thawley all morning. Quickly, Petra walked over to Thawley's console and looked around. There was no obvious place to hide her pad in proximity to the console, but then inspiration struck her. She took the pad out of her pocket and buried it beneath a few crumpled-up papers at the bottom of a wastebasket. The pad was already programmed to search the console for evidence of the man named Abel—whoever he was—so all she had to do was come back in a few hours and retrieve it.

In the middle of the afternoon she returned to the workroom and found it still empty. She went over to the wastebasket and reached down to get the pad.

"What are you doing?"

Petra, her heart skipping a beat, abruptly straightened up and turned around, concealing the pad behind her. She saw Mrs. Thawley standing at the foot of the stairs.

"Oh," Petra said, "I was just going to empty out some of the wastebaskets down here."

"Well, never you mind with that. Just get yourself over to Cabin Four. We've got another guest arriving in half an hour, and I want you to make sure that cabin sparkles."

"I'll get right on it, Mrs. Thawley," Petra promised, smiling obediently.

"You do good work, child. Just keep it up."

"Thank you, Mrs. Thawley. I certainly will."

Petra stood there for a few agonizingly slow seconds

until Mrs. Thawley finally nodded to her and made her way back up the stairs. Petra stuck the pad in her pocket and took a deep breath. Covert operations!

At dinner that evening, Petra found out who the new guest was. She was sharing server duties with Gina Chang, another of the bar girls, and got her first look at Maddie Mitchell, the representative from Prizm, as she was serving drinks. Petra had an odd, uneasy notion that Mitchell was staring at her, but tried to take no notice of it.

Maddie Mitchell was a tall, very slim, thoroughly gorgeous brunette in her thirties, wearing a black skirt slit to the hipbone and a sheer blue blouse that did almost nothing to hide her very small breasts and dark, pointed nipples. She reminded Petra of Gloria in her seemingly boundless confidence in her own beauty and abilities. The other corporate reps deferred to her, and even Claude Rankus seemed to be beguiled by her charm and intelligence. Petra was able to overhear only a little of their conversation, but it seemed that the Prizm rep was there to keep an eye on local events and possibly to cut some sort of deal with the Lodge or the other corporates. In any event, Mitchell was a new player in the game, and Gloria would want to know about her arrival.

Throughout dinner, Petra tried to monitor the conversation without being too obvious about it. She gained a general impression that Sherwin Lund of Excelsior and Gaspar Norfleet of Servitor were fencing with Maddie Mitchell, while Thomas Shoop of Imperium seemed content to watch and listen. Petra knew that Prizm stood to be the big loser if one of the other corporates began full-scale development of the Sylvania Fergusite deposit, but Mitchell acted as if it were Servitor and Excelsior who were in peril. Was it merely a ploy, or did Prizm have an ace up its corporate sleeve? Maybe it was simply the magnetic personality of Mitchell herself that created the impression. She was witty, incisive, and unperturbed by the sallies of Lund and Norfleet. Petra found herself liking the Prizm rep.

As she was clearing the dessert course, Petra's reaction to Maddie Mitchell took a sudden and shocking turn in a totally unexpected direction. She felt Maddie's eyes on her as she bent over the table, with her ridiculous French maid's outfit revealing her breasts as she did so. She glanced up into Maddie's brown eyes for a moment, then quickly gathered up the dishes and started to return to the kitchen; Maddie's voice stopped her in her tracks.

"I want *that* one," she said.

Petra couldn't help turning around. She saw Maddie's long, delicate forefinger pointing at her.

Claude Rankus seemed momentarily shocked, as well, but quickly recovered. "Of course, my dear. See to it, would you, Mrs. Thawley?"

Mrs. Thawley was suddenly at Petra's side, a firm grip on her elbow. "Come along, Petra," she said.

Petra stood rooted in place.

"Now!" hissed Mrs. Thawley, increasing the pressure on Petra's elbow.

"But . . . you mean . . . ?" Petra wasn't quite certain she understood what was happening.

Rankus turned in his chair and gazed at her with an impatient frown. "Take her to Cabin Four, Mrs. Thawley," he said, with the firmness and clarity of a general ordering a lieutenant to take a hill.

"Wait!" cried Petra. "I'm just here to clean and serve. I'm not . . . I mean, the other girls . . ."

"You are here to do what is required of you," Rankus told her sternly. "Let's have no more of this foolishness. You will go where you are told, or you will never work here again."

Mrs. Thawley applied enough force to her grip to get Petra in motion toward the kitchen. Petra looked back over her shoulder in mute appeal, but Rankus had already turned back to the table. Maddie Mitchell simply gazed at her with a thin, superior smile.

As she marched Petra off to Cabin Four, Mrs. Thawley lectured Petra on the duties of those who served the Lodge. There was no distinction between cleaning a bedroom and making herself available for a guest's pleasure in that same room. Any woman who worked in a place like the Emporium should understand and accept that requirement. Petra's protests that she was not a prostitute but simply a waitress left Mrs. Thawley unmoved. She roughly shoved Petra into Cabin Four, then locked the door behind her.

Petra, stunned and afraid, thought furiously. She had not expected anything like this, and she didn't think that Gloria would have knowingly sent her into such a situation. She could simply refuse to have anything to do with Maddie Mitchell, storm out of the cabin as soon as the door opened, and, if necessary, walk back down the mountain to Greenlodge. It didn't seem likely that Rankus would forcibly detain her against her will; if nothing else, that might poison his relationship with the Emporium and its new proprietor, who just happened to be the Dexta representative on this planet.

On the other hand, a flat refusal would end Petra's usefulness at the Lodge. She had already gathered what seemed to be worthwhile information, although she didn't know what, if anything, the pad had acquired concerning the man named Abel. Gloria thought it important to her plans—whatever they were—to have a spy at the Lodge, and Petra had agreed to accept the job. Yet the job never included mandatory sex with anyone—at the Emporium or the Lodge, male or female. But now . . .

The door opened, and Petra whirled around to face Maddie Mitchell, who closed the door behind her.

"Your name is Petra?" she asked.

"Yes . . . but listen, this isn't . . ."

"Yes, I know. You're just a serving girl."

"Yes!"

"Then serve me." Maddie pulled off her blouse, then unfastened her skirt and let it drop. She was wearing nothing underneath it, and stood before Petra with an expectant look on her face.

"I . . . I can't . . ." Petra stammered.

"I won't hurt you, if that's what you're worried about."

"No . . . no, I didn't . . . that is . . ."

"Mr. Rankus expects it of you," Maddie reminded her. "He wouldn't like it if you disappointed me."

"I know, but this isn't what . . . what I expected. All I've ever done here is clean toilets!"

Maddie smiled wolfishly. "Then this would be a step up, wouldn't it?"

"No! I mean . . ."

"You find me less appealing than cleaning a toilet?" Maddie raised an eyebrow.

"That's not what I meant," Petra protested. "I just meant that I didn't sign up to have sex with anyone."

"You accepted employment here, and according to Claude, that means you agreed to do whatever was required of you."

"Yes, but . . ."

"Then take off your clothes, Petra. I won't bite."

Petra shut her eyes and tried to think. This was insane. And yet, if she didn't go along with Maddie's desires, her mission to Sylvania would be a failure. Spirit only knew what impact that failure might have on the entire course of events on this world. She couldn't let Gloria down . . . but how much could Gloria ask of her? How much did she owe Gloria? Would *Gloria* do this?

Silly question, she thought.

"Would you like me to take your clothes off for you?" Maddie asked.

If Maddie started stripping her, Petra realized, she would certainly find the pad. And if that happened, the consequences might be much more serious than simply being fired. Reluctantly, Petra began unbuttoning her maid's uniform. She carefully laid it on a side table, fearing that the pad would make an audible thump if she simply dropped the outfit.

"Those too," Maddie said, indicating with her eyes the frilly black panties Petra wore.

"No," Petra said. "I can't do this!"

To Petra's surprise, Maddie backed off. "Oh, all right," she said. "I just wanted to see if you were game."

"Well, I'm not!" Petra gasped. She darted around Maddie and retreated across the room.

"And here I thought Dexta people were made of sterner stuff," said Maddie.

"*What?*"

Maddie smiled. "Relax, Petra. I know who and what you are, and why you're here."

"You do? But—"

"I'm your contact, Petra. Or you're mine. Anyway, I need you to relay messages to Gloria. I can't use the comm without being overheard, and it would look suspicious if I kept running down to the Emporium to meet with her."

Petra's head was swimming. "You mean," she asked, "that all of this was a sham?"

"Not for a moment," Maddie replied. "I really do want you, Petra, and I had hoped that you might want me. But I can see now that you don't. A pity, really. I thought we had gotten beyond all of that centuries ago, but I guess you're one of those throwbacks who see something shameful about this."

"Uh . . . no . . . uh, not really."

"Have you ever been with a woman?"

"No . . . I just don't . . . I don't *feel* that way. And anyway, I just didn't want to be forced into it, with anyone."

Maddie nodded. "I can understand that, I suppose. Still, you and I are going to have to *act* like lovers, Petra, even if you insist on playing the shy virgin in reality. We'll have to share the bed tonight, of course, but nothing will happen unless you want it to. And in the morning, I'll tell Rankus that you were entirely satisfactory, and that I want the arrangement to continue throughout my stay here. That way, you won't have to sleep with anyone else, and I'll have a secure line of communication with Gloria."

Petra took a deep breath, then let the air out slowly. She felt immense relief, although the arrangement Maddie had described still seemed vaguely troubling.

"How much has Gloria told you about . . . about what we're doing here?" Maddie asked her.

"Umm . . . who's *we*?"

Maddie nodded to herself. "I see," she said. "If Gloria thinks it best to keep you in the dark, then I'll do the same. And it's for your own good, Petra. If things go wrong . . . well, the less you know, the better off you'll be."

Petra found herself feeling irritated with Gloria. She had accepted the fact that there was more going on than Gloria had told her, but it rankled, somehow. She wanted to know more.

"Is Prizm involved in some sort of plot with Dexta? Or Gloria?"

Maddie smiled. She was a remarkably attractive woman, perhaps even the equal of Gloria, although of a different type.

"Ask me no questions, Petra, and I'll tell you no lies. Come here and sit beside me, at least. We can't conspire properly from opposite sides of the room." Maddie patted the bed next to her. Petra walked slowly across the room and cautiously sat down. Maddie patted her on her thigh as if to reassure her. If that was the point of the gesture, it failed utterly.

"Petra," Maddie said, her voice dropping to little more than a whisper, "I've learned something that Gloria needs to know. Servitor and Excelsior are going to bring in a transport with a thousand people on it. They'll set up a camp outside of town, and every one of those people will register as voters."

Petra's eyes widened slightly. Suddenly, she felt like a real spy again.

"That would just about clinch the registration, wouldn't it?" she said.

"If it doesn't, they'll bring in another thousand," Maddie said. "They intend to get the territory incorporated just as soon as possible. I don't know the date of the first shipment, but it will probably be within a couple of weeks."

"I'll tell Gloria," Petra said. "Is there anything else she needs to know?"

"That's all I have for the moment. But ask Gloria to tell me all she can about her end of things. I'm a little in the dark up here."

"Aren't we all?"

chapter 13

THE LODGE UTILITY SKIMMER DELIVERED PETRA
and the other girls to the Emporium the next morning.
Petra didn't follow the others to their tent, but went off
in search of Gloria. After a nervous, sleepless night, she
was feeling drained and weary and more than a little
odd; she desperately needed to have a talk with Gloria.

She learned from one of the workmen that Gloria
was inside the Emporium, where Petra was not allowed
to go. She waited outside, feeling too conspicuous in her
skimpy maid's uniform with the pad bulging in her
pocket.

Gloria appeared at the front entrance, wearing her
gravity-defying jeans and nothing else. She seemed to
know immediately from the expression on her assistant's
face that something was wrong.

"Let's go for a little walk," Gloria said. "I can't let
you inside, and I don't want to talk in one of the tents
where we could be overheard."

"But won't we attract attention being together like
this?"

"Why? You're just another of my employees. And people are used to seeing me walk around town like this."

They might have been used to it, but they certainly didn't take it for granted. As they strolled down the main street—mud-free for once, after a week of dry weather—every head turned to follow their progress. People waved and said hi, and Gloria happily returned their greetings.

"Here," Petra said, handing her pad to Gloria. "I shouldn't be seen with this."

Gloria took it and used a little hook attachment to hang it from one of her belt loops. "Did you get anything?"

"I haven't had a chance to check. But if there was anything there about Abel, we should have it now."

"Good work, Petra. Did you have any problems?"

Petra looked around quickly. People were staring at them as they made their way down the street, but no one was within earshot.

"Uh . . . not a problem, exactly. I was . . . uh . . . approached . . . by Maddie Mitchell, the rep from Prizm. She says I'm supposed to be her contact with you."

Gloria brightened. "She's here? Great. I've been expecting her, but I didn't know when she would arrive."

"You know her?"

"We met back on Earth last month. And I left a message for her about you at the Palmyra Station. Did she have any messages for me?"

"Yes. She said to tell you that Servitor and Excelsior are bringing in a shipload of a thousand people to be registered. She doesn't know when they're due, but thinks it will be within a couple of weeks."

Gloria nodded. "I've been expecting them to do something like that," she said. She paused for a second to say hello to a passing boomer.

"Gloria?" Petra asked when they were alone again. "There's more going on here than just registering voters, isn't there?"

"Did Maddie tell you something?"

"No. She said that the less I know, the safer I'll be."

"She's right. I'm sorry I can't tell you more, Petra. I don't like keeping things from you. It's not that I don't trust you—you know that, don't you?"

"Sure I do," Petra said, smiling at her boss. "And I trust you, too. But did you know . . . about Maddie?"

Gloria looked at Petra for a few seconds, then caught on. "Ah," she said. "I see."

"She said she wanted me, and Rankus sent me to her cabin. At first, she tried . . . well, never mind about that. Anyway, Maddie says it will make a good cover for us, and it will keep me from having to sleep with anyone else."

"But you slept with her?"

"No!" Petra replied. "We just spent the night in the same bed, is all. But . . ."

"But she did want you."

Petra sighed and shook her head. "Spirit, Gloria! Ever since I got to this planet, I've been fending off men who want to sleep with me, women who want to sleep with me, women who want me to sleep with men, and men who want me to sleep with women!"

"And you haven't slept with anyone, have you?"

"Should I have?" Petra asked forlornly.

"That's entirely up to you, Petra," Gloria told her. "Look, I would never ask you to do that, although I admit that I knew there was a chance something might happen at the Lodge. But I trusted you to handle it, and I see that you have. Still, if things get too uncomfortable for you, I won't hold it against you if you decide to back out."

"I won't do that, Gloria. I said I'd do this job, and I will."

Gloria frowned and chewed on her lower lip for a moment. "I can tell you this much, Petra," she said. "This job we have may be the most important thing you and I will ever do. The whole future of the Empire may be riding on it. There's not much that I wouldn't do to ensure our success, but I can't ask that from you, Petra. The last thing I want is to see you hurt in any way."

Petra gave an artificial laugh. "I knew the job was dangerous when I took it," she said. "But . . . I don't know, Gloria. There are some things . . . I mean, I'm not like you."

Now it was Gloria's turn to laugh. "Be glad of that, kiddo," she said. "Let me tell you something, Petra. Every man on this planet wants to fuck me—hell, every man in the Empire wants to fuck me. But if you asked all the men at Elba's on any given night to choose between you and me, a lot of them would choose you."

"That's ridiculous," Petra responded.

"No," Gloria insisted, "it's not. Oh, I suppose most of them would grab me first for a night or two, but you're the one they'd want to take home to meet their parents and spend the rest of their lives with. You're a genuinely nice person, Petra. I'm not."

"That's not true," Petra objected. "You're nice, Gloria. I mean, most of the time."

"When it suits my purposes, yes," Gloria acknowledged. "And when it suits my purposes, I can also be entirely cold-blooded and ruthless. That's the real difference between us, Petra. You know what happened that first day with Grunfeld, don't you? I dressed in a way that invited Grunfeld to try something. And when he did, I let him stick his grubby finger inside me—and then I broke that finger, plus another one, and kicked a couple of more asses in the bargain. All of that didn't just *happen*, Petra. I planned every bit of it, right down to throwing Karl Cleveland out the window by his beard. Cold-blooded and ruthless, you see?"

"Yes, but—"

"There's no 'but' about it. Even if you knew Qatsima, could you have done that, Petra?"

"Umm . . ."

"We both know the answer. You're right. You *aren't*

like me, and you shouldn't try to be. Oh, I think it might be good for you if you loosened up a bit. Elba saw that. I just wish *you* could see that."

"You think I should have sex with Maddie?"

"Let's just say that I don't see any reason why you shouldn't. She's a wonderful lover, you know."

Petra looked at her. "You . . . and she . . . ?"

"Of course. Maddie has the same genetic . . . advantages . . . that I do, and sex with her is something very special. So why shouldn't you have sex with her? Or with anyone else around here? Back on Mynjhino, you were with Ricardo, and then with Bryce, our favorite news weasel. Why not with Maddie, or a boomer, or maybe with one of the Dexta team? I think Palmer Ellison has his eye on you."

"He *does*? I mean . . . uh . . . well, I'll think about it, Gloria. I really will."

"Whatever you do," Gloria said, "I promise I won't tell your mother."

Petra returned Gloria's grin. "Well," she said, "at least that's one less thing to worry about."

She was about to let the matter drop, but a thought occurred to her, and she turned to look at her boss. "Gloria?" Petra said. "Could I ask you a personal question?"

"Of course you can, Petra. You're my best buddy, you know."

"What do you *want*?" Petra asked. "I mean, in life?"

Gloria chuckled. "Now you sound like *my* mother. Do you mean, do I want a husband and children? I don't know . . . maybe, someday. There's still plenty of time for that. But if you mean what do I want to achieve in my life . . . ?"

"Yes."

"Petra," Gloria said, "I intend to run Dexta someday."

Petra nodded. "I thought maybe that was it."

"Norman Mingus will be gone someday, although I dread the prospect. I want to be his successor, although

Charles would stop the stars in their courses—and he can—to prevent that from happening. But it's what I want, and I'll do whatever I have to in order to get it. I told you, I'm cold-blooded and ruthless, and I have absolutely no sense of shame. Sex is my trump card, Petra, and I'll use it any way I have to. I mean, what's the point of being the most desirable woman in the Empire if I don't use that to get what I want?"

"I guess you're right," Petra said.

"And what about you, Petra? What do you want?"

"I guess," Petra said after a moment's thought, "what I want is to go on being your best buddy and gal Friday. And when you're in charge of Dexta, I'll be right there outside your door, guarding the gate to the castle." Petra giggled, then added, "Because that would make *me* the most powerful woman in the Empire!"

Gloria laughed, then stuck out her hand and shook Petra's.

"Deal," she said.

THE GRAND REOPENING OF ELBA'S EMPORIUM was the biggest social event in the brief history of the town of Greenlodge. Two or three thousand people jammed the street outside, and everyone wanted in. That was clearly impossible, so Gloria arranged things so that a group of one hundred would be admitted every ten minutes and allowed to stay for a half an hour—long enough for a quick guided tour, a free drink, and an invitation to register to vote. The hookers and bar girls led the tours, while Dexta people manned the main desk for registration. Meanwhile, Gloria and Althea stood on a platform in front of the building, taking turns describing the new amenities now offered by the Emporium.

The boomers in the street didn't seem to mind the long wait because Gloria wore nothing but a gold chain around her hips, with a gem-studded brooch that drew attention to her crotch without actually concealing much of it. Althea, like the bar girls and hookers, was entirely nude. Like carnival barkers, Gloria and Althea offered a slick line of patter about the wonders of the revamped Emporium and the great advantages of voter registration. Among the advantages, as previously promised, were a hug and a kiss from Gloria and, for one day only, a chance to win a night with Althea.

It amused Gloria to see how quickly and completely Althea had thrown herself into her new role. Snob though she was, Althea luxuriated in sex—of any kind with anyone. During her years at Dexta, she had famously humped her way through most of the Imperial family—including Charles, before, during, and after his marriage to Gloria. She was even more uninhibited than Gloria, and her lack of discrimination had hurt her career at Dexta, as had her bitchy personality and tendency to lose sight of the forest for the trees. For Gloria, Althea served as a useful object lesson in the dangers of giving in too completely to her own carnal appetites.

She had hoped Ted Oberlin would show up for the festivities, but he was nowhere in sight. In his absence, she was tempted to match Althea and offer herself as another door prize for registering, but that might get in the way of her job. She didn't want boomrats fighting over her.

Instead of Oberlin, Kevin Grunfeld showed up in a skimmer, along with two of his pukes—and Myron Vigo. The skimmer parked at the edge of the crowd, and the occupants got out and looked around. The boomers soon noticed them and grudgingly cleared a path for them.

"Welcome to our Grand Reopening, Mr. Mayor—and Mr. Vigo," Gloria said from the platform.

"You ain't reopenin' nothin'," Grunfeld snarled. "This here establishment is officially closed for violations of the fire safety code."

The boomers reacted with a chorus of boos and catcalls, but Grunfeld simply stared at them until they quieted down.

"I didn't realize that Greenlodge had any such code," Gloria said.

"It does," Grunfeld assured her.

"He's quite right, Ms. VanDeen," said Myron Vigo. "It's not explicit, but the Town Charter includes a provision which adopts, in toto, with appropriate local exceptions, the existing health and safety codes of Palmyra City."

"But for some reason, you've never chosen to enforce them until now," Gloria pointed out.

"Irrelevant," said Vigo. "Today, we *are* enforcing them."

"And we're shuttin' down your Emporium," added Grunfeld.

"Just how do you know we're in violation of your code?" Gloria asked.

"Shit, are you kiddin'?" Grunfeld guffawed. "That whole place could burn down if someone just dropped a seegar on the floor. Surprised it ain't already. See, we don't want no tragedies in our town. So you just get everybody out and shut them doors."

The grumbling from the boomers increased, but Gloria remained unperturbed. "Mr. Mayor," she said, "Mr. Vigo, I suggest you accompany me on a little tour of our new and improved Emporium. I think you might find a few surprises." Gloria descended from the platform and beckoned the local establishment to follow her inside.

She ushered them into the anteroom just inside the front door. The Dexta staffers at the desk watched them in silence, and a tour group of a hundred boomers, led by Petra, backed away to give them some space.

"Anybody got a match?" Gloria asked. "And something to burn?" A boomer obligingly provided her with a matchbox and a copy of one of the flyers that had been circulated to advertise today's event. Gloria struck the match, ignited the crumpled-up paper, and tossed it at one of the walls. A second later, to the sound of a snake-like hiss, a jet of blue chemical fog gushed out of the wall and instantly extinguished the blaze.

"We've made a few changes," Gloria said proudly. "You see, Grunfeld, we don't want any tragedies, either. If someone were to try to burn this place down—accidentally or otherwise—they wouldn't get very far."

Grunfeld frowned, then turned to Vigo. "You gonna let her get away with this?"

Vigo smiled toward Gloria and shrugged. "It seems we have no choice. I'm assuming, of course, that your fire prevention system extends throughout the building."

"It does."

"Well, we'll just see about that!" Grunfeld was about to bull his way through the crowd into the main room, but Vigo caught his arm and restrained him.

"I don't think that will be necessary, Kevin," he said. "I doubt that Ms. VanDeen has missed anything."

"Not a thing," Gloria affirmed. "But there are some other points of interest that I think you might like to see." Gloria gestured to the left of the front door, toward the entrance to the general store. There, a tanklike metal structure ten feet high and four feet in diameter stood embedded in a thick concrete base.

"What the fuck is *that*?" Grunfeld demanded.

"That," said Gloria, "is our new plasma recharger."

"Your *what*?"

"As I said. The second one on the planet, but the only one that's available for general use. Nobody has to sell out their claim to use *our* recharger, Grunfeld. All they have to do is register to vote. And the highboys seem to like the idea." She looked toward the front desk. "How many have signed up so far?"

"Seventy-two, Gloria," Jillian Clymer said with evident pride.

"Shit, they can't do this, Vigo!" Grunfeld insisted.

Vigo shook his head apologetically. "I'm afraid they

can, Mr. Mayor. The local exception for *your* recharger would apply here, as well." Vigo smiled at Gloria. "Tell me, Ms. VanDeen, are there any other surprises we should be aware of before we go?"

"Oh," said Gloria, "nothing that would concern the local government. Just the usual amenities. Some new and better slot machines. A new VR booth. It has a program that comes highly recommended—History's Greatest Women. You can make love with Helen of Troy, Cleopatra, Catherine the Great, Marilyn Monroe, Xantha of Delta Albus . . ."

"What?" asked Vigo. "Not Gloria VanDeen?"

"Actually," she said, "there seems to be a recent addition to the program of some blonde named Gloria. Surprised me, I can tell you. Not to be compared with the real thing, of course, but I may just want to take some legal advice about this, Mr. Vigo."

Vigo grinned and bowed theatrically. "At your service, Ms. VanDeen. Appropriating your name and image for commercial purposes without your consent would, of course, be actionable. You might have a good case—and a profitable one, I shouldn't doubt. I'd be happy to represent you, my dear."

"What the fuck are you talkin' about?" growled Grunfeld.

"Nothing that concerns your immediate purposes, Mr. Mayor. I think we're about finished here. Thank you for the tour, Ms. VanDeen."

"Anytime," Gloria said.

Grunfeld stomped out of the Emporium with a look on his face that left no doubt about what had happened inside. The boomrats on the street roared as Gloria stepped back outside and waved to them.

THE NEXT DAY, WITH THE DEXTA TEAMS OFF IN search of votes and with Althea taking charge of the Emporium, Gloria got into a skimmer and headed upriver, wearing nothing but a pair of sandals and a utility belt around her hips. From the belt hung a registration pad on her left flank, and a sheathed bush knife on her right. The pad was for business, and the knife was for anything else that might arise. She knew she had pushed Grunfeld close to his breaking point and intended to be prepared for his inevitable attempt to teach her a lesson.

After more than a week of constant work and no sex, Gloria felt as if she were approaching her own breaking point. If she didn't get relief soon, she really would offer herself in the Emporium's rooms. But that would only cause problems. It was important for her to seem totally available while still keeping above it all, like some sort of goddess. The boomers, she believed, preferred her that way. She could attract their support and devotion only by maintaining her position as an idealized embodiment of sex, not by becoming its hot, sweaty reality.

Yet she seriously needed that hot, sweaty reality. Wandering around the town nearly naked most of the time had stoked her internal fires to the boiling point, and today's expedition in the altogether was going to cause steam to come out of her ears. Petra once said she didn't know whether to envy her or pity her. Gloria didn't have the heart to tell her that it should be envy—definitely, envy. She was an enhanced human being, after all, and normal humans simply couldn't understand what that was like. It had taken her years to understand it herself. But Mynjhino had somehow changed everything for her, and she had come to realize that the glamorous, daring, totally public sexual icon she had become was what she was always meant to be. She was like some primal force of nature, unbound, unleashed, unlimited in her potential. And she would harness that force and use it to run the Empire itself, someday . . . someday . . .

But first, there was the little matter of Sylvania. And the Fergusite deposit that could destroy that Empire.

• • •

SHE PULLED INTO PIZEN FLATS SHORTLY BEFORE
noon. The riverrats dropped what they were doing and
swarmed around her as she made her way to King Gus
Thornton's royal campfire. She greeted them warmly,
some of them by name, and happily gave Gus a kiss that
curled his whiskers. He squeezed her bare bum and
sighed in contentment.

"Sorry I missed the grand reopening," Gus told her,
"but you know how it is when ya got responsibilities."

"Sure do, Gus. What do you say, could you buy a girl
lunch and some coffee?"

Gus gestured to the rickety wooden throne and invited her to take a seat. "Rustle up some grub for Miz
Gloria," he commanded to no one in particular. His order was obeyed within seconds, and Gloria sat down to
enjoy a fried chicken leg and a cup of the potent brew
that passed for coffee in Pizen Flats.

"You folks hear we got a recharger at the Emporium
now?" she asked between bites.

There was general assent. "The highboys are pretty
damn excited about that," Gus said. "Hell, we got a couple of old plasma drills around here, too. Might just take
'em into town to get jazzed up again."

"You're more than welcome. Our price is reason-
able, and all you have to do is register to vote."

Gus frowned, and there were some unhappy mut-
ters from the assembled riverrats. "Same damn deal as
Grunfeld," someone complained. "Just sugar-coated."

"Go with Grunfeld," another agreed, "ya lose your
claim. Sign up to vote, ya wind up losin' your claim."

"Not true, boys!" Gloria stood up and gestured emphatically with the drumstick. "Listen to me. Whether
you register or not, this territory will wind up being incorporated within a month. Excelsior and Servitor are
bringing in a shipload of a thousand people in a couple
of weeks, and all of them are coming here to register.
And if that's not enough, they'll bring in a thousand
more, and a thousand more after that."

That produced general commotion. No one sounded happy. Ted Oberlin pushed his way through the mob to face Gloria. He paused a moment to run his eyes over her naked body, smiled at her for a second, then spoke.

"If that's true . . ." he began.

"It is."

"Then why are you here? Why do you want *us* to register?"

"Because the more of you boomers who register, the fewer people the corporates will bring in. And those people will do more than just register. They'll start filing claims, too. Ted, you know what that would mean."

Oberlin nodded, pursed his lips, and thought for a moment. He turned to face the other riverrats.

"She's right," he said. "Look, boys, from what Gloria just told us, incorporation is inevitable. That means that the only thing that matters now is the fight over Eminent Domain."

"Eminent fuckin' Domain!" someone snorted. "Just an excuse to grab our claims and throw us out, all legal-like. Whatever we do, we're gonna lose!"

"No!" Oberlin shouted down the grumblers. "We can win! And I know how we can do it. Listen to me, some of you know I studied law. Well, I think I see a way for us to win the Eminent Domain battle. Let me just think about it for a little while, and I'll tell you what I have in mind. It'll work, dammit, I know it will! Just give me some time to get this organized, okay? And in the meantime, I think the best thing all of us can do is get registered with Gloria . . . and collect our hugs and kisses! And I'm gonna be first!"

Before anyone could mount a protest, Oberlin stepped next to Gloria. She took the registration pad from her belt, quickly scanned his retina, then handed him the pad and a stylus. He scrawled his name, then wrapped her in his arms and collected on her promise.

"I'll be at the falls tonight," she whispered in mid-clinch. "Can you get a skimmer?"

"I will," he vowed, "if I have to build one out of tin cans and twigs!"

He broke away from her, then called out, "Okay, boys! Who's next?"

"*I* am!" declared Gus Thornton. "By the divine right of kings!"

"'THE WOODS ARE LOVELY, DARK, AND DEEP,'" Gloria said to herself as she walked into the forest in the bowl by the falls, " 'and I have promises to keep.' "

Minus her sandals and belt, she padded forward on the soft mosses and looked around. There was no sign of anyone, but she was certain she wasn't alone. When she had gone far enough for the forest to absorb the roar of the falls, she stopped.

"All right, Abel!" she called. "I know you're here. I know you can hear me. Come out! You and I have to talk!"

Silence. Not even a voice . . . or the Voice.

"Come out and talk to me, you old fraud! I need your help!"

And suddenly, he was there.

"Fraud, is it?" he said. "That's a fine thing to call someone, when you need their help."

Gloria simply smiled at him.

chapter **14**

GLORIA WATCHED AS THE COMPACT, RED-FACED, curly-haired man who called himself Sam Russell accepted a metal canister about the size of a large can of tomato juice from a dusty, bearded highboy. He tapped a button on the big, black plasma recharger beside him, causing a curved panel to pop open. Russell inserted the canister into the recharger, fiddled with a connection for a moment, then closed the panel and hit another button on the recharger. Nothing visible or audible happened, but Russell kept his eye on a digital display for a few seconds. Then he opened up the recharger, removed the plasma containment canister, and handed it back to the highboy, whose smile was visible under his dark whiskers.

"Damn," he said. "Haven't used that drill in near about six months! A pleasure doin' business with ya."

As the boomer left, Gloria glanced at Wilmer DeGrasse, who was manning the front desk. DeGrasse nodded; the boomer had been duly registered.

She also looked quickly at the man named Sam. He gave her a barely perceptible nod, which she returned.

Out on the street, Gloria got into a skimmer next to Palmer Ellison. Tellemacher's initial assignment of two-person teams had proved to be ineffective. Ellison and Jillian Clymer had done well, Randolph Alexander and Pearl Shuzuki had been barely adequate, and the gloomy pair of DeGrasse and Sintra Garbedian had been an outright disaster. Garbedian tried to be a good soldier, but his heart clearly wasn't in it; DeGrasse, meanwhile, seemed to have his mind on other things these days, namely, Lulu Villegas. Gloria decided to re-arrange things, breaking up the permanent teams and rotating desk duty among the seven, while the other six, including Tellemacher, spent the day in the field. Today, she was spelling Garbedian, who claimed he was not feeling well.

Gloria let Ellison drive. She was a highly skilled driver, and back home, she drove her Ferrari with de-light and enthusiasm; she had even won a couple of skimmer rallies. However, she had noticed that some people seemed to get very nervous when riding with her. She couldn't imagine why—she was in complete control, after all—but in deference to the shakier nerves of others, she reluctantly relinquished the controls from time to time.

They crossed the river and headed up into the hills on the western side of the valley. The highboys were more thinly scattered there than on the east side, where the slopes were higher and less encumbered by trees. They soon found three of them working a small outcrop with picks and shovels. It developed that they had sold their plasma drill months ago after its charge ran out rather than surrender their claim to Grunfeld. They were making a steady return, they said, although the work was backbreaking. They had heard about the new recharger at the Emporium, but they had decided not to get a new drill because they figured they would be run off their claim by the corporates before long. They couldn't quite see the point of registering, not even for a kiss and a hug from Gloria, and in the end, Gloria and Ellison moved on without having accomplished anything.

"It's like fishing," Ellison explained as they moved cautiously along the ridgeline. "You make your cast, jiggle the bait for a while, and if you don't get a bite, move on to the next good spot. Some of these guys just love to argue, so it's best to avoid getting into an extended debate with them."

"You've caught more than your share, Palmer," Gloria said.

"It's Pug," he said with a slightly embarrassed grin.

"Pug?"

"Short for Pugnacious. I used to get into a lot of fights at school."

"Did you win them?"

"Most of them. I try to make a habit of winning."

Gloria nodded. "That's a good habit to get into."

Gloria was wearing a pair of thin, white, hip-hugging shorts and an unbuttoned blue shirt, and Ellison kept glancing in her direction. That had not mattered on the river, but along the ridgeline, where there were trees to dodge and sudden changes in elevation, his inattention was enough to make Gloria a little nervous. After their next stop—again, no takers—she decided to take the controls herself and Ellison obediently slid over.

At their third stop, they found only a single lonesome highboy, clacking away at the rocks with a hammer. They had to hike a considerable distance up the slope from where they had parked to get to him, and when he saw them, he stood up and grinned at Gloria. "Damn," he said, "it's my day for company. You're the second bunch come through here today."

"We are?" Gloria asked. "Who else was here?"

"Couple o' city types," the highboy answered. "New boots, not hardly broken in. You could tell their feet hurt."

"Who were they?"

"Said they were from Excelsior. Offered me ten thousand crowns for my proxy, damned if they didn't!"

"And did you take it?"

"Do I look like some kinda idiot?" he demanded. "Damn right I took it! Ten thousand crowns! And they said when the Eminent Domain deal goes through, I'd probably get another hundred thousand for my claim! How 'bout *them* apples?"

Gloria and Ellison looked at each other. "At that price, they could get the proxies for just about every claim in the valley for ten or twenty million," Ellison calculated.

"Cheap at twice the price," said Gloria.

"What's that?" the highboy asked. "You sayin' I got hornswoggled?"

"You sold low," Gloria told him. "Sorry, but it's the truth."

The highboy sagged visibly, sank, and plopped down on a rock. "Shit," he said. "Never been no damn good at the business end o' things. Shoulda known better."

"Well," said Gloria, "as long as you sold your proxy, you might as well register to vote. That will speed things up, anyway. The sooner we get people registered, the sooner you'll get paid for your claim if the corporates have their way. But next time, don't take the first offer you hear."

The boomer accepted Gloria's logic and registered. "Might just go on down to your new Emporium, Miz Gloria," he said, trying to salvage something from his day. "Play a little poker, get some decent grub . . . hell, can't let them crowns burn a hole in my pocket, now can I?"

On their hike back down to the skimmer, Ellison said, "It's amazing any of those boys hang on to a penny."

"A few do, most don't," said Gloria. "It's always that way in a boom, they say. Between cards and girls, he'll probably drop most of that ten thousand at the Emporium tonight. Sad, really. I'd cut prices, but I have a payroll to meet and a Comptroller to satisfy."

"Getting softhearted, Gloria?"

"I have my moments," she conceded.

"Then," said Ellison, "maybe I should take advantage of the moment while it lasts." He suddenly put his arms around her, pulled her close, and kissed her.

Gloria didn't quite resist, but didn't cooperate, either. When he slid his hand inside her shirt and began stroking her breasts, she finally backed away. Ellison stood there looking at her, his face revealing a combination of desire and doubt. He was a good-looking young man, with short brown hair, a sharp nose, and active blue eyes flecked with gray.

"I'm crazy about you, Gloria," he said. "Maybe I shouldn't have done that, but I don't regret it."

Gloria thought for a moment, then said, "If you want to fuck me, Pug, you can. We'll do it right now, down under those trees."

Ellison looked as if he couldn't believe his luck. "Really? You mean it?"

"Absolutely," Gloria told him. "Of course, if we do this, then you'll never be able to work for me again."

Ellison's brow creased. "What do you mean?"

"I mean that I like you, Pug, and I like your attitude and ability. I was going to ask you to come join the OSI when we got back to Manhattan. I think you'd be a real asset to the Office. But I'm not going to have sex with you or anyone else who works for me. Too many complications."

"Uh . . ." Ellison had, in seconds, plunged from the summit of joy into the crevasse of indecision.

"You can fuck me or work for me," Gloria said. "But you can't do both."

Ellison thought about it for several seconds, but both of them already knew what his decision would be. Finally, he kicked at a loose rock and sent it bouncing down the slope.

"Shit," he said.

Gloria smiled and patted him on the shoulder. "Don't worry about it, Pug. One roll in the pine needles with me just isn't worth it."

"Yeah," he said, "I guess you're right."

"You're smart and ambitious, and I'll be glad to have you on my team. You should go far at Dexta—if you avoid temptation."

"That won't exactly be easy if I'm working for you," Ellison pointed out. "You are temptation personified."

"You'll get over it. People do, you know. Anyway, there are plenty of other women around who would be happy to be with you. I saw you looking at Petra the other night."

"Petra? Uh . . . yeah, she's quite a lady. You think she'd be interested in me?"

"Find out for yourself, Pug. What do I look like, Cupid?"

They returned to the skimmer. Gloria congratulated herself on having done her good deed for the day.

PETRA, BACK FROM ANOTHER SESSION AT THE Lodge, was waiting in Gloria's office when she returned to the Emporium that evening. Gloria was covered with dust and wanted nothing more than a hot bath and some cold beer. She sat down at her desk—now complete with a computer console—and started taking off her boots and socks.

"How'd it go?" Gloria asked.

"No problems," Petra told her. "Another message from Maddie. She said that the other two trustees of the Lodge were due to arrive this afternoon. They're younger men who inherited their spots on the board from their deceased fathers."

"Interesting," said Gloria. "I get the feeling old Claude is about to be sold out."

"Maddie said the same thing. She thinks Excelsior

and Servitor have cut some sort of deal with the other trustees, but she doesn't know any of the details. But you'll probably find out soon enough. Here." Petra pulled a square envelope from her pocket and handed it to Gloria.

"Ah. I'm invited to dinner tomorrow night. I guess the two new trustees want a look at me."

"Who wouldn't?" Petra asked.

Gloria peeled off her socks, got to her feet, and removed the shorts and shirt. She wiggled her toes and sighed. "How are you getting along with Maddie?" she asked as she gathered up her clothes, setting loose a small dust storm in the office.

"Um . . . we . . . uh . . . manage."

"Well, don't let her bully you."

"I won't."

Gloria headed for the door to her own room, but paused for a moment.

"I spent the day with Pug Ellison out in the field."

"Pug?"

"Short for Pugnacious, he says. He's really quite a nice guy, and very promising. I've invited him to join OSI permanently when we get back to Manhattan. Maybe you ought to look him up and have dinner with him tonight. I'm sure he'd be glad to get the lowdown on what it's really like to have me for a boss."

"You think so?"

"Sure do. Enjoy your dinner. I'm gonna go get wet."

Gloria went into her room, shut the door behind her, and smiled. Two good deeds in one day!

WHEN SHE ARRIVED AT THE LODGE THE NEXT evening, Gloria was considerably surprised to find Raul Tellemacher already there. The explanation for his presence was soon forthcoming. It seemed that Tellemacher and Joe Pollas, one of the two younger trustees, were old school chums. Pollas was another wealthy ski-bum type; Sidney Taplin, the other new trustee, was older and more serious-looking. Both Pollas and Taplin made a production out of welcoming Gloria, while Rankus, Vigo, and Ogunbayo were more subdued.

Rankus, in fact, looked older and wearier than he had the last time Gloria had seen him. His skin had a grayish cast to it, and his eyes had lost some of their usual fire. Gloria realized that he was dying. Vigo had said that he was ill, and the prospect of losing control of the Lodge and his beloved Sylvania was probably sucking the remaining life out of him. Gloria felt no particular pity for him, but thought it sad that everyone around Rankus was probably waiting impatiently for his demise.

The four corporate reps—Shoop, Lund, Norfleet, and now, Mitchell—also extended their greetings. Maddie pretended not to know her, but made a show of fondling Petra's buttocks when she came in to serve drinks. Maddie was stunning this evening in a long, very sheer white dress that was slashed in a wide V from her neck nearly to her crotch, while Gloria wore a little black minidress that kept no secrets.

"I really must come down to your famous Emporium some evening," Maddie said to Gloria. "Are all your girls as pretty as Petra?"

"We have something for everyone," Gloria said noncommittally. "You gentlemen are welcome, too."

"Our guests rarely . . . *descend* . . . to the level of the town," Rankus said, making it clear what he thought of the Emporium and its denizens.

"Really? I'd think the Lodge would get a little boring at times. After all, you three gentlemen have been here for weeks, now. Although I gather that you've been keeping busy."

"How, exactly, did you gather that, Ms. VanDeen, if I may ask?" said Lund.

"Up in the hills yesterday, I discovered that some of your Excelsior people have been going around buying up proxies from the miners. Getting them very cheaply, too, from what I hear."

"*Carpe diem,*" Lund replied. "The price will only go up as we get closer to incorporation. I assume you've heard by now that we're bringing in a thousand people next week."

Gloria turned to look at Thomas Shoop, the Imperium representative. He was quieter than the others, but Gloria wasn't sure if that meant he was playing his cards closer to the vest, or was just naturally reticent. He was of medium height, a little overweight, and had a face that might have been mass-produced on one of Imperium's assembly lines.

"Is Imperium busy seizing the day, as well, Mr. Shoop?" Gloria asked him.

"If we are," Shoop answered, "we won't advertise the fact."

"Well, even if you don't have people out in the valley, maybe you should try to find the time to get out there yourself," Gloria suggested. "See it before it's gone."

"That, Ms. VanDeen," Rankus declared, "is the most intelligent thing I have yet heard you say. It will be gone, you know. These fine gentlemen—and Ms. Mitchell, as well, should Prizm prevail—will soon bring in their planet-raping machines and turn this paradise into a pit. I'm grateful I shall not live to see it."

"As usual, my old friend," said Myron Vigo, "you're being too hard on yourself, and everyone else. The Lodge and Overhill will survive—and so will you, Claude, if you'll just perk up a bit."

Rankus's only response to that was a wordless snort.

"Gloria," said Joe Pollas, "Raul tells me that the voter registration drive is going very well."

"It's proceeding as planned," Gloria affirmed. She gave Tellemacher a short, not very subtle glare. "Tell me, Mr. Pollas, don't you share some of Claude's reluctance to see the corporates come in?"

"Please, call me Joe. And yes, I admit I've felt a twinge or two about it. I spent every summer here when I was a kid. Used to go prowling along the ridges, boating in the river. We even have a little ski lodge, way up in the mountains, although we never got around to fixing up a real ski run. You know, I even found Fergusite crystals up in the hills. Pretty green things. If only I'd known!"

"Praise whatever powers there be that you didn't," said Rankus, "or we'd have lost our planet a dozen years ago."

"Now, Claude," Pollas soothed, "we aren't really losing it. We'll still have the Lodge and the lake—and I intend to bring my children here someday."

"Your father would have horsewhipped you for selling out to these corporate Visigoths!" Rankus said with some heat.

"My father would have made the same deal as I have," Pollas responded. "And he'd have horsewhipped *you* if you had tried to stop him!"

Myron Vigo stepped between the two and tried to pour a little oil on the troubled waters. "I knew Old Joe for seventy years," he said, "and I never once saw him horsewhip anyone. Other than the occasional horse, mind you. Ms. VanDeen, how goes it at your new and improved Emporium?"

"We seem to be flourishing," Gloria told him.

"I apologize for Grunfeld's behavior the other day," said Vigo. "And I'm not surprised that you anticipated our little ploy. Still, we do what we must. I expect Claude will insist that we challenge every registration."

"I will," said Rankus.

"I've told him that it will be a waste of time, but Claude is within his rights." Vigo turned to look at the corporate reps. "We may also be challenging some of your proxies. I'm a lawyer," he added with a self-conscious grin, "so it is my sworn duty to make everything as difficult and expensive as possible for everyone."

"Joe," Gloria said to Pollas, "you alluded to some sort of deal with the corporates? Might I inquire . . . ?"

"Certainly. Nothing secret about it. When the boom first started, some of us planned ahead and acquired some proxies from the first wave of miners, who needed financial support that we were able to provide."

"I should have expected that from you and young Taplin here," growled Rankus, "but it grieves me that Ogunbayo was in on it. I expected more than that from you, Rahim."

"You're just annoyed that you didn't think of it first, Claude," Ogunbayo blithely responded. "In any case, Gloria, we do have a considerable number of proxies among us, and our friends from the corporates will find it necessary to secure our cooperation if they expect to get the necessary 60 percent for Eminent Domain proceedings."

"And what of Prizm?" Gloria asked, turning to Maddie. She didn't want to make their connection conspicuous by too obviously ignoring her. "Will you be involved in the proxy battle?"

"Oh"—Maddie smiled—"we'll have a horse in the race."

"A damned dark one," put in Gaspar Norfleet. "Face it, Maddie, you're already beaten."

"Music to my ears, boys," she responded. "A key part of our strategy is to rely on the usual myopic overconfidence of our competitors—especially Servitor. That's what got your ass whipped on Mynjhino, isn't it, Gassy?"

"Only thanks to Ms. VanDeen's rather unfortunate intervention," Norfleet said, nodding his head toward Gloria. "I trust that won't become a factor here, as well. Dexta is here to register voters, not to meddle in corporate or Imperial affairs. Isn't that right, Mr. Tellemacher?"

"That's our assignment," Raul agreed. "Of course, I'm not the boss. What about it, Gloria, are we going to be doing any meddling?"

Gloria gave him a frosty gaze. "We'll do what we've come here to do," she said simply.

"Was running a whorehouse part of the assignment?" he asked. "I don't recall hearing you mention that back on Earth."

"When there's something I think you should know, Raul, I'll be sure to tell you."

"Hah!" barked Pollas. "Put you in your place, didn't she, Rowdy?"

With that, the party repaired to the dinner table, where the conversation continued in much the same vein—a high-level fencing match in which no actual blood was drawn but points were scored. Gloria spoke in glowing terms of her visits to Rankus Falls, although she didn't mention Old Abel or the Voice. Rankus warmed to the topic, and went on at some length about the early days on Sylvania, when he and a small group of friends had been the only humans on the planet. When he began to repeat himself, Vigo gently steered the conversation in another direction.

The future was becoming clear to all of them. Rankus's days were numbered, his influence waning, and only Vigo's continuing support kept him in the game at all. Soon, the requisite number of voters would be registered, an Imperial Governor would be appointed, and the business of dividing up the Fergusite spoils would begin in earnest. The initial jockeying for position among the corporates, and the proxies held by Pollas and the other trustees, would determine the shape and flow of the battle to come. There was little Gloria could do—directly—to influence the course of events, but she wondered if some indirect influence might be possible.

Following dinner, Gloria went out to the veranda to drink in the night scene, and was quickly joined by Shoop, Lund, and Norfleet. Maddie Mitchell made as if to join them, but Gloria gave her a quick, subtle headshake. Maddie understood, and retired.

"It really is a magnificent planet," Gloria said.

"You've missed a lot by rooting yourselves here in the Lodge, gentlemen."

"I'm not here as a sightseer," said Lund.

"Too bad," Gloria said. "I'm planning a little expedition back to the Falls tomorrow. I was hoping I could persuade you all to come with me. That's if you don't mind camping out overnight."

"Spirit!" Lund grunted. "Next, you'll be asking us to toast marshmallows over a campfire."

"Great idea!" said Gloria. "I wonder if we have any marshmallows down at the Emporium general store? I know we have some hot dogs."

"Hmm," Norfleet pondered. "Peking duck's on the menu here for tomorrow night. Quite a choice."

"Menu and your obvious charms aside, Gloria," Lund said, "I see no point in your little nature tour. I believe I'll pass."

"I admit, I am tempted," said Norfleet. "But I'm not exactly the wilderness type. I didn't even camp out when I was a boy."

"And what about you, Mr. Shoop?"

Shoop granted Gloria one of his rare smiles. "I *like* hot dogs," he said.

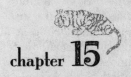

chapter 15

GLORIA CRAWLED TOWARD THE LIGHT. THE BLUE-
green glow far ahead of her seemed impossibly distant,
and the dark rocks around her seemed to close in on her;
they seemed to suck up the very air she breathed.

"This is *not* claustrophobia," she whispered to herself. "I do *not* have claustrophobia!"

"What was that, Gloria?" Sam Roosa asked from behind her. His words echoed faintly back and forth along
the length of the tunnel.

"Nothing, Sam," she assured him.

The tunnel was no more than four feet in diameter
and extended for a good hundred feet, from ten feet beneath Room 9 to the position of the plasma recharger
under the entrance anteroom of the Emporium. Roosa
and his team had used their drills to carve out the pas-
sageway during the week of renovations, and no one was
the wiser. Althea was aware that something odd was going on in Room 9, but was smart enough not to ask questions. One of the two recharger operators—Sam or his
assistant Dwayne—was nearly always shut up in the

room while the other manned the desk, and it was rare
to see either of them take time for a meal or a drink.
They also ignored the girls.

Gloria took deep breaths and forced herself to keep
moving. It wasn't really necessary for her to be there,
but since she was in charge of the operation, her sense
of duty compelled her to see the underground works for
herself. Anyway, she was curious about how it all fit together. A few minutes in a dark, dank, dim enclosed
space beneath the surface of the planet would surely do
her no harm. None at all. After all, she was an enhanced
human being and therefore not subject to the failings of
mere mortals, whose skin might feel clammy and whose
breath might become labored in a narrow, constricted,
gloomy, downright spooky place where they might easily
be trapped beneath tons of rock and dirt if anything
went wrong. Those were symptoms of claustrophobia,
which Gloria definitely did *not* have—no sir!

She forced herself to move forward, sensing Roosa
close on her heels behind her. At last, she arrived at the
cubical gallery that had been cut away around the vertical shaft. The gallery was about ten feet on a side and six
feet high, and would have seemed roomy but for the array of controls and monitoring equipment that had been
installed there. Gloria slid away from the tunnel exit to
make way for Roosa, who scrambled into the gallery after her.

A photosensitive cylindrical shield encased the vertical shaft in the center of the gallery. Its darkened surface let through only a small fraction of the intense light
produced by the plasma beam coursing down from
above, but even that was enough to leave Gloria momentarily dazzled. She sat there blinking while Roosa
got to his feet and methodically moved around the
gallery, checking readings on each of the instruments.
He came back to where he had begun and sat down on
the cold stone floor next to Gloria.

"So," he asked her, "what do you think? Did you get your money's worth?"

"I don't know," she replied. "Did we?"

"I think you probably did," Roosa said. "At any rate, we're doing exactly what we came here to do. Eckstein's estimates were pretty damned good. He said we'd hit the Fergusite layer at a hundred meters, and we hit it at eighty-nine."

"Is there any way to tell if we're having the desired effect?"

"Not directly," Roosa said. He pointed at the shaft. "Obviously, we can't get down there, but we did send a drone down before we went operational. Got some samples back, and Eckstein was right on the button again. The Fergusite matrix is just about the density he predicted, which means that we should be getting the results we'd hoped for. Otherwise, the amount of energy we've pumped down there would be melting the bedrock by now."

Gloria thought of something. "I don't get it," she said. "Why doesn't the constant plasma beam destroy the lattice of the Fergusite directly below it? Wouldn't that ruin its energy transference properties?"

"It would, if the beam didn't move and always struck the same spot. In fact, we've altered the recharger so that the beam slowly moves in an ever-widening spiral. Right now, the spiral is about six centimeters in diameter. And, of course, we've only affected the upper layer of the deposit. By the time we're through here, the spiral will be more than a meter in diameter, at a depth of three of four meters into the Fergusite layer."

Gloria nodded. "So the plasma energy is dispersing throughout the Fergusite layer?"

"Seems to be. We've probably ruined all the Fergusite crystals within a couple of kilometers of here. That should amount to maybe 1 or 2 percent of the entire deposit." Roosa grinned suddenly. "Think of that—we've already destroyed about twenty trillion crowns' worth of the stuff!"

"The greatest act of vandalism in history," Gloria noted.

"Something to tell our grandchildren."

"Hardly! Sam, this goes to our graves with us."

Roosa frowned but nodded in agreement. "I suppose so."

"Have any problems come up?" Gloria asked him.

"None that we can see. If we had hit any major obstructions in the deposit, we'd be getting a gradual buildup of energy—heat, in other words. Our monitors would detect it, but so far there's no sign of it. As best we can tell, the energy is being dispersed at a fairly steady rate throughout the Fergusite layer."

"So you'll be able to tell if we do hit something?"

"For now, yes," said Roosa. "But in a week or two, the dispersal field will be so wide that there won't necessarily be any feedback where we can detect it. According to Eckstein, the joker in the deck would be any igneous intrusion that cuts all the way across the deposit. That would keep us from getting at the rest of the layer."

"And what would happen in that case?"

"Eckstein said that the energy being distributed by the Fergusite would eventually melt the intrusion. That might get it out of our way, or it might just bring down the overlying rock and continue to block us. It might also cause some earthquakes."

"I see," Gloria said. She hadn't counted on anything quite that dramatic.

"The second problem Eckstein mentioned," Roosa continued, "is that the density of the matrix might change as we get deeper into the deposit. From the samples we've taken and the analysis Eckstein did of the surface deposits, the density is just right to allow us to do our little trick here. That is, the average density of the Fergusite crystals within the matrix is such that it permits direct energy transfer between the crystals. But we have no way of knowing if that density remains constant throughout the entire layer. If it changes too much in either direction, that could shut off the energy transfer and ruin our little plot."

"So," said Gloria, "if the density remains constant, if the layer is fully contiguous, and if there are no igneous intrusions, then we'll succeed."

"You forgot one big *if*," Roosa reminded her.

"What?"

"If no one finds out what we're up to."

Gloria gave him a weak grin. "Well, yes," she said. "There's that, isn't there?"

GLORIA AND THOMAS SHOOP ARRIVED AT PIZEN Flats just in time to see the end of the brawl. It wasn't really much of a brawl, considering that the highboys were outnumbered by about four to one, but they put up a good fight against the riverrats for a few minutes. Noses were bloodied, some teeth were lost, and one of the highboys might have had a rib cracked, but no serious damage was done except to the pride of some who thought they were better brawlers than they turned out to be.

As they got out of their skimmer, Gloria and Shoop saw a couple of good punches landed, but the scene resembled a rugby scrum more than it did a battle. People began to notice Gloria's arrival, and most of them quickly decided that they would rather watch her than roll around in the mud with other miners. The commotion gradually subsided, and the riverrats and highboys stood around the campsite breathing hard and feeling, perhaps, a little foolish.

"What's all this, then?" Gloria asked Gus Thornton. The King of Pizen Flats was a little bloody but clearly unbowed by the festivities.

"Just sortin' out what's what, is all," Gus explained.

"We were discussing some of the finer points of the law," Ted Oberlin amplified. His hair was mussed, but he did not seem to have suffered much damage. He started to smile at Gloria, but his face froze when he saw that she was accompanied by another man.

"Law, my maiden Aunt Matilda!" shouted one of the highboys, wiping some blood from his chin. "These god-damn riverrats are tryin' to *steal* what we got comin' to us!"

"What you got comin', Slick," a riverrat responded, "is another ass-kickin'!"

"Why don't you just try it?" the highboy challenged.

The brawl might have resumed then and there had Gloria not exercised one of her lesser-known talents. She stuck two fingers into her mouth and loosed a shrill, piercing whistle that echoed across the valley. Anyone who hadn't already been looking at her turned now to do so.

"Hey, boys," she called, "Give it a rest! Gus? Why don't you take a stab at explaining this, and everybody else just shut up, okay?"

Everybody else did, reluctantly.

"Well, Miz Gloria," Gus said, "it's like this. These highboys here decided to come down and tell us what they thought about our plans. Didn't think much of 'em, and said so. And then we told 'em what we thought about *their* plans. Took a whole bunch o' tellin', what with their heads bein' so hard. But I think we made our point."

The riverrats noisily agreed with Gus for a few moments, while the highboys registered their dissent.

"And what are these plans that everyone is so excited about?" Gloria asked.

"Best let Ted tell ya, Miz Gloria," Gus said, "since he's the one that thunk 'em up."

At the urging of the other riverrats, Oberlin stepped forward and launched into an explanation. "We're going to refile our claim, Gloria," he said. "Right now, there are fifty people at Pizen Flats, but only one claim. But these ten or twelve highboys here have maybe six or seven claims among them. So we're going to redress the balance."

"Redress yer ass!" shouted one of the highboys. "They just wanta steal the damn Eminent Domain vote."

Undeterred, Oberlin continued. "This may seem like just a disorderly encampment, Gloria, but it's really the Pizen Flats Mining Company. Everyone here has a share in it. In order to work the rivers properly, you need a division of labor and some room to spread out. So, in the beginning, it seemed best to incorporate and file a single claim on this stretch of the river. But we've decided to adapt to the changing circumstances."

"I see," Gloria said. "And how will you do that?"

"We're going into town tomorrow to dissolve the company. Then each of us will file individual claims, dividing up the same land that the company held. That way, each of us will have a voice in the Eminent Domain battle. At the same time, we're sticking together and re-organizing ourselves as the Pizen Flats Cooperative Association. We'll share the profits, same as before, but we'll retain our individual claim rights."

"And that's just plain wrong!" declared one of the highboys. "You can't change the rules in the middle of the game, dammit! Us highboys work hard up on the slopes to make a go of our claims, while these sissies on the river take it easy with their damn company. Well, if that's how they wanted to do it, fine. We got no problem with that. What we got a problem with is them tryin' to turn one claim into fifty all of a sudden, just 'cause it's convenient now. That just ain't right!"

"But it's legal, Fred," Oberlin reminded him, "and that's all that really matters."

"Is that true, Miz Gloria?" the highboy asked. "Can they get away with doin' this?"

Gloria silently mulled it over for a few moments, then said, "I think they probably can, Fred. But there are still a lot more highboys than there are riverrats at Pizen Flats."

"But it ain't just Pizen Flats," Fred insisted. "This

legal-talkin' bastard here's been gettin' *all* the river camps organized and fixin' to do the same damn thing!"

"Is that true, Ted?"

"I've been trying, Gloria," he told her. "Not all of the camps have decided yet, but we're making some progress. If we get everyone together on this, we should have at least 40 percent of the total claims by the time we're through. And *that*," he added triumphantly, turning to face the other riverrats, "will be enough to keep the corporates from taking our land!"

The riverrats roared. Gloria glanced at Shoop to see how he was taking the news, but his face remained impassive, as always.

Gloria was proud of Oberlin for what he had accomplished, but she harbored no illusions. The dream of 40 percent was likely to prove a chimera. Too much power and money was aligned against the riverrats. When the price the corporates were willing to pay for proxies went high enough, even the most loyal members of the Pizen Flats Cooperative Association would find themselves sorely tempted to sell out. Still, Oberlin might round up enough votes to make the Eminent Domain battle interesting, and she supposed that there was even a chance that they would win. If only she could have counted on that, her underground plot would never have been necessary.

When things had settled down, Gus Thornton invited Gloria and her guest to share some lunch. Gloria introduced Shoop to the riverrats, but identified him only as a friend who wanted to see the river and the falls. In the present atmosphere, telling them that he was from Imperium could have been risky. As it was, only Ted Oberlin seemed upset by Shoop's presence.

The Pizen Flats men were eager to hear Gloria's approval and enthusiasm for their plans, but she explained to them that she had to remain strictly neutral. Nevertheless, she wished them well. She also urged them to be cautious. The brawl with the highboys had reminded her that the game was beginning to get very serious.

Without being obvious about it, Gloria tried to avoid Oberlin; that proved to be easy, since he had decided to retreat into a sulk. Men were such babies—but that was not exactly a revelation to Gloria. She wondered if Shoop had noticed the dirty glances he was getting from Oberlin. It was hard to tell about Shoop, but Gloria expected to get to know him much better before the day was through.

THE FOREST, THE CANYONS, AND THE FALLS LEFT Thomas Shoop even more speechless than usual. But, Gloria thought, the quality of his silence had changed. It no longer seemed to flow from reticence, but rather, from awe. His eyes wide, his lips slightly parted, he let Gloria show him the natural wonders of Sylvania with scarcely a word. Finally, Gloria parked the skimmer on the bank to the side of the falls at her usual campsite, and they got out.

"We'll set up the tent here," Gloria said. "Later, we'll start a fire. But for now, I think I'm going to take a swim. Care to join me?"

"In *there*?" Shoop asked, amazed, as he pointed toward the churning river. It was the first time Gloria had managed to impress him.

"I do it whenever I'm here," she said. "It's fun."

"I'll take your word for it," Shoop said. "From where I'm standing, it looks cold and dangerous."

"That's what makes it fun!" Without further preamble, Gloria stripped off her shirt and shorts and plunged into the frigid waters of the Rankus River. Shoop sat down on the bank to watch.

Gloria paddled back and forth with vigor, then turned to float on her back for a while, being careful to give Shoop a good view. She knew he wanted her, but his natural reticence seemed to extend to the matter of sex.

Neither of them had brought up the subject, although the prospect of sharing the same small tent tonight made the outcome obvious and all but inevitable. At least, Gloria assumed as much.

She felt a little uneasy about it. She was never reluctant to have sex with a man for whom she felt an attraction, even a total stranger if the circumstances were right. But a deliberate and, yes, cold-blooded, seduction of a specific man for a specific purpose went somewhere beyond her comfort zone. She would have preferred another approach to Shoop, but she had to work with what tools she had. Considering what was at stake, this was no time for half measures. And maybe something good would come from it, she thought. Maybe Thomas Shoop would enlist in her cause merely because she was a fabulous lay, and because her cause was right.

And then again, maybe not. Just in case, she did not intend to count on sex alone. The seduction of Thomas Shoop would involve two stages, only one of which depended on the sexual appeal of Gloria VanDeen. The second would rely on the clever fraud of a wizened old wood gnome. At least, it would if Old Abel was on the ball . . .

Gloria gave Shoop a cheerful wave and pointed toward the falls. Then she dived deep, swam submerged until her lungs were ready to burst, then surfaced behind the cascading curtain of water. She crawled up onto a big, slippery boulder and waited while Abel orchestrated his illusion.

At first, Gloria had sincerely believed in the Voice. Part of her had desperately wanted it to be real, and for her theory to be true. If the Voice were a Sylvanian cousin of the Spirit, then the universe would finally make sense and life itself would resonate with some deeper, holier meaning. The appeal of such an idea was primal, and for the first and only time in her life, Gloria had believed that she understood the force that drew people to religions and some conception of God. If only it were all true!

But the skeptic in her could not ignore the doubts that Oberlin had planted. If the Voice knew that Gloria could prevent people from hurting it, then why did it have to ask her who she was? A very human sort of mistake, Ted had suggested. And Gloria was unable to persuade herself that he was wrong.

If there was a key to the mystery of the Voice, it had to be Old Abel. She resolved to clear away some of the mist that shrouded his origins and even his identity. So she dispatched Petra on her spy mission, and was rewarded with the answer, whole and complete.

Stored in Preston Thawley's employment files at the Lodge was a record of everyone who had ever worked there, all the way back to the very beginning, twenty years earlier. Not only was there an "Abel Brookshire" listed among the laborers who had built the Lodge, there was even a copy of his employment application and his résumé. Abel Brookshire, it seemed, had worked for more than forty years on Palmyra and several other worlds—as an audio engineer.

When she finally confronted Abel, he had given her a crooked smile and a wink, then admitted that her suspicions were correct. He had come to Sylvania in search of a place to retire, and had immediately fallen in love with this pristine world. When the work on the Lodge was complete, he had simply drifted into the forests with a minimum of supplies and a pad loaded with all his favorite books; *Walden* was near the top of the list. He had survived for years in contented solitude, learning all there was to know about his new home.

When the boom began, he told her, he had realized that the life and the planet he had come to love were dangerously, perhaps fatally threatened. So, using the skills from his former life, he had invented the Voice. He bought the equipment he needed on Palmyra, had it delivered to Elba's, and set about spooking the boomers.

It was easy enough for an audio engineer to employ microamplifiers and resonators to create an ethereal whisper that seemed to come from everywhere and nowhere. His intimate knowledge of the valley allowed him to come and go unseen, planting his nearly invisible devices in places he knew were frequented by the miners.

He managed to scare off some of them, and even those who stayed began to treat the valley with a measure of respect. He concentrated on the highboys, who did the most damage, and had some considerable success among them. For the less destructive riverrats, his message was less a threat and more an entreaty. He realized that he would never be able to get everyone to leave, but he hoped that he could slow down the boom and delay the inevitable until after he was gone.

"I was afraid I might be getting a little too cute when I tried it on you," he told Gloria. "Ignorant boomrat miners don't ask too many questions, but I knew you were a smart cookie. Should have known better."

"You almost had me," Gloria admitted. "I really wanted to believe in the Voice."

"But then that young bastard Oberlin caught me out."

"You heard that conversation?" Gloria asked him.

"O' course I did. Got that whole campsite area bugged. That damn Oberlin kid spotted my mistakes right off. Shouldn't have asked you who you were. Never did that before. In fact, I never even tried to start a conversation with anyone. Just tried to scare 'em. But I knew you were important, and I guess I wanted to show how clever I was—you know, just sorta grandstandin' for a pretty girl. So I had the Voice ask you some questions first, kinda like breakin' the ice, ya know? But I forgot that the Voice wouldn't have *had* to ask. Damn stupid of me. So, now that ya know, what are ya gonna do about it?"

What Gloria decided to do about it was to enlist Abel in her scheme. So, as Gloria sat under the falls, shivering, Thomas Shoop was going to have his own encounter with the Voice. Fraud, pure and simple, she thought. It might even work.

When she judged the time was right, Gloria slid back into the water, dived under the falls, and swam back to the bank. As she clambered up the rocks, she saw Shoop standing there watching her, his mouth hanging open.

"Did . . . did you hear it?" he shouted to her above the roar of the falls.

"I couldn't hear anything where I was. Why, what did you . . ." With what she thought was the right combination of curiosity and dawning comprehension, Gloria let her eyes widen and looked at Shoop in feigned wonder. "You heard the Voice?" she cried.

"I . . . I think so," Shoop responded. "Rankus talked about it, but I . . . I never really believed it. Until now."

Gloria gathered up her clothes and began walking toward the campsite. Shoop trailed along after her, staring at her magnificent nude body and trying to find the right words for the moment.

"What did it say to you?" Gloria asked him. She reached into her pack, pulled out a towel, and started drying herself off.

"It just said, 'Don't hurt me.' It said that twice."

"That's about the same as it said to me," Gloria told him.

"You've heard it too?"

"Just once. I brought you here because I wanted to hear it again, and I hoped you would hear it, too." She smiled at him as she spread her towel on the grass, picked a log out of her pack, and ignited it. "I'm glad you heard it, Thomas."

Shoop dazedly plopped down next to her and shook his head. "I never . . . . I mean, in my whole life, I never . . ."

Gloria patted him on his thigh. "I know," she said. "Me too."

He broke into an embarrassed grin. "I would never have believed it," he said.

"Believe it," Gloria told him. "Believe it, and accept it." Gloria put her arms around Shoop's shoulders, drew him close, and kissed him. After a moment, Shoop kissed her back. Moments later, he was fondling her breasts and she was unzipping his jeans. His penis was already hardening as she set to work, determined to make a believer out of Thomas Shoop.

LATER, AS THE SUN WENT DOWN, THEY SAT before the fire roasting hot dogs that they had skewered on long sticks. Shoop had put his clothes back on, but Gloria remained completely nude and totally available.

"Officially," Gloria said, "I have to be scrupulously neutral. But unofficially—personally—after I heard the Voice, I became utterly and unreservedly committed to saving this planet. I think the Voice is kind of like the Spirit, back home—sort of a planetary entity, a consciousness. It wants our help, Thomas."

"It wants a lot, then," Shoop commented. "I'm in awe of this place, Gloria, and if the Voice doesn't want me to hurt it, I sure as hell won't. But you know as well as I do what's going to happen here, and nothing you or I can do will prevent it."

"Are you sure of that?"

Shoop removed his hot dog from the fire for a moment and turned to look Gloria in her eyes. "I'm just a regional rep, Gloria. Can you imagine what would happen if I went back to Earth and told the Imperium Board that we should turn our backs on mining a quadrillion crowns' worth of Fergusite just because some disembodied voice wants us to?" Shoop gave a short, cynical laugh. "They'd have me committed!"

"Maybe you don't have to tell them," Gloria suggested. "Maybe there are things you can do right here that would help save Sylvania."

"Even if there were," Shoop replied, "you're forgetting that Imperium isn't the only player in this game. Or were you planning to bring Lund and Norfleet here and seduce them, too?"

"I would if I thought it would help. Please don't take that personally, Thomas. I truly like you, and I was glad that you were the only one who accepted my invitation. Lund and Norfleet are not my idea of fun dates. But I'd gladly fuck everyone on the boards of each of the Big Twelve if I thought that would save this place."

Shoop contemplated his roasting hot dog for a few moments. When he judged it sufficiently blackened, he clamped a bun around it, removed it from the stick, squirted some mustard on it, and took a bite.

"I don't know the details," Gloria said, "but just from watching Lund and Norfleet, it was easy to see that they've got some sort of deal, probably in conjunction with Pollas and some of the other trustees. It's an obvious match. Servitor has the financial resources and the influence at Court. Excelsior is one of the smaller of the Big Twelve, but it has the equipment for the job and wants to catch up with Imperium and Prizm. If they get the concession, that would leave Imperium out in the cold."

"Maybe not," Shoop said. "We know they have the inside track, but we think we can get enough proxies to force Servitor and Excelsior to let us in on the deal."

"What if you worked with Prizm and the riverrats? If you combined your resources, you might be able to get more than 40 percent of the proxies and block development altogether."

"And what would be in it for Imperium? Prizm would naturally like to prevent exploitation of the Fergusite, and the riverrats want to keep their claims and go on doing what they've been doing. But what would Imperium stand to gain?"

"Maybe a deal with Prizm? A piece of their existing Fergusite operations?"

Shoop said, "Hmmpf."

"I'm serious," Gloria insisted. "Why not try it?

Instead of a small piece of the Servitor-Excelsior deal, Imperium could get a big piece of a partnership with Prizm. It would make sense for Prizm to save half a loaf instead of getting none, and you could get your half of the loaf without having to risk a big investment on the mining operation."

Shoop took another bite of his hot dog. After some more beer, he said, "I'd hate to have to try and sell that to the Board. I admit, there's a certain plausibility to the argument. But it would put Imperium at odds with the Emperor, and that could have a detrimental effect on everything else we do."

"You'd have Dexta's support. I can tell you in strictest confidence that Norman Mingus is seriously concerned about the potential effect of using Sylvanian Fergusite on a large scale. Its quality is uncertain, and if significant problems arose, that could undermine the stability of the Empire itself."

"That doesn't seem to concern the Emperor," Shoop pointed out.

"Charles is only interested in the profits and graft he can make on the Sylvania deposit. He's a selfish and shortsighted man, Thomas. Believe me, I know."

Shoop laughed. "I guess you would," he agreed. "But I still don't think the Imperium Board would be thrilled to find themselves facing the Emperor's wrath. They would never go along with this."

"Maybe they would if you presented them with a *fait accompli*. If you and Maddie Mitchell can work out a deal between yourselves to block Servitor and Excelsior, that would give Prizm and Imperium time to formalize it. That would be worth trying, wouldn't it? To save Sylvania?" Gloria looked at him hopefully, nude and glowing in the firelight.

Shoop stared at her for a minute, then shook his head and smiled. "Why do I get the feeling that you've presented *me* with a *fait accompli*?"

"Because," Gloria explained, "you're a very perceptive man." She threw their hot dogs into the fire and continued her seduction of Thomas Shoop. She no longer felt the least bit uneasy about it. In fact, she thoroughly enjoyed it.

So did Thomas Shoop.

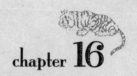

chapter **16**

GLORIA AND SHOOP GOT A LATE START THE
next morning. They almost didn't get started at all; both
of them would have preferred to spend the entire day in
the idyllic setting. With or without the Voice, Gloria felt
a reverence for the place that defied rational analysis.
And it wouldn't hurt to let Shoop share that feeling.

For all his reticence, Shoop had proved to be an ardent and creative lover. Gloria shared some jigli with
him over breakfast, and they spent a long hour or two on
the bed of soft, springy mosses until Shoop was utterly
exhausted. Gloria practically had to scoop him up and
pour him back into the skimmer.

By the time they got back to Greenlodge, the
boomers from Pizen Flats had already arrived. Their
fleet of battered old utility skimmers was parked at
river's edge, and all fifty of the riverrats were gathered in
front of City Hall. Gloria parked her skimmer next to
the Emporium, then walked over to City Hall with
Shoop trailing along behind her.

She saw Mayor Grunfeld, flanked by Hank Frezzo

and Noz Gnozdziewicz, standing on the front steps, sneering defiantly at the mob. It was easy enough to figure out what was happening. Gloria saw that the occasion would call for a little more of her star power, so she unbuttoned her shirt to reveal her breasts more completely and tugged her low-riding shorts even lower. Still riding the jigli high, heart racing, nerves tingling, she plunged into the crowd and made her way to the base of the steps.

There, she found Ted Oberlin angrily trying to stare down Grunfeld, who reacted to her arrival with a snort of contempt.

"You just stay outta this, VanDeen," Grunfeld warned her. "Ain't none o' Dexta's business. This here's a *local* matter!"

"Local, hell!" Oberlin responded. "Our claims and legal filing have to be registered with the District authorities on Palmyra."

"Then take 'em to Palmyra!"

"We don't have to do that. We have every right to make the initial filings right here, with the existing local government. Unfortunately, that means you, Grunfeld. Whether you like it or not, you have to accept our filing."

The riverrats cheered heartily, but Grunfeld remained unimpressed. He pointed an index finger at Oberlin (splints gone, his middle fingers seemed to have healed) and shook it menacingly. "I don't have to do a fuckin' thing, kid," he snarled. "And I don't need some snot-nosed punk tellin' me what the law says. *I'm* the law 'round here, and you best not forget that."

"You're wrong," Gloria said politely.

"I told *you* to stay the fuck outta this!" Grunfeld reiterated.

"I'm afraid I can't, Mr. Mayor," Gloria replied, unperturbed. "You've misrepresented the situation, and I can't let that stand. *You*, Mr. Mayor, are not the law. You are merely the local representative of the law, charged with obeying and enforcing it. If you are incapable of performing that function—"

"Horseshit! I can perform any damn function I want, and you can't say no different!" Grunfeld turned to Frezzo and said, "Hank, go bring Vigo out here. 'Bout time that old bastard earned his cut." Frezzo obediently went inside City Hall and returned a moment later with Myron Vigo at his side.

Vigo emerged into the sunlight, blinked a few times, then noticed Gloria. He smiled and bowed slightly in her direction. "Ah," he said brightly, "Ms. VanDeen! You're looking exceptionally lovely this morning. I was hoping you would be here."

"At your service, Mr. Vigo," Gloria said. "And I'm glad to see that Mayor Grunfeld has a qualified legal advisor present. It seems that he could profit from your guidance. I don't think he fully understands his responsibilities."

"Aw, cut the crap, Vigo," Grunfeld snapped. "Just tell 'em."

"Exactly what would you like me to tell them?" Vigo inquired.

"Tell 'em this is local business, goddammit! And Dexta can just go fuck itself, 'cause it ain't got no damn excuse to horn in on this."

"Ah." Vigo nodded, then turned back to Gloria, still smiling. "My learned colleague may have expressed it a bit crudely, Ms. VanDeen, but I believe he has grasped the nub of the matter. The filing of routine claims and legal documents is, of course, a purely local matter and not subject to interference by Imperial or Dexta representatives. But I'm sure you already know that."

"Of course, Mr. Vigo," Gloria agreed. "That's entirely true. However, if I understand what's going on here, it would seem that Mayor Grunfeld is, for some reason, refusing to accept these claims and filings."

"You got that right, VanDeen. Ain't nobody filin' *nothin'* here today!"

The riverrats responded with a volley of jeers and catcalls. Gloria quieted them by ascending the first couple of steps of City Hall and letting them get a good look at her. She smiled at them and held up one hand for a few seconds.

"Settle down, boys," she said. "We'll get this cleared up, I promise you."

"Ain't nothin' to clear up," Grunfeld said.

"Oh, but there is," she assured him sweetly. "Tell him, Mr. Vigo. Remind him of the constitutional responsibility of local government to conform with and efficaciously carry out all of the lawful requirements enumerated in the *Imperial Code*."

"Ms. VanDeen—"

"Aw, shut up, Vigo! Listen here, all of ya! Dexta ain't got nothin' to say about any o' this! You keep buttin' in, VanDeen, an' I might just hafta place you under arrest for . . . for . . . uh, *indecent exposure*!"

That produced a cascade of jeers and laughter from the riverrats, and even an amused titter from Vigo.

"Oh really?" Gloria asked innocently. She hooked her thumbs in the top of her shorts and slowly pulled them downward until her exposure was, if not indecent, then nearly complete. "I certainly don't want to violate any local ordinances, Mr. Mayor. Perhaps if you could show me the relevant sections of the local statutes, I'd be able to comply with them more precisely. As it stands, I don't know if I'm allowed to expose my breasts"—she casually removed her shirt and tossed it into the crowd to the sound of lusty cheers—"or my—"

"Now, you just cut that out!" Grunfeld demanded, realizing he was being unfairly upstaged. "I'll arrest you for incitin' a fuckin' riot, then! You and every one o' these . . . uh . . . rioters. What we got here is a disorderly assembly. That's what we got here, a fuckin' disorderly assembly!"

Gloria doffed her shorts and threw them to the crowd, as well. "What about it, boys?" she shouted. "Are you planning to start a riot? If you are, I'm afraid I'll have to put my clothes back on!"

"Hell, no!" cried one leather-lunged riverrat. "We ain't gonna start no riot!"

"Then I can count on you all to be well behaved and orderly, can't I?"

"Bet yer sweet ass, ya can!"

"Then would you please prove that to the Mayor? Would you all just sit down and be quiet as church mice for the next few minutes?"

As a man, without a word, the boomers sat down in the street, even though some of them had to do it in mud puddles. They sat there, heads tilted up to keep their eyes on Gloria, as quiet and orderly as a convention of Sunday school teachers. Gloria turned back to look at Grunfeld.

"There you are, Mr. Mayor. No riot. No disorderly assembly. No reason at all to ignore the legitimate requests of these peaceful citizens. Isn't that right, Mr. Vigo?"

Vigo scratched his balding head for a moment. "Um," he said thoughtfully, "I admire your, uh, technique, Ms. VanDeen. And I confess that I see no cause for anyone to be arrested, at the moment."

"Aw, fuck you, Vigo! What the hell good are ya?"

"There you are, Mr. Mayor," Gloria said. "Even your legal advisor concedes that there has been no violation of the law. Except, perhaps, on your part. So why don't you just get your Town Clerk to start registering the filings of your constituents?"

"Town Clerk?" Grunfeld looked around in confusion for a moment. "Noz? That's you, ain't it?"

"Me? Hell no! I think it's Hank."

Frezzo shook his mangy head. "Ain't me. I think that's Luther. I," he added with evident pride, "am the Commissioner of Health and Human Services!"

"Well, then," Grunfeld growled, "why don't you just

go and fetch the honorable Mr. Luther Dominguez, Town Clerk, and get his distinguished ass out here?"

"Can't, Boss," Frezzo protested. "Ain't here. Remember? You sent him over to—"

"Keep yer mouth shut! Fuck this shit." Grunfeld glared at Gloria. "There, ya see? There ain't no Town Clerk here today. Don't matter what the law is or ain't, we got no clerk to record this shit!"

"I see," said Gloria. "Then you're telling us that the legally constituted government of Greenlodge is presently incapable of performing its designated functions and duties?"

Vigo saw what was about to happen, but before he could intervene, Grunfeld smugly answered Gloria's question. "That's what I'm tellin' ya," he declared. "So all you bastards might just as well go back to your fuckin' mud pies." He folded his arms in satisfaction. "Ain't gonna be *nothin'* registered here today, and that's all there is to it!"

"Not quite," Gloria said. Vigo sighed and shook his head.

"Mr. Mayor," Gloria said formally—or as formally as she could, standing naked in front of a crowd that had swelled to hundreds—"you have just affirmed, in front of witnesses, that the government of Greenlodge is presently incapable of performing its lawfully designated functions and duties, as regards the registration of legal documents. Therefore, I, in my capacity as senior Dexta representative in this jurisdiction, under the provisions of Chapter Thirty-nine, Paragraphs One through Eight of the *Dexta Code*, declare that henceforth and until such time as local authority may be reestablished, all necessary functions of local government will be carried out by Dexta personnel. I'll require you to surrender immediately all relevant documents, records, and computer files. Failure to do so will result in seizure of said records and the arrest and imprisonment of any responsible local officials who are in noncompliance with

Dexta regulations. Penalties may include prison terms not to exceed five years, and fines of not less than one hundred thousand crowns."

Gloria paused for breath. Everyone stared at her in amazed silence for a moment. Then the crowd started to cheer, but Gloria calmed them down with a single look. She turned back to face Grunfeld. "Let's have those records, Mr. Mayor."

Grunfeld looked for a second as if he were about to swing at her, but thought better of it. He appealed to Vigo for support, but Vigo simply shook his head.

"She's got you," he said.

Without so much as a parting sneer, Grunfeld and his men stormed back into their seat of government, slamming the door behind them. The riverrats leaped to their feet and cheered like madmen.

"Deftly done," Vigo told Gloria. "Spirit save lawyers from clients who can't keep their mouths shut! I might have outfoxed you yet, Ms. VanDeen, if not for the stupidity of our distinguished Mayor. Oh, well. I'll have those records for you within the hour."

"Thank you, Mr. Vigo. We'll be setting up operations at the front desk of the Emporium, just as soon as I recall our field teams."

"It won't change anything, you know. Not in the long run."

"We'll see, Mr. Vigo."

"Indeed we shall. And Ms. VanDeen? If I may add a word of purely personal advice, please be careful. Grunfeld is a loose cannon. There's no telling what he may do. I'm afraid that Claude is no longer able to control him."

"Who does, then?" Gloria asked him.

Vigo started to say something, but stopped short. Then he shook his head sadly and went into City Hall.

Gloria descended the steps, the cheers still ringing in her ears. Oberlin walked along beside her as she headed toward the Emporium. "Thanks," he said. "You probably saved our bacon."

"Just doing my job."

"You couldn't have done it with your clothes on?"

"Probably," Gloria chuckled. "But you know what I am, Ted. Don't expect me to be something else just because you and I have been close."

They came upon Shoop at the edge of the crowd, and paused. "You truly are amazing," he said, smiling. "I have to get back to the Lodge now, Gloria. But I just wanted to thank you for . . . for everything. I promise you, I'll think about what you said."

Gloria gave him a quick kiss, and he departed. Oberlin didn't look happy. "The Lodge?" he said. "Who the hell is that guy, anyway?"

"He's the rep from Imperium," Gloria told him.

"Imperium? A corporate rep?"

"Ted, it was necessary. Don't ask me for explanations I can't give you."

"No explanations necessary!" Oberlin fumed. "The great Gloria VanDeen can fuck anyone she wants, and doesn't have to explain it to anyone! But did you have to take him *there*? To the falls? To *our* place?"

Gloria suddenly understood. Men were so incredibly, instinctively, bullheadedly territorial! Even if they knew they couldn't possess *her*, they wanted to possess the *place* where they'd had her. Stu Eckstein didn't want her to take anyone else up to their alpine meadow, and now Ted Oberlin wanted exclusive rights to the falls. The wonder was that they didn't go around pissing on bushes to mark their turf!

"Ted," she said, "don't make an issue out of it, okay? I'm going to be very busy for the next few days, but after that, maybe we can—"

"Sure! You bet! I'll just take a number, okay?"

"Ted—"

But Oberlin had already whirled away from her and stomped off in the opposite direction.

Gloria sighed. Sometimes, she reflected, it was not easy being the Sweetheart of the Empire.

• • •

THERE WAS A LOT OF SKIMMER TRAFFIC TO AND
from the Lodge that day. Petra tried to keep track of it as
she went from cabin to cabin, making beds, sweeping
floors, and scrubbing toilets. Myron Vigo had left early
in the morning, and somewhat later, Thomas Shoop returned. Then Vigo came back, and a few minutes later,
Petra saw Joe Pollas and Sidney Taplin depart.

That afternoon, when she went out to the swimming
pool to serve a drink to Maddie Mitchell, she noticed
that Pollas's skimmer was back, along with a utility skimmer from town. Maddie was lolling in the sun on a
chaise lounge big enough for two, naked and shiny with
perspiration. Petra put the drink down on a table next to
Maddie and asked if there would be anything else.

Maddie pushed her sunglasses up and smiled at
Petra. She looked around and saw that they were
alone, except for two of the Overhill boys working in
the yard beyond the pool. They pretended they were
too busy to look.

"Yes, Petra," Maddie said. "Would you put some lotion on my back, please?" She rolled over onto her stomach and wiggled around for a bit to get comfortable.

"Yes, Ms. Mitchell," Petra said obediently. She sat
next to Maddie on the chaise, poured some lotion on her
hands, and began massaging it into Maddie's flesh over
the knobby projections of her shoulder bones and rib
cage. Maddie was downright skinny, Petra thought, and
sleeping with her could be more than a little uncomfortable. She had sharp knees and elbows to go with her
sharp tongue.

But sleeping was still all that they had done together. Maddie never stopped trying, but Petra believed
that she had come to terms with the situation. It was
flattering, in a way, that Maddie wanted her, but she had
lately come to realize that Pug Ellison wanted her, too,
and that she wanted him. They hadn't done anything

about it yet, but Petra was scheduled for an evening off later in the week.

"Don't miss anything," Maddie said when Petra paused at the lower reaches of her spine. Petra pursed her lips, then moved on, pouring more lotion onto Maddie's suntanned buttocks. Maddie gave a little moan of pleasure as Petra ran her hands over her, and sighed in seeming contentment. It was no different than cleaning a toilet, Petra told herself—just another chore to be performed.

When Petra believed she was finished, Maddie suddenly rolled over onto her freshly oiled back. "Now," she said, "do my front."

"Maddie!" Petra gasped.

"Just do it!" Maddie said in an urgent whisper. "People are watching. Mrs. Thawley is at one of the windows. Remember, you and I are lovers, and this isn't anything you haven't done before."

"The hell it isn't!" Petra whispered back. But she didn't see how she could avoid it, so she reluctantly poured some lotion onto Maddie's chest. She swirled it around over her sternum, took a deep breath, and went to work on Maddie's small breasts and dark, pointy nipples. The boys in the yard found that their work took them a little closer.

"Try to act like you're enjoying this," Maddie said softly. "After all, why shouldn't you?"

The fact was, Petra realized, she *did* enjoy it. She could no longer deny that she felt an odd attraction to Maddie. The woman was drop-dead gorgeous and exuded a sexual aura that Petra found herself unable to ignore. There was a delicious tang of naughtiness about all of it. And Weehawken, after all, was still five hundred light-years away.

"That's better." Maddie sighed as Petra moved downward to her flat, sensuous belly. "It's not so awful, is it?"

"I never said I thought it was awful," Petra replied.

"I just didn't want to be maneuvered into something I didn't really want to do."

"Lower, please." Petra hesitated, then ran her slick palm over the tangle of Maddie's dark pubic hair. She felt an odd thrill as she did so, but resisted when Maddie asked her to go even lower.

"I don't think you're going to get a sunburn *there*," Petra told her. "Now, if there's nothing else . . ."

"There *is*!" Maddie whispered. "Something's going on here."

Petra leaned close to her and said, "What?"

At that moment, Mrs. Thawley emerged from the house and came out onto the deck. "Petra," she said, "we need you in Cabin Six."

"Oh, no, Mrs. Thawley," Maddie objected. "Surely, you can spare Petra for a little while. After all, you said she would be at my disposal."

"Well, yes, Ms. Mitchell," Mrs. Thawley said, "but that doesn't mean we can spare her indefinitely from her regular duties."

"Oh, just another half hour or so," Maddie insisted. "Really, Mrs. Thawley, I don't see what's so important about Petra's scrubbing another toilet right this minute. I'd hate to have to complain to Mr. Rankus."

Mrs. Thawley frowned, hesitated, then said in an unhappy tone, "Very well, then, Ms. Mitchell. Half an hour, then." Mrs. Thawley briskly walked back indoors.

"Take off your clothes, Petra," Maddie said, smiling wickedly. "You could use some sun."

"Oh, no! If you think I'm going to—"

"Just do it!" Maddie hissed. "Dammit, we're being watched, so we have to make this look good!"

Petra half suspected that this was just another of Maddie's ploys, but out of the corner of her eye, she saw motion in one of the Lodge windows. Mrs. Thawley, no doubt. Gritting her teeth, Petra pulled her maid's uniform off, dispensed with her panties, and lay facedown on the chaise next to Maddie.

Maddie leaned over her and began spreading lotion across her back. "Listen," she said softly, "I saw Grunfeld and two of his men arrive here about an hour ago. And that's not all. I know they went upstairs—to see Rankus, I assume. But I have a sneaking suspicion that they're also meeting with Pollas and Taplin. And somebody else. I heard another voice, but I didn't see who it was."

"What do you think it's about?"

"I don't know," Maddie said, "but it smells to high heaven." Maddie finished with Petra's back and slid her palms downward over her round buttocks. Petra couldn't help flinching. She also couldn't help feeling a warm sense of pleasure welling in her groin. Yikes, she thought, I'm really letting her do this . . . and it's not so bad!

"Now roll over," Maddie commanded. That was more than Petra was prepared for, but Maddie wouldn't take no for an answer, and physically turned Petra onto her back.

"Maddie . . ."

"Just listen to me. In a few minutes, you and I are going to have a lovers' spat."

"Why not right now?" Petra asked. "Dammit, Maddie."

"Just go along with it for now and stop whining! Act like you enjoy it even if you don't."

Maddie began massaging the lotion onto Petra's pert breasts. Her pink nipples were erect, and she felt her breath coming in short, urgent gasps. Spirit, how did she get herself into this? And how could she let herself enjoy it so much?

"After we have our quarrel, I'll tell Mrs. Thawley that I don't want you here tonight. That should leave you free to go back down to town this evening and tell Gloria what's happening."

"But what is happening?"

"I've told you all I know for sure." Maddie spread

more lotion over Petra's belly and smiled as she rubbed it in. "Petra, I hope you're enjoying this as much as I am."

"Uh, Maddie, please, I don't—"

"Oh, shut up. Now that I've finally got my hands on you, I'm not going to stop now. And don't pretend that you don't like it. I know better!" Maddie's hand darted downward, through Petra's brown pubic curls. Petra's pelvis lurched upward in sudden pleasure, and she had to gasp for breath.

"After a couple of days, I'll tell Mrs. Thawley that I've changed my mind and want you back, okay? And maybe by then, you'll even want me. But let me give you something to think about in the meantime."

Maddie's fingers stroked Petra's vaginal cleft, parted her labia, and plunged in. Deftly, expertly, she massaged Petra's swollen clitoris until Petra, stunned, fascinated, and strangely helpless, exploded in an orgasm so intense that she cried out in sharp, electric ecstasy. Maddie continued what she was doing and Petra lost herself in the strange, surreal moment.

"Aww, ain't that cute?"

Maddie and Petra both looked up and saw Kevin Grunfeld and two of his men standing on the deck, grinning.

"What the hell are you doing here?" Maddie demanded.

"Oh, just shut up, lady. This ain't got nothin' to do with you." At the nod of Grunfeld's head, his two men advanced and seized Petra, each grabbing her by an arm and yanking her bodily off the chaise lounge.

"Stop it!" Maddie screeched, while Petra screamed incoherently. "Mrs. Thawley, what is the meaning of this?"

"Just stay the fuck out of it, lady," Grunfeld snarled as his men dragged Petra back into the Lodge. "You don't," he added as he paused at the door, "maybe next time, we'll come and get *you!*"

• • •

GRUNFELD DISAPPEARED INSIDE. MADDIE LEAPED
to her feet in pursuit, but was met at the door by a stern-
faced Mrs. Thawley, her arms folded across her chest.

"Now, now, Ms. Mitchell," Mrs. Thawley said,
"there's no need for you to be upset. This is a matter of
internal security at the Lodge and none of your concern."

"The hell it isn't. I want to see Rankus right now!"

"Mr. Rankus is indisposed this afternoon. I'm sure
he'll be happy to listen to you when he's feeling better.
After all, you are his guest, and he wants nothing more
than for his guests to be content."

"Get out of my way, you old cow," Maddie threatened. "I'm not about to let—"

Maddie was astonished to find herself suddenly in
the powerful grip of the old cow. Mrs. Thawley held
Maddie's arm behind her back and force-marched her
to the chaise longue. Mrs. Thawley threw her back
down onto it.

"Now, then," said Mrs. Thawley, "would you care for
another drink, Ms. Mitchell? Or shall I have some of our
people come and confine you to your cabin?"

"What are you going to do to her?" Maddie demanded.

"That's none of your concern. Would you care for
iced tea? Or perhaps, something a little stronger?"

Maddie settled for something a little stronger. Out
in the yard, the two boys went about their labors, as if
they had seen and heard nothing.

chapter 17

GLORIA KEPT HER EYES ON SLIM JIM ZUNI THAT evening as she ate dinner with Jill Clymer. After the high of her performance on the steps of City Hall, and the drudgery of an afternoon of bureaucratic punctilio, she felt mentally drained. What she needed was an early evening and some uncomplicated sex; Slim Jim looked like just the man for that.

One of the professional gamblers who leased a table from the Emporium, Slim Jim Zuni was a very tall man with dark hair and eyes and gaunt, almost cadaverous features. He was quiet and well-spoken, and carried himself with an air of confidence that Gloria found very attractive. No one seemed to know him very well, but everyone said that he ran a clean game. His long, nimble fingers handled playing cards expertly, and Gloria found herself wondering what else he could do with them.

Her sex life lately had been active, but unusually taxing. With Stu Eckstein, there had been a sense of desperation, as befitting the desperate risks they were sharing. Ted Oberlin was an attractive and engaging young man, but she had been actively trying to control him and keep him from leading some harebrained anti-registration drive. And with Thomas Shoop, it had been pure manipulation from the start. She didn't regret anything she had done, and she honestly liked each of the three men, but she longed for a good dose of pure pleasure without any attendant baggage. Tonight, she hoped, Slim Jim Zuni would provide it.

Jill Clymer distracted her with a question. "Aren't we supposed to be neutral?"

"Huh? What? I'm sorry, Jill, what did you say?"

"I asked if we weren't supposed to be neutral in everything going on around here. I mean, you didn't seem very neutral at City Hall today, Gloria."

"The boomers have rights," Gloria replied. "And protecting them is part of our job. As for neutrality . . . Spirit, Jill, how can anyone be neutral about a reptile like Grunfeld?"

"Point taken," said Jill. "Still, I think we need to be careful about what we do."

"Agreed. We have been, and we will continue to be. I wasn't taking sides today, I was just keeping the game fair."

"Maybe you should wear a striped jersey, then," Jill grinned. "Or *something!*"

Gloria returned her grin. "People expect me to be a little outrageous," she said.

"And you're happy to meet their expectations."

"I loved every second of it, Jill. And so did all those boomers. When I make myself the center of attention like that, I get to control the agenda. Instead of a riot, we wound up with the rule of law firmly established. It's all about physical authority, I think. Grunfeld and his thugs are big, tough bruisers and they use their physical strength to get what they want. I use *my* body to help me get what *I* want—a different kind of body, a different kind of strength, but it works. And Grunfeld can't compete."

"Not on your terms," Jill agreed. "But he can on *his* terms. Isn't what you do kind of risky?"

"I can take care of myself," Gloria assured her, "and I made sure that Grunfeld knows it."

"So I heard. Still, I'd be a little more careful if I were you. Grunfeld's bound to try something, especially if you keep publicly humiliating him."

"I'm counting on that," Gloria said with smug confidence. "If he takes me on, he takes on Dexta. Then I can bring in the Bugs and put that bastard away for keeps. I'm the bait in the trap, Jill."

Jill shook her head dubiously. "Dangerous job, Gloria. You know, sometimes the rat gets away with the cheese."

"Not if the cheese is smart. I'm not just a lump of Limburger, Jill. I'll be okay."

With that, Gloria rose to her feet, bade Jill good night, and casually sauntered across the room to the table where Slim Jim Zuni was dealing a hand of five-card stud to some optimistic boomrats. Gloria watched for a moment as Slim Jim proved once again that a pair of sevens were enough to beat a busted flush and an inside straight that went unfilled. As he pulled the chips across the table, Gloria whispered a few words in Slim Jim's ear, then retired to her room.

Ten minutes later, he arrived. "What took you so long?" Gloria asked him.

"I like to take my time, ma'am," he said, then proceeded to prove it.

"GLORIA! I NEED YOU OUT HERE!"

Althea's urgent voice at the door brought Gloria back from her interlude with Slim Jim. She forced herself to get out of bed and went to the door. She opened it and stood there, nude, in front of Althea and two goggle-eyed teenage boys.

"Gloria, something has happened at the Lodge!"

"What?" Gloria's sex-softened senses abruptly became fully alert.

"I'm not sure, but it seems that Grunfeld and his men have taken Petra."

"Spirit!"

"These two young gentlemen," Althea said, indicating the boys standing behind her, "work at the Lodge. They say that Maddie Mitchell sent them here to tell you."

"Tell me what? What happened?"

One of the boys shyly stepped forward, trying but failing to keeps his eyes on hers, instead of her breasts and belly. "My name's Ed Watson, ma'am," he said. "And this here's Ramdath Knipper. We work up at the Lodge."

"Yes, yes," Gloria said impatiently. "Tell me what happened!"

"Well, ma'am, it's like this. We was workin' in the yard out by the pool. And Miz Petra came out, and she and Miz Mitchell were, well, they was sorta doin' stuff to each other, you know? And then, all of a sudden, Grunfeld and two of his guys—"

"It was Noz and Hank," Ramdath put in.

"Yeah, anyway, they just grabbed Miz Petra and carried her inside. And Miz Mitchell tried to stop 'em, but then Miz Thawley stopped *her*. Told her they'd lock her up in her cabin if she tried to do anything."

"So then," Ramdath said, "Miz Mitchell just kinda pretended that she didn't care no more, and just had herself another drink. But when Miz Thawley left, Miz Mitchell called to us. Told us we should get down here to the Emporium and tell you what happened, and so, that's what we done."

"Miz Mitchell said you'd give us a hundred crowns apiece," Ed Watson added.

"Thanks for coming, boys. Now, this is important. Do you know where they took Petra and what they did with her?"

"No, ma'am," Ramdath said. "They probably took

her to one of the cabins, but we don't know which one, or what they done there."

"And who else is at the Lodge?"

"Don't know for sure, ma'am," said Ed. "Mr. Rankus is feelin' poorly today, they said, so I expect he's upstairs in his room. And Mr. and Miz Thawley are there."

"Saw Mr. Shoop come back," Ramdath added. "But he looked kinda tired, like he was just gonna go to his cabin and sleep. Didn't see him again."

"Mr. Pollas and Mr. Taplin were there," Ed added. "And some other guy I don't know—didn't really get a good look at him. And, lemme see, I think Mr. Lund and Mr. Norfleet went down to the lake for the day. Didn't see them around. Didn't see Mr. Vigo or Mr. Ogunbayo, neither."

"Anyone else?"

"Not that we saw, ma'am. We was outside, though, so could be there's some more inside. Ma'am? I sure hope they don't do nothin' to Miz Petra. She's a real nice lady."

"She sure is," Gloria agreed. "Thank you for coming, boys. Althea? Give these young gentlemen two hundred crowns apiece, and—" Gloria paused and looked very carefully at Ed and Ramdath.

"How old are you two?"

"Sixteen, ma'am!" Ed declared.

"Both of us!" Ramdath insisted.

Gloria nodded. "And give them anything else they want. Understand?"

Althea grinned. "I understand perfectly."

"But first, find Pug Ellison and tell him to meet me downstairs. Tell him to bring his plasma pistol."

"Will do. And Gloria? Be careful!"

Gloria quickly slithered into a bodysuit. "Anything I can do to help?" Slim Jim Zuni asked her.

"Just keep an eye on things around here," Gloria told him as she fastened a utility belt low around her hips and attached her holstered plasma pistol.

"You be careful, Gloria. I mean that. If you run into Grunfeld, don't turn your back on him, not for a second."

"If I run into Grunfeld," Gloria replied, "I'll kill him."

GLORIA GUNNED THE SKIMMER STRAIGHT UP the side of the mountain, ignoring the road and its complicated switchbacks. Skimming above a steep slope like this required a delicate touch on the controls and precise attention to the mass-repulsion output, but Gloria had no time for caution and no doubt about her abilities. Beside her, Pug Ellison seemed to have quite a few doubts.

"If you flip us over, we won't be any help to Petra," he pointed out.

"I'll get us there, Pug. Don't worry about that."

"If you say so," Ellison said, sounding as if he didn't quite believe her. "But what are we going to do once we get there? I mean, there's only two of us. Maybe we should have brought some of the others?"

"Who?" Gloria snorted. "Garbedian? DeGrasse?"

"Well, then, maybe some of the boomers. They'd be glad to help."

"We don't have time to recruit an army. You and I will do better than a disorganized mob. Just stay sharp and do as I tell you. And don't hesitate to use that pistol if you need to. This isn't some brawl in a school dormitory, Pug."

"I know that. If those bastards have hurt Petra—"

Gloria almost lost it for a second, and the skimmer pitched upward until it was nearly vertical. Her fingers danced over the controls, reducing lift on the forward repeller and increasing it on the aft. The nose of the skimmer came down abruptly and tapped against the ground before rebounding. Gloria quickly restored equilibrium and resumed their dash up the mountainside.

When she saw the lights of the Lodge two hundred

yards ahead, she cut power and brought the skimmer to a halt. She and Ellison jumped out and scrambled up the slope. "Front door," Gloria told him. "I'll go in first, you come in behind me a couple of seconds later."

Gloria had planned to open the door with a Qatsima kick, but found that it was already open. She dived into the Lodge, rolled on the plush carpet, and came up to a kneeling firing position, her pistol leveled at the first person she saw, who turned out to be Preston Thawley. Mrs. Thawley stood on the other side of the room, looking surprised and outraged. Ellison charged in a second later and spun around, waving his pistol, looking for someone to shoot.

"Where is she?" Gloria demanded as she got to her feet.

"I have nothing to say to you, Ms. VanDeen," Thawley said. "And I don't know what you think you're doing, bursting in here like—"

"*Where is she?*" Gloria advanced on Thawley and stuck the barrel of the pistol against the side of his head. Thawley started to make a move of some sort, but thought better of it.

"You'll get nothing from me," Thawley repeated.

"Really? We'll see about that. Pug, watch him. If he tries anything, burn him."

"Gladly." Ellison grabbed Thawley by the back of his collar and held the pistol firmly against his spine.

Gloria crossed the room and roughly seized Mrs. Thawley by her upper arm. "Where is she?"

"I won't tell you anything!" Mrs. Thawley insisted.

Gloria broke her arm.

Mr. Thawley instinctively lunged forward as his wife howled in pain, but Ellison held on and restrained him. Gloria grabbed Mrs. Thawley's other arm. "*Where is she?*" Gloria demanded.

"Cabin Six," Mrs. Thawley sobbed. "She's in Cabin Six!"

"Pug," Gloria ordered, "stay here and watch them!"

"Like hell!" Ellison bashed Mr. Thawley on the back of the head with the butt of his pistol, and Thawley unceremoniously collapsed. Mrs. Thawley howled again, so Gloria treated her the same way.

Gloria dashed down a long corridor that connected the main Lodge with each of the cabins. The corridor curved to the right, following the contours of the ridge; as far ahead as she could see, it was deserted. When she reached Cabin Four, she slowed down, flattened herself against the inner curve of the wall, and advanced cautiously, with Ellison following her.

When they were opposite the door of Cabin Five, Gloria made a sudden rush ahead, once again diving and rolling. But the corridor was still empty. She savagely kicked at the doorknob of Cabin Six, and the door flew open. Ellison bulled his way past her, ready to fire at anything or anyone. There was no need. The only person inside the cabin was Petra.

Gloria felt her heart in her mouth as she looked down at the bloody bedsheets and the small form curled up on them. At first, she thought Petra was dead, and for a moment, her mind stopped functioning. But then, Petra moaned and slowly turned her head.

"I knew you'd come," Petra whispered in a muffled, indistinct voice. Her face was swollen almost beyond recognition, her eyes were narrow slits, and her jaw hung at an odd angle. There were fresh red bruises and raw lacerations all over her body, and she was bleeding at the crotch.

Ellison made an animal noise, and Gloria could only gasp. She bent over the bed and cupped Petra's puffy cheek in her hand.

"Petra, Petra! I'm so sorry! I—"

Behind her, Gloria heard a thump, and she whirled to see Ellison pitching forward to the floor. Hank Frezzo, Noz Gnozdziewicz, and two men she had never seen before stood there, plasma pistols in their hands and hateful grins on their faces.

"We knew you'd come, too." Frezzo laughed. "Boss said you'd be here, right about this time."

"Where is he?"

"Oh, he'll be along, Miz Gloria, don't you worry none 'bout that. He's got some business to tend to first, ya see, but he'll be along. No way he'd miss *this!*"

The two men she didn't know grabbed Gloria by her arms and pinned them behind her. Then Noz unfastened her utility belt and took her gun. He took Ellison's, as well, pausing to give the unconscious man a kick in the ribs.

They walked Gloria out of the cabin and down the corridor to the next cabin. She squirmed and tugged instinctively, but the men who held her were too strong, and she had no Qatsima moves adequate to the situation. She cursed herself for charging into the Lodge the way she had, with no help, no backup. Spirit! What had she been thinking?

In Cabin Seven, they began tying her arms to the bedposts. "No," commanded Frezzo. "The other way 'round. I think Miz Gloria's the type that likes it up the ass. What about that, Miz Gloria, you like it that way?"

Gloria tried to spit in his face, but missed.

Frezzo laughed. "Just one o' them days when nothin' goes right, eh, Miz Gloria? Now, just so ya don't get too scared, gotta tell ya that the Boss gave us strict orders. So we ain't gonna cut ya or bruise ya none. Not the way we did that little spy o' yours. No, we're gonna be real gentle with Miz Gloria VanDeen of Dexta. Ain't that right, boys?"

"Right," said Noz. "We're gonna fuck you every which way there is, but we ain't gonna hurt ya none."

Gloria shut her eyes tightly and choked back a sob. Fear and horror gripped her as never before. She felt Frezzo moving around on the bed behind her. The moment seemed unreal, unnatural. This couldn't be happening—and yet it was.

One of the two strangers suddenly burst into the

cabin. "A whole bunch of skimmers headed this way!" he shouted. "Let's get the fuck out of here—*now*!"

"Shit!" cried Frezzo. He scrambled off the bed, grabbed his clothes, and disappeared.

Gloria took a deep, relieved breath and tried to calm herself. It was over. Over. She was still alive, and it was over.

Spirit! How could I have been so stupid? Stupid! Smug and arrogant and stupid!

Long minutes later, Jill Clymer came through the door. Slim Jim Zuni and Thomas Shoop were with her. Each of them paused to look and react, then Slim Jim swiftly moved to the bed and began loosening her bonds.

"Petra—"

"We know," said Jill. "Althea and some woman named Maddie are with her. My God, Gloria, are you all right?"

"I will be," Gloria told her. "As soon as I get my hands on Grunfeld and his pukes." Zuni released her hands, and Gloria jumped out of bed and raced through the corridor to the next cabin. There, she found Pug Ellison staggering with Petra in his arms, wrapped in a sheet. He insisted on carrying her himself, but he was still groggy and couldn't resist when Zuni took her from him.

"I've already called the Emporium and told them to get a doctor," Althea said. "Gloria? Did they . . . ?"

"Forget about what they did to me," Gloria snapped. "All I want to think about is what I'm going to do to them!"

They all followed Zuni down the corridor and out of the Lodge to where a half dozen skimmers were parked. A swarm of boomers from the Emporium stood there, looking angry. "Bastards got away!" someone shouted. "Took off into the hills in a black skimmer. No way we can follow them at night."

Thomas Shoop laid his hand gently on Gloria's

shoulder, and she whirled around. "Gloria," he said, "you have to get a grip. I know how you must feel—"

"You have no idea how I feel!"

They laid Petra in the back of a utility skimmer, and Gloria and Maddie got in next to her, while Zuni drove. Petra was unconscious and still bleeding. Gloria cradled her head in her lap and tried to blink back tears. There would be plenty of time for tears later. Shoop was right, she had to get a grip. She had to think.

"They locked me in my cabin, and Shoop in his," Maddie said. "I don't know what the hell happened here, but I think Rankus may be dead. Your friends from the Emporium finally came and let me out. They got worried and mounted an expedition to help you. Spirit, Gloria, why the hell didn't you bring enough people with you in the first place?"

Gloria looked up at Maddie and stared at her for a moment, without saying anything.

Petra stirred and moaned faintly. Gloria gazed at her friend's battered face and choked back a sob.

"Gloria?"

"I'm here, Petra. We're taking you to a doctor. You're going to be fine. Don't try to talk. Everything is going to be fine."

"No . . . Gloria. I heard them. They're going to attack the camp. The one at Pizen Flats. Tonight . . ."

Petra seemed to sigh and lay still again.

chapter 18

ABEL HEARD THEM COMING.

He had bugged virtually the entire valley, and not much happened there that escaped his notice if he paid attention. Unfortunately he hadn't been paying attention that afternoon, or he would have had time to warn the boomers at Pizen Flats.

He couldn't spend *all* of his time with his monitors and equipment. As usual, he had been out and around, enjoying the valley and the life that flourished there. Two chicks had hatched in the nest of the eaglelike birds that made their home in the tall trees at the base of the western slopes. And the creatures that he thought of as foxes had been out of their den, teaching their young kits to hunt.

It was early evening by the time he returned to his own den, deep in a camouflaged cave that no one had discovered in twenty years. People thought he lived like an animal, and he supposed that was true enough. He often slept in makeshift burrows and lean-tos, or out in the open under the stars. But even animals had safe and comfortable places to hide, and Abel was no exception. With a small fusion reactor to provide power, light, and heat, and money enough to buy small amenities, Abel lived better than most of the pathetic boomrats out on the slopes and rivers.

He fixed himself a light dinner and read a chapter of Parkman's *The Oregon Trail* while he ate. Then he switched on his console and dutifully scanned a digest of the day's events in the valley, as recorded by the innumerable listening devices he had planted over the years. There was a big to-do at City Hall, and he enjoyed reading Gloria's back-and-forth with Grunfeld. Quite a gal, that Gloria.

The business about refiling claims at the Emporium proved to be boring, although he was interested to see that the bunch at Pizen Flats had actually gone ahead with their plan. They had been debating it for days, and Abel had had his doubts that they would ever get around to doing it. The boomrats were big on talk, but usually pretty short on action. But the Oberlin kid had finally made them see the light.

Nothing else of note seemed to be happening at the Emporium. Lulu Villegas had a little trouble with one of the boomers who seemed to have some unusual notions about sex, but Althea had straightened things out quickly enough. Abel had grown to like Althea and her silky, superior voice. In some ways, she did a better job of running the Emporium than Elba had. Maybe, the next trip into town, he'd see about Althea for himself.

The digests from the Lodge caught his attention. There were annoying gaps in his records from the Lodge, however. He'd bugged the place when he helped build it, but that had been twenty years ago, and some of the equipment had given out in the meantime. Still, he gathered that something was wrong up in Rankus's quarters; maybe the old bastard had finally kicked the bucket. It was hard to tell.

Then, there were a lot of people coming and going,

lots of whispered conversations and elliptical comments. There were just too many gaps to be sure just what was going on, but he was certain, at least, that Grunfeld and some of his men had been there. And later, there had been some sort of altercation outside near the pool, but it was impossible to tell who had done what to whom. But there were some screams that might have come from Petra, that spy Gloria had planted in the Lodge.

Abel wondered if he should somehow alert Gloria. The digests from the afternoon at the Lodge were already several hours old, however, so he decided to read through the more recent events before making a move. What he read alarmed him, but he feared that it was already too late to do anything about it.

Switching on the live monitors, he heard the distinct thrum and whine of skimmer engines, at least three or four of them, all apparently headed toward Pizen Flats. Spirit, what to do?

He had to warn them . . . somehow.

GUS THORNTON POURED SOME MORE BOOZE into Ted Oberlin's coffee. "Drink up, son," he said. "You earned it!"

Other riverrats gathered around the campfire echoed the sentiment. Oberlin couldn't help blushing a little. He raised his cup high and said, "Here's to the Pizen Flats Cooperative Association!"

Everyone drank to that.

"And here's to Ted Oberlin!" shouted one of the riverrats. "For someone who didn't know a sluice box from a shit hole when he got here, he turned out pretty damn good!"

Everyone drank to that, too, and Oberlin could only grin in embarrassment. Pizen Flats was a hell of a long way from Philadelphia, and yet, for the first time in his life, he felt as if he had found a home. These were good people. Good people.

His own people, the family he had abandoned in anger and defiance two years before, were not good people. That was a hell of a thing to say about your own flesh and blood, but it was true. Selfish, stiff-necked, mean-spirited, and cold. They had expected him to be the same way, but somehow he hadn't been. He saw other possibilities in life, and broader horizons than a law office on Chestnut Street. And he longed for the warmth that he saw in others but never in his own family. To his amazement and pride, he realized that he had finally found it here, five hundred light-years from Chestnut Street, among people his family would have found contemptible.

Oh, they'd sock you in the jaw over some imagined slight or insult, but afterward they'd help you up, dust you off, and lend you their last crown. They looked after each other and genuinely cared what happened to a person. They were crude, semiliterate bumpkins, most of them, but they had a sort of wisdom that came from somewhere deep inside. They knew when you were happy, and they knew when you were hurting.

He had never said a word to any of them about his relationship with Gloria, but all of them seemed to know. So when they saw Gloria with that Shoop character, and saw how Ted reacted, they knew he was hurting. No one actually said anything about it, but they all seemed to try to prop him up and keep him smiling through his pain.

And, he supposed, he *was* being pretty silly about it. She was Gloria VanDeen, for Spirit's sake! Ex-wife of the Emperor, no less. And yet, she had shared a few passionate evenings with him, Ted Oberlin, in the most beautiful place in the galaxy! What the hell did he have to complain about? If he lived to be two hundred, the thought of Gloria and their time together would always bring a warm smile to his face.

He resolved to go back into town tomorrow, find Gloria, and apologize to her for having been such an idiot. Maybe they would even steal a few more evenings together before her business here was ended and the tides of the Empire swept her away from him forever.

Well, maybe not tomorrow, but soon. He had business of his own to take care of. There were dozens of other camps up and down the river that were considering doing the same thing that the Pizen Flats people had done. He needed to get them copies of the template he had created, so they could refile their own claims. All they would need to do would be to fill in the proper names and locations, then take the forms into the Emporium to be properly registered.

He knew that the odds were still against them. He had no illusions about the power of the corporate interests that wanted to rape this valley, and the nabobs at the Lodge and their pet apes who wanted to terrorize and dominate everyone who lived here. But if a solitary woman like Gloria could stand up to them and prevail, then who was to say that a united front of boomers— riverrats and highboys alike—could not do the same?

It could happen, he told himself. He could *make* it happen! The thought made him as happy as he had ever been in his life.

He held his cup out to Gus. "Gimme another shot, Your Highness," he said. "I feel like howling at the moons tonight!"

Before Gus could pour him some more booze, the Voice spoke to them.

It came from everywhere and nowhere, but for once, it did not whisper. It shouted.

They are coming! They are coming! Protect yourselves! Protect yourselves!

But before anyone could do anything, the blue-green bolts of plasma crisscrossed the campsite. The thunderclaps they caused echoed across the valley, drowning out the words of the Voice.

• • •

THEY PUT PETRA ON THE BED IN ALTHEA'S FIRST-
floor room. Doc Harkins, the drunken old sot who minis-
tered to the broken bones and bellyaches in Greenlodge,
was already there, waiting for them. Gloria watched in agonized silence as he ran his instruments over her ravaged
body. Petra was still unconscious and her breathing was
ragged and shallow. Twice on the trip down the mountain,
it had seemed to stop altogether, and Gloria pressed her
lips to Petra's and tried to breathe life back into her.

"Massive hematoma, apparent fractures of occipital
and mandibula. Fractures of left radius and ulna.
Trauma to nose and eyes. Probable rib fractures. Vaginal
and rectal bleeding. Probably some internal bleeding,
but I can't be sure."

"Will she live?" Gloria demanded.

Harkins shook his head in an indeterminate motion.
"She should, if we get her to a hospital. There's not
much I can do for her here."

"Althea, find the Cruiser pilot! We're taking her to
Palmyra!"

Jill Clymer came in as Althea departed. She paused
to take a look at Petra, then turned to Gloria. "I can't
raise anyone at Pizen Flats on the comm," she said.

"Shit!"

"Calm down, Gloria. It may not mean anything.
Pizen Flats is at extreme range for the comm without a
satellite link, and it's nestled down in the valley."

Gloria pushed her way past Jill and went out onto
the main floor of the Emporium. The boomers fell silent
and turned to look at her.

"Listen to me, everyone!" she shouted. "Grunfeld
and his men are going to attack the camp at Pizen Flats!
I need everyone with a plasma pistol and a skimmer to
meet me out front in ten minutes. If you don't have a
gun or a skimmer, then find someone who does. We
need your help, and we need it now!"

The boomers stared at her in shocked silence for
several seconds, then scrambled to their feet and

headed for the doors. Gloria ran upstairs to her own room and allowed herself a minute in the shower, as hot as she could stand it. Then she threw on jeans, a shirt, and some boots and raced back downstairs. She bumped into Raul Tellemacher at the foot of the steps.

"Where the hell have *you* been all day?" she demanded.

Unperturbed, Tellemacher replied, "Out with DeGrasse, registering voters at the far end of the valley, like a good little bureaucrat. We never heard the recall signal. What's happening?"

"Just grab your pistol and come on. I don't have time to explain!" Gloria dashed outside and found at least fifty or sixty boomers and a couple of dozen skimmers assembled there.

"I don't know what the situation is at Pizen Flats," she cried, "but be prepared for anything! But do not fire your weapons unless fired upon, without a specific order from me! Does everyone understand?"

"We're with ya, Gloria!" someone shouted.

"Then let's go!"

Gloria shoved Pug Ellison out of the driver's seat of their skimmer, powered up, and headed for the river. The armada from the Emporium followed close behind.

THEY WERE TOO LATE. AS THEY ROUNDED A bend in the river and came within view of the point of land known as Pizen Flats, they saw the flames and smoke, glowing orange in the firelight, billowing upward from the scorched remains of the tents and shanties. There was no sound but the whine of their engines and the slap of waves against the shore.

Gloria grounded her skimmer and leaped out, borrowed pistol at the ready. But there was nowhere to aim, nothing to shoot.

She tripped over the first body, barely ten yards from the river. It had no head.

Pug Ellison helped her to her feet. As other boomers rushed past them, they paused for a moment and stared at the corpse. There was no way to identify it, but it was someone Gloria had known, someone she had kissed and hugged and laughed with just days ago.

She forced herself to move on, the sick feeling in the pit of her stomach growing stronger with each step. There were more mangled bodies, burned and dismembered, the closer she came to the center of the camp. Then she saw Gus Thornton's "throne," and in it, a headless, legless torso.

It was too much for her. She doubled over and vomited.

Others, not far from her, were doing the same.

The boomers were a tough lot, but few of them had ever experienced anything like this. A handful of older men, who had served in the war with the Ch'gnth, forty-odd years earlier, recognized the sights and smells, but even they had a hard time accepting what lay before them.

The massacre of Pizen Flats was thorough. There were no survivors. Someone with a strong stomach and a sense of order eventually counted forty-nine bodies. One of them was Ted Oberlin's.

Gloria stood above it and stared at the wreckage of what had been a marvelous young man. Half his head was burned away. The lips that had kissed hers and the eyes that had stared at her with hunger and passion were gone. The magnificent brain that had helped her solve the mystery of the Voice and had rallied the riverrats was spilling out of his shattered skull and onto the ground.

She felt someone's arm around her waist. "Gloria," Jill Clymer said softly, "come with me."

"No," Gloria told her. "I need to . . . I need . . ."

"There's nothing you can do. There's nothing anyone can do now."

Gloria didn't have the strength to resist. She let Jill

guide her back to the riverbank and sit her down in the front seat of a skimmer.

She could not tell what she felt at this moment, could not give a name to the emotions that flooded through her. Anger, hatred, disgust, despair, horror, pain . . . all of them were present, and much more. And beyond it all was the certain, undeniable truth that everything that had happened on this terrible day had been her fault.

Petra . . . Ted . . . Gus . . . and so many others . . . all had paid the price for her arrogance and smug certainty that she could handle anything. She was Gloria VanDeen! Heroine of Mynjhino! Sweetheart of the Fucking Empire!

Spirit save her!

She began to sob. She knew people were watching, but she could not help herself. At last, something that the great Gloria VanDeen could not control. Herself!

Poor Ted. The last time she had seen him—just hours ago—he had been angry with her. She had toyed with his emotions because it suited her purposes, and now he was dead and she could never, never make it up to him and tell him how much he had really meant to her, what a special man he was!

And good, gentle, genial Gus, the King of Pizen Flats. Another special man. Everyone who knew him loved and respected him. And most of those people were dead, too, vaporized into clouds of uncaring ions drifting in the night winds. Dead, all dead.

If only . . . if only . . . if only *what*? What could she have done, should she have done, to prevent all of this from happening? If only she hadn't gone out of her way to antagonize Grunfeld. Maybe then . . . but would it have mattered?

Dammit, *she* was supposed to have been the bait in the trap! The rats hadn't gotten the cheese, not quite, but the moment of helpless horror on that bed had been the worst of her life—and that was *nothing*! *Nothing!*

She would go through it all again, a hundred times, a thousand times, if it would bring back the riverrats of Pizen Flats, if it would erase the terrible hurt that had been done to Petra.

Petra! At least she was still alive—Spirit, she *had* to be alive!—but would life ever be the same for her? How could she have been so stupid, so uncaring, to send her closest friend, the person she loved above all others, into what was so obviously—obvious *now*!—a dangerous trap? Would Petra ever be able to forgive her? Would she ever be able to forgive herself?

The tears and sobs would not stop, but gradually she became aware that a small crowd had gathered around her. Dexta people, and Slim Jim Zuni, and a few other boomers. Most of them were keeping a respectful distance, but the sight of proud, confident, glamorous Gloria VanDeen, weeping uncontrollably, was, in a strange way, as upsetting as anything they had seen on this awful night.

She forced herself to rally. There would be plenty of time for tears. Later, later . . .

Gloria looked up, wiped away a string of mucous dangling from her nostril, and tried to focus her blurred vision.

"Gloria?" Jill Clymer asked softly. "We need to make some decisions."

Gloria nodded. "I know," she said in a choked voice.

"The . . . bodies," said Jill. "Some of the boomers want to get them buried as soon as possible."

"No," said Gloria. "We need . . . no, wait . . . yes, we should do that. But first, I want someone to image the entire scene. Every bit of it. And someone will have to try to identify everyone, if we can. I know it's asking a lot, but . . ."

"We'll take care of it, Gloria," said one of the boomers. "Don't you worry about it. We know these folks, and we'll do right by 'em."

"And I'll do the imaging," said Pug Ellison.

"Thank you. And . . . Jill? I can't think. What else?"

"Well . . . what do we do about Grunfeld? Should we organize search teams, or what? For that matter, how do we even know it *was* Grunfeld? I mean, all we have is Petra's word for it."

Gloria's eyes narrowed and she stared at Jillian for a long, tense moment. Then she said, "That's good enough for me."

Jill nodded. "I didn't mean anything by that, Gloria. It's just that . . ."

"I know. I'm sorry, Jill."

"It might not be enough for an Imperial Court," Raul Tellemacher pointed out. "I don't mean to be indelicate, and Spirit forbid that it should happen, but if Petra can't testify . . ."

"Shut your mouth, Raul! Just shut it. I'm going to Palmyra with Petra tonight, and she's going to be fine!"

"And who's in charge here while you're gone?" Tellemacher wanted to know.

"Jill is," Gloria said.

"I'm senior," Tellemacher protested.

"Fuck your seniority!" Gloria sprang to her feet and looked ready to attack Tellemacher, but she regained control quickly. "I can appoint any deputy I want, and Jill is it. You'll take orders from her and no one else. I should be back in a day or two, and I'll be bringing Internal Security and Imperial Marshals with me. In the meantime, I want every outgoing ship, commercial or private, searched before departure, just in case Grunfeld and his pukes try to get away. And get someone up to the Lodge to image the scene there. Take statements from Maddie Mitchell and Thomas Shoop, and those two boys. And find out what's happened to Rankus. If you can find Mr. and Mrs. Thawley, put them in custody. Beyond that, it's business as usual, understand? Althea will run the Emporium, and you'll go on registering voters and filing legal documents. Is everybody clear on that?"

"Got it, Gloria," Jill said. "Is there anything else?"

Gloria shook her head, then sagged back down into the skimmer.

"Just one more thing," she said. "Would someone please get me back to town? I don't think I'm in any shape to drive."

"I'll take you," said Slim Jim Zuni. "Just leave everything to me."

chapter 19

THE DEXTA CRUISER LANDED AT PALMYRA CITY
in the middle of the night. They had radioed ahead after
reentering normal space, and an ambulance was waiting
to meet them, along with Jennifer Astuni from the
Dexta office. Gloria had hovered over Petra throughout
the eight-hour trip, but Petra never stirred.

Gloria went with the ambulance and breathed an
inner sigh of relief when trained and competent medical
personnel began attending to Petra. At the hospital, a
team of specialists took over and rushed Petra into a
treatment room. Gloria tried to follow, but was barred
from access. Jennifer Astuni pulled her away and led her
to a waiting room. She collapsed onto a couch, and, in
spite of everything, immediately fell into a troubled and
exhausted slumber.

When she awoke, Sabaru Graff and Stu Eckstein
were there. Eckstein sat down next to her and put his
arm around her shoulders. Gloria shrugged him off, got
to her feet, and insisted on seeing the head of the medical team that was treating Petra. Jennifer assured her

that he had already been summoned. Gloria paced around the small room in agitation, ignoring all attempts by the others to get her to sit down.

When Dr. Hamdoon arrived, he was smiling and pleased with himself. "She'll be fine, Ms. VanDeen. There is no permanent damage, and I anticipate a full recovery."

Gloria's relief was such that she couldn't breathe for a moment. Finally, she was able to whisper, "Can I see her?"

"She's still under anesthesia."

"I want to see her."

"Very well." Dr. Hamdoon led the party down a long corridor and into a recovery room. There, Gloria saw Petra, swathed in bandages and connected to a multitude of tubes and wires, breathing slowly and regularly. She stared at her in silence for several moments, privately thanking the Spirit for keeping her friend alive.

"There was some serious trauma and considerable bleeding in the cranial cavity due to the fractured occipital," Hamdoon explained. "If you hadn't gotten her here when you did, there could have been permanent brain damage. As it is, I'm confident that we've avoided that. As for the rest—well, it looked worse than it really was. We've administered nanomeds, and they are already repairing the damage cell by cell. Within a month, she'll be as good as new. No scars, no disabilities. However," he added, "considering what she endured, she will undoubtedly need psychological counseling."

Gloria thought about that for a moment, then said, "No."

"What's that, Ms. VanDeen? Perhaps you don't understand—"

"I understand perfectly. But I can't permit that. Petra was doing confidential work for Dexta, and I can't have her talking about that to some shrink."

"But," Hamdoon protested, "her psychological recovery will require—"

"It doesn't require talking to unauthorized personnel. That's final. If she needs to talk to someone, she can talk to Jennifer Astuni."

"With respect to Ms. Astuni, she is not qualified—"

"By the time she's needed, she will be. Jennifer? I want you to take a crash course in counseling. Arrange it with Dr. Hamdoon and the staff here, all right?"

"Whatever you say, Gloria."

"This is highly irregular," Hamdoon said, frowning, "and I can't be held responsible for—"

"It's my responsibility," Gloria said firmly. "When will Petra be conscious?"

"I'd like to keep her under for at least the next day."

"Fine. I'll be back tomorrow morning. Thank you for everything, Dr. Hamdoon."

"Just a moment, Ms. VanDeen. I understand that you were assaulted as well. I'd like to examine you before you leave."

"Not necessary, Doctor. As you can see, I'm fine."

"What I see," said Hamdoon, "is a young woman in a state of nervous exhaustion and post-traumatic stress. Not to mention denial. I'd like to give you a complete physical and some appropriate medication. And whether you think you need it or not, I strongly recommend that you receive counseling, as well."

"Thank you for your opinion, Doctor. I'll see you tomorrow." Gloria brusquely turned and marched away down the corridor, with the others bringing up the rear.

AT THE DEXTA OFFICES, JENNIFER HAD BREAK-fast delivered, and the four of them sat around a conference table drinking coffee and picking at their meals. Gloria described for them the recent course of events on Sylvania and answered their questions. Eckstein had little to say, realizing that Gloria would make a private report to him later on. Graff kept frowning and shaking his head, but it was unclear whether his disapproval applied to the situation on Sylvania or to Gloria's conduct there.

"What I need now," Gloria concluded, "is an Internal Security team and some Imperial Marshals. They'll accompany me back to Sylvania on the Cruiser."

"I see," said Graff. "And just how many will you need?"

"A dozen Bugs, and at least three or four Marshals."

"Out of the question," Graff replied. "This isn't Earth or one of the big colonies, Gloria. Our full Internal Security staff on Palmyra only totals sixteen. As for Marshals, there aren't half a dozen on the entire planet."

"All right then, you've got sixteen Bugs, I'll take eight. And two Marshals."

"I can let you have four, at most. The Imperial Marshal's office will have to make its own decisions on personnel allocation."

Gloria turned her weary gaze toward Graff. "You don't seem to understand, Mr. Imperial Secretary," she said. "That wasn't a request, it was an order."

"That would leave us seriously shorthanded here. I can't possibly—"

"You can't possibly mean to say that you intend to disobey my order," Gloria interjected.

"Now, look here, Ms. VanDeen. I know Secretary Mingus is very taken with his notion of an Office of Strategic Intervention. But we in the local offices have responsibilities, as well, and I cannot believe that Mr. Mingus ever intended that we should be stripped of essential personnel just to satisfy the momentary needs of this OSI of his."

"If you want to know what Secretary Mingus intends, I'll be happy to order you back to Earth immediately so you can hear it from his own mouth."

Before Graff could respond, Jennifer smoothly intervened. "You'll have your eight Bugs, Gloria. And I'll call the Marshal's Office."

"Good," Gloria said. "Also, I want a 'round-the-clock Internal Security guard put on Petra's door at the hospital."

"Now, really!" Graff sniffed. "I understand your

concern, but I don't see what possible need there could be for such a misallocation of personnel. She'll be perfectly safe here."

"Secretary Graff," Gloria said, slowly and patiently, "Petra is the only surviving witness who has knowledge of the massacre at Pizen Flats. Whoever planned that crime is undoubtedly aware of that."

"But I thought it was clear that it was Grunfeld. And he's still on Sylvania."

"We don't know where he is for certain. And I have serious doubts that Grunfeld was the only party involved in the massacre. Two of the men who assaulted Petra and me were strangers, not part of Grunfeld's gang. They had to have come from somewhere, at someone's orders. Grunfeld may have carried out the massacre, but he didn't plan it."

"Then who?" Graff demanded.

"I don't know, yet," Gloria replied. "But it had to have been one or more of the corporate representatives on Sylvania and the Lodge trustees."

"The Lodge trustees?" Graff cried in genuine alarm. "You can't be serious!"

Gloria was beginning to lose her patience. "Look at me, Graff," she snapped. "Do I look as if I'm not serious?"

Graff did look at her, and seemed startled by her intensity. Nevertheless, he insisted on making his point. "Ms. VanDeen, you are talking about members of five of the most prominent and powerful families on Palmyra. Claude Rankus, if he still lives, as well as Myron Vigo, Rahim Ogunbayo, Sidney Taplin, and young Joe Pollas."

"I know exactly who I'm talking about, and that's precisely why Petra needs a full-time guard."

"She'll have it," Jennifer assured her.

"This is outrageous," Graff muttered. "Do you have any idea of what you are suggesting? The ramifications and consequences of placing these citizens under suspicion? This is *not* Sylvania, it's Palmyra, a settled and civilized world! I'll not have you going about making wild and unsupported accusations just because you and your assistant were badly treated. I believe you are placing your personal desire for revenge above your duties as a Dexta officer. If you persist in this, Ms. VanDeen, I shall file the strongest possible protest with Secretary Mingus!"

"File to your heart's content, Secretary Graff. And, in the meantime, I'm also going to need a judge. Is there a reasonably honest and competent Imperial Judge on this planet who doesn't have ties to your precious prominent families?"

"There is," said Jennifer.

Graff gave her a startled look. "You can't mean—"

"I do," said Jennifer. She turned to Gloria. "Judge Otis Kershaw. He's the maverick on the local Imperial bench. He's been here forever and hates everyone impartially."

"Good. Get him, and tell him to pack for a trip to Sylvania. But first, we'll need warrants to investigate the finances of each of the Lodge trustees, as well as those of Kevin Grunfeld. Get your Financial people on it immediately. I'm specifically interested in any transactions between the trustees and Grunfeld. Also, any transactions involving Excelsior, Servitor, or Imperium. I want a preliminary report before I return to Sylvania."

"Now you've gone too far! Really, Ms. VanDeen," Graff objected, "Judge Kershaw is 130 years old—"

"So is Norman Mingus," Gloria reminded him.

"I only hope that Secretary Mingus is not as befuddled as Judge Kershaw. The man is an irresponsible, shoot-from-the-hip, troublemaking scoundrel. I really must put my foot down, Ms. VanDeen. Assignment of Imperial Judges is not even a Dexta matter, as I'm sure you must know. It's the exclusive province of the Imperial Governor, and I can assure you on his behalf that such an assignment will not be forthcoming. And speaking of the Governor, I can also assure you that he will be deeply upset by the actions you intend to take and the aspersions you are casting upon the Lodge trustees. I intend to take this matter up with him at the earliest opportunity."

"You won't have that opportunity, Graff," Gloria told him icily.

"And just what do you mean by that?" Graff demanded.

"The problem with Imperial Secretaries," Gloria said, "is that too many of them think that their primary responsibility is to ingratiate themselves with the local power structure and keep them happy. In fact, their primary responsibility is to do, efficiently and without complaint, whatever Dexta requires of them. You've made it clear that you are incapable of doing that, Mr. Graff. Effective immediately, I am removing you from your present assignment. You will report back to Dexta Headquarters to make yourself available for reassignment. And, Mr. Graff, by immediately, I mean you are to take the very next ship leaving the Orbital Station for Earth. There should be one this afternoon, so I suggest you return to your quarters and start packing."

Graff blustered and sputtered. "You have no authority—"

"I'm a Ten, you're a Twelve, Graff, and the OSI Charter gives me all the authority I need. Now get out of my sight. I will not have you hanging around, creating problems for me. You are not to attempt to communicate with any of the Lodge trustees, their families, or representatives. And if you are not off-planet by this afternoon, I'll have the Bugs put you in detention. Jennifer? Congratulations, you're the new Imperial Secretary."

"Thank you," Jennifer said. She looked at Graff. "Shall I call you a cab?"

GLORIA SPENT THE REST OF THE DAY TENDING to endless details and trying to think of anything else that needed to be done. She had arrived on Palmyra wearing the same jeans and shirt that she had been wearing when she left the Emporium, so she dispatched a Dexta worker to acquire shoes, a skirt, and a blouse. The resulting outfit was the most conservative one she had worn in years, although in a concession to her public image, she left the loose gray blouse unbuttoned to the waist. She didn't even want to think about sex at the moment, but sex was an essential part of her arsenal and she knew it would be an asset in the meetings she had scheduled.

First, she met with the Chief Imperial Marshal in his office and explained the situation on Sylvania. The massacre was, of course, a violation of the *Imperial Code*, and the Chief was properly outraged and cooperative. He assigned two Marshals to accompany her back to Sylvania, with the promise of two more to come, if necessary.

Next, she sat down with the eight Internal Security officers who had been hastily assembled from all over the planet. The massacre itself was an Imperial matter, but the assaults on two Dexta representatives were a violation of the *Dexta Code* and came under the aegis of the IntSec Bugs. The massacre and the assaults were obviously related, so the Imperial and Dexta investigations would proceed in harness. Gloria explained to the Bugs what she expected of them, and they were eager to get started. There wasn't really a lot to keep them busy on Palmyra, aside from essentially bureaucratic matters, and they welcomed an opportunity to flex their muscles and put their training to use. Moreover, the Bugs were personally incensed by the assaults; their main task was the protection of Dexta personnel, and they tended to view an attack on one as an attack on all.

THEN, IT WAS ON TO A HASTILY ARRANGED luncheon with Imperial Governor Vincent DiGrazia. He was a sturdily built, suavely handsome man, who was delighted to meet Gloria and eager to be of assistance. He was momentarily unsettled by the sudden loss of his Imperial Secretary, but quickly recovered. Imperial Governors were political appointees, and DiGrazia had made a career out of being pleasing and accommodating to anyone who seemed to have more power than he did. Technically, Dexta had no authority over an Imperial Governor, but DiGrazia was not about to stand up to Gloria VanDeen. If the Emperor himself couldn't control her, DiGrazia had no intention of trying.

When Gloria made it clear that some of Palmyra's leading families were under suspicion, DiGrazia was not happy. He didn't want to annoy the very people he had so assiduously cultivated during his time in office there, but if any of them were involved in the massacre, he was determined not to be tainted by his association with them. The wind had changed suddenly, and DiGrazia was an experienced political sailor who knew when to trim his sails.

He had no objection to assigning Judge Kershaw to Sylvania; in fact, he was glad to have an excuse to get him out of his hair, if only temporarily. The cantankerous old jurist had been a thorn in the side of every Imperial Governor of Palmyra for the past thirty years.

DiGrazia's only real disappointment was that he had been hoping to get some media mileage out of his meeting with Gloria, but she had quickly squelched his plans. Word of the massacre would be released in due course, but Gloria told him that she wanted to keep the media away from Sylvania (and from her) for as long as reasonably possible.

HER FINAL MEETING OF THE DAY WAS WITH Judge Otis Kershaw, a white-haired, bushy-eyebrowed, craggy-faced relic who ogled her partly exposed breasts with the relish of a man a century younger. Gloria noticed, and subtly maneuvered to give him a better view as she sat across from him in the Dexta offices, explaining why he was needed. Kershaw nodded gravely when she described the basis for her suspicions of the Lodge trustees.

"Vicious bastards, the lot of 'em," Kershaw said. "Wouldn't put it past any of 'em. You'll get all the warrants you need, Ms. VanDeen."

"We'll also need you on Sylvania for several weeks, Judge. I want you available in case of challenges to the voter registration—although if Rankus really is dead, I doubt there will be any challenge. After that, there will be Eminent Domain hearings, and I'd like you to oversee those, as well."

Kershaw nodded. "Will I have any time to do some fishing?"

"All the time you want," Gloria assured him.

"Good. Been there a few times as a guest at the Lodge, but I preferred it down in Greenlodge. Is Elba still around?"

"Elba has retired, but I think you'll find the Emporium in good hands."

"In that case, Ms. VanDeen, I'm all yours, for as long as you need me."

WHEN HER MEETINGS HAD FINALLY CONCLUDED, Gloria squirreled herself away in a vacant Dexta office and began writing reports to go out on a courier. She wrote formal reports for the OSI office and Mingus, but spent most of her time on a long, private, encrypted report for Mingus's eyes only.

After spelling out everything that had happened on Sylvania since her arrival, and providing a progress report on Roosa's work, she at last unburdened herself to the Dexta Secretary.

"Norman," she wrote, "I feel awful about what's happened. I'm afraid I've made a mess of everything. The massacre might never have happened if I hadn't been so damned sure I could handle Grunfeld. I might even have provoked him into it by humiliating him in public so often. There's probably a lot more to it, as I've outlined, but I can't even be sure of that much. And I don't know if I can forgive myself for what happened to Petra. She had no training as an undercover operative, and I had no business sending her up to the Lodge to be a spy. I was an idiot, and Petra paid the price.

"Spirit knows, I'm flattered by your confidence in trusting me with this assignment. But with so much at stake, I wonder if you made a good decision. I was just too damned smug and sure of myself, too busy being the glamorous Gloria VanDeen! I can't undo the damage I've already done, and I'm frightened by the thought that I'll do more. People have died because of me! Maybe I'm just not ready for that kind of responsibility. I feel that I have failed you, Norman, and I will understand completely if you decide to relieve me of my present assignment. Don't let your personal feelings for me interfere with what you must do. As you pointed out when you gave me this job, the future of the Empire is at stake. Do what you must!"

AFTER A LONG DAY, EXHAUSTED AND DRAINED, Gloria finally accompanied Stu Eckstein to his apartment, where he cooked her a meal that she hardly touched. Later, they sat together on the couch and she gave him a full account of events on Sylvania. She also brought him up to date on Sam Roosa's progress.

"Sounds good," said Eckstein. "There are bound to be at least some intrusions in the Fergusite layer, but I think it's unlikely that we'll be completely blocked."

"When are you going to start taking samples?"

"The Survey Office is already trying to get me moving. I gather that some of the corporates have been giving them some heat about the delay. But I think I can use the massacre as an excuse to put it off a few more weeks."

"It's an ill wind that blows no good," Gloria observed sourly.

"In any case, I can plot Roosa's results over time and use that to begin the sampling in spots where the Fergusite has already been ruined. But this is still going to be hit-or-miss, Gloria. Even if the plasma injection goes perfectly, there will still be isolated patches of Fergusite that are unaffected."

"You mean that all of this might be for nothing?"

"I didn't say that. I just meant that it won't be a case of simply taking a couple of samples and declaring the entire layer worthless. And don't forget, the corporate geologists will be looking over my shoulder the whole time."

"Corporate geologists, and maybe corporate assassins," Gloria pointed out. "Two of the men who assaulted me were total strangers. They had to have been sent there by one of the corporates."

"Or maybe just by someone at the Lodge. They have their own interests to protect."

"True," Gloria conceded. "What I don't understand, though, is why they did it when they did. Grunfeld and his men are effectively outlaws now. He's cut himself out of the spoils."

"Not necessarily. He probably already cut a deal and sold all of his claims and proxies to someone. The massacre was probably part of the deal. At a minimum, what happened at Pizen Flats is going to make the other riverrats think twice about refiling their claims. That could be enough to tilt the Eminent Domain results to the corporates. And there's one other thing, Gloria. I hate to bring this up, but have you considered what would have happened if your friends at the Emporium hadn't gotten worried and gone up to the Lodge to find you?"

Gloria thought about it for a few seconds, then nodded grimly. "They'd have taken Petra and me away and killed us," she said.

"In which case," Eckstein said, "there would have

been no witnesses to connect Grunfeld to the massacre. They'd probably have blamed it on the highboys—they did have that brawl with the riverrats, after all. Grunfeld would still be in business."

"He counted on me charging up to Lodge all by myself, with no backup. And I did, dammit. Spirit, I fell for it, hook, line, and sinker! I've been a complete idiot, Stu. Mingus should relieve me."

Eckstein looked at her carefully. "Is that what you want?" he asked.

Gloria didn't know how to answer his question, so she ignored it. "What I want," she said finally, "is a good night's sleep. Alone, Stu."

"I understand," he said, "but—"

"Yes, yes, I know what you're going to say. I've been through a terrible experience, but all I really need is for a good, strong, tender, loving, sensitive man to take me in his arms and make everything right again. I know. But not now, Stu. Not yet."

"When you think the time is right, Gloria, let me know. In the meantime, the bedroom is yours, and I'll sleep on the couch."

Gloria managed a weak smile. "It may be a while," she told him.

"I'm not in any hurry," he said.

She leaned toward him and kissed him. "You're a good man, Stu."

"But a man, nonetheless."

"They're not my favorite sex at the moment," Gloria conceded. "When those bastards were about to rape me I felt . . . Spirit, I can't even describe what I felt. The only thing that saved me was sheer dumb luck. I can't even imagine what it must have been like for Petra."

"You can't blame yourself for that. It wasn't your fault."

"Wasn't it?"

Eckstein shook his head. "You did what you thought

you had to do. Nobody's right all the time, Gloria. Not even you."

"Lately, I haven't even been right *some* of the time."

"It will average out eventually. Everything does, you know. Trust me, I'm a scientist. I know about things like that." Eckstein put his arm around her and held her close.

THE NEXT MORNING, GLORIA RETURNED TO THE hospital. She sat down in a chair next to Petra's bed and waited to be noticed. Petra was awake but groggy and far from alert. Her face, where it wasn't covered with bandages, was still red and swollen.

"Gloria?"

Gloria reached for Petra's hand and squeezed it. "I'm here, kiddo," she said.

Petra's voice was slurred and strained; she had to speak through her teeth, since her broken jaw was secured in the shut position.

"Where am I?" she mumbled.

"You're in a hospital on Palmyra. Don't worry, you're going to be fine. The doctors say you'll make a complete recovery."

"Recovery from what?"

"Um . . . what's the last thing you remember?"

Petra thought about it for several moments before responding. "I was in the skimmer on the way up to the Lodge. What happened? Did we crash?"

Gloria hesitated before saying anything. It might be a blessing if Petra had no memory of the assault, but it would also mean that there was no one who could connect Grunfeld to the massacre.

"Petra," Gloria said, "someone at the Lodge found out that you were spying on them. Do you remember that?"

"Uh . . . no. Is that what . . . what happened to me?"

Gloria nodded. "They beat and raped you, Petra.

I'm so sorry. I should never have sent you there. It's all my fault."

"No," Petra protested weakly. "I knew the risks."

"So did I, and I sent you there anyway. It was a stupid thing to do, and I just hope that you can forgive me somehow." She squeezed Petra's hand harder. "I just don't know if I'll ever be able to forgive myself."

"No . . . no . . . you were just doing your job. And I was doing mine. If they found out I was a spy, I must have screwed up."

"No! You didn't screw up, Petra—I did!"

Petra considered that for a moment. Then she said, "If you screwed up, then what are you doing here, holding my hand? Get that beautiful ass of yours back to Sylvania and fix things!"

"Petra—"

"Just do it! How am I ever going to become the most powerful woman in the Empire if you just sit here blaming yourself? Get back to work this instant, you hear me?"

Gloria found herself grinning at her assistant. "Yes, ma'am," she said.

GLORIA SPENT MOST OF THE DAY MEETING WITH the Dexta Office's Financial staff as they sorted through a mass of computer records. Nothing incriminating leaped out at them. The likelihood was that any payoffs to Grunfeld would have been handled through offworld accounts, probably via banks on New Helvetia, where privacy was considered a sacred (and very profitable) trust. Still, a careful analysis of the records of the Lodge trustees might lead to other accounts. Realistically, the whole investigation would have to be taken over by Dexta Headquarters on Earth, and would undoubtedly take months. Nevertheless, Gloria urged the Palmyra staff to keep at it and send her regular reports after she returned to Sylvania.

She was planning to leave that night, along with the Marshals and Bugs, but first, she returned to the hospital to say good-bye to Petra. As she walked down the long corridor to Petra's room, Gloria was overtaken by a harried and apprehensive-looking administrator.

"Ms. VanDeen?" she said. "I'm sorry to have to tell you this but . . . Ms. Nash is gone."

"*Gone?*" Gloria gasped. "You mean, she's . . . ?"

"I mean, she's *gone.* She disappeared from her room about an hour ago. We have no idea where she is."

chapter **20**

GLORIA MET IN THE ADMINISTRATOR'S OFFICE
with Dr. Hamdoon and Glenn Wong, the hastily summoned head of the Palmyra Dexta Internal Security Office. The administrator, a Ms. Suharto, seemed to regard
Petra's disappearance as a bureaucratic tragedy, Hamdoon
viewed it as a frustrating medical development, and Wong
saw it as a major crime that had occurred in his own back-
yard. The Bug who had been assigned to guard Petra's
door had been found, drugged and unconscious, under
her bed; someone had evidently slipped something into
his coffee.

To Gloria, it was like the latest phase of a nightmare
from which she was unable to awaken. It echoed what
she'd felt when Grunfeld's thugs had tied her to that
bed—this couldn't be happening, and yet it was.

"Medically," Dr. Hamdoon opined, "we had already
done everything necessary to assure her recovery. Quik-
Knit will repair her fractures within a few weeks, and
the bone braces for her wrist and jaw will dissolve when
their work is done. The nanomeds will complete their

repairs of her various wounds. My concern is that she may receive insufficient post-treatment care—proper changing of bandages, prevention of infection, and so forth. Also, of course, there would be a heightened risk of reinjury, were she to be subjected to any further trauma."

"But she will recover?" Gloria asked.

"All things being equal, assuredly so."

"We can't count on those other things being equal, Doctor," said Wong. "I've already alerted the local police and Internal Security on Palmyra Orbital Station. But the kidnappers had a head start, so there's no telling where they've taken her by now. They could be anywhere on Palmyra, or even off-world."

"I want a full report on departures from the Orbital Station," Gloria told him.

"Already in the works. But Palmyra is a very busy port. During the critical window, there were probably half a dozen commercial departures, and probably several private vessels, as well."

"And they could be headed anywhere."

"Too true."

"Well, it's a big Empire," Gloria said, "and we can't do anything about it now if they've already gone off-world. Let's focus on what we *can* deal with. Did anyone in or near the hospital see anything that could help us?"

"The police are already working that angle," said Wong. "They'll be here soon to start interviewing hospital workers. And I'm going to bring in my own officers— at least, the ones you aren't taking with you to Sylvania—to begin our own investigation."

Gloria turned to Ms. Suharto. "How could they have gotten in and out without being noticed?"

Suharto shrugged. "It's hardly unusual to see a patient being carted down the corridor on a gurney," she said. "It would be unlikely to attract any notice. And Ms. Nash's room was at the far end of the Pollas Wing, near the doors—"

"The *what* wing?" Gloria demanded.

"The Pollas Wing. Named for one of our founders, Joseph Pollas. Why?"

Gloria sighed. "I suppose you have a Rankus Wing, too," she said.

"As a matter of fact, we do. Why, is that important?"

"It may be. Do the Pollas and Rankus families still have ties to the hospital?"

"Of course," said Suharto, as if that were obvious.

"Young Joe Pollas is on our Board," Dr. Hamdoon volunteered. "I played golf with him just last month, in fact. Surely, Ms. VanDeen, you aren't suggesting that *he* had anything to do with this?"

"For now, Dr. Hamdoon," Gloria said tersely, "no one on this planet is above suspicion. And that includes you and Ms. Suharto, and your entire staff. Mr. Wong and his people will want to talk with each one of you. And if anyone in this place is less than a hundred percent cooperative, I'll see to it that they spend the next ten years on a high-gravity prison world. Do you understand?"

They earnestly assured her that they did. Gloria stalked out of the hospital, feeling as angry and frustrated as she ever had in her life.

THAT NIGHT, GLORIA AND THE BUGS, THE Marshals, and Judge Otis Kershaw flew back to Sylvania. On their approach, she caught sight of the gleaming bulk of the Sylvania Orbital Station, already nearing completion. When it became operational, within a few weeks, the equation on Sylvania would change. The corporates could bring in their immense Extractors and ready them for the task ahead on the surface. On the plus side, communications between Sylvania and Palmyra would become much easier. From the Orbital Station, it would be possible to launch fast, unmanned, reusable messengers, and even faster one-way (and therefore more expensive) couriers.

Of course, improved communications would also mean that the media would arrive in strength. So far, the story of a voter registration drive on a backwater world—even if Gloria VanDeen was involved—had attracted scant attention. The difficulty and expense of getting news from Sylvania—not to mention the lack of first-class (or any) hotel facilities—had prevented the major media groups from sending their representatives to cover what was not a very exciting story to begin with. But with faster and cheaper communications possible, and the lure of a massacre, the media would soon be swarming all over Sylvania. Gloria dreaded the prospect. She would once again be thrown into the spotlight, and she was afraid that it would get in the way of her job. Worse, there was the possibility that some eager beaver might stumble onto the secret of Room 9 in the Emporium.

THE CRUISER LANDED AT GREENLODGE IN midmorning. Gloria led her charges through the muddy streets to the Emporium, where she planned to assign them rooms. Althea would undoubtedly complain about what that would do to the profit margin, but it couldn't be helped. Gloria intended to give Judge Kershaw her own room, the best in the house, and then double up with Althea.

News of their arrival got to the Emporium before they did, and Jill Clymer ran out to meet them. "Gloria!" she cried breathlessly. "Thank the Spirit you're back! How is Petra?"

"She's—" Gloria suddenly froze. Out of the corner of her eye, she noticed the tall, beefy figure of Mayor Kevin Grunfeld shambling toward the Emporium.

"That's Grunfeld!" she shouted to the Marshals and Bugs, pointing in his direction. "Get him!"

The khaki-clad Marshals and gray-clad Bugs sprang into action and flocked to Grunfeld like white corpuscles mobbing an intruding bacterium. They physically dragged an unresisting Grunfeld back to where Gloria was standing.

Grunfeld calmly stroked his mustache, smiled, and greeted her in a friendly manner. "G'mornin', Miz VanDeen," he said. "See ya brought some friends back with ya."

Gloria was so incensed, she struggled to find the words to express herself. The unexpected sight of Grunfeld walking around as free as a bird all but unhinged her.

"Gloria," Jill Clymer said, "I don't—"

"What the hell is this bastard doing here?" Gloria exploded. "Why don't you have him locked up?"

"For what?" Grunfeld asked innocently. He looked at the Bugs holding his arms. "Hey, boys, lighten up a bit, would ya?"

Gloria stepped closer to confront Grunfeld. He was a foot taller than she was, so she had to tilt her head back to look up into his eyes. "You know what for," she told him, trying to keep her voice under control. "You abducted, raped, and assaulted Petra. You almost killed her! And you *did* kill forty-nine people at Pizen Flats!"

"*Me?*" Grunfeld asked, seemingly amazed. "*I* did all them things? How ya figure that, Miz VanDeen?"

"Petra told us it was you, Grunfeld. You and your pukes." In fact, Gloria was all too aware that on that awful night, Petra had not actually mentioned Grunfeld's name. And now, her memory of those events was gone . . . and so was she! Gloria felt an unnamable rage boiling within her at the very sight of Grunfeld.

"Petra?" Grunfeld asked. "Ya mean that pretty little gal that got herself all busted up? Now why in hell would she say a damnfool thing like that? Ya think mebbe she got her brains scrambled?"

That was almost more than Gloria could take. If they had been alone, she would probably have killed him. As it was, her body trembled with the unspent energy of the Qatsima moves she yearned to unleash.

"Ms. VanDeen," Judge Kershaw interjected. He was no fool, and could see that Gloria was on the verge of an explosion. "If Mayor Grunfeld has any explanation he wishes to offer, perhaps we should hear it now. No charges have been filed against him as yet, and before I issue a warrant, I'd like to get a handle on this thing. Mayor Grunfeld, do you wish to make a statement?"

"Hiya, Judge," said Grunfeld. "Nice to see ya again. Thanks for rememberin' that I got some rights. Seems these Dexta folk forgot about that."

Kershaw was not impressed by Grunfeld's cheerful demeanor. "Your statement?" he said.

"Ain't got no statement, 'zackly. I guess ol' Myron Vigo will tend to the legal particulars. But I will say what happened. And I never raped nor assaulted nobody. Not that Petra gal and not nobody up to Pizen Flats. No sir."

"We have a witness who saw you abduct Petra at the Lodge!" Gloria insisted.

"Abduct? Hell, I didn't abduct her. I arrested her."

"*Arrested her?*" Gloria screeched. Jill Clymer put her hand on Gloria's shoulder.

"Sure," said Grunfeld placidly. "Arrested her on suspicion o' murderin' poor ol' Mr. Claude Rankus."

"*What?*"

Grunfeld looked at the judge. "Hey, how'm I gonna say what happened if ya let this gal keep interruptin' me?"

"Ms. VanDeen," Kershaw said, "please try to restrain yourself. Continue, if you would, Mayor Grunfeld."

"Thankee, Judge. Y'see, I got a call from the Thawleys that somethin' terrible had happened up at the Lodge, so I went up there to investigate. Found ol' Mr. Rankus sittin' in the easy chair up in his room, half his head blowed off. Had one o' them antique pistols o' his in his hand, like he done it to himself. But it looked kinda fishy to me—o' course, I ain't no trained investigator, like these here Marshals. So I said to myself, 'Kevin, you'd best just clamp a lid on this whole business until we can get us some Imperial Marshals here from Palmyra to look into this all legal and proper.' And that's what I done."

"And why did you arrest Ms. Nash?" asked Kershaw.

"On account o' she was a suspect. Wasn't hardly nobody up there at the time, just the Thawleys and that Petra gal, and a couple of them corporate reps—Miz Mitchell and Mr. Shoop. Didn't seem like they was suspects, but just to be sure, later on I locked both o' them in their cabins. Just like I locked up Miz Petra in one o' the cabins. Seemed like the best thing to do, seein' as how we ain't got no proper jail facilities down here in Greenlodge. Then, that night, Mr. Pollas went off to Palmyra to fetch the Marshals. But I guess he didn't need to do that, after all." Grunfeld offered the Marshals an ingratiating grin.

"I know about Pollas," Gloria said. The records they had obtained at the Palmyra Orbital Station showed that Pollas had arrived there in his yacht several hours before Gloria's Cruiser. They also showed that he had departed the Station barely an hour after Petra's disappearance from the hospital.

"Then," said Grunfeld, "I 'spect you'll be talkin' to him soon enough. He'll back up everything I've said."

"And," Kershaw continued, "I assume you will maintain that you had nothing to do with the massacre at Pizen Flats."

"O' course! Wasn't anywhere near Pizen Flats that night. To tell ya the truth, I was in Overhill that night, visitin' a little gal I know there. She'll tell ya I was there the whole damn night."

"Of that," said Kershaw, "I have no doubt." He turned toward Gloria. "Ms. VanDeen? Is there anything else?"

"Frezzo and Gnozdziewicz," she said. "They and two other men raped and assaulted Petra. They also . . . they also assaulted me later that night."

"You?" Grunfeld sounded astonished. "Y'mean someone assaulted *you*, Miz VanDeen? That don't hardly seem possible! You don't look like nobody so much as mussed a hair on your pretty little head!"

"They didn't beat me the way they did Petra. They just manhandled me and tied me up. They were going to rape me, but they didn't get the chance."

"You don't say? Well, knowin' the kind o' woman you are, you must've been real disappointed."

Jill clamped both hands on Gloria's shoulders and held her back.

"Where are they?" Gloria demanded.

"Hank and Noz? Ain't seen them around, the last couple o' days. Don't rightly know where they are. You fixin' to have them arrested for what you say they done to ya? Now, *that* might be real interestin'. Now, I don't know for a fact, but I 'spect ol' Hank and Noz would just say that you begged them to fuck ya, like ya been fuckin' half the men in the Territory. Runnin' 'round naked, fuckin' like a mink . . . you got yourself quite a reputation, Miz VanDeen. Wonder what a jury would say about this here 'rape' ya say almost happened to ya? Might be real interestin'. Anyway, I ain't seen Hank and Noz."

"Under the circumstances," Kershaw said quickly, before Gloria could respond, "I don't believe I see sufficient evidence to justify issuing a warrant for Mayor Grunfeld's arrest at this time. Release him, if you would, gentlemen. However," he added with a stern gaze directed at Grunfeld, "the investigation of the incidents here has just begun. Mayor Grunfeld, you are instructed not to attempt to leave this jurisdiction without first obtaining the consent of this court—meaning me. Ms. VanDeen? Gentlemen? I suggest that we get settled in our rooms and meet in half an hour. Perhaps we can begin to sort this out."

"Thankee, Judge," said a grinning Grunfeld. "Pleasure havin' ya back in town."

• • •

THAT AFTERNOON, GLORIA RETURNED TO THE Lodge in the company of Judge Kershaw, the two Marshals, and Greg Remchuk, commander of the Internal Security detachment. Myron Vigo met them at the door and ushered them into the dining room, where Joe Pollas, Sidney Taplin, Rahim Ogunbayo, Thomas Shoop, and Maddie Mitchell were already sitting around the big table. There was no sign of the Thawleys.

Vigo was more subdued and less witty than usual as he made the appropriate introductions and bade everyone to take a seat. "Ms. VanDeen," he said, "before we get started, I feel that I should inform you that we may be filing charges against you and Mr. Ellison for your actions several nights ago."

After a day of unpleasant surprises, Gloria barely even reacted to this one. But Judge Kershaw asked what charges Vigo intended to file.

"Unlawful entry and felonious assault against poor Mrs. Thawley, for starters. We may have more to come," Vigo replied.

"And just where is poor Mrs. Thawley?" Gloria asked.

"She and her husband are on medical leave," Vigo explained. "Mr. Pollas took them to Palmyra that same night."

Gloria looked at Pollas, who returned her level gaze. "Is that true?" she asked.

"It is. Mrs. Thawley needed medical attention which she could not receive on Sylvania. Her husband naturally accompanied her. In addition, it was necessary to transport Mr. Rankus's body back home for cremation and interment in the family crypt."

Kershaw's bushy eyebrows shot upward. "Cremation? Are you aware, Mr. Pollas, that your actions may constitute tampering with evidence in a capital case?"

"Well, we couldn't just *leave* him here, you know!"

"As for the cremation," Vigo quickly added, "that

was the wish of his family. A complete postmortem was conducted beforehand, not that there was any doubt about the cause of death. Before removing the body, we carefully imaged the scene. The pistol is still here, and you are welcome to it."

"Mr. Pollas," the judge said, "while you were on Palmyra, why did you not report the death of Mr. Rankus to the proper authorities?"

"I did. I met with my family attorney, Bill Bullock—you know him, Judge. I gave him a complete statement. He said that he would bring the matter to the attention of Judge Hasbrouk the following day, and I assume that he did. Apparently Judge Hasbrouk didn't feel it was necessary to inform you."

"He might at least have informed the Imperial Marshal's office," said Marshal Boris Morales.

"Maybe you left Palmyra before he did," Vigo suggested.

"Speaking of leaving Palmyra," Gloria said, "you left just a few hours before we did, Mr. Pollas. But I didn't see your yacht in the harbor."

"I seldom use the harbor, Ms. VanDeen. I generally use the lake. It's there now."

Gloria looked at Morales and Remchuk. "Get people down there as soon as you can. I want that yacht examined microscopically."

"For what, if I might inquire?" asked Vigo.

"For any evidence that Petra Nash was aboard it. She was kidnapped from the hospital on Palmyra an hour before Mr. Pollas's departure." Gloria stared at Vigo and waited for him to respond. Vigo appeared mildly surprised and concerned.

"Kidnapped, you say? I'm very sorry to hear that, Ms. VanDeen. All the more so because I was hoping we could get a definitive statement from her about what transpired here. But surely you aren't suggesting that Mr. Pollas had anything to do with her abduction."

"She's not suggesting any such thing," Kershaw quickly assured him.

"The hell I'm not!" Gloria had been trying to keep a rein on her temper ever since her arrival at the Lodge, but Vigo's bland pronouncements were pushing her close to her limit.

"The fact is," Marshal Morales put in, "we would want to examine every vessel that left Palmyra in the hours following the disappearance of Ms. Nash. Since your vessel qualifies, Mr. Pollas, and since it is close at hand, we intend to examine it just as soon as Judge Kershaw issues the warrant."

"Which I will as soon as we are finished here," Kershaw said. "But first, I'd like to return to the events of the night in question. I suppose the Thawleys gave you their version of events, Mr. Vigo. Would you be good enough to share that with us?"

"Certainly. As instructed by Mayor Grunfeld, they locked Mr. Shoop and Ms. Mitchell in their cabins—"

"They forcibly dragged me into mine!" Maddie Mitchell interjected.

"And I was already in mine, asleep," said Shoop. "I didn't even know anything was happening."

"Where were Lund and Norfleet?" Gloria asked.

"They apparently spent the day down on the lake, sailing," said Vigo. "They've grown quite fond of it, I gather. Afterward, I understand that they had dinner in Overhill and spent the night there with . . . uh . . . friends."

"We'll want to talk to them, as well," said Morales.

"Certainly," said Vigo. "I believe they are down on the lake again today. Of course, I don't represent them, but I'll tell them."

"If we could get back to the Thawleys . . ." Kershaw prodded.

"Yes," said Vigo. "They stated to me that at about eight o'clock that evening, Ms. VanDeen and a young man later identified as Palmer Ellison, a Dexta employee, broke in the front door—"

"It was already open!"

"Ms. VanDeen, if you please!"

"Sorry, Judge."

"—burst in the front door, aimed plasma pistols at Mr. and Mrs. Thawley, and verbally and physically abused them. Ms. VanDeen then broke Mrs. Thawley's arm."

"I don't suppose she happened to mention the four men who were already here. The men who beat and raped Petra."

"No, Ms. VanDeen, they didn't," Vigo said. "However, Mr. and Mrs. Thawley had been upstairs in the private quarters ... uh ... cleaning up some of the mess. If the four men you allege assaulted Ms. Nash were here, the Thawleys did not see or hear them."

"What happened next, Mr. Vigo?" Kershaw asked.

"After Ms. VanDeen attacked Mrs. Thawley, she and her husband went down to Overhill to seek medical attention. They remained there until departing on Mr. Pollas's yacht later that evening."

Kershaw turned to Shoop and Mitchell. "Did either of you hear the four men in question?"

They shook their heads.

"So, the only remaining witness who actually saw them is you, Ms. VanDeen."

"And Petra!"

"And Ms. Nash, of course. Unfortunately, her testimony is not available at the moment."

"Spirit!" Gloria cried in exasperation. "You can't be telling me that you doubt their existence. They beat Petra half to death!"

"I assure you, Ms. VanDeen," Kershaw said calmly, "I am well aware of that fact. Clearly, Ms. Nash was criminally assaulted. As you know, I've already issued warrants for Frezzo and Gnozdziewicz and the two unknown men. However, unless someone here has anything new to volunteer, it seems to me that we have taken this investigation as far as it will go, for now. No? Very well, then. Marshal Morales, Mr. Remchuk, and their people will be meeting with each of you individually in the days to come. I expect each of you to make yourselves available, and not to leave the planet without first informing me. I think that's all for today. Ms. VanDeen? Gentlemen?"

Judge Kershaw got to his feet and the others followed. Gloria paused to look at Vigo.

"Nicely done, Mr. Vigo," she said. "But forty-nine people died at Pizen Flats that night. And Petra knew it was going to happen, because she heard about it right here in the Lodge."

"I wish you the best of luck in your investigation of that tragedy, Ms. VanDeen," Vigo said smoothly. "It is my earnest hope that you will find the parties responsible for the—"

"Put a cork in it, Vigo!" Gloria snarled. "I already *know* who was responsible. And I'm going to prove it!"

THAT EVENING, WHEN SHE RETURNED TO HER office in the Emporium, Gloria found a folded piece of paper on her desk. On it, printed in block letters, was a single sentence:

"IF YOU WANT HER BACK, STAY OUT OF THE WAY!"

chapter 21

GLORIA SAT ALONE IN HER TENT, SPOONING
cold beans out of a can and staring at the driving rain
outside. A beautiful day had suddenly turned miserable
as soon as she arrived at the falls—an apt metaphor, she
thought, for her entire mission to Sylvania.

Nearly three weeks had passed since the massacre
and Petra's kidnapping. By precise calculation, exactly
zero progress had been made since then toward solving
either crime. Petra could be anywhere in the Empire—
although Gloria was convinced that she was right here
on Sylvania—and the same could be said for the killers.

The two Marshals and eight Bugs had made a dili-
gent effort to investigate everything that had happened,
but every result so far had been negative—in one case, a
little too negative. The search of the Pollas yacht had
turned up no trace, macro- or microscopic, of Petra, no
hairs or blood or sweat or miniscule fragments of her
DNA. Strangely, the search had also turned up no evidence that the Thawleys—or even Joe Pollas himself—
had ever been on the yacht. Indeed, there was no

evidence that any living being had ever been aboard the vessel.

Boris Morales explained to Gloria that there existed a class of chemical oxidants that were wonderfully efficient at destroying every organic molecule they encountered. Some of the oxidants also had the useful property of breaking down to their basic components, which were nothing more sinister than atoms of hydrogen, oxygen, and nitrogen. Dispersing such a substance within a confined area, such as the interior of a space vessel, would quickly and efficiently destroy literally everything that was not made out of metal, plastic, stone, or composite.

Someone had clearly used some such substance in the Pollas yacht. That seemed highly suspicious to Gloria and Morales, but there was, Pollas maintained, a perfectly innocent explanation. The corpse of Claude Rankus, it seemed, had been not only messy, but smelly. Upon his return to Sylvania, Pollas, in the interests of sanitation and good scents, had set off an oxidant dispersal packet inside his yacht. Of course, it never occurred to him that in the process, he might be destroying evidence.

Judge Kershaw had agreed with Gloria that Pollas had been attempting to cover his tracks. However, he disagreed with her that this somehow constituted incriminating evidence, in and of itself. "His explanation is as phony as a three-crown note," Kershaw said, "but it's valid. Absent additional evidence, there's nothing that can be done with what you have. It's the dog that didn't bark. It may be curious that the dog didn't bark, but not barking is not a crime." Having said that, Judge Kershaw then went fishing.

Pollas also managed to shed no light on the identity of the third person, heard but not seen by Maddie Mitchell, early that afternoon in the Lodge. Maddie had seen Pollas and Taplin, and was certain she heard a third person, but Pollas maintained that no one else had been there at the time. Probably, he suggested, the mysterious third person was simply Mr. Thawley. Maddie was certain that it had not been either one of the Thawleys, but the voice had been too distant and muffled for her to offer any positive identification.

Thomas Shoop had been no help at all. He had returned to the Lodge that morning in a state of exhaustion after spending the night at the falls with Gloria. He fell asleep around noon and didn't wake up until that evening, when the rescue team from the Emporium arrived and unlocked his door.

If events at the Lodge remained murky, the details of the massacre were all but impenetrable. Plasma bolts left no identifying physical traces; the killings at Pizen Flats could have been accomplished by one or many plasma pistols or rifles. They could even have been done by plasma drills mounted on skimmers. That, in fact, was the favored explanation being pushed by the Lodge and Grunfeld.

It was obvious, they maintained, that the massacre had been carried out by highboys, still angry over having been beaten up by the riverrats the previous day. The highboys felt threatened by the refiling of the Pizen Flats claims. Turning one claim into forty might overturn the majority of claims, now held by the highboys, and cost them the money they expected to make from Eminent Domain payments. The massacre at Pizen Flats was not only retaliation, but a warning to every other riverrat camp.

If it had been a warning, it had proved to be an effective one. The other camps along the river had been considering following the Pizen Flats example and refiling their claims; after the massacre, none did. Whether it was highboys or Grunfeld or (as some conspiracy theorists maintained) a return to hostilities by the long-since-defeated Ch'gnth, the killers remained at large. As long as they did, the other riverrats had no desire to provoke another massacre.

The Bugs and Marshals had investigated the possibility that the highboys were the culprits, but found no evidence that pointed one way or another. The highboys who had been involved in the brawl at Pizen Flats all had mutually supporting alibis for their whereabouts the night of the massacre.

The Bugs had also conducted a thorough, if not exhaustive, search of Overhill. Without specific evidence, Judge Kershaw refused to issue search warrants that would have permitted the Bugs to make a clean sweep. Nevertheless, they established a presence in Overhill, kept a watch, and made themselves unpopular, but they turned up no evidence or witnesses who could shed any light on Petra's whereabouts. On both the night of the massacre and the night of Pollas's return, no one in Overhill had seen or heard anything.

Gloria finished her beans and restrained an urge to toss the empty can out into the rain. Instead, she dutifully packed it away in her kit bag. Might as well respect the environment for as long as it lasted.

It wasn't likely to last much longer. The Orbital Station, though construction was not yet complete, was finally operational. Gloria had learned from Shoop that the first of Excelsior's immense Extractors was due to arrive shortly.

Excelsior had already established a presence on the ground. The first shipment of a thousand people had arrived two weeks earlier. They quickly set up a tent city on the outskirts of Greenlodge. Soon thereafter, strangers began filing into the Emporium to register as voters. The total count was over forty-five hundred, and the target figure of five thousand was within easy reach. Soon, Charles would be able to appoint an Imperial Governor and legally incorporate the Territory of Sylvania. Well, Gloria reflected, at least Charles couldn't complain about the job she had done getting the voters registered. If nothing else, that one aspect of her mission to Sylvania had gone swimmingly.

But the *real* mission had suddenly run into problems. Sam Roosa, looking tired and worried, had told her the previous night that they were beginning to detect evidence of a buildup of heat at the bottom of the shaft. Somewhere far beneath the surface of the planet, the transfer of energy from the plasma recharger was being blocked. The problem might be temporary, or it might become worse—there was no way to know. All they could do was keep pumping energy into the Fergusite layer and wait to see what happened.

If the sabotage operation failed, the only way to block the corporates' mining operations would be to prevent them from getting 60 percent of the proxies in the Eminent Domain hearings. But without the refiling of claims by the riverrats, that seemed an impossible goal. Shoop and Mitchell had already agreed that it would be pointless to pool the proxies of Prizm and Imperium without a substantial increase in the number of claims by the riverrats.

Gloria knew that she could have done more. She could have visited the camps and rallied the riverrats—as Ted Oberlin would have done. She could have promised protection—even if the Bugs and Marshals weren't numerous enough to provide it—and encouraged them to reorganize their companies and refile their claims. If enough of them did, it might still be possible to keep Excelsior and Servitor from amassing 60 percent of the proxies.

But Gloria had done nothing. She had stayed out of the way.

Guilt gnawed at her. Guilt over her role in determining the fate of this special and spectacular valley. Guilt over what had happened to Petra . . . and what might yet happen to her.

Was saving this valley worth sacrificing Petra's life?

Was saving Petra's life worth sacrificing this valley?

And, of course, there was still the minor matter of the future of the Empire . . .

• • •

ASIDE FROM EVERYTHING ELSE, GLORIA HAD very personal demons with which to wrestle. Dr. Hamdoon had said that she was in denial, but Gloria knew that she was denying nothing. She was all too aware of what had happened . . . and what had *almost* happened. The memory of it clawed at her mind with razor-sharp talons.

Frezzo, Gnozdziewicz, and the two unknown men had not been seen. Conceivably, they had found a way to get off-world, possibly with Pollas on that same night. Yet Gloria was convinced that they were still on Sylvania, just as she was certain that Petra was there. Possibly they were even the ones who were holding her hostage; find them, find her. Gloria sometimes found herself fantasizing about what she would do to them if she caught them . . . *when* she caught them.

Rape was something that had never worried her. Growing up rich and privileged at Court, it had never really been a consideration. During her marriage to Charles, there had usually been security guards close at hand. When they were away from Court, Charles himself had been all the protection she needed; like everyone in the line of succession, he had been trained from an early age in the most sophisticated and deadly forms of martial arts. After she left him, she took up Qatsima and quickly became an expert in that graceful but violent discipline.

But even Qatsima had been useless against four large, powerful, and thoroughly depraved brutes. They had seized her without difficulty, leaving her feeling helpless, humiliated, and stupid. Gloria VanDeen, the sexiest woman in the Empire, nearly hoist on her own petard! Or maybe on Frezzo and Gnozdziewicz's petards—she wasn't sure exactly what a petard was. Sex had always been her strong suit, her trump card, useful on every occasion, in every situation. She had become, she realized, smug and arrogant about it, so proud of herself that she couldn't or wouldn't see the inevitable fall that awaited her.

Sometimes she wondered if she would ever feel the same about sex. She had gone without it since that awful night, although Slim Jim Zuni and even Althea had made some thinly veiled advances. She knew that she was no candidate for a convent; yet, for the first time, she found that she associated sex and guilt. In the age of Spiritism, that was not only unusual, but—for Gloria—almost inconceivable.

At some level, she understood that if she was ever to enjoy sex again, the way it was meant to be enjoyed, she would have to do something about the guilt. But the guilt would never go away if anything happened to Petra.

If? Something had *already* happened to her, something infinitely more horrible than anything Gloria had experienced. She couldn't imagine what it had been like for her. It would be a blessing from the Spirit if Petra's memory of that night never returned; but Gloria's memory of it never left her. When she remembered the sight of Petra, curled up on that bloodstained sheet, Gloria felt physically ill.

Gloria ran her hands through her damp hair. At times, she felt like yanking it out by the roots. At other times, she just wanted to roll up into a ball and cry. Tonight, alone in the rain, far from everyone, she began to cry.

No one but Abel heard her.

THE NEXT MORNING, FEELING DRAINED AND defeated, Gloria headed back to town through another storm. The rainy season was beginning on Sylvania's only continent, and the landscape was rapidly turning to thick, gooey mud. When she came to the point of land at Pizen Flats, Gloria veered the skimmer all the way to the opposite side of the river. She didn't ever want to see the place again.

Approaching Greenlodge, she saw that two freighters had arrived overnight. More of Excelsior's "voters," she figured. Well, they would have a jolly time pitching their tents in the gumbo.

By the time she parked outside the Emporium, the rain was coming down in sheets. In her optimism the previous day, she had neglected even to pack a jacket. Just getting from her skimmer to the front door of the Emporium left her soaked to the skin.

Inside, she found a small, rather unruly mob waiting for her in the anteroom. The media had arrived on Sylvania.

They aimed their imagers at her and shouted questions. Gloria stood passively inside the front door, taking in the scene while the media reps focused on her. She was wearing only a thin white tee shirt and brief, hip-hugging shorts, now drenched, plastered to her skin, and utterly transparent. Gloria normally enjoyed parading her body before the media, but in light of recent events, she could take no pleasure in it on this day.

"Ms. VanDeen! Is it true that you not only run this bordello, but also work in it as a prostitute?"

"Ms. VanDeen! Is it true that you were raped by the gang that committed the massacre?"

"Ms. VanDeen! Why is Dexta operating a whore-house?"

"Ms. VanDeen! Can we get rooms here? It's the only half-decent place to stay on the whole goddamn planet!"

Ms. VanDeen suppressed a sigh. Trust the media to concentrate on the essentials.

She held up her hands for a few moments until the media reps settled down. "Welcome to Sylvania," she said, managing a smile. "I'm not going to take your questions now, but we'll set up a briefing for you tomorrow. As for rooms—you're on your own, folks. We don't have enough to go around, so you'll have to check the boardinghouses or pitch your own tents. Furthermore, although you are welcome to sample whatever the Emporium has to offer, you will not be permitted to go inside with your imaging equipment. In fact, you'll be searched, and anyone caught violating this rule will be permanently banned from the Emporium. People come here to relax and enjoy themselves, and I am not going to subject them to the glare of the media. Our customers are entitled to their privacy, and it *will* be respected! That's all I have for you now."

With that, Gloria pushed her way through the crowd in the anteroom amid a cacophony of complaints, questions, and more complaints. When the media reps attempted to follow her into the main room, Ernie the Bouncer stood in their way, and no one was inclined to dispute his authority.

Inside, Gloria found another surprise awaiting her. Arkady Volkonski, OSI's Coordinator for Internal Security, had arrived, bringing six more Bugs with him. A further surprise was the presence of Dina Westerbrook, deputy to OSI Administrator Grant Enright.

"Mingus thought you could use a little help," Volkonski explained. "Jillian has already brought us up to speed on where things stand."

"Did she mention that we don't have anywhere to put you?"

Volkonski, a dark, glowering Russian, known for his single, unpunctuated eyebrow and his ingrained sense of irony, shrugged expressively. "No problem," he said. "We brought our own tents. Internal Security is prepared for anything."

"In that case, once you get settled, we'll discuss assignments. Welcome to Sylvania, Arkady. And you, too, Dina. Are you here as den mother for Arkady and his juvenile delinquents?"

"More or less," Dina said. "But we need to talk. Maybe this evening?"

"Fine, we'll have dinner. Right now, I just want to get a hot shower and some dry clothing. Arkady? I'll see you in half an hour, okay?"

"Anywhere, anytime."

• • •

THAT EVENING, GLORIA MET DINA FOR DINNER in a small, semiprivate room of the Emporium, just off the main room. Gloria felt uncharacteristically shabby in her jeans and old sweatshirt when she saw Dina, looking ethereally beautiful in a thin, nearly transparent, pale blue dress, which she had fastened only at the waist. Although she was a Dexta Tiger, Dina's choice in apparel was normally more subdued; but tonight, her small breasts and pink, erect nipples were almost totally exposed, and her sparse nether hair flashed in and out of view as she walked to the table and sat down to join Gloria.

"You're looking great, Dina," Gloria observed. "Field duty must agree with you. That's sort of a new look for you, isn't it?"

"No," Dina said with a little laugh, "an old one."

"Oh?"

"Twenty-five years ago," Dina said, "I was Gloria VanDeen before there *was* a Gloria VanDeen."

"I didn't realize I was infringing on your copyright," Gloria said, amused.

"Oh, it's not mine. I think it goes back to Cleopatra or Helen of Troy or someone. You and I are just the latest in a long, long line."

Gloria poured them some wine, picked up her glass, and proposed a toast. "Here's to our distinguished forbears, then. Spirit bless 'em."

After they had ordered dinner, Gloria spent a few moments staring at Dina. She was at least fifty, but antigerontologicals made her look no more than a mature, worldly thirty. She had delicately sculpted Nordic features, very fine blond hair, and wintry, blue-gray eyes. Gloria had always thought Dina looked a little sad—haunted, perhaps—but that night she seemed to have rekindled some forgotten inner flame.

"So," Gloria said, "you were me before I was?"

"I was the up-and-coming Tiger of my era," Dina

affirmed. "I was screwing all the best men in all the best nightclubs and flouncing around in the nude when you were still just a twinkle in the eye of some gene-twister. I've got the same genetic advantages that you do, Gloria. The S-complex, I think they call it in the business."

"I didn't realize you knew about me."

"I can tell. Takes one to know one, you might say."

"You seem to have learned to control it," Gloria pointed out. "Better than I do, at least."

"Experience helps, of course," Dina conceded. "But I wouldn't worry about it, Gloria. As far as I can see, you're doing just fine."

Gloria took a sip of wine and looked down at the tablecloth. "Maybe you haven't caught up on current events, then," she said.

"No," Dina said, "I heard. They tried to rape you. And you are busy castigating yourself because you think your sex appeal somehow constituted an invitation. I did the same after it happened to me. One of the reasons Mingus sent me here was to offer you some sage advice, but I don't really think you need it. You know as well as I do that rape is not about sex, it's about violence and domination. It had nothing to do with how sexy you are. Those thugs raped Petra, they tried to rape you, and they'd have raped their own grandmothers if they thought the situation called for it."

"I suppose you're right."

"You know I am. Don't let this spoil sex for you, Gloria, or screw up your life. Your body has its own needs that have nothing to do with what your brain might want. Thanks to that old S-complex, you and I need, want, and revel in sex. That's a fact that we both have to live with. I just hope that you're not going to be as big an idiot as I was and spend years blaming yourself for something you couldn't possibly have controlled."

Gloria smiled self-consciously. "Is it all right if I spend a few weeks being an idiot?"

"Mandatory, in fact," Dina told her. "But no more

than that. I mean it, Gloria. You know what the Spirit said. Do not deny yourself Joy—it's the wellspring of happiness."

Gloria looked at her. "Is that what happened to you?" she asked. Gloria had never inquired, but she was aware that something had happened to Dina, years earlier—something that had derailed her Dexta career. Before Gloria tapped her for OSI and had her promoted, Dina had been a Thirteen for twenty years, and seemed to have a reputation within Dexta as damaged goods.

Dina shook her head. "No, not exactly. The rape was part of it, I suppose. But what mainly screwed up my life was something else entirely. You see, Gloria, I wasn't un-lucky enough to marry a future Emperor, the way you did. What I did was much, much worse. I had an affair with Norman Mingus."

"Ah," said Gloria.

"Ah," Dina agreed.

Gloria waited. "Well?" she said, finally.

Dina closed her eyes for a moment and smiled, as if recalling a pleasant dream. "It was wonderful for a while," she said. "Oh, we tried to be discreet, but people at Dexta knew. They always do, somehow. Norman was between wives at the time, and I thought I had a good chance to fill that position. But he thought I had a bright future at Dexta, and didn't want to compromise my use-fulness. Dexta always comes first with him, you know."

Gloria nodded. "I know," she said.

"And then," Dina said, sighing audibly, "he sent me on a secret mission. Something like the one he's sent you on, I suppose. He didn't tell me what you're really doing here, Gloria, and I'm not going to tell you about my own mission. Just that it was very important and very sensi-tive. I was twenty-nine years old, and suddenly the fu-ture of the Empire was in my hands—or so it seemed at the time. I suppose it wasn't, really—I mean, it seems to have survived, despite the fact that I made a mess of everything. You see, Gloria, I failed. Failed the Empire, failed Dexta, failed Norman. Worst of all, I failed my-self." She looked Gloria in the eye. "And that is why Norman sent me here. To tell you that you mustn't fail the way I did, Gloria. You *mustn't*!"

"I see," Gloria said.

"No, you don't."

"I don't?"

Dina shook her head. "Gloria, failure happens to everyone, sooner or later. My mistake wasn't failing—it was the *way* I failed. The reason I failed."

"And what was that?"

"I lost faith in Dina Westerbrook. I got scared. Overwhelmed by the responsibility. The great big Em-pire depends on little old *me*? I let it get to me, Gloria, and once that happened, I was lost. Every time some lit-tle thing went wrong, it seemed like a catastrophe. Every time something big went wrong, it felt like Ar-mageddon. And so the failures just kept snowballing, getting bigger and bigger until finally, the failure was complete. I failed because I came to believe that it was no longer possible for me *not* to fail. Do you understand what I'm saying?"

"I . . . I think so."

"You've had some failures lately, Gloria. Big ones."

"Whoppers."

"The massacre. Petra. The assault. Any one of those things would be enough to knock you back on your heels. All three together would probably have destroyed any normal person. But Gloria—you *aren't* a normal person! You can't afford the luxury of reacting like a nor-mal person. I lost faith in Dina Westerbrook, but you *can't* lose faith in Gloria VanDeen! Yes, I know—in the middle of the night, when you're all alone, you're still just a frightened little girl. But that little girl has grown up to be Gloria VanDeen, and now you've got to *be* her! The Gloria VanDeen that makes strong men tremble and awes the Empire with her beauty, strength, and courage. You created that Gloria VanDeen, and you can't let anything that happened prevent you from being her. *Don't fail, Gloria. Don't let yourself fail!*"

Dina's words struck Gloria with a force that was almost physical. She realized suddenly that ever since the awful night when everything had gone wrong, she had been waiting for the next disaster to strike. She expected things to get worse, and so they had. Petra had been kidnapped. Grunfeld and the barons of the Lodge had gotten off the hook. The rapists and murderers had gotten away. Sylvania was about to be strip-mined, and the Empire was going to be held together by dangerous, low-grade Fergusite. And she had done *nothing*! Failure begat failure and still more failure, and she had watched it all happening, feeling too small and helpless to do anything about it.

Dina reached across the table and squeezed her hand. "I know exactly how you feel," she said. "But you can't let it throw you, the way it did me. I may have been the first Gloria VanDeen, but I don't want you to become the next Dina Westerbrook."

Gloria looked at her and managed a smile. "I don't know," she said. "The Dina Westerbrook I see tonight seems to be doing pretty well."

"After a brief twenty-year time-out."

"What happened, Dina? To you, I mean?"

Dina hesitated, and for a moment a wistful expression came over her. "I told you that I failed myself. I mean that literally. After I screwed up my secret mission, I gave myself a failing grade—in life. I figured that I was worthless, and spent years proving myself right. Norman ended our relationship, not because I botched my mission, but because he couldn't stand being around me, the way I was. He can't abide losers, you know. He's been a winner all his life, and he didn't have the time or inclination to hold my hand and nurse me back to health."

"Why did you stay in Dexta all these years?" Gloria

wondered aloud. "It must have been tremendously painful for you."

"It was—and that was just what I deserved. I wanted to make sure that I was punished for all my failures. But there was something else. I think I was hoping for a second chance—from Norman or Dexta or just life, I don't know. And finally, Gloria, you gave it to me. Why did you ask me to join OSI?"

"I knew you a little from Sector 8," Gloria replied, "and I thought you were dependable and a good worker. And . . . don't take this wrong, but I think I pitied you. I didn't know your story, but I knew you were a Tiger who had made a mistake somewhere along the way. And I knew that the same thing could happen to me someday. I suppose I thought that if I could help you, maybe someday someone would do the same for me. I just didn't expect the day to come so soon, or for the someone to be you."

"Partly me, partly Norman," Dina said. "When he got your courier, he asked me to come up to his office. It was the first time I had been alone with him in twenty years. He told me he needed my help. Imagine how I felt when I heard that! And then he explained that things were going badly for you, and asked me to come here and talk to you. He thought I might be the one person who could get you back on track."

Gloria smiled. "Wise man, that Norman Mingus."

Dina returned the smile. "And so, here I am. I hope I've done some good."

"More than you know."

"I'm glad. So stop feeling sorry for yourself, kid. Let us see the *real* Gloria VanDeen—every bit of her! The Empire just can't afford to have a Gloria VanDeen who mopes around in sloppy old sweatshirts."

"You're right." Gloria laughed, and promptly removed the offending garment, leaving her in nothing but her low-slung jeans. She got to her feet and took Dina by the hand.

"Come on," she said. "I want to introduce you to some people here. But I warn you, Althea will want you to work the rooms."

"I may just take her up on that. I've got a lot of catching up to do."

chapter 22

GLORIA SPENT THE NIGHT WITH SLIM JIM ZUNI.
She fixed some jigli tea and consumed enough of the potent aphrodisiac to overwhelm any lingering reserva-
tions she might have had concerning sex. Slim Jim
needed two cups of the tea just to keep up with her, and
by the time they finally drifted off to sleep, he was exhausted and she was feeling like herself again.

Slim Jim was a curious man, in some ways. He was a
marvelous lover, and yet he played at love in much the
same way he played cards. He held his hand close to his
vest and didn't reveal much of himself, retreating behind his poker face whenever Gloria tried for something
more than physical intimacy. She didn't really mind, but
she wondered about him.

The next morning she met with the media for the
promised briefing. Still tingling with the jigli high and
determined to follow Dina's advice, she let the Empire
see the Gloria VanDeen they expected to see—all of
her. She wore only a sheer white camisole top, unlaced
to fully reveal her breasts, and a smart-fabric band skirt,

set for maximum transparency and less than minimum coverage. It rode so low on her hips that her blond pubic thatch was partially exposed.

If yesterday's near nudity before the media had been inadvertent and unwanted, today's was calculated and invigorating. She wanted everyone to see—and to convince herself, in the bargain—that she was unintimidated by the assault on her, and that sex was and would continue to be a vital element in the complete VanDeen package. She had succeeded at Dexta and on Mynjhino by playing to her strengths, not by denying what she was, and she was now more determined than ever to succeed on Sylvania the same way. Gloria stood before the media reps and smiled as they ogled her with eyes and imagers, drawing strength and energy from their attention.

Her briefing was brisk and businesslike. She brought the media reps up to date on the voter registration drive and estimated that the five thousand figure should be reached within the next week or two. Concerning the massacre at Pizen Flats, she would say only that the incident was under active investigation by both Dexta and the Imperial Marshals and, therefore, she could make no comment on it. For the same reason, she refused comment on reports of the assault and kidnapping of a Dexta official.

When asked directly about the assault on her, she did make a comment. "Yes," she said, "it's true. I was assaulted by four men, two of whom were then employed by the Mayor of Greenlodge. I don't know the identity of the other two. All four men have since disappeared, although I have reason to believe that they are still on Sylvania. They attempted to rape me, but were prevented by the timely arrival of my friends from the Emporium. If they are listening, I'd like to invite them to take another shot at me. I would welcome the opportunity to meet them again."

"Ms. VanDeen," said a shocked media rep, "let me

get this straight. Are you saying that you *want* them to rape you?"

"No, I'm saying that I want them to *try*. Of course, being the cowards that they are, I doubt that they'll have the balls to make the attempt. Nevertheless, they know where to find me if they're game. That's all I have for you today. Thanks, and check with Jillian Clymer about the schedule for future briefings."

LATER THAT DAY, GLORIA SNEAKED OUT A SIDE door of the Emporium and walked to City Hall through a light rain. The boomers, tired of waiting for municipal government to do something, had taken it upon themselves to lay out wooden plank boardwalks around town, so she made it to City Hall without having to tramp through the ubiquitous mud. She entered the building and encountered Grunfeld's three remaining pukes in the hallway—Karl Cleveland, Luther Dominguez, and Anselmo Maharaj. "Hi, boys," she said cheerily as she let herself into Grunfeld's office.

Grunfeld was in his chair, feet propped up on his desk, apparently snoozing. Gloria cleared her throat and said, "We have to talk, Grunfeld."

The Mayor opened his eyes, noticed Gloria, then took his feet down and stared at her. The rain had left her minimal garments entirely transparent, and Grunfeld's gaze fixed on her fully revealed crotch. Gloria let him look.

"You want it, don't you, Kevin?" Gloria said. "A shame you missed your chance that night at the Lodge. What did Hank and Noz tell you about me?"

Grunfeld started to say something, but caught himself. He met her eyes and gave her a wary smile. "Didn't say nothin' that *I* heard, Miz Gloria. Didn't see 'em no more. You must think I'm real stupid."

"Not as stupid as they are. In fact, I think you're probably smart enough to see that time is running out. In about two weeks, this territory will be incorporated, and the new Imperial Governor will have the authority to pull the plug on your little kingdom. And, of course, by then the big shots up at the Lodge will probably have sold you out, anyway. You've served your purpose, Kevin, and now you're becoming an embarrassment. The media are here, you know."

"Yeah," he said. "They been comin' 'round here all day, askin' for interviews. Ain't made up my mind about that, yet. Mebbe I could use a little good publicity."

Gloria gave a short, sharp laugh. "Good publicity? Kevin, I don't quite know how to tell you this, but they'll make you look even worse than you really are. That would be a stretch, I know, but they're capable of it. From one end of the Empire to the other, you'll be known as a stupid, brutal, small-town tyrant. They'll ask you questions you don't want to answer, they'll try to embarrass you, and they'll make you lose your temper. You'll probably end up slugging one of them, which is just what they want. That'll look great on the news vids."

Grunfeld thought about that for a moment. "Don't suppose I could arrest them, could I?"

"What am I, Kevin? Your new media advisor? I'm on the other side, remember?"

"Ain't likely I'd forget that," he said.

"But that doesn't mean we have to be enemies all the time," Gloria told him. "It doesn't mean that you can't fuck me. You can, you know. All you want. You won't even have to rape me. I'll give you the best fuck of your life, Kevin, the best fuck in the Empire. And you know I can do it."

Slowly, Gloria removed the camisole and tossed it onto a chair. Then she hooked her thumbs in the band skirt and pulled it still lower until, finally, she stepped out of it and dropped it on the chair.

Grunfeld appeared to have frozen in place, but Gloria noticed tiny beads of perspiration breaking out on his forehead. He breathed hard, then said, "You must think I'm some kinda complete idiot. Last time I stuck somethin' in there, you busted it!"

"Not this time, Kevin. This time, I promise you, we'll both enjoy it."

Grunfeld gave her a wolfish smile. "Miz Gloria," he said, "I could sit here all day watchin' ya. I really could. That's gotta be the best pussy in the Empire, and you gotta be the best fuck in the galaxy."

"It is, and I am," she said.

"So whaddya want from me?" Grunfeld demanded.

"Petra," Gloria said.

"Petra? That cute little bitch what got herself kidnapped?"

"That's right, Kevin." Gloria looked Grunfeld in the eye. "I get Petra back, safe and unharmed, and you get me. You can have me for a full week, and I'll do anything and everything you want. I might even teach you a few things, Kevin. Here, let me give you a preview."

Gloria got out of the chair, went around the desk, and knelt next to a flabbergasted Grunfeld. She unfastened his fly and pulled out his turgid organ. For the next thirty seconds, Grunfeld sat there in dazed rapture, a look of utter astonishment on his face.

And then she was away from him, standing on the other side of his desk. "Like I said, Kevin—the best."

"Spirit's holy shit!" Grunfeld exclaimed. "You ain't gonna *leave* me like this?"

"Just a preview, Kevin, just a preview."

"Yeah, but—"

"Think about it, Kevin." Gloria slipped back into her wisps of clothing as Grunfeld gasped for air and tried to make up his mind what to do.

"I get Petra, you get me," she said. A second later, she was out the door and gone.

THAT EVENING, KARL CLEVELAND SHOWED UP at the Emporium and approached Gloria at the table where she was finishing a late dinner with Jill Clymer and Dina Westerbrook. Cleveland carefully kept his distance and said, "Boss wants to see ya."

"I'll just bet he does." Gloria laughed.

"He's in his office," Cleveland said.

"Tell him I'll meet him on the pier in fifteen minutes."

"That's not how he wants it."

"That's how it's going to be. You go and tell him, then come back here with Luther and Anselmo. The three of you stay here, and drinks are on the house. My friend Arkady Volkonski and some of his friends will keep you company. When I come back, you can leave."

"Boss ain't gonna like that," said Cleveland.

"Tough," said Gloria. "Go tell him."

Fifteen minutes later, Gloria walked out onto the pier. The rain had stopped and a few stars were visible, along with one of Sylvania's two small and unimpressive moons. There was a slight chill in the air, but Gloria had not bothered with any additional clothing. She saw Grunfeld standing in a pool of light on the nearly deserted pier and approached him.

Grunfeld looked more wary and less smug than usual. His mustache seemed to droop a bit, and his eyes had the look of long and sustained worry.

"Evening, Kevin," Gloria said pleasantly. "Made up your mind?"

"Still thinkin' 'bout it," he said. His eyes swept over her nearly nude body. "You sure do make it tough on a man."

Gloria smiled. "What's so hard about it? You want me, don't you?"

"That ain't the point. It's the price that bothers me."

"You know the price, Kevin. Release Petra and I'm yours."

"And how do I know I can trust you?"

"How do I know I can trust *you*? Release her, and that will establish a basis for some trust."

"Look, I ain't sayin' I know anything. But it just might be that I could find out where she is and maybe set her loose. But I gotta have some guarantees. Mebbe you got it in mind to turn around and arrest me for assault and kidnappin', soon as I let her go."

"No evidence," Gloria pointed out. "The kidnapping occurred on Palmyra, and you weren't there. And you weren't directly involved in the assaults that night at the Lodge. Oh, I heard your men talking about how you would love fucking me when you got there, but that would never stand up in court. And, of course, you have your alibi, don't you? That girl in Overhill?"

"That's right, I do. And ain't nothin' gonna shake her story."

"Shake it, no, probably not. But you know, Kevin, the Bugs and Marshals have questioned her three times, and each time, her story came out a little different. Of course, we both know it's all bullshit, anyway. After all, how likely is it that you would spend the night with your girl in Overhill, when you thought I was there for the taking at the Lodge? The only reason you weren't at the Lodge that night is because you had important business elsewhere—at Pizen Flats."

Grunfeld snorted in contempt. "There, ya see? How in hell am I supposed to trust you when ya pull shit like that? I ain't about to let you pin Pizen Flats on me."

Gloria shrugged. "I probably won't have to. At the appropriate moment, your friends at the Lodge will do that."

Grunfeld pivoted sharply and walked a few steps away from her. When he turned back toward her, he looked angry. "You got it all figured out, don't ya?"

"Kevin, it's blindingly obvious. You know too much, and they need a fall guy for the massacre. You see any other candidates around? Here's how it will go, Kevin. They'll invite you up to the Lodge for a meeting, and as soon as you get there, they'll kill you. Then Vigo will tell the Marshals some perfectly plausible story about how you threatened them or tried to blackmail them, or you were drunk and dangerous. Whatever. They won't try to make it look like suicide, of course, the way they did with Rankus. In fact, while they're at it, maybe they'll blame you for that, too."

"Bullshit. He was dead when I got there."

"As a matter of fact, Kevin, I believe you. And I just can't buy Rankus as a suicide. He may have been sick, but I think he was prepared to fight it out to the very end. But then his friends got tired of waiting for him to die, so they gave nature an assist."

"Damn right they did. Found that old bastard just sittin' there in his easy chair, that old gun in his hand and his brains blowed out. Never seen a man got shot by one o' them bullet-pistols before. Real mess. I know damn well he didn't do it to himself, but I don't know who really did it. If I did, mebbe I'd tell ya. But I don't."

Gloria nodded. "But you do know a lot of other things, Kevin. Right now, your only way out is to start talking, before they kill you. I'm prepared to offer you a deal."

"What kind of deal?"

"You testify against them, and you walk. I'd have to talk to Judge Kershaw and the Marshals about it, but I think they'd go for it. You give us the person or persons at the Lodge who ordered the Pizen Flats massacre, and you'll go free. Why not be smart, for once in your life, Kevin? You don't owe those bastards a thing."

Grunfeld tugged at one end of his mustache for a moment. "You're pretty smart, Miz Gloria," he said. "But it could be that you ain't got everything figured out as good as you think. Mebbe I got some leverage o' my own."

"Or maybe you just think you do. What you do have, Kevin, is 3.7 million crowns in a bank on Palmyra, and another account on New Helvetia. We don't know yet how much you have in that one, but we we'll find out eventually. You could have a pretty good life with that kind of money, if you don't go on being greedy and stupid. Get out now, while you still can."

"Mebbe I can get out without your help. Mebbe I don't need nobody's help. I ain't as stupid as you think I

am. I can figure things, too, Miz Gloria, and I ain't about
to let any o' those bastards at the Lodge sell me out."

"Kevin, Kevin," Gloria said, "Myron Vigo has been
outsmarting people a hell of a lot smarter than you for
nearly a century. That's what he *does*, for Spirit's sake!
Whatever angles you think you've figured, he's figured a
dozen more."

Grunfeld said nothing for nearly a minute. Gloria
waited patiently.

"I gotta think 'bout this some more," he said at last.

"Have it your way. But don't take too long. And in
the meantime, the deal for Petra still goes. Don't take
too long making up your mind about that, either. I know
she's still on Sylvania. If we find her first, the deal's off,
and the only way you'll ever fuck me is in your dreams."

TWO DAYS LATER, THE IMPERIAL GEOLOGICAL
Survey team landed. They arrived in a Land-Air-Sea-
Space (LASS) vehicle, similar to those used by the Imperial Marines but about a quarter the size. The vessel
splashed down in the river because a water landing was
more economical of fuel, but it could just as easily have
landed on Main Street or on top of a mountain.

Stu Eckstein and his crew of five greeted Gloria at
the Emporium. Gloria threw her arms around him and
gave him a bearish hug. His five geologists had to settle
for handshakes, and glared at their leader with a mixture
of admiration and envy. There were no rooms available
at the Emporium, or anywhere else in town thanks to
the crush of new arrivals, so Eckstein and his people decided to stay aboard their LASS.

Eckstein took Gloria on a brief tour of the vessel,
whose mission was to take samples from the Fergusite
layer beneath the valley and surrounding mountains.
Plasma drills, powered by the LASS's fusion reactor, unfolded from the fuselage and would be used to create
boreholes down to the Fergusite. A variety of drones

would then be sent down the holes to collect samples and make measurements. The samples would be delivered to the onboard geological laboratory for analysis.

"First," Eckstein explained, "we need to map the area in several wavelengths and get a better picture of the lay of the land. The existing geological maps are just first-order work, not really good enough for sampling purposes. Then, once we've got everything plotted, we'll start drilling holes and taking samples."

"How long will it all take?" Gloria asked.

"A couple of weeks to get a representative set of samples. Then we'll use that data to map the quality of the Fergusite layer. It's bound to vary from place to place, but we'll be able to establish upper and lower values as well as an average value for the layer as a whole. And that will determine whether it's worth mining."

Gloria nodded. "The geologists from Excelsior, Servitor, and Imperium are already here," she said. "They're staying up at the Lodge, but as soon as they find out you're here, they'll be all over you. 'Eager' doesn't begin to describe them."

"No one from Prizm?"

"Maddie Mitchell says Prizm is willing to accept the IGS results and doesn't feel the need to kibbitz. They seem to have developed a fatalistic attitude about the whole thing."

"So have I," said Eckstein, looking around to make sure they were alone in a corner of the LASS. "I've had a report from Sam Roosa. It doesn't look very promising."

"I know," Gloria said. "Isn't there anything you can do?"

"Hard to say. I want to get down there and check out the readings as soon as possible."

"No time like the present. The Emporium's not very busy during the day, so we can get into Room 9 without attracting attention."

"Lead on," said Eckstein.

• • •

THEY FOLLOWED SAM ROOSA THROUGH THE tunnel to the gallery on hands and knees. Gloria again felt the symptoms that she refused to believe had anything to do with claustrophobia, and was relieved to arrive at the larger space of the gallery. Eckstein immediately surveyed the instruments, looking and sounding like a doctor making rounds in a ward full of seriously ill patients.

"I don't like it," he said when he was finished. "Too much heat buildup, and it's lasted too long."

"That's what I thought," Roosa agreed.

"We should have melted any small igneous intrusion by now. It's possible that there's a break in the layer itself, and the energy just isn't getting to most of the Fergusite."

"Can we do anything about that?" Gloria asked.

Eckstein shook his head. "We'd need to map the break and set up operations on the other side of it. Under the circumstances, I don't see any way to do that."

"But at least we've ruined all the nearby Fergusite, right?"

"Maybe." Eckstein pointed toward the blue-green glow of the plasma beam. "Nothing like this has ever been done before, for obvious reasons," he said. "It should work, in theory, but reality is a hell of a lot sloppier than theory. What worked in my computer sims may not work at all in the ground."

Gloria frowned. "You never mentioned that," she said.

"I didn't think I needed to. Anyway, I didn't want to discourage you—and I still don't. This may yet work, and if it doesn't, there may be another dodge we can try. I need to think about that some more. In the meantime, though, if I were you, I'd concentrate on winning the Eminent Domain vote. Right now, that looks like our best bet."

"Then we're in worse trouble than you think, Stu.

After the Pizen Flats massacre, the riverrats were too scared to refile their claims. As far as I can tell, there's a solid majority of claims that will go with the corporates."

"Sixty percent?"

"Probably, but there's no way to be sure. This isn't an exact science either, you know."

"Then you'd better start changing some minds, Gloria."

"I know, I know." But she also knew that if she did anything at all to rally the riverrats, it could cost Petra her life. If she couldn't tempt Grunfeld into accepting her deal, she wouldn't dare let herself be seen taking an active role in the Eminent Domain battle.

Stay out of the way, they had told her.

GLORIA SPENT THAT NIGHT WITH ECKSTEIN AT the Emporium. She was happy to be back with him. He didn't have the youth and energy of Ted Oberlin or the virtuosity of Slim Jim Zuni, but she felt more comfortable with him. She wasn't in love with Stu Eckstein, but she liked him a great deal and admired his intelligence and courage; after all, he was taking the same risk she was. With poor Ted, there had not been time enough to establish that deep a bond, and Slim Jim was content to keep an emotional distance between them. Eckstein was an attentive and intuitive lover, and had the maturity to keep things in perspective. Gloria nestled in his arms and slept well.

The next afternoon, the Dexta team crowded into Gloria's office and watched over her shoulder as she downloaded the day's results from the pads of each registration team. They had been working Overhill of late, where resistance to registration had abruptly faded following the death of Claude Rankus. With each new data set, the total number of registered voters climbed toward five thousand. When the computer tallied the data from the final pad, the total number flashed in red on the console screen: 5007.

The weary bureaucrats shouted and whooped. They had succeeded in their mission and were justly proud of themselves. There were handshakes, hugs, and kisses all around, and Gloria promised them free drinks, free dinner, and free anything else that they might choose to sample from the Emporium's wares. But, happy as they were, most of them had only one question in their minds.

"When can we go home?" Sintra Garbedian asked.

"Soon," Gloria told them. The answer was not well received.

"What does 'soon' mean?" demanded Wilmer DeGrasse. "We were brought here to do a job, and we've done it. We should be allowed to return to Earth immediately."

"We're not quite done, people," Gloria explained. "There may still be some refiling of claims before the Eminent Domain hearing, and we'll have to handle that. So for now, we stay."

"And when will this hearing happen?" Garbedian wanted to know.

"As soon as Charles appoints an Imperial Governor and formally incorporates the territory. Then the Governor can accept the Eminent Domain petitions from the corporates and set a date for the hearing. From what I've heard from HQ, it seems that the Governor-designate is already on his way here. So I'd guess you'll be here another two or three weeks, at a minimum."

The groans were almost as loud as the cheers had been a few moments before.

"If it's any consolation to you," Gloria said, "I want you to know that I intend to give each of you the highest possible commendation for your service here under difficult and trying conditions. I expect you'll all be looking at promotions when you get back to Manhattan."

That mollified them, and the Dexta people made

their way out of her office and down to the main room for the promised free dinner and drinks. Gloria lingered in her office alone. She was proud of her team—but one member of it was still missing.

"Petra," Gloria said aloud, "I'll get you back. I swear it!"

chapter 23

THE FOLLOWING MORNING, STU ECKSTEIN AR-
rived at the Emporium lugging an armful of hard-copy
images acquired from the LASS. "It's all in the computer, of course, but I like to be able to see it all at once,"
he explained to Gloria. "Got a couple of tables where I
can spread this out?"

They shoved two large tables together in a corner of
the main room and Eckstein proceeded to lay out the
images, as carefully as Slim Jim Zuni dealing a hand of
cards. When he had finished, the eastern side of the
Rankus River Valley was revealed before them, in all its
complexity.

"This is just visible wavelengths," said Eckstein, "but
it helps me to study the way it all looks to the naked eye.
My colleagues tell me I'm old-fashioned, but for my
money, the best geological instrument in the galaxy is still
a Mark-One Eyeball. You need to get a feel for the gestalt
of a place and see how it all fits together before you can
really hope to understand the subsurface structures.
Synclines, anticlines, plutons—the works. See there?

That pile of scree at the base of the cliff tells me volumes about the geological history of that area."

"Uh-huh," said Gloria, who didn't know anticlines from antimatter. To her, the images looked pretty, with their sweeping blend of greens and browns, but seemed to convey no more information than an abstract artist's painting. She was impressed by Eckstein's ability to glean useful data from the apparent chaos.

Gloria pointed to one corner of the array. "And this is Greenlodge?"

"In all its glory," Eckstein affirmed. "And that misshapen monstrosity is the Emporium, as seen from twenty kilometers overhead."

"Hey, careful how you talk about the Emporium, pal!" Gloria objected. "I think it has a certain dynamic . . . uh . . . grace. And this is the Lodge, over here?"

"Right, and Overhill just beyond it."

"Funny, it looks much closer than it seems from the ground."

"The straight-line distance is only about six kilometers, but you have to travel twice that far to get there in a skimmer."

Gloria gestured at the images. "And this is the ridgeline where the highboys work?"

"That's right. To the east and north, the Fergusite layer is mostly submerged, although I think there may be a couple of outcrops on the slopes of that second ridgeline, and maybe a few more as you get up into the mountains."

"I see," said Gloria. Something caught her attention in one of the images, and she pointed to it. "What's that?"

"What?" Eckstein looked to where she was pointing. "Oh, that? Some sort of small structure on the southwest face of this mountain. I hadn't really noticed it before— I tend to concentrate on the rocks."

"What sort of structure?"

"Beats me. I didn't even realize there was anything up there, that far from the river. Looks like it might be a house, but I don't know why anyone would build one there. See how close it is to the snow line? A few more weeks into the rainy season, and it'll be half-buried in snow."

"*Spirit!*" Gloria covered her mouth with her hand and stared, wide-eyed, at the image.

"What?" Eckstein asked her.

"It's a ski lodge!" she cried. "Pollas's ski lodge! He mentioned it once, but I forgot all about it!"

"So?"

Gloria turned to face Eckstein. "That's where she is," she exclaimed. "That's where they've taken Petra!"

Eckstein was not immediately impressed. It seemed to him that Gloria was overinterpreting the data. "What makes you think so?"

"Where else could she be?" Gloria insisted. "The Bugs have searched Greenlodge, Overhill, and every mining camp in the valley. And, Stu—it's *Pollas's* ski lodge! It all fits! That's the only place he could hide her."

Eckstein thought about it, nodded, and turned to say something to Gloria. But she was already gone, racing across the Emporium to find Arkady Volkonski.

GLORIA EASED THE SKIMMER UP THE FINAL slope. Ahead she could see the wooden structure of the ski lodge, with its steep roof and gingerbread architecture. It was downright cute, she thought. Beyond, the mountain rose swiftly, with the snow line just a couple of hundred meters above the house. The top of the peak was cloaked in gray clouds.

It had taken her over three hours to pilot the skimmer to this spot. The course she followed had been plotted from the geological images in order to find the most accessible route for a skimmer. Still, it had been a difficult journey. She made it over the first ridgeline with few problems, but the second ridge was steeper and offered little in the way of gentle slopes and unobstructed passage. After negotiating an annoying but necessary series of switchbacks to gain elevation, she picked her way through a narrow, boulder-strewn defile that led to the other side of the ridge and a long, nearly straight valley. She followed that to the northeast, toward the towering peaks in the distance.

As she drove, Gloria thought about what Eckstein had told her that night in his apartment on Palmyra: eventually, everything averages out. After so many mistakes and so much arrogance and stupidity, it seemed to her that she had finally done something right. Still, luck had its own role to play in the course of events. If she hadn't taken an interest in Eckstein's images, if she hadn't spotted the little structure on the mountainside . . . well, that didn't really bear thinking about. She *had* spotted it, and that was all that mattered.

Petra was there. Gloria felt it as a certainty. Her friend was going to be all right; she was certain of that, too.

And, as a welcome bonus, she wouldn't have to spend that week with Grunfeld. The little preview in his office had been bad enough; a week with that monster would have been dreadful beyond imagining. The offer was necessary, and she had been prepared to live up to her part of the bargain. Fortunately, Grunfeld had been too stupid to seize the opportunity.

When the ski lodge was in view, she carefully parked the skimmer behind a cluster of tall, pinelike trees and got out to walk. The air was thin and bracing, and Gloria wished that she could have worn something more than the molecules-thick white bodysuit she had on. But she knew she would need every possible edge for what was coming, and the bodysuit was slick and almost impossible to grip securely. For the same reason, she had set the suit's transparency at 90 percent and left the pressure seam open in front all the way to her crotch; bare breasts and belly might win her a crucial second of distraction, and a second was all she needed. At least, she hoped so.

As far as she could tell, there was no one outside on

guard duty. In a way, that was good; it implied that they were securely overconfident. On the other hand, it meant that all four of them would be inside. She had no doubt that all four men who had assaulted her and Petra would be there. She would be disappointed if they weren't.

She paused at the front door. She had noted another door on the right side and presumed that there was a rear exit, as well. Curtains obscured the view through the windows. After considering a dramatic, kick-the-door-open entrance, she decided to settle for a sharp knock on the door. That, in itself, ought to have been a considerable surprise.

A few moments later, the door opened and she saw Hank Frezzo standing there, plasma pistol in hand. Frezzo's eyes widened.

"Hello, Hank," she said, and walked past him into the building.

Noz was standing behind Hank, and exclaimed, "What the fuck are *you* doing here?" The other two men from the lodge were also there—a tall, skinny man with red hair and a red beard, and a shorter, huskier man with a shaved face and shaved scalp. They stood rooted in place, and could not have been more surprised if Santa Claus had suddenly dropped down their chimney.

Gloria looked around, engraving the details of the interior in her mind. To the right of the large, central room there was a kitchen, mostly hidden by the angle of the walls. Directly ahead, she saw a hallway that presumably led to bedrooms and a bathroom. Just to the left of the hall was a massive stone hearth, with a fire crackling away. Along the left wall sat a large sofa. A dining area and table was to her immediate right and a vidscreen was on the wall to her left, with a few chairs and a coffee table scattered aimlessly throughout the room. The place looked a bit sloppy but expensive and comfortable. Pollas probably liked it there.

Frezzo shut the door behind her and continued

staring at her. The bald man took a step toward her. "You got your full share of nerve," he said. "I'll give you that."

"I think she just misses us," Noz snickered, once he had recovered from his surprise. "Wants another go-round."

"What I want," Gloria said, "is to make a trade. Let Petra go, and you can have me. But first, I have to see for myself that she's all right. Where is she, back there?"

Gloria pointed toward the hallway, and without waiting for anyone to respond, started walking in that direction. The red-haired man obligingly stepped out of her way. The first door on her left was open, and she saw that the room was empty. The first door on her right was closed. She kicked it open.

"*Gloria!*" Petra screeched.

They threw their arms around each other and hugged so hard it hurt. Gloria had to push her away so she could get a good look at her. Petra seemed fully recovered, as far as could be determined simply by looking. The nanomeds had done their job, and her face was unmarred, her body apparently sound. Her hair was straight again and back to its natural shade of brown. She was wearing only a much-too-large green flannel shirt that came down almost to her knees.

"How are you, kiddo?" Gloria asked her.

"I . . . I'm fine. Really! But what are you doing here?" A fearful expression crossed her face. "They didn't take you, too, did they?"

Gloria shook her head and smiled. "No chance of that," she said.

"That's what you think, bitch," said Red, from behind her. "Both of you, get out here."

Gloria put her arm around Petra's back and gently ushered her into the main room. "Don't worry," she said. "Everything's going to be fine."

The bald one frowned, then shook his head. "I don't like this," said Baldy. "Noz, get outside and keep a watch. I don't think she's dumb enough to have come here alone."

"Fuck you," Noz replied. "I ain't missin' this!"

"Just do it," Baldy snapped. It was clear to Gloria that he was the man in charge. It figured; no one in his right mind would have put Hank or Noz in charge of anything.

Noz stared at Baldy for a moment, then reluctantly went to the door and stepped outside.

"Now," said Baldy, "suppose you tell me just why you think I should let *her* go and keep *you*, when I can keep both of you?"

"You don't need Petra," Gloria replied. "The whole point of kidnapping her was to keep me from doing anything to screw up the Eminent Domain vote for Pollas, right?" She watched Baldy carefully, but his face betrayed no reaction. "Well, if you've got me here, I can't do anything, can I?"

"If I let her go, she'll just go straight to those Bugs you've got in town and tell them where to find us."

"She won't if I tell her not to."

"You expect me to believe that? You must think you're dealing with complete idiots."

"No," said Gloria, "as far as I know, I'm only dealing with two complete idiots. Red, I don't know about, and you seem to have at least a few brains under that shiny dome of yours. Let Petra go, and I promise you, she won't tell anyone where I am. Right, Petra?"

Petra looked very uncertain. "Uh, Gloria . . ."

"*Right*, Petra?" Gloria repeated, giving Petra a nudge with her left elbow.

"Uh . . . right. If you say so."

"I say so."

"I still don't buy it," said Baldy. "Why don't I just keep both of you?"

Noz abruptly reentered the lodge. "There ain't nothin' out there," he declared.

Baldy turned on him. "Just keep watching, dammit!"

"Fuck you," Noz responded. "I'd rather watch *her*." He pointed at Gloria. "You said we couldn't touch the other bitch, and we didn't. Nobody said we couldn't have the VanDeen cunt."

"Is that true, Petra?" Gloria asked her. "They didn't harm you?"

"Nobody laid a hand on me," she said. "Actually, they were kind of nice to me, in a creepy sort of way. Once I could walk again, they even let me outside sometimes."

Gloria looked at Baldy. "Thank you," she said. "I know it couldn't have been easy keeping these morons in line."

"Watch that talk, Miz Gloria," Hank cautioned. "We let you off easy, last time. Could be, we'll give you a taste o' what we gave Petra, this time 'round."

"You're welcome to try, Hank," Gloria said evenly. "But if you keep waving that plasma pistol around, there might not be anything left for you."

Hank looked at the pistol, then sheepishly tucked it into his belt.

Gloria looked into Baldy's eyes. The man was no fool, and very soon, he was going to make his decision. There was no doubt what that decision was going to be.

She willed herself into a Qatsima-state and took the measure of the moment. The discipline involved mind as much as body, and Gloria felt herself moving into the deep-focus mentality that the Qatsima masters had taught her. While continuing to stare at Baldy, she registered the precise location of everyone, everything in the room. Petra was to her left, tense and breathing rapidly. Ahead of her stood Hank, on the far left, then Noz, Baldy, and Red, lined up about two meters away from her, a meter apart.

"Petra," Gloria said, "you know what they say. If you can't stand the heat, get out of the kitchen. What about it, Baldy? Think you can stand the heat?"

"What the hell is that supposed to mean?"

Instead of answering, Gloria took a half step forward, her eyes still locked with Baldy's. They were four and she was one, but she was focused and concentrated and knew exactly what she intended to do, while they were uncertain and uncoordinated. Advantage: VanDeen.

Gloria suddenly thrust her arms straight out to the sides. The motion provoked consternation and confusion among the four, but they held their ground and watched her carefully. She slowly moved her arms up in a circular, windmill motion, and four sets of eyes could not help following them.

With no preamble, Gloria abruptly launched herself in a flying kick that planted her right heel squarely in the soft groin of Hank Frezzo. Even before Frezzo toppled over backwards, Petra, taking her cue, was dashing toward the kitchen and its door to the outside.

Gloria rebounded from Hank, whirled to her left and around, coming out of the spin in a double-scissors-kick move. Noz, Baldy, and Red all ducked back and out of the way, as Gloria had intended. That gave her room to slide to the right, to the fireplace. She grabbed a long, brass poker and waved it menacingly as the three men maneuvered to trap her in the corner to the right of the hearth. Trapped she may have been, but she was precisely where she wanted to be—no one could get behind her.

Noz was now on her left, Red in the center, and Baldy on her right. They crouched slightly and spread their arms a little, as if expecting her to attempt a break through their loose line. She swung the poker back and forth and made short, thrusting feints with it, keeping them at a wary distance until they could figure out how to handle her. Across the room, a supine Hank Frezzo was moaning and clutching himself.

"You're gonna get it now, bitch," Noz promised her.

Baldy suddenly saw a blur of motion to his right, out of the corner of his eye. "Watch out!" he shouted to Noz, who turned just in time to see the cast-iron frying pan come crashing into his face, swung with all the force in her small body by a vengeful and single-minded Petra.

Before Noz hit the floor, Gloria took a backhand swipe at Baldy with the poker, hitting a glancing blow on his right cheek, and almost simultaneously launched herself into another flying kick that connected with Red in precisely the same spot she had connected with Hank.

With no one blocking her way to the left, Gloria quickly danced past the collapsing Red, pausing on her way past to give him an elbow to his nose. Out of the corner of her eye she saw Hank, on the floor, trying to rally and reaching for the pistol in his belt. Petra saw him too and dashed over to him with the frying pan. Its impact on his face produced a resounding, satisfying *clang*!

Gloria gave Baldy an evil grin. "You're outnumbered," she told him. "You want to give up now, or do I need to break a few bones first?"

Baldy put his hand to his cheek and wiped away blood from where the poker had struck him. He looked at the blood in his hand, then looked up at Gloria and returned her grin. "Take your best shot, bitch," he snarled.

"Aw, hell," said Gloria. "This is too easy. Here, catch!"

She tossed the poker high into the air, almost to the ceiling. Baldy instinctively reached upward with his right hand to catch it. Before it came down, she was on him, snaring the splayed-out little finger of his right hand in her right fist. She quickly broke it and yanked his arm downward. As he howled in sudden pain, she got a grip on his right thumb with her left fist, and broke that, too.

Baldy flailed for her with his left hand but couldn't catch up with her as she pulled him around by his right. Then she raised his arm, ducked under it with a twisting move and came up on the other side of him with a final application of torque that snapped his right wrist. He bellowed in pain and outrage and Gloria, behind him now, planted a hard kick in the back of his right knee, dislocating it. He fell forward and Gloria was on him, her knee impacting on his spine.

"Frying pan?" Petra asked.

"No thank you," Gloria said politely. Instead she simply picked up the poker again and savagely slashed him across the right side of his face three more times, turning his cheek to hamburger and scoring the fourth broken nose of the day.

Arkady Volkonski suddenly stuck his head inside the door. "Internal Security, anyone?" he asked.

"You're early, dammit!" Gloria snapped.

"Well, I didn't want you ladies to have *all* the fun," Volkonski said. Six gray-clad Bugs came through the door behind him and stationed themselves over the more or less inert forms of the four men.

Then Pug Ellison managed to force his way through the crowd and ran to Petra. She threw her arms around him. "My hero!" she cried.

"What's he doing here?" Gloria demanded.

Volkonski shrugged. "Couldn't keep him off the LASS," he said. "Young love, you know."

Volkonski and his Bugs got things organized, and in short order Hank, Noz, and Red, their arms bound behind them, were sitting on the sofa in varying degrees of consciousness and pain. Baldy, with his broken arm, was left unshackled, but was seated on a wooden chair with Bugs on both sides of him.

Arkady nodded toward Baldy, then looked at Gloria. "This is the leader?"

"Seems to be," Gloria affirmed.

Volkonski kicked him sharply in his good knee to get his attention. "You know who we are?" he asked.

"Fucking Bugs," Baldy responded. He tilted his head back in an effort to staunch the continuing flow of blood from his nose.

"That's right," said Volkonski. "We're fucking Bugs, otherwise known as Dexta Internal Security. We have an

Empire-wide reputation for our dedication to the rigid enforcement of all three thousand pages of the *Dexta Code*. We are known for our integrity and adherence to the law. What is not widely known, however, is that we only play by the rules when someone is watching. No one is watching now."

Baldy untilted his head and looked at Volkonski. "What the hell is that supposed to mean?"

"No one knows we're here," Volkonski told him, "and no one knows *you're* here. Figure it out. You see, we Bugs take a very dim view—in fact, an *incredibly* dim view—of anyone who assaults one of our people. And you four idiots assaulted *two* of our people. Rafferty? Show them what we think of people who do things like that."

One of the Bugs nodded and unceremoniously grabbed a log from next to the hearth and used it to shatter Red's kneecap.

"You fucking people are crazy!" Baldy shouted above Red's agonized screams.

"We don't appreciate verbal `abuse, either," Volkonski informed him. "Gloria? I note that you broke this man's arm."

"Plus a thumb and a finger," Gloria amended.

"Ah, yes, so I see. One of your Qatsima moves? I'm sure my men and I could profit by a demonstration. Would you be so good as to show us how you did it?"

"Certainly. Gentlemen?" She looked toward the two Bugs flanking Baldy. They grabbed him by his upper arms and yanked him to a standing position.

Baldy, grimacing from his accumulated pains, stared at Gloria in something very close to horror. "You can't *do* that!" he screamed.

"Don't be silly," she said. "Of course I can." She snatched his left little finger and thumb and, as the Bugs held him, deftly repeated the maneuver that had broken Baldy's right wrist. The crack of the bones in his left wrist sounded like a firecracker going off.

The Bugs deposited Baldy back in his chair. He doubled over, gasping for air. Volkonski straightened him up by grasping his broken nose in a viselike grip and pulling. Baldy nearly passed out from the pain.

When he had recovered slightly, Volkonski stooped over and addressed him, face-to-face, from a distance of a few inches. "Now, then," he said. "Do you understand your situation? We are going to ask you some questions. You are going to answer them. If we don't like your answers, or if we think you are holding anything back, we are going to break more of your bones. There are, I believe, some 206 of them in the human body. I think we could probably break about a hundred of them without actually killing you. It might be interesting to find out, don't you think? Or would you prefer to talk?"

Broken and bleeding, the man in the wooden chair talked.

chapter 24

"DO YOU, VINCENT HASTINGS, AFFIRM THAT THE statement you are about to give is by your own free will and not made under duress or coercion?"

Baldy started to laugh in Volkonski's face when he heard that, but evidently thought better of it. "I do," he said. His nose had stopped bleeding and was taped up; he sounded as if he had a very bad case of hay fever.

"Will you describe for us the actions taken by you and your confederates—Henry Frezzo, Herbert Gnozdziewicz, and Franklin McDonald—at approximately 8:00 P.M. on the evening of June 15, 3217, Standard Calendar, at a place known as the Lodge on the planet Sylvania?"

Hastings glared at his captors for a moment, than began reciting in a dull monotone the details of the assault on Petra and Gloria. Petra, hearing for the first time what she still didn't remember, listened with an increasingly angry expression on her face. Pug Ellison stood close behind her, his hands on her shoulders.

"Now, Mr. Hastings, would you tell us how you came to be on Sylvania at that time?"

322 • C.J. RYAN

"I was hired by some guy on Palmyra," he said.
"Don't ask me his name because I don't know it. Just
some guy. Gave me ten thousand crowns in cash and
promised me another forty for doing a job on Sylvania. I
asked him if I could bring along Frank McDonald to
help, and he said okay. They only paid Frank twenty-
five. We took a freighter to Sylvania."

"Where did you go following your arrival?" Volkonski
asked him.

"Well, first we went to this place called the Emporium. We had a few drinks and—"

"I think you can skip that part for the moment. Did
you then proceed to the Lodge?"

"Yeah."

"And who at the Lodge instructed you in the duties
you were to perform?"

"The guy who runs the place," said Hastings.

"Pollas?" Gloria interjected eagerly. "Vigo?"

"No," Hastings said, "the guy who *runs* the place.
Thawley."

"Thawley!" Gloria exclaimed. She approached
Baldy and looked at him carefully. "You don't expect us
to believe that Thawley was running the show, do you?"

"Believe whatever the fuck you want. You asked me
who gave us our orders, and I told you. It was Thawley.
I saw that Pollas guy once or twice, and Vigo, but I
never said anything to them and they never said anything to me."

"Damn!" Gloria was sure Baldy was telling the
truth, and the truth was not what she wanted it to be.
She should have expected it, she told herself. Pollas and
Vigo were too smart to let themselves become directly
involved. Thawley was the obvious middleman.

"Mr. Hastings," said Volkonski patiently, "do you expect us to believe that you were brought from Palmyra
and paid fifty thousand crowns simply to assault and
rape two Dexta officials? What else were you expected
to do to earn your money?"

"There was some other stuff," Baldy admitted after a moment's hesitation. "But we never got around to doing any of it, so you can't hang *that* on us."

"Hang what on you?"

"Thawley said we should attack some of the miners' camps along the river. The way they did at Pizen Flats that night. Only we never did that."

"Why not?"

"They gave us something else to do a couple of days later." He nodded toward Petra. "Someone I'd never seen before showed up with her in a skimmer late at night and told us to bring her here and keep her here. Also told us not to touch her, and we didn't. She'll tell you that herself."

"I see," said Volkonski. "Now, as to these massacres that you didn't get a chance to commit, did you receive any specific instruction as to where, when, and how from Mr. Thawley?"

"No. Thawley told us to coordinate it with the other guy."

"What other guy?"

"That big clown down in Greenlodge. The guy who did the Pizen Flats job."

"And which big clown would that be?" Volkonski inquired.

"Who do you think?" sniffed Baldy. "That idiot mayor. Grunfeld."

KEVIN GRUNFELD PACED BACK AND FORTH IN his small office. Too damn small, he thought. It felt more like a cage than an office.

It would be neither cage nor office much longer; that much, at least, was clear to him. VanDeen, damn her, had been right—time was running out. He had thought that he had planned everything with care and precision, and that the deals he had made would protect him. He knew enough to bring down Pollas and Vigo and the fat cats at the Lodge, and a couple of those corporate bastards, to boot. They wouldn't dare try to sell him out, because that would just be cutting their own throats.

Grunfeld had written down everything and stashed it all in a place where no one would ever find it. And that, it had lately occurred to him, could be a problem. If no one could find it, then it would pose no threat to anyone if he were dead. He needed a way to make sure that his story would automatically surface if anything happened to him, but that was no easy thing to arrange. For starters, he had to make sure that his account could not come to light *before* he was dead. But there was no one on the whole Spirit-forsaken planet that he could trust!

Karl Cleveland had been with him the longest, and was as close to being his friend as anyone—which was not very close, now that he considered it. Cleveland was reliable but not exactly trustworthy, and he sure as hell wasn't very smart. He'd make his own deal with the Lodge, or get suckered by Vigo, probably both. As he continued pacing, Grunfeld arrived at the suspicion that Cleveland had probably *already* sold him out. Luther Dominguez, too.

In a strange way, he realized, the only person on the planet that he trusted at all was Gloria VanDeen. She had offered him a deal that was almost too good to be believed, and yet he did believe it, up to a point. She was tough, but when she stared at him with those too-blue eyes of hers, it was almost impossible not to believe that she meant what she said. She might fight him, humiliate him, embarrass him, or tempt him, but he didn't think that she would lie to him.

And just why did he think that? Because she was the greatest piece of ass in the fucking galaxy, that was why!

"Kevin, you poor stupid bastard," he said aloud. "You're thinkin' with your cock."

Which she had counted on, of course.

He stopped pacing, sat down behind his desk, propped his head up on his elbows, and pulled idly at the ends of his drooping mustache. Spirit, how had he gotten himself into this fix? And how could he get out of it?

He didn't see how he could avoid making the deal with VanDeen. He could sit down with her and the Bugs and Marshals and the Judge and tell them everything he knew about what had been going on. And then he would walk . . . free to enjoy his millions on some faraway world where Pollas and Vigo would never find him. At least, VanDeen said he would walk, if the Judge and Marshals went along with it. But would they? Would they let him walk away from the massacre at Pizen Flats?

Grunfeld was no humanitarian, but he had never felt good about Pizen Flats, not from the first moment the plan had been explained to him. Oh, there was a certain mad, frenzied exhilaration about it, he couldn't deny that. Burning all those people and knowing he would get away with it had loosed some primal, predatory joy within him. Slaughter for its own bloody sake had some instinctive appeal to it; it must have, or else why did it keep happening, again and again, down through the ages?

And yet, he'd had nothing against those people. Hell, he'd even liked Gus Thornton, a bit. He didn't much care for the idea of them all being dead, for no good reason except money. And was it really about the money? Grunfeld already had more of it than he'd ever dreamed possible. He was a fucking *rich man*, incredible as that still seemed to him. Did he really need the extra money that had been promised to him—enough to kill forty-nine people for it?

If not the money, then what? What kept him here, long after he should have cashed in his chips and gotten out of the game?

What it came down to, he realized, was that Greenlodge was the only home he had ever known. He

had drifted his way here and always figured that someday he'd drift somewhere else. Instead, he had stayed,
and had put down something very like roots. He enjoyed
lording it over the town and the people, and hated to
think that he would have to give that up. But more than
that, he had grown attached to the place itself—the
tranquil river and the soaring peaks in the distance, and
the slow, unhurried rhythm of the changing seasons. He
didn't want to leave.

What he really wanted was the Emporium. Damn
Elba, for not selling it to him! It was a good place to
while away the hours and days. Good food, drinks, a
hand of cards, a few laughs, all the pretty whores a man
could ask for. But then VanDeen aced him out and
Dexta took it over—Dexta! Spirit, how could such a
thing have happened?

And then, that miserable night after VanDeen
broke his fingers . . . they had laughed at him. Laughed!
At him—Mayor Kevin Grunfeld! No one had ever
laughed at him before, or if anyone did, they didn't
laugh for long. After that night, he couldn't even go back
to the Emporium for a drink or a whore. VanDeen had
ruined everything for him.

VanDeen. Spirit, what ill wind had brought her
breezing into his life? He had always thought he could
handle any woman—except maybe Elba—but VanDeen
was more than *any* man could handle. Even the Emperor. It made Grunfeld feel oddly proud that he had
something in common with the Emperor.

He could have her for a week. He had no doubt that
she'd live up to that part of the deal. The bitch was sex-
mad, he could tell. Oh, she was just trying to use him to
get her friend back, but there was more to it than that.
She could have said he could have her for a day, but instead she'd said a week. She wouldn't have said a week if
she didn't feel at least something for him. And lately,
she'd taken to calling him "Kevin," as if she actually

liked him a little. Maybe she even wanted that week as much as he did. Maybe . . .

Grunfeld leaned back in his chair and sighed. The goddamn woman had turned his brain to mush! Like him? Shit, she despised him!

But . . . a week. A week. Alone with Gloria VanDeen, the most beautiful woman in the Empire, the sexiest bitch in existence. Spirit, how could he *not* take a deal like that?

It would mean selling out Hank and Noz, of course. He didn't mind selling out those two assholes they'd brought in to "help" him—as if he couldn't handle everything himself. But if he sold out Hank and Noz, how long would it be before Karl and Luther did the same to him, if they hadn't already?

One thing was becoming crystal clear. Before this was over, somebody was sure as hell going to get sold out. And Kevin Grunfeld, Honorable Mayor of Greenlodge, was the one man that *everyone* could sell out. It could come from above or below, but it was bound to come.

There was only one possible answer.

"I'll do it," he said aloud. He'd take VanDeen's deal, and even if *she* sold him out, too, maybe he'd at least get his week with her first. A week with that golden body and that hypnotic face and flowing blond hair . . .

His dreams of Gloria were abruptly interrupted by the reality of her. She stood in his doorway and smiled at him.

"Time's up, Kevin," she said.

Grunfeld didn't move. He sat there, staring at her for long moments, then slowly nodded.

"Figures," he said. "Just now made up my mind to take your deal. Don't suppose I can still get that week with you?"

Gloria shook her head. "We have Petra back," she told him. "And the men who had her have been talking a blue streak. No deals, Kevin. It's all over."

Behind Gloria, Grunfeld could see a couple of the

Bugs out in the hallway. Well, it had been a pretty good run while it lasted. Grunfeld pushed his chair back, got to his feet, and walked out from behind his desk.

"We could've had a helluva week," he said to her, managing a weak smile.

"It might have been interesting," Gloria conceded. "But right now, you have a date with Judge Kershaw. If you cooperate and tell us everything you know about the Lodge and Pizen Flats, it will go easier on you."

"Fat chance of that!" Grunfeld laughed.

"Don't be so sure, Kevin. You're not the one we really want. We want Pollas and Vigo, and you can give them to us."

"Mebbe I can," Grunfeld agreed. "And mebbe I'd turn up dead about two seconds after I started talkin'. I'd need a bunch o' protection."

"You'll be in Dexta custody, at least initially," Gloria assured him. "You'll be completely safe."

"Hah! Ya think so? Then there's shit you ain't got no idea about, Miz Gloria. I don't think I like my chances with Dexta."

Gloria spread her arms and asked, "What other chance do you have, Kevin?"

Grunfeld smiled. "One, mebbe," he said, and then threw himself into the window behind him. He crashed through wood and glass and splatted down onto the mud outside.

The impact momentarily knocked the wind out of him, and it took a few moments for him to get moving. He slopped around in the mud, immediately lost his footing, and went down face-first. By the time he was on his feet again, Gloria had raced out the front of the building and into the alley. She tackled him on the fly, and they both went down. They rolled over each other and all but vanished in the mud.

He was on top of her, and Gloria could gain no leverage for a Qatsima move. His weight pressed her down deeper into the gumbo. As she took a last gulp of air, he put his hand over her face and pushed until the mud closed over her completely.

It crossed Grunfeld's mind that he could drown her in the mud. Kill her, right there in the alley in the middle of town. It seemed a shame, somehow, and anyway, he had more urgent things to do. Two Bugs had come after him, sloshing their way toward him, plasma pistols drawn. He rolled away from Gloria and kicked out at the first Bug as he came in range. Grunfeld's kick missed, but in trying to avoid him, the first Bug lost his balance, slid back into the second one, and both of them went down in the mire. One of them lost his pistol; it went flying up into the air and Grunfeld lunged for it. He flopped through the ooze like an alligator on a riverbank and managed to seize the pistol securely in his grip.

Gloria emerged from the mud, gasped for air, then tried to wipe the gunk out of her eyes. Grunfeld, pistol in one hand, grabbed for her with his other. She tried to squirm away from him, and he could get no grip on her muddy, slick bodysuit. She twisted around to crawl away, but Grunfeld managed to get a handful of her hair and brought her up short with a firm yank.

Grunfeld scrambled onto the firmer ground, keeping the pistol pointed in the direction of the two Bugs in the mud, dragging Gloria with him. He got himself to his feet and pulled Gloria to hers. Then he stuck the barrel of the pistol against her head and moved backward, toward two skimmers parked on the other side of the alley.

Volkonski and three other Bugs had arrived at the scene, pausing at the far end of the mud puddle, ten meters away. Their plasma pistols were drawn, and they were taking dead aim on Grunfeld.

"No," Gloria shouted, sputtering out mud. "We want him alive!"

"You want *her* alive," Grunfeld added, "you put them pistols down. Throw 'em in that puddle. *Now!*"

The Bugs hesitated, but Volkonski finally tossed his

pistol into the mire, and the others followed suit. Grunfeld, still holding a firm grip on Gloria's hair, pulled her along with him to the skimmers.

"I oughta burn your fuckin' head off, Miz Gloria, I really oughta," Grunfeld told her.

Gloria twisted around and looked at him over her shoulder. "You don't want to do that Kevin," she said.

Grunfeld looked into the intense blue eyes staring at him from her mud-smeared face. Even now, she was the most beautiful thing he had ever seen, and his heart ached to think that he would never really have her. Not for a week, not for a night, not for a second. He could keep anyone else from having her, he could pay her back for all the misery she had caused him. He could . . .

No, he realized suddenly. He couldn't.

"Shit," he said. "We coulda had ourselves a time." With that, Grunfeld gave her a hard shove that sent her reeling back into the mud.

He ran for the nearest skimmer, got in, and started moving. Volkonski and the Bugs made for the puddle to retrieve their pistols, but Grunfeld aimed the skimmer straight at them, and they dived headfirst into the muck. Grunfeld zoomed past them and headed for the river.

First the river, then . . . then *what*? *Where*? He wondered if it even mattered now. There was no way he could get off of the planet, and yet there was nowhere *on* the planet that he could hide. The mountains, maybe. Sure, why not? Upriver, then. He would run, and they would chase. He didn't have to run *to* something—running was its own excuse. Just keep running. What else was left?

GLORIA GOT TO HER FEET AND DASHED TO THE second skimmer. She jumped into the driver's seat and nearly slid right out of it. Righting herself, she started it up and took off in pursuit of Grunfeld. He had gunned his skimmer across Main Street and headed toward the river, scattering boomers right and left as he went. They had no sooner pushed themselves back up out of the mud than they had to dive back into it to avoid Gloria.

Grunfeld headed upriver at top speed, keeping barely a meter above the water to gain maximum force from the mass-repulsion unit. Gloria did the same, but found she could not gain on him. He was already a good three hundred meters ahead of her, throwing up a rooster tail of spray.

Where Grunfeld thought he could go, Gloria could not imagine. Had he made himself a hidey-hole somewhere up in the mountains, she wondered? He could have cached supplies enough to last for quite a while, she supposed, but to what end? So he could live like a hunted animal for a few months? Maybe. Grunfeld operated more on instincts than intellect, and he was fleeing instinctively now.

But he hadn't shot her.

And somehow, she had known that he wouldn't.

He was a swine for sure, a cold-blooded, sadistic killer with no redeeming characteristics except, perhaps, a poorly developed sense of humor. And yet, Gloria knew—instinctively, maybe, like Grunfeld—that there was some strange link between them. She had read somewhere that the hunter feels some sense of identification with the prey, so perhaps that was it.

At one point, Grunfeld veered to the left, toward the west bank of the Rankus River and a side stream that came gushing down from the slopes. Gloria angled to cut him off, and Grunfeld turned back to the right and upriver again. She realized that he was searching for alternatives as he fled, and had no plan, no destination.

Gloria glanced back over her shoulder and saw, a kilometer to the rear, a makeshift fleet of three more skimmers in pursuit. Volkonski and the Bugs, obviously. Wherever Grunfeld went to ground, he would soon have company. Gloria just hoped that Volkonski could control his Bugs and keep from killing Grunfeld. He was the only link between the massacre and the

Lodge—except for Preston Thawley, who was on far-away Palmyra, or perhaps even farther away by now. Or perhaps, simply dead. Gloria suspected the latter. Mr. and Mrs. Thawley were of no further use to the barons of the Lodge, and they knew far too much.

So it was Grunfeld. They *had* to take him alive.

THEY SPED PAST PIZEN FLATS WITH NEVER A pause and continued upriver toward the cul-de-sac of the falls. With Gloria close behind and the Bugs spread out across the river to the rear, Grunfeld had no hope of escaping by doubling back, and ahead lay nothing but the massive wall of the mountains. They emerged from the final, narrow canyon into the bowl at the head of the river, and Grunfeld slowed for a moment before making for the east bank, near the campsite Gloria had used. He grounded the skimmer on dry land and got out quickly. Looking back at his pursuers, he paused to fire a harmless bolt from his plasma pistol, then ran toward the craggy rocks that flanked the falls.

Gloria was only seconds behind him. She parked the skimmer next to his and ran after him through a gentle, misty rain. Heavy gray clouds cloaked the peaks to the north, and the falls itself seemed to plunge from out of nowhere, like a detail of an immense, unfinished landscape painting. She saw Grunfeld climbing the rocks like some large, mud-colored lizard ascending a stucco wall.

She quickly reached the base of the escarpment and clambered up onto the first tier of smashed boulders. Grunfeld was perhaps twenty meters above her now, making his way steadily upward. The higher he went, the steeper the climb became.

"Kevin!" Gloria called to him, straining her voice to make it heard over the roar of the falls, "where the hell do you think you're going?"

He paused and looked down at her with an inscrutable grin. "Gonna hide in them clouds up there!" he yelled. "Then I'm gonna float away on 'em."

It might have been a joke, but Gloria realized there was a kernel of truth to it. If Grunfeld could climb high enough to disappear into the overhanging clouds, they would lose track of him, and it might take days or weeks to find him again.

"Kevin," she shouted, "come down here before you hurt yourself!"

"You come *up*!" he laughed, then turned back to the rocks and resumed his ascent.

Gloria shook her head, but knew she would have to follow him. Her bodysuit had built-in treads on the soles of the feet, but they were not designed for mountain climbing. The rocks were slippery in the rain and spray from the falls, just ten meters to her left, and she had little experience at this sort of work. Still, Grunfeld was no mountain goat himself, yet he was making steady progress. The incline was still fairly gradual here, and the jumble of cracked and shattered boulders offered a profusion of foot- and handholds. Farther up, above the pile of debris that had fallen from the unseen cliff top, the granite face of the native rock looked sheer and unscalable. Grunfeld couldn't get away, but he might very well kill himself trying. Gloria went after him.

She followed his path, finding the going difficult but not impossible. Twice, her feet nearly slipped out from under her, but she managed to grab on to outcrops with her hands and pull herself back up. She craned her neck and saw Grunfeld another thirty meters above her, perhaps fifty meters from the base of the debris pile.

"C'mon, Kevin," she cried. "You're not gonna make me come all the way up there, are you?"

"Why not?" he shouted back at her. He almost sounded as if he were enjoying himself.

Gloria looked down and saw Volkonski and the Bugs assembled below her. Two of them had started to follow her up the rocks, but she called, "No! Stay there, all of you. I can handle this myself!"

"Don't be crazy, Gloria," Volkonski yelled. "He can't get away!"

Grunfeld heard him and replied by firing off a bolt from his pistol that sent the Bugs scattering for cover.

"Stop that, Kevin," Gloria demanded. "You're being stupid again."

Grunfeld laughed heartily. "Why change now?" he asked. He stuck the pistol back into his belt, boosted himself onto a ledge, and strained for a grip on the next outcrop. Gloria sighed, then resumed her own climb. Handholds were getting harder to find now, and the surface was wet and slick. She pressed herself as close as possible to the rock face and kept climbing. A downward glance was a mistake, she discovered. Of course, she didn't have acrophobia, just as she didn't have claustrophobia. Heights didn't frighten her a bit—but *falling* from them did. She took a deep breath, found a likely foothold, and moved upward.

Tilting her head back, she saw Grunfeld struggling on the slippery surface. He braved a vertical jump and managed to get a secure handhold on a narrow ledge above his head. Huffing and puffing from the unaccustomed exertion, he was able to boost himself upward until he could stand on the ledge. Above, the going got even more difficult.

"Kevin!" Gloria shouted. "Come back down while you still can! Tell you what, I'll give you an hour with me. We'll go off into the woods alone and fuck our brains out for an hour! How's that sound?"

Grunfeld looked back down at her. "Sounds like a trick."

"No trick, I swear. C'mon, Kevin, you know you want me. This is your last chance."

"An hour, huh?"

"Absolutely!"

Grunfeld laughed. "You really want me that bad? Shit, could be you're gettin' so ya like me a little?"

"Could be, Kevin," Gloria agreed, but added, "Everyone knows I have terrible taste in men. I mean, look at the man I married!"

"Hah! Ya had a fuckin' emperor, and now ya want the miserable Mayor of Greenlodge?"

"I'm just a sucker for a man with a title, Kevin."

Grunfeld thought about it for a few seconds, then shook his head. "Ain't got no title now," he said. "Just an ex-mayor. Ex-everything. Naw, I don't think so, Miz Gloria. Been swell knowin' ya, but I think I'd best move on."

"Dammit, Kevin!"

But Grunfeld had already begun his next ascent. He wedged his left foot into a narrow crevice in the rock and pushed upward. He clawed at the slick rock surface and found a projecting rock that seemed to offer a secure grip, but when he put his weight on it, the rock broke away from the cliff face. Grunfeld windmilled his arms frantically, searching for a grip somewhere in thin air. He found none.

Gloria watched in dismay as Grunfeld toppled over backwards and plunged downward. He struck the cliff face halfway down and ricocheted toward the base of the falls. His splash was lost in the thunder and spray of the cascading water.

Forty meters up, Gloria gritted her teeth, took a deep breath, then pushed off. She tried for a graceful swan dive, but rotated a little too far over; instead of hitting the water cleanly, she smacked it hard with her back and rump.

The impact stunned her momentarily, and the next thing she knew, she was deep under the water below the falls, gliding downward through a ghostly, bluish-green radiance. She had spent so much time swimming there that the scene was familiar to her, although she had never dived so deep. Maneuvering to halt her downward motion, she desperately looked around in search of Grunfeld.

She spotted him languidly drifting toward the bottom, perhaps twenty meters away from her. She stroked and kicked, feeling the painful pressure in her ears and the beginnings of urgent need in her lungs. Gloria strained every muscle and pushed herself to her physical limits, closing the distance to Grunfeld in seconds.

She snagged him under his collar with her left hand and immediately began kicking toward the surface. The big man's inert weight tried to pull her back down, and her upward progress was agonizingly slow. She would never reach the surface in time with him in tow, never. The light was just too far away. But she had to try, so she closed her eyes and stopped tormenting herself with the sight of the impossible distance she had to go. She retreated into a Qatsima mind-set, tranquil and patient. Time was merely an illusion, distance a mirage. All moments, all places were one . . .

Gloria broke the surface, opened her eyes, and filled her lungs. The turbulence from the falls pulled her back down again, but she maintained her grip on Grunfeld and began kicking toward shore. Gaining distance from the riotous waterfall, she managed to get her head above water again and gasped hungrily for more air. The shore was just ahead.

Two Bugs plunged into the frigid water and helped her pull Grunfeld to the rocky riverbank. He lay on his back, eyes wide-open but unseeing. Gloria wasted no time, and pressed her lips against his, forcing precious air into his lungs. Again, and then again, and still again.

"Breathe, Kevin!" she yelled at him. "Dammit, breathe!"

She felt hands on her shoulders, trying to pull her away. She fought them and again put her mouth to Grunfeld's, trying to breathe for him. In, out . . . dammit, Kevin . . .

"Gloria!" Volkonski shouted at her above the thunderous falls. He put his fingers under the back of the neck of her bodysuit and pulled her upward.

"Let me go!" Gloria screeched.

"Gloria, it's no use!" Volkonski insisted. "Look at him, Gloria. His neck is broken."

She did look, and for the first time noticed that Grunfeld's head was tilted away from his body at an impossible angle. Volkonski was right—it was no use. Grunfeld was gone. And gone with him was everything he knew and would never say.

chapter 25

SIR HARTWELL BOSWORTH, NEWLY APPOINTED
Imperial Governor of Sylvania, surveyed his realm from
the heights of the Lodge and wondered if it consisted of
anything more than rain, mud, and Fergusite. His arrival
and ceremonial investiture had been a fiasco, with a
drenching downpour reducing the welcoming committee
to a handful of Dexta functionaries and a couple of gofers
from the Lodge. None of the local population—*not
one!*—had bothered to show up, and the absence of comsats and communications facilities made it impossible to
spread the news of his coming except by word of mouth.
In the end, the formal proceedings had been held aboard
the Imperial yacht that delivered him. The Territory of
Sylvania was officially incorporated into the Empire and
entrusted to Sir Hartwell's care before an audience of five
and a few media reps; most of the media had gratefully
departed from Sylvania after the massacre story wrapped.

One of the five was Gloria VanDeen, about whom the
Emperor had given him abundant warning. She had
quickly lived up to her advance billing by inviting him and

his retinue to a reception at a place called the Emporium, about which he had also been warned. He had icily declined the invitation, with the observation that a whorehouse was hardly an appropriate venue to begin his term in office. "Why in the world not?" VanDeen had replied.

Fortunately, the trustees of the Lodge had forwarded an invitation to make his headquarters in the now-vacant upper floors of their establishment. Since the only alternatives were the Emporium or the cramped quarters of his yacht, Bosworth had hastily accepted. Now, as he endured a boring and rather makeshift reception in the main room at the Lodge, he reminded himself that his appointment to this soggy, backwoods world would last no more than a few months, if all went well.

This was his fourth Imperial Governorship, his second for Charles, and he knew precisely what was expected of him and what he stood to gain from a smooth performance. Bosworth was one of a more or less hereditary class of Imperial retainers, worthy individuals from the right families who stood ready to serve the Emperor in any appropriate manner. His father and grandfather before him had been Imperial Governors, and one of his great grandfathers had been Chamberlain to Alfonso II.

In an interview before leaving Earth, Charles had explained matters to Bosworth in considerable detail. His task was clear: oversee the Eminent Domain hearing, grant the mining concession to the corporates, and see to it that the operation got off to a swift and efficient start. Since the outcome of the Eminent Domain hearing was assured, and since the deal for the mining concession had already been struck, he would really have very little to do other than show the Imperial flag and keep all of the players in line. For that, he would receive the thanks of a grateful Empire and ten million crowns, payable to his account on New Helvetia.

It all seemed easy enough, even if it meant enduring months on this truly awful planet. The trustees of the Lodge were an obsequious, oily bunch, eager to please and thoroughly transparent—small-time hustlers from the third-tier world of Palmyra. He supposed that he could endure their company for a few months, since there seemed to be no alternative.

The only bright spot was the presence of at least three extraordinarily beautiful women. One of them, alas, was Gloria VanDeen, and the Emperor's warning about her had been explicit. "Don't even think about fucking her, Bosworth," Charles had snarled. "Well, you won't be able to avoid *thinking* about it, but don't *do* it, you hear me? She'll wrap you around her little finger and cause Spirit knows what mischief. Look, but don't touch, understand? That's an order from your Emperor!"

Bosworth was content, for the moment, just to look. VanDeen had come to the reception wearing an entirely transparent dress, deeply slashed in front and rear to freely reveal every bit of her magnificent body. Imperial orders notwithstanding, he had every intention of fucking her before he left this otherwise dismal world, and from everything he had heard about her, he rather fancied that he would get the chance to do just that. Already, she had given him rather obvious encouragement with her flirtatious behavior and an invitation to visit her at the Emporium.

Still, VanDeen was dangerous, so Bosworth shifted his gaze to the other likely candidates. One was a Prizm representative named Maddie Mitchell, tall, thin, dark-haired, and blatantly sensual. She was wearing a navy blue jacket which she had left wide open, and matching, low-riding pants that rode unnervingly low on her hips. Her nipples were as impressive as VanDeen's, and she had the same 'please-fuck-me-immediately' look in her eyes. However, the word on Mitchell was that she preferred women.

That left his new, interim Imperial Secretary, an icy blonde from Dexta named Dina Westerbrook. She was a bit older and more knowing, and would certainly be aware of what he expected from her. She wore a black skirt slit to the hipbone and a sheer white blouse, unbuttoned to reveal her small, eager tits. Her manner was formal but enticing, and he fully expected to have her in the sack by the end of this very long and tiresome day.

Bosworth nibbled some rather ordinary canapés, sipped the mediocre champagne, and allowed himself a sigh of resignation. One does what one must, he reminded himself, and ten million crowns was more than adequate compensation for a few months of enforced boredom. Still, he felt that after this assignment, Charles would owe him something a little better the next time.

He saw Norfleet and Lund, two of the annoying corporate reps, approaching him and mechanically switched on his condescending smile. Weasels, both of them, but major players in the unfolding scheme of things around here. A quadrillion crowns at stake, Charles had said, so it was necessary to put on a good face for Excelsior and Servitor and their smug little minions. He stole another look at VanDeen's spectacularly bare ass across the room, then greeted Lund and Norfleet as if there were nothing more important in the Empire than keeping them happy.

AT THE FAR END OF THE RECEPTION AREA, Gloria glanced over her shoulder at Imperial Governor Bosworth, then resumed her conversation with Dina Westerbrook. "Loyal retainer," she said, "prominent family, skilled politician, total jerk. I never met him in Rio, but I heard about him. He'll expect his new Imperial Secretary to do his work for him by day and warm his bed at night."

Dina shrugged. "He's not bad-looking, though, in an overbred sort of way."

"Said to be a skilled if somewhat eccentric lover. You don't *have* to screw him, you know."

"I know. But it might be useful, don't you think?"

"Hmmm." Gloria considered that for a moment, then said, "Useful, maybe. But not essential. He won't be making any decisions on his own, I can assure you of that. He's just here to implement the deals that have already been made. I'd fuck him myself if I thought it would help, but I doubt that it would."

"No problem," Dina said. "I'll handle him. I may even take a run at Lund and Norfleet, too, for whatever that may be worth."

Gloria laughed. "You're really plunging into this assignment, aren't you?"

"Gloria," Dina said, "I've waited twenty years for another chance, and now that I have it, I'm not going to be shy about using everything I've got. I may even teach you a few tricks." Dina winked at her, then glided across the room to join the corporate reps and the new Imperial Governor.

Maddie Mitchell joined her and nodded toward Dina. "One of the sisterhood, isn't she?"

"She's got what we've got," Gloria agreed.

"Lucky her. Lucky us. I've been hoping that you and I could find some time to renew our relations, Gloria. I've thought about you a lot."

Gloria gave her a warm smile. "We've both been pretty busy lately," she said.

"How's Petra?" Maddie asked. "I'm sorry I haven't had a chance to see her since her return."

"She's doing fine," Gloria said. "Physically, she's completely recovered. She still doesn't remember much that happened that day, which is probably just as well. She says she does have some disconnected recollections of being out by the pool with you, however. Finally got her, huh?"

Maddie shook her head. "Not really. Not the way I wanted her."

"Too bad. You've missed your chance, then, I think. She and Pug Ellison seem to have started something pretty torrid."

"Really? Good, that's just what she needs. And what

about you, Gloria? How are you getting along with our geologist friend?"

Gloria smiled. "Just fine, thank you. Although he's been pretty busy with the sampling and . . . other things."

"And how are those 'other things' going?"

"Not very well, it seems. We may have some serious problems. Right now, I think our best bet is for you and Shoop to come up with something."

"That's not a very good bet, then. You haven't heard? An Imperium VP just arrived the other day. The proposals about a Prizm-Imperium deal that Shoop sent back have not met with overwhelming favor at the home office. I think the VP is here to ride herd on Thomas, although he says he's just observing. Unless you can come up with a hell of a lot more proxies for the Eminent Domain vote, I doubt that there will be any deal."

"I see. Well, I may be able to get a few. Now that Petra is safe and the Bugs are here in force, I intend to do a little drumbeating among the riverrats. If I can get them to refile the way they did at Pizen Flats, we may come up with several hundred more proxies for our side. *May*, I emphasize."

"That would certainly help," Maddie said. "And I'll do what I can with the Imperium Veep. Not my type, you know—but he seems to think that I'm *his* type. I'll just close my eyes and think of Prizm."

"Do you suppose," Gloria wondered, "there was ever a time when people made major decisions simply on the merits of the case, and not because of money, politics, and sex?"

"You, my dear," Maddie said, giving Gloria a chaste peck on the cheek, "are an idealist!"

GLORIA HAD MANAGED TO AVOID DIRECT EN-counters with any of the Lodge nabobs, but Myron Vigo finally cornered her alone, offering his usual charm, wit, and innocent smile. She was weary of fencing with him and decided to stop pretending that he was anything other than what he was.

Vigo took a moment to stare at Gloria's fully exposed breasts and blond pubic delta. "Enchanting dress, Ms. VanDeen," he said. "I must say that I find your penchant for public nudity most diverting."

"Thank you, Mr. Vigo," Gloria replied. "But it's not simply sexual display, you know. Back on Mynjhino, the natives said it signified that I was an honest woman with nothing to hide."

"Indeed," said Vigo, "I'm certain that's true. I hope you're enjoying the festivities, such as they are."

"Not as much as you are. But then, I suppose it must be very satisfying to commit mass murder and think that you've gotten away with it."

For a second, Vigo seemed on the verge of reacting with anger, but he quickly collected himself and countered with more charm and wounded innocence. "Ms. VanDeen," he said, "you disappoint me. You've gotten your killers, and it would be presumptuous in the extreme to accuse others of being involved. Grunfeld is dead. The case is closed, is it not?"

"Not," Gloria said firmly. "What's presumptuous is to assume that Grunfeld was acting on his own. Now that he's dead, Judge Kershaw issued a writ to get us access to his account on New Helvetia. Who knows what might turn up there?"

"Indeed," said Vigo. "Yet you act as if you already knew. Whatever transactions may have been recorded, personally, I would doubt that they would point you in any particular direction."

"Meaning that you've covered your tracks."

"Meaning, Ms. VanDeen, that even an idiot like Grunfeld would be unlikely to leave any incriminating evidence behind."

"There's still the question of all the claims and proxies he accumulated. We still don't know who wound up with them. Do you, Mr. Vigo?"

Vigo gave her a thin, cautious smile. "If I did, I certainly wouldn't be at liberty to discuss the matter, now would I?"

"So Grunfeld sold them to you and your pals? With something extra to pay for the massacre, no doubt."

"Really, Ms. VanDeen, I would be a little more circumspect, if I were you. Loose talk like that could put you on the receiving end of a truly prodigious lawsuit. As an attorney, allow me to advise you to refrain from publicly slandering people simply on the basis of your unfounded suspicions. The consequences could become quite ugly."

"Well, mass murder is an ugly business, isn't it? Permit me to ask you, as an attorney, if you think that the Special Circumstances statutes would apply in this case."

"The death penalty?" Vigo asked. "I should think that it might, indeed, be applicable in such a case, and it wouldn't surprise me at all if the Imperial Justice Department asked for it in the prosecution of Grunfeld's gang. But that's mere speculation on my part. After all, I'm not a criminal lawyer."

"Too bad. You might need one before this is finished."

"I rather doubt that, Ms. VanDeen," Vigo replied. "But before I take my leave of you, allow me to give you one piece of advice that you would be foolish not to heed."

"Oh? And what would that be, Mr. Vigo?"

Vigo winked at her. "Try the lobster bisque. It's superb."

GLORIA SPENT THE NEXT DAY ON THE RIVER, visiting the camps of the riverrats and spreading her gospel of refiling their claims. With Grunfeld and his pukes gone and the Bugs patrolling the valley, she assured them of their safety. She hoped she wasn't being overconfident on that score, but figured that it was unlikely that the Lodge would attempt any new attacks at this stage.

The riverrats' response was not everything she had hoped for, but they still had a week to make up their minds before the filing deadline. The corporates had already filed their Eminent Domain petition with the Imperial Governor, and Bosworth was setting everything in motion. Judge Kershaw would preside at the hearing in ten days' time.

Gloria roamed through the camps along the river wearing nothing but thin white shorts and a flimsy shirt, both of which were quickly rendered transparent by the daylong drizzle. She was free with her hugs and kisses and let the boomers take liberties with her that even she might have considered too familiar under normal circumstances. But the circumstances were anything but normal now; they were in the home stretch, and in order to accomplish the mission Mingus had given her, she would need to employ every advantage she could muster. If letting the riverrats grope, paw, and ogle her would result in even a few more votes in the Eminent Domain hearing, she was more than willing to subject herself to their attentions.

EVENING FOUND HER HUDDLED WITH ECKSTEIN and Roosa in the gallery beneath the plasma recharger, pondering the gloomy geological news. The results from the first sampling runs had been more than a little discouraging. The Emperor and the corporates were willing to accept an impurity rate in the Fergusite of between ten and twenty parts per billion, despite all the risks that entailed. Eckstein's initial results showed an average impurity rate of about sixteen parts per billion.

"I thought we'd do better than that," Eckstein admitted. "And some samples are as high as thirty PPB, so it's not as if we haven't accomplished anything. But the average for the areas we've covered so far is still well within the acceptable limits the Emperor established."

"So all of this"—Gloria swept her hand around to encompass the gallery and the shaft—"is a bust. We've failed."

Eckstein shrugged. "We sure as hell haven't succeeded. But it's not over yet."

"We only have a week to go," Roosa pointed out. "I don't see how we can accomplish much in that amount of time."

"Not the way we're going about it now," Eckstein agreed. "But there's one other thing we can try. There are problems with it, but my simulations show there's a chance that it could work."

"Forgive me for saying this, Stu," Gloria said in disgust, "but your simulations seem to stink."

"I never guaranteed anything," Eckstein reminded her. "And I'm not promising results now. But there is something else we can try, if we're willing to take some risks."

"Such as?"

"We'd need to use the second recharger— Grunfeld's. But that's in City Hall."

"Dexta runs City Hall now, Stu," Gloria pointed out. "We've moved all of our operations over there. If you're worried about security, I can get Arkady to put a couple of Bugs on it. No one will know anything is going on."

Eckstein nodded. "Okay, that takes care of one problem. Sam, how long to adapt the second recharger?"

"Maybe a day," said Roosa. "And another day to drill a shaft down to the Fergusite. But even with two plasma streams, I don't see how we're going to accomplish much in the five days we'll have left."

Eckstein grinned. "For what I have in mind," he said, "five *minutes* will be enough."

Roosa looked at him, and comprehension slowly dawned in his eyes. He shook his head. "You can't be serious!" he objected.

"I think it would work," Eckstein insisted.

"Spirit! You must be out of your mind!"

"Maybe. But I still say it would work."

"*What* would work?" Gloria demanded.

Roosa pointed his finger at Eckstein. "This maniac," he said, "wants to blow us all to kingdom come!"

"Not quite, Sam. You're forgetting something. With *two* rechargers, we can set up an interference pattern. See?"

Roosa frowned, his brow furrowed in deep thought for several moments. "Hmmm," he said.

"It's just a question of synchronizing the wave patterns so we get a nulled-out region between the two discharges. Then the overload will be forced into the surrounding Fergusite."

"Can we get that kind of precision?" Roosa asked dubiously. "You're expecting a helluva lot from a jury-rigged system."

"We can do it," Eckstein insisted. "We'll start out at low energy levels and fiddle with the pattern until we've got it synchronized. Then we gradually increase the energy until we're ready for the final overload."

"Yeah . . . yeah . . . maybe . . ."

"Maybe *what*?" Gloria shouted in frustration. "All this may be perfectly obvious to you technical types, but I have no idea what you're talking about."

Eckstein turned to her, an eager smile on his rugged features. "Look," he said, "it's really very simple, Gloria. You know how two waves can cancel each other out, right? If the waves are synchronized properly, you get an interference pattern."

"Uh . . . okay. So what?"

"So we can do that with the two plasma rechargers. That would create an area between here and City Hall, maybe a few hundred meters in diameter, where the energy input into the Fergusite layer would do no damage at all."

"And that's good?"

"It's essential. Look, the reason our results so far

have been poor is because we are limited in the amount of energy we can pump into the layer below us. If we put in too much, it will simply break down the local Fergusite crystal structure to the point where no further energy transfer to the rest of the stratum is possible. So we've had to do it gradually, to preserve the energy transference properties of the Fergusite. But with an interference pattern established to protect the stuff directly below us, we can inject far more energy, which would be transferred throughout the entire Fergusite layer."

"And that would be enough to ruin the rest of the Fergusite?"

"Absolutely," Eckstein assured her.

Roosa cleared his throat. Gloria and Eckstein looked at him. "Tell her the rest of it," he said.

Gloria looked back at Eckstein and raised her eyebrows.

"Well," Eckstein told her, "there is one minor drawback to this plan."

"Which is?"

"Which is," Roosa put in, "that the three of us spend the rest of our lives on a prison world for high treason."

"I didn't say it was perfect," Eckstein said. Roosa gave a snort of derision.

"Wait a minute," said Gloria. "If we do it this new way, you're saying we'll be caught? Why?"

"Because," Roosa explained, "doing it this way will blow the roof off City Hall and the anteroom of the Emporium. Literally. That might tend to draw a certain amount of attention to what we've been doing."

"You see, Gloria," Eckstein said, "we don't have time to be subtle. We'll have to zap the entire layer all at once with one, final, gigajoule overload. That energy will spread throughout the Fergusite layer and destroy it. But it will also seek out every line of escape, so to speak."

Roosa pointed his thumb toward the shaft. "It will blast straight up through this shaft and the one under City Hall. I expect people would notice that."

"Ah," said Gloria, understanding at last.

They sat in silence for a full minute, each of them contemplating the risks, the stakes, and the future. At length, Gloria said, "I'm in."

"I'll send my man Dwayne away the day before we do it," Roosa said. "At least that will give him a head start."

"And you'll go with him, Sam," Eckstein said. "I won't need you for the finale. We can't do it manually, in any case. I'll rig a remote to blow both rechargers at the same instant."

Roosa shook his head. "You'll still need someone on the second recharger to make final adjustments to the flow. Anyway, I don't want to miss this. It ought to be one hell of a show."

"A show?" asked Gloria.

"Plasma beams shooting into the sky like Empire Day fireworks," said Roosa.

"Hmmm," said Gloria, a smile beginning to form on her face.

Eckstein stared at her. "What?"

The smile was complete. "I have an idea," she said.

GLORIA WALKED QUIETLY THROUGH THE MISTY forest near the base of the falls. She was nude, as she had been most of the day as she went from camp to camp, drumming up support for refiling.

Now, she padded over the soft, wet mosses of the forest floor; when she was far enough into the forest that the roar of the falls was no more than a dim, muted thunder, she stopped and looked around.

"Abel!" she called. "We have to talk. I need you!"

And suddenly, Abel stepped out from behind a tree, grinning.

"Been expectin' you," he said.

chapter **26**

GLORIA'S WAS NOT THE ONLY VOICE HEARD IN
the valley that week. There was another voice, ethereal
and haunting, that seemed to come from everywhere
and nowhere . . .

"You must not hurt me!"

It echoed from the high ridges and murmured along
the streams and rills. It spoke to solitary, frightened men
and raucous campfire assemblages, to highboys and
riverrats, to humble townspeople and self-important
dignitaries. It was heard in the Emporium, and it was
heard in the Lodge.

It was even heard, one damp afternoon, on the golf
course in Overhill, where Thomas Shoop was allowing
himself to be outplayed by the visiting Imperium Vice
President, Oswald Hanratty. The corporate veep was
just about to stroke a fifteen-foot putt to save par when
the Voice interrupted his concentration and caused him
to miss the putt.

"You must not hurt me!"

At first annoyed, then puzzled, Hanratty looked

up, turned to Shoop, and asked, "What the hell was *that*?"

"It's the Voice!" cried Shoop. "I *told* you it was real. I *told* you!"

Hanratty looked around, as if expecting to find the source of the Voice in the fairways or sand traps. "That was it?" he asked Shoop. "That's all?"

"Well what did you expect? A heavenly chorus? For Spirit's sake, Ozzie, that's the Voice I've been telling you about. It's real, dammit—*real*!"

"Uh . . . well, I did hear *something*, but . . ."

"You heard the Voice, Ozzie! I know you and everyone back at headquarters thought I was crazy, but now you know I'm not. Dammit, Oz, you can't just ignore this!"

Hanratty thought about it for a moment, then shook his head. "The Board would just think that I've gone crazy, too."

"But we both know that's not true," Shoop protested. "Listen to me, Oz. I don't know what the Voice is, and neither does anyone else. Some people say it's Sylvania's version of the Spirit, and that makes about as much sense as anything else. All I know for sure is that it's real, and we can't ignore it. We cannot let this planet be raped! And you and I can do something to prevent it."

"You mean the deal you want to make with Prizm?" Hanratty walked over to the hole and backhanded his ball into it for a bogey. He leaned over to pick up the ball, when the Voice spoke again.

"You must not hurt me!"

Hanratty stood up quickly, looked around again, then thoughtfully ran his palm across the back of his neck. The little hairs there were standing on end.

"Spirit!" Hanratty breathed.

Shoop looked at him. "Oz?"

"Spirit," Hanratty repeated. He shook his head. "I don't know how in hell we're going to sell this to the

Board, but I guess I'm willing to try it. Let's go talk to Mitchell."

Hanratty strode off the green toward their waiting golf cart. "You don't want to finish the round?" Shoop asked him.

"Shit, no," Hanratty declared. "After that, I'd be afraid to take a divot!"

THE EXCELSIOR EXTRACTOR FINALLY ARRIVED in the harbor one afternoon, and people flocked to the shoreline to stare at the behemoth. It was as if a large, angular island had suddenly appeared in the bay.

The Extractor was an immense cube, half a kilometer on a side. With its Ferguson Distortion Generators, it was capable of interstellar transit, although its gargantuan mass meant that it had to poke along through the ether at a mere five light-years per day. It could float in an ocean, or sink beneath one and ponderously rove across the seafloor. But its true home was on the surface of a planet, and no planetary surface touched by an Extractor was ever again recognizable.

The business end of the Extractor was the gaping maw on its leading edge, four hundred meters wide and a hundred high. Its perimeter was studded with precisely aligned arrays of mass-repulsion units and plasma drills that, working in tandem, were capable of turning mountains into gravel. As the juggernaut moved forward, the landscape ahead of it was shattered and smashed, then scraped into the maw for processing. Anything of value was sorted and stored within the machine; everything else was ejected from the rear, like the droppings of dinosaurs. An Extractor was the ultimate expression of humankind's instinct for transforming its environment. The Excelsior Extractor now floating in the harbor would not merely destroy the Rankus River Valley. It would erase it.

And four more Extractors were already on their way to Sylvania.

BILL TRENGGANU NEVER HAD MUCH LUCK. HE tried not to whine about it too much, but it was the Spirit's own truth that he rolled snake eyes more than his fair share of the time. You could ask people, and they'd tell you.

He'd been born on Dalmatia IV, way the hell on the other side of the Empire from Sylvania, a good twelve hundred light-years distant. It was a drab, gray splotch of a world, with nothing to recommend it and nothing to keep a man there except maybe gravity. He never got much of an education—hadn't really wanted one, he'd admit—and spent a dozen or so years working at odd jobs before settling in as a skimmer mechanic. He married and started putting a few crowns away toward the day when he'd have his own shop. But then his wife ran off with his best friend and took most of his money when she left. Never saw it coming. Unlucky.

Bill tried again with another wife. Same damn thing happened.

By that point, Bill figured it was time to change his luck. He'd heard about the big boom on Sylvania and decided he couldn't do much worse there than he'd been doing on Dalmatia. So he sold everything he owned and borrowed what he could from friends and relatives, then made his way across the Empire to Sylvania.

He didn't know the first thing about mining, or geology, or Fergusite, or much of anything else, really. He thought he knew a little about poker, but soon learned otherwise at the Emporium. After a few weeks on the East Ridge, he had run out of supplies, had run afoul of other highboys, and had yet to see so much as a speck of Fergusite. Changing planets didn't seem to have changed his luck.

Half-starving, he stumbled into the riverrat camp at

Crooked Elbow Creek one day, and they took him in. They put him to work on the sluice boxes, scooping and hauling sand from the bottoms, and they gave him food to eat and a dry place to sleep. And after six months, they gave him a share in the Crooked Elbow Company.

It looked as if his luck was finally changing; but it wasn't, not really. No sooner did he get a share of the company than the whole shooting match looked like it was going to go south. Grunfeld, Dexta, the corporates, the Empire . . . they weren't about to let Bill Trengganu or anyone like him get a piece of the pie, and maybe not even any crumbs. The only way his luck could have been worse, he figured, would have been if, instead of Crooked Elbow, he'd stumbled into Pizen Flats.

There had been a lot of talk about re-filing the Crooked Elbow claims, but after the massacre at Pizen Flats, enthusiasm for that idea all but vanished. Not until the final week before the deadline, when Gloria VanDeen showed up—in the flesh, and lots of it—did talk of refiling revive. Bill didn't see what difference it would make, one way or another; he was certain that he and everyone else along the river would get screwed, no matter what they did.

The only reason he agreed to go along with the majority at Crooked Elbow and refile their claims was because Gloria VanDeen was offering herself as a prize. The names of everyone who refiled would go into a hat, she said, and the lucky boomrat whose name was drawn would win a night alone with her. Bill, who knew he was not a lucky man, never figured on being the winner, but maybe he'd know the guy who did win and get the inside story.

But then, Bill's luck finally changed. He won.

He was so astonished by this turn of events that he didn't even know how to react. When Gloria took him to dinner at the Emporium—champagne, prime rib, oysters, the works—he found himself all but tongue-tied and could only stare at her across the table, wondering how this could be happening to him. She smiled and tried to put him at ease, but the sight of that incredible face and that magnificent, all-but-naked body was almost more than he could handle. He knew all about how to deal with bad luck, but good luck was a new one on him. And luck just didn't get any better than this!

Then she took him by the hand and led him up to her room. He made a mess of things, naturally—just couldn't contain himself. But she didn't seem to mind, and couldn't have been nicer about it. And when they tried again, everything was just about perfect.

Bill left the Emporium the next morning smiling as he had never smiled before. And never again would he complain about his luck. He knew he'd had a lifetime's worth of good luck in a single night. Couldn't ask for more than that.

THE DEXTA TEAM GATHERED AROUND A LARGE table in the Emporium to celebrate the end of their labors on Sylvania. The Governor's deadline had passed, the last claims had been filed or refiled, and there was nothing left for them to do but eat, drink, and dream of Earth.

By midevening, the drinks had taken full effect, and even the most reluctant of the big-bucks bureaucrats were feeling mellow and forgiving about their sojourn on Sylvania. The work had been tedious and the living conditions primitive, but they felt a certain pride in what they had accomplished, and some of them had even found unexpected rewards on this backwater world.

Petra and Pug Ellison sat next to each other, gazing into each others' eyes and pawing one another in undisguised heat. No longer a bar girl, Petra was still nearly naked in a plunging minidress she had borrowed from Gloria, her small breasts and pert nipples fully in view and available for Pug's pleasure. The two had been inseparable since Petra's rescue, and their natural appetite for sex had been enhanced by Gloria's gift of a packet of potent jigli. Gloria wanted Petra to enjoy sex as much as she did herself, if that was possible; even though she had no memory of the rape and assault, Petra was aware that it had occurred, and might have become skittish about sex, if not for the welcome presence of the ardent Pug Ellison. Gloria watched Pug stroking Petra's bare breast while she nibbled his earlobes, and smiled beneficently.

MORE SURPRISING THAN PETRA'S RECOVERY was Wilmer DeGrasse's apparent conversion. Lulu Villegas, naked Emporium whore, sat in the lap of the erstwhile Christian moralist, licking his beet-red face.

"Lulu is coming back to Earth with me," DeGrasse explained, in evident embarrassment. "I'm . . . that is . . . she . . . we . . . uh, we're going to be, uh, married!"

The Dexta staffers roared their approval and laughed in delight. Lulu had hit the Mother Lode and was the envy of her colleagues in the rooms. For his part, De-Grasse had discovered that perhaps money *could* buy happiness, after all. He would have to come up with some appropriate cover story for his family—could he pass Lulu off as a missionary, he wondered?—but he had no doubt that true love would conquer all. True lust, in any case, had conquered Wilmer DeGrasse.

GLORIA SAT ALONE AT THE HEAD OF THE TABLE, pleased that her charges had performed so well and apparently held no grudges against her. She had pushed them hard, bullied them when necessary, and achieved everything the Emperor had insisted upon. Officially, at least, there could be no cause for Imperial displeasure over the Sylvania mission.

Unofficially, there would no doubt be repercussions over the way Gloria had spent the final week. She had abandoned Dexta's professed neutrality in her campaign to get the riverrats to refile their claims before the Eminent Domain hearing. Her justification, publicly, was that the Pizen Flats massacre had represented a failure by Dexta to control the course of events, and her refiling efforts were simply an attempt to right the wrong that had been done and to restore the natural balance of forces. It was a flimsy argument, but that was her story, and she intended to stick with it.

The manner in which she had pursued the refiling campaign was likely to cause further outrage in some quarters of the Empire. She had offered herself as a prize in a lottery for those who refiled, and had faithfully paid off to a bedraggled boomer named Bill Trengganu. It was only right, she thought, that one of the boomrats should get to spend a night with her, and under the circumstances, her only regret was that she hadn't been able to do the same with more of them. If things turned out badly here, she was going to live the rest of her life on a prison world; she didn't want to spend the coming decades wondering if she could have done more. And Bill had been a nice man. Most of the boomers were. She wondered again if maybe she should have worked the rooms. By now, practically everyone seemed to assume that she did, anyway, and that she had indiscriminately screwed every riverrat she could find. Maybe, she thought, I should have.

She was alone this evening, since Eckstein was off on another sampling expedition. In any case, it seemed wise for them not to be seen together more than necessary. Their plans had already been set in motion, and the second recharger was in synchrony with the first. Now, all that remained was to wait for the Eminent Domain results and find out if their fireworks display would be necessary.

Gloria wore only an oversized blue shirt, mostly unbuttoned. Feeling a buzz from the drinks and a tingle from the jigli she had smoked during the day as she made her final rounds of the camps along the river, Gloria looked around the table at her team. Spirit, she was proud of them! Effete, rich jerks, many of them, and yet they had rounded into shape and turned into effective team players. Jill Clymer, looking dazzling tonight in a see-through dress that showed off her ample bosom to maximum advantage, had been a rock—loyal, dependable, and relentlessly competent. Randolph Alexander and Pearl Shuzuki had performed close to the limit of their modest abilities and had caused no problems. Gloomy Sintra Garbedian had surprised her with his willingness to work. Wilmer DeGrasse had done his job, as well, perhaps inspired by his new outlook on life. Young Pug Ellison had been impressive, and would be a welcome addition to the permanent OSI team—especially so for Petra. Even Raul Tellemacher, who had put in a brief appearance at the party, then left, had worked diligently. And, of course, Althea had performed above and beyond the call of duty—and loved it.

They were telling war stories. Pearl Shuzuki had a good one about the old boomrat who insisted that he never signed his name to anything unless he was stone-cold sober—which he hadn't been, by his reckoning, in about twenty years. Garbedian followed with the tale of his travails the day the skimmer broke down high on a ridge, and he and Jill Clymer had been forced to hike miles back down to the river in a pouring rain.

"At least you weren't alone," Wilmer DeGrasse told him. "One day, Tellemacher left me all by myself on the ridge for three or four hours. Just took off in the skimmer and said he'd be right back. I would have tried walking back, but I had no idea which way to go. Thought I'd have to spend all night there, but Tellemacher finally came back. Said it was all a mistake, and he was terribly sorry. Imagine!"

Gloria suddenly snapped to full alertness. "Wilmer, when did that happen?"

"What? When? Oh, I don't know, a month or so ago.

Come to think of it, I believe it was the day when . . . when everything happened."

"The day of the massacre? The day Petra and I were assaulted?"

DeGrasse looked abashed. "Well, as a matter of fact, it was. And here I am, complaining about what happened to *me* that day. I'm sorry, Gloria, I didn't—"

Gloria abruptly sprang to her feet and dashed out of the Emporium.

A MAN SHE HAD NEVER SEEN BEFORE OPENED the door to the Lodge. Gloria shoved him out of her way and marched inside. There, she found Tellemacher and Pollas seated comfortably before the fireplace, feet propped up, sipping brandy. She halted in front of Tellemacher's easy chair and glared at him.

"You incredible bastard!"

Tellemacher looked up. Gloria had not bothered to fasten more of the buttons of her shirt and stood before him all but fully exposed. He carefully inspected her body before meeting her angry eyes.

"You're wasting your time here, Gloria," Tellemacher said affably. "We don't have any claims we want to refile. But if you'd like to fuck us, like you did all those boom-rats, I don't think we'd have any objections."

"Anytime," Pollas agreed.

"Shut your mouth, Pollas," Gloria told him. "I don't have anything on you—yet. I'm here for this piece of filth."

"That would be me, I take it," said Tellemacher.

Gloria slowly shook her head. "I knew you were a lowlife," she said. "I've known that for years. But it never occurred to me that you would be capable of something like this."

"Like what?"

"You were here that day. You were the third voice Maddie Mitchell heard. It was you, Tellemacher. *You* were the one who told them about Petra!"

"Me? Gloria, you wound me, you truly do! What makes you think a thing like that?"

"You left DeGrasse up on the ridge that day. You lied when you told me that night that you never heard the recall after the Pizen Flats people came in to refile. You heard it, all right. And you knew the refilings would force the Lodge to respond. But there was something they needed to know first. So you came here and told them—that Petra was from Dexta and was here as a spy. It was you, Tellemacher. It couldn't have been anyone else!"

Tellemacher shifted his weight in the easy chair and brought his feet down. "You're jumping to conclusions, Gloria."

"It's the only conclusion possible. So much was happening then that I never thought to check your story with DeGrasse. But as soon as I found out that you left DeGrasse alone that afternoon, it all fit into place. I never thought it was you before, because I assumed that you were accounted for. But you weren't. You left DeGrasse on the ridge, and you came here to warn your friends about Petra."

"Hogwash," said Tellemacher.

"You know," Gloria said, "I always wondered why you agreed to come on this mission. You could have found a way to weasel out of it. Did someone *send* you? Was it Charles? Or one of the corporates? Or maybe just your family? It wouldn't surprise me if they had their greasy tentacles in the middle of this."

"Oh, now you're just being insulting. My family's greasy tentacles happen to be in the middle of *most* important things in the Empire. What does it matter why I came? I did come, and I did my job. Even you can't deny that."

"Your job didn't include selling out a Dexta colleague."

Tellemacher shrugged. "Petra was taking a chance just by being here. You knew that, and yet you sent her.

They were bound to find out about her sooner or later. You can't prove I had anything to do with it."

"I'll prove it," Gloria promised. "But right now, I don't have to. I already have everything I need to bring you up on internal Dexta administrative charges. DeGrasse will state that you left him alone for three to four hours that afternoon. And you lied to me about the recall signal. I've got you cold, Tellemacher—dereliction of duty and making false statements to a superior."

Tellemacher got to his feet and stood in front of her. Still seated, Pollas said, "Really, Ms. VanDeen, surely, these are trivial matters. Aren't you making a mountain out of a molehill?"

Gloria gave Pollas a quick, frosty glance, then turned back to Tellemacher. "I can see that your friend doesn't know how we handle molehills in Dexta. Maybe you should explain it to him."

"No," said Tellemacher, "you do it. You'll enjoy it more."

"Damn right, I will. You see, Pollas, Dexta washes its own dirty laundry, according to the *Dexta Code*, not the *Imperial Code*. Tellemacher will be hauled before a Dexta Board of Inquiry. He'll be entitled to an advocate, of course, but as soon as the Board hears that he is under suspicion of betraying a Dexta undercover agent, they'll ship him off to a prison world without so much as blinking an eye. No trial. No appeal."

"I see," said Pollas. "Frightening."

Gloria looked Tellemacher in the eyes. "I'm taking you into administrative custody, Tellemacher. If you want to try to escape, this will be your only chance. Be my guest, Raul. Please."

Tellemacher laughed and shook his head. "No thank you, Gloria," he said. He reached into his back pocket, pulled out his pad, and tapped a couple of keys on it. Then he held it out to Gloria. "Here," he said, "this is my letter of resignation. You can't take me into custody because I am no longer *in* Dexta."

Gloria ignored the pad. "Nice try," she said, "but you should know better than that. Your resignation doesn't become effective until it's endorsed by your immediate superior, which is me, in case you've forgotten."

"It may be you at the moment," Tellemacher conceded, "but three months ago, back on Earth, when I wrote this letter, it wasn't you. It was your old pal Hector Konrad, Administrative Supervisor for Sector 8. If you'll bother to read it, you'll see that there's a paragraph stating that my resignation becomes effective immediately upon transmission to the appropriate authority in whatever jurisdiction I may find myself. I've just transmitted it to your pad, Gloria. As of this instant, I am no longer in Dexta."

Gloria angrily snatched the pad from Tellemacher and read the letter. The provision was there, as he had stated it. It was certainly unusual, perhaps even unique, but the endorsement by Konrad made it legal. She couldn't touch him.

She flung the pad back at him. He caught it, smiled, and tucked it back into his pocket.

"You son of a bitch!"

"Undoubtedly. You never met any of my family, did you? Detestable people. They steered me into Dexta because they thought it would be useful for the family, and my older brothers and sisters already had the prime slots in the bank and business. So Raul, that flighty ski bum, wound up in Dexta, very much against his will. But no more, thank the Spirit! Don't worry about me, Gloria. You see, I've already lined up another position."

"Indeed," said Pollas. "I think congratulations are in order. Ms. VanDeen, say hello to the new Executive Vice President of Pollas Enterprises."

Tellemacher and Pollas grinned at her. Gloria stood there before them, steaming, furiously trying to think of something to say.

"Care to have a drink with us to celebrate my entry

into the private sector?" Tellemacher looked immensely pleased with himself.

"This isn't over," Gloria said.

"I think it is," said Tellemacher.

"You're wrong." Gloria pivoted on her heel and stormed out of the Lodge to the sound of laughter.

GLORIA RETURNED TO THE EMPORIUM, WOKE up Arkady Volkonski, and dragged him out of his bed. Volkonski was disappointed to find that she wanted information rather than sex, but he answered her questions in considerable detail. He didn't ask her why she wanted information on this particular subject matter. As an Internal Security officer, he was well aware that it could be dangerous to know more than was necessary.

Following her session with Volkonski, Gloria packed a small bag, roused the Dexta Cruiser pilot, and headed for the pier. She told Petra that she would be back in a day, in plenty of time for the Eminent Domain hearing.

Upon her arrival on Palmyra, she went first to the Dexta offices and met with Jennifer Astuni. From Jennifer, she learned that the local police had found two bodies that had been identified as those of Mr. and Mrs. Preston Thawley. They had been dead for several weeks. Gloria was not surprised.

Then she went to the hospital where Petra had first been treated, then abducted. She had a brief and contentious meeting with Dr. Hamdoon and Ms. Suharto, the hospital administrator. Gloria questioned them closely about a suspected discrepancy in the hospital's inventory. They were relieved when she said that in return for their cooperation and continued silence, she would forgo filing charges. All she needed was to collect a little evidence. They were happy to comply and vastly relieved when she departed as swiftly as she had arrived.

Late the next night, Gloria was back on Sylvania.

chapter 27

GLORIA SAT ALONE IN THE FORMER OFFICE OF the late Mayor of Greenlodge, staring at the walls. She had been there most of the night, following her return from Palmyra. It was her office now. Grunfeld and his pukes were gone, Rankus was dead, and the new Imperial Governor was an empty suit. Gloria VanDeen was the new power on Sylvania, and yet she had sat there half the night feeling utterly powerless.

And scared.

She had not felt this frightened since she faced down a marching army on a dusty road on Mynjhino. Her knees had actually been trembling that day. But then, at least, it had all been right there in front of her. She could see what was happening and knew what needed to be done. But now, today on Sylvania, she had already done every last thing it was possible for her to do, and still it was not enough. Whatever happened—with the Eminent Domain vote or the plasma rechargers—was beyond her power to influence. She could only wait helplessly—like everyone else—for the future to unfold . . . a future she might very well spend on a prison world.

If the future was unknowable, it didn't make her feel any better to contemplate the past. Spirit, had she done *anything* right on this miserable planet? Dina Westerbrook may have pulled her out of a slough of despond, but mere words could not erase the deeds that had been done. So many lives lost that needn't have been; perhaps, an entire world lost. And with it, maybe, the Empire.

If only she had been smarter, less arrogant and full of herself. If only she had . . . *what*? If only *what*? Hindsight might have provided additional perspective, but it offered no answers.

Petra suddenly appeared at the office door. She paused there for a moment, then walked on in and closed the door behind her. "It's time," she said.

Gloria looked up at her assistant. Petra was positively glowing, in full and radiant bloom. For once, she even outshone her famous boss. Gloria, determined not to be the center of attention today, was wearing a relatively conservative charcoal-gray jacket which, buttoned at the waist, covered her breasts most of the time, and a matching miniskirt that concealed her crotch with an inch or two to spare. But Petra was wearing a very sheer, pale green shirt, unbuttoned to the waist, that left her small, round breasts almost completely uncovered. And her dark green miniskirt was as revealing as any that Gloria owned.

Was it Pug's influence, Gloria wondered. Or Elba's? Whatever the reason, Petra seemed to have hit her stride and was displaying a confidence Gloria had never seen before. She hadn't mentioned Weehawken in weeks!

"You look nice today, Petra," Gloria told her.

"And you look tired," Petra responded. "Have you been sitting here all night?"

"Most of it," Gloria shrugged. "Big day today."

"And, of course, sitting here all night worrying about it will make everything turn out right."

"Probably not," Gloria conceded. "Petra, I have screwed up everything I've touched on this damned planet. *Everything!*"

"I see," said Petra. "So if the vote comes out wrong today, it's all your fault, huh? And the people who died—or got hurt—were all your responsibility too, I guess. And if the Extractors rip up this valley, that'll be on your head, as well, right?"

"Petra—"

"Oh, shut up, Gloria," Petra said in evident disgust. "Spirit, you rich people! One way or another, for good or ill, everything is about *you*, isn't it? Us poor people know better, but you richies just don't get it, do you? Well, listen up, Gloria, I've got some news for you. The galaxy does *not* revolve around *you*!"

Petra stood there and stared down at Gloria. Stunned by her words—and the fact that she had said them—Gloria stared back at Petra, seeing her gray-green eyes and determined face in a new light. Petra, the cute, funny, flighty little assistant—who was, in fact, two years older than Gloria and had overcome obstacles in life that Gloria could hardly imagine. They locked eyes for a long, silent moment, and Gloria could think of nothing to say.

Then Petra broke the tension. Her face relaxed into a broad smile and she said in her familiar giggle, "It revolves around *me*!"

"Maybe it should," Gloria laughed as she got to her feet. She threw her arm around Petra's shoulders, and together they marched outside over the planks and mud and down the street to the Emporium.

THE MAIN ROOM OF THE EMPORIUM WAS crowded to the rafters as Judge Kershaw gaveled the Eminent Domain hearing to order. Kershaw sat behind a table covered in green baize (from one of the gambling tables), positioned in front of the west wall of the building. The table—or improvised judge's bench—was mounted on a riser to give him a commanding view and authoritative presence. Facing the judge were three tables: one on his right, for the representatives of Excelsior and Servitor, who had initiated the Eminent Domain petition; one on the left for Dexta personnel and the judge's two legal clerks; and one in the center for the new Imperial Governor and his Imperial Secretary. Behind them, hundreds of chairs were occupied by boomers of all descriptions, each of whom held at least one certified claim or proxy. Additional chairs had been set up on the second-floor balcony, around three sides of the main room.

At the judge's far left, near the door to the anteroom, a table had been provided for the media. The event had drawn a flock of media reps back to Sylvania, but they had also been attracted by the frequent appearances of the Voice. Word of the Voice had begun to circulate throughout the Empire, and it was causing a considerable stir. The Universal Church of the Spirit had been especially interested, since the Voice seemed to many to be a local manifestation of the Spirit Herself. The UCS Bishop of Palmyra, an old fishing buddy of Judge Kershaw, had come to see—or hear—for himself, and was seated with the media, where he was readily available for interviews and theological speculation.

"This hearing will come to order," Judge Kershaw said in his gravelly voice. The babble in the Emporium gradually died away.

"Now, then," said Kershaw, "let me explain a few things before we get started. We are using makeshift facilities here, and I'm well aware of the normal function of this establishment. However, that does not mean that we will act as if we were in a bawdy house, even though it happens that we are. The bar is closed and will remain closed until we're done here. Anyone creating a disturbance of any sort will be ejected by the Dexta security people—those muscular-looking gentlemen in gray. I trust that will not become necessary." The judge slowly shifted his gaze to every part of the room, high and low, making it clear to one and all that he meant exactly what he said.

"Very well," Kershaw continued. "As to the business before us, as you know, we meet today to consider an Eminent Domain petition filed by the Excelsior Corporation, which seeks to condemn certain properties and mining claims on this planet for the purpose of conducting large-scale extraction operations."

Some of the boomrats bravely offered hisses and boos. Kershaw whacked the gavel against the table. "I warned you about that," he said. "I won't warn you again."

Kershaw checked something on his pad for a moment, then looked up. "There are precisely 2640 individually filed and certified claims involved in these proceedings. In order for the Eminent Domain petition to be granted, 60 percent of them, or 1584 claims, must vote in favor of the petition. We will go through the list of certified claimants in alphabetical order. Fortunately, quite a number of claims are held by proxy, and I gather that the proxy holders will be doing most of the voting. Even so, it's likely to take all day for us to get from A to Z. So settle in and get comfortable—we're going to be here a while. Is there any business before we get started?"

At the table on the judge's right, Myron Vigo got to his feet. "Good morning, Your Honor," he said, smiling.

"Morning, Mr. Vigo. I gather that you are representing the petitioners? Okay, what have you got?"

"A point of inquiry, Judge. What will be the procedure regarding challenges?"

The judge lifted his bushy eyebrows. "Why? You intend to file some?"

"Possibly," said Vigo.

"I see. In that case, the procedure will be that each challenged claim will have to be examined. I see the

Imperial Geologist sitting at the Imperial Governor's table. Good morning, Dr. Eckstein."

Stu Eckstein got to his feet. "Good morning, Judge Kershaw."

"Dr. Eckstein," said the judge, "you have the only reliable maps of this region. In the event of a challenge to a claim, we will have to rely on your good offices. How long would it take you to examine a challenged claim?"

"Well, Your Honor," said Eckstein, "we'd need to check the map, then go to the site itself to make the necessary measurements, assuming that it's the size or location of the claim that is in dispute. Then, depending on the outcome, we might very well be forced to measure all the surrounding claims and make appropriate adjustments. If the challenge is in regard to whether or not a claim has been 'improved'—that is, whether it's a 'proved' claim—that would also require on-site examination to determine whether the claim meets the legal standards."

"And how long would all of that take?"

Eckstein spread his arms. "Days? Weeks? Hard to say, Your Honor. It would depend on the circumstances."

"I see. Thank you, Dr. Eckstein." Kershaw looked at Vigo. "Well, Mr. Vigo?"

Vigo gave the Judge an abashed smile. "Under the circumstances," he said, "I rather doubt that we'll be making any challenges."

"Glad to hear it," said the judge.

"However, we do reserve the right to make challenges regarding legal ownership and the assignment of proxies." Vigo sat down again.

"So noted," said Kershaw. "Now, if no one else has anything to say, let's get on with this. The clerk will call the first name."

One of Kershaw's clerks got to his feet and came around to the front of his table. He was a slight, harried-looking man with a high-pitched voice. He checked his pad and said, "Aaron, Levander B."

A disheveled, dusty boomer got to his feet near the rear of the room. He looked momentarily lost, then slowly made his way forward. The clerk scanned his retina with the pad and nodded. "Identity confirmed," he said. "Claim Number 0974 confirmed. How do you vote on the petition?"

"I'm for it," said Levander B. Aaron.

"Claim 0974, aye," said the clerk.

Levander B. Aaron looked toward the corporates' table. "When do I get my money?" he asked.

"All in good time, Mr. Aaron," the judge assured him. "Now take your seat, or leave, if you wish."

"Yessir." Levander B. Aaron returned to his seat.

"Abelard, Gerald C.," the clerk called.

Gerald C. Abelard held twelve proxies. He voted aye and quickly sat down again. Only 2627 claims remained.

GLORIA SAT AT THE DEXTA TABLE AND TRIED not to fidget. Petra sat next to her, keeping track of the running count on her own pad.

Before the hearing began, Sam Roosa had informed Gloria that he had sealed off the tunnel to Room 9 the previous night and that both rechargers were humming along in synchrony, awaiting only a final signal from Eckstein. The interference pattern that had looked so good in Eckstein's simulations was just as good in reality, and there was every reason to believe that the plan would work. There was also every reason to believe that if it did, unless people bought the diversionary cover story she had devised with Old Abel, the three of them would be charged with treason.

The cover story seemed increasingly threadbare as the time for its employment drew near. She knew that the only realistic hope they had to avoid a prison world was for the Eminent Domain vote to fall short of 60 percent. Then, there would be no need to light up the skies of Sylvania with the pyrotechnics Eckstein had planned, no need to destroy the Fergusite layer. The boomrats could go on producing their trickle of Fergusite without danger to the Empire, as long as the corporates were prevented from unleashing a flood of the stuff. But there was simply no way to predict the outcome of the vote, and she found herself checking Petra's running tally every few minutes. After the first hour, with 310 claims counted, the ayes had a comfortable margin of 207 to 103.

As the morning wore on, the nays staged a rally as a number of riverrat proxies were counted. She was pleased to see that the riverrats were presenting a nearly united front. With few exceptions, the miners from the river camps were voting no, while the highboys were voting yes. By the end of the second hour, the vote stood at 342 ayes, 262 nays.

During the third hour, a boomer with a long black beard and a wild look in his eyes somehow managed to evade both Ernie the Bouncer and the Bugs. He ran into the room, stopped before the judge, and shouted, "I want to change my vote!"

Two Bugs immediately grabbed him by each shoulder and started to drag him away, but the boomer put up an energetic resistance and loudly appealed to the judge. "You gotta let me change my vote, Your Honor! You gotta!"

"I don't gotta do anything," Kershaw told him. "However, as long as you're here, perhaps you could tell me why you think I should do that."

The Bugs relaxed their grip on him, and the boomer looked up at the judge. "My name's Floyd Givens, Your Honor, and I work up on the West Ridge. I give my proxy to my friend Eddie Dawkins. That's him, sittin' over there. And we was both gonna vote yes on this Eminent Domain deal, on account o' we wanna get paid something for all the work we put in on them worthless holes. You see how it is, Your Honor?"

"I think I do," said Kershaw.

"But then last night," Givens continued, "I heard the Voice! Heard it plain as day, I did. It said not to hurt it, and I'll be damned if I'm gonna! No sir. So you gotta let me change that vote—and you oughta change yours, too, Eddie! I want to vote no, Your Honor, and screw the money. I don't want to mess with that damn Voice!"

"I appreciate your position, Mr. Givens," Kershaw said. "However, your proxy vote has already been cast, and once a vote has been counted, it cannot be changed."

"But that ain't fair!" Givens protested.

"It may not be fair," Kershaw conceded, "but it is the law. Sorry, Mr. Givens. Gentlemen, if you would escort Mr. Givens to the exit, we'll continue."

The Bugs took their cue and started dragging Givens away. He bellowed to the heavens, if not to the judge, "It ain't my fault! I ain't the one that wants to hurt you. Ya gotta understand that! It ain't my fault."

As the Bugs removed Givens, the Spiritist Bishop got up from the media table and followed them out. Curious, Gloria slipped out of her chair and joined them in the anteroom.

There, Gloria listened as the Bishop closely questioned Givens about his experience with the Voice. It was a frequently heard story in the valley by then, the usual tale of a voice coming from everywhere and nowhere, asking not to be hurt. Abel was playing it just right, Gloria thought, repeating the same simple, urgent message to one and all.

When he was finished with Givens, the Bishop came over to Gloria and introduced himself. "Glenn Arkwright, Ms. VanDeen," he said, taking her hand. "I'm very pleased to meet you. Tell me, have you heard the Voice?"

"Indeed, I have," Gloria told him.

"And what did you think of it?"

"When I first heard it," Gloria said, "I thought that it must have been something a lot like the Spirit on Earth. I wondered if every planet had one."

Arkwright seemed delighted by her answer. "Just so!" he exclaimed. "It's a fascinating question, isn't it? Certainly, there are scores of stories of similar phenomena on worlds throughout the Empire. But this may be the first case that has been so extensively witnessed and documented. I believe that it has profound implications for the future of Spiritism."

"Oh?"

"We live in a very skeptical age, Ms. VanDeen. There are many, I'm sure you are aware, who doubt the reality of the Spirit. They think Her Visitations were just smoke and mirrors, arranged by a band of cynical manipulators. But events here on Sylvania are, I believe, powerful evidence to the contrary. The Spirit is universal, and will follow humanity throughout the galaxy. Let the cynics scoff about what happened eleven hundred years ago—but they cannot deny the reality of what is happening here today on Sylvania! It is nothing less than another manifestation of the Universal Spirit."

"I see," said Gloria.

The Bishop seemed to realize that he was getting carried away, so he brought himself back to basics by taking a good, close look at Gloria. "May I say, Ms. VanDeen," he went on, "that I believe that you, yourself, are a powerful force for the advancement of Spiritism? Oh, I know you have your critics, but I suspect they are motivated more by envy than reason. You are a living example of the Spirit's words—'Do not deny yourself Joy, for it is a gift unto humankind and the wellspring of happiness!' Your own appearance and actions are but a reflection of the Spirit's. You are proud and unashamed, and that is as it should be. I congratulate you and thank you for your affirmation of the creed of the Spirit!"

"Uh, yes . . . well . . ."

"I tell you," Arkwright said with enthusiasm, "I don't

believe that it is mere coincidence that you are here to be a witness to this newest manifestation of the Spirit. I believe the Spirit intended that you should be here to welcome Her to this world, for She has no finer testament to the power and righteousness of Her message. Bless you, Ms. VanDeen, bless you!"

Gloria returned to her seat in the main room, feeling distinctly uneasy about what she had just heard. She had no desire to be a secular saint in a religion that had no saints, an icon for a religion that had no icons. And for the first time, she began to think about the wider implications of the Voice—the fake Voice.

She was just in time to hear the clerk finish reading the very long list of claims whose proxies were held by Excelsior. There were 236 of them. Sherwin Lund voted yes.

The next big block of proxies belonged to Imperium. Seated a row back from the Dexta table, Shoop, Hanratty, and Maddie Mitchell sat together, in apparent accord. But Hanratty kept shaking his head and mumbling to himself about how he was going to explain this to the Board. Voice or no Voice, making a deal with Prizm would shut Imperium out of any possible deal with Excelsior and Servitor. Nevertheless, when Imperium was called, Thomas Shoop stood and delivered 187 votes against the petition.

With the tally standing at 655 ayes and 521 nays, Kershaw called a lunch break. The bar was closed, but the Emporium offered free sandwiches and coffee for everyone. People got to their feet, stretched, lined up for sandwiches or the restrooms, and gathered in roving clumps, discussing the prospects for the petition. Gloria noticed the Emporium's retinue of professional gamblers clustered at the back of the room, apparently making book on the outcome. She walked over to them and caught Slim Jim Zuni's eye.

"What are the odds, Jim?" she asked him.

Zuni smiled enigmatically. "Even money," he said.

"Right now, I'll settle for that."

"I hope you get what you want, Gloria," Zuni said. "But remember, there's no such thing as a sure thing."

Gloria went outside to take in a little of the rare rainy-season sunshine. She unbuttoned her jacket and let the strong breeze flap it open to expose her breasts, while her miniskirt rippled revealingly. Everyone noticed and enjoyed the view, and Gloria enjoyed watching them enjoying it. Don't deny yourself joy, she thought. It's the fucking wellspring of happiness . . .

She had always wanted to believe in the Spirit, but she suddenly wondered if she ever could, now. People like Arkwright believed in the Voice the same way they believed in the Spirit, because it offered them something that they wanted and needed in life. But the Voice was nothing more than a convenient bit of fakery, and if that was true of the Voice, she realized, it was probably also true of the Spirit. She felt strangely guilty about her role in propagating both illusions.

If she was a living testament to the creed of the Spirit, as Arkwright had said, did that make her a coconspirator in the millennium-old fraud of Spiritism? And did her plotting to spread the word of the Voice compound her crime?

And yet . . . was it such a crime? Spiritism had clearly been a force for good throughout its history—not even the most ardent cynics could deny that. And she truly believed that what she was doing on Sylvania was for the ultimate good of the Empire and humanity. If people like Arkwright were determined to incorporate the Voice into the gospel of Spiritism, was that such a bad thing? And if her own explosive sexuality seemed to be an affirmation of the words of the Spirit, did that harm anyone?

Gloria stared at the distant peaks beyond the valley, now dazzling white with their seasonal snowcaps. It was such a beautiful world. It would be worth preserving for its own sake, she thought, even without the imperative of the Fergusite problem. So . . . did the end justify the means? She laughed to herself at the thought. If things didn't go right today, it was the sort of philosophical conundrum that she could debate at her leisure during the coming decades on a prison world.

THE AFTERNOON SESSION WENT A LITTLE FASTER, as large blocs of proxies were cast. Rahim Ogunbayo proudly cast his 43 ayes, then Joe Pollas stood with a satisfied smirk on his face for several minutes as the clerk read off 253 claim numbers. Maddie Mitchell followed with 217 proxies cast against the petition on behalf of Prizm.

The grandson of Claude Rankus looked uncomfortable with the entire process. Nevertheless, he voted aye with the family's 57 proxies.

Gaspar Norfleet cast the last of the corporate proxies for Servitor. He gave Gloria a meaningful stare, as if he wanted her to appreciate the fact that this was partial payback for what she had cost the company on Mynjhino. Servitor voted aye, 249 times.

After Sidney Taplin and Myron Vigo voted their own proxies, the magic number of 1584 was within view. Nevertheless, the riverrat coalitions held steady, with thirty votes here and forty votes there. It was increasingly clear that the final tally was going to be very close.

Gloria tried to keep her composure as the clerk wound down through Watanabe, Watkins, Williams, Winters, Wolowiscz, Yarrow, Young, Yung . . . When Zachary Zane cast his three votes nay, it was all she could do not to stand up and cheer. There was a discernible babble slowly rising throughout the room, and Judge Kershaw had to whack his gavel a few times to keep order.

The ayes were stalled at 1578—six votes short—and when Bob Zimmermann cast 14 nays, there was an audible intake of breath in the Emporium. Then an old highboy named Elbert Zinn got up and listened as the clerk read off his seven claim numbers. Zinn looked around the room for several moments, then shook his head. "Shit," he said, "I ain't gonna be the one to do it. I vote no."

The room erupted in whoops and hollers, but Kershaw banged his gavel again. He looked toward the clerk who said, "There is still one name remaining." Instantly, the big room was dead silent.

"The final name," said the clerk, pausing to enjoy the moment, "is Zuni, James M."

Gloria felt her heart leap, but it froze in midflight as she watched Slim Jim make his way to the front of the room. She had never been able to read him, and she couldn't now. Yet there was something in the deliberate movement of his cadaverous frame that sent a chill coursing through her.

"Identity confirmed," intoned the clerk after Slim Jim's retina was scanned. "Nine claims, numbers 0341, 0569, 0579, 1094, 1542, 1543, 1544, 2009, and 2241. How do you vote?"

Slim Jim turned to look at Gloria and the Imperium and Prizm reps behind her, then turned the other way to look at Pollas, Lund, and Norfleet. Vigo was suddenly on his feet. "Your Honor," he cried, "I request a short recess!"

Kershaw chuckled. "I can't imagine why," he said. He looked over at Shoop and Mitchell. "Any objection?"

"We second the motion, Your Honor." Shoop said.

"Thought you might," said Kershaw. "Very well, then, we are in recess for the next ten minutes. Mr. Zuni, why don't you make use of the office over there? Have fun."

Gloria practically hurdled the table and beat everyone to Slim Jim. She looked up at him, into his unreadable dark eyes, and said, "Jim, you can't!"

Slim Jim remained unflappable. "Gloria," he said calmly, "I told you that there was no such thing as a sure thing—but I've got one now. I could have sold my proxies, but I knew there was a chance that it would be close, so I played a long shot, and for once, it came in. This is *it* for me, Gloria. The pot of a lifetime, and I'm holding aces. I'm going to take the best offer."

"But . . ."

"Right this way, Mr. Zuni," said a smiling Myron Vigo as he clutched Slim Jim's elbow and led him toward the office. Pollas, Ogunbayo, Rankus, Taplin, Lund, and Norfleet followed along. Mitchell, Shoop, and Hanratty brought up the rear. As they disappeared into the office and the door shut behind them, Gloria sat down again and propped her head up on her elbows.

Petra touched her arm. "Gloria? Slim Jim won't sell you out. I know it!"

Gloria shook her head sadly. "Slim Jim," she said, "will do what's best for Slim Jim. Spirit knows how many millions those proxies of his are worth right now. But he'll go with the high offer, whoever makes it. That *is* a sure thing."

Twenty very long minutes later, Slim Jim Zuni emerged from the office, still maintaining his poker face. But behind him, Mitchell, Shoop, and Hanratty look stunned, while Myron Vigo wore an expression of supreme satisfaction.

Slim Jim stood before the clerk. He glanced toward Gloria, gave her an apologetic smile, then turned back to face the clerk.

"How do you vote?"

"I vote yes," said Slim Jim.

It was several minutes before Judge Kershaw could gavel the room back to order. Then the clerk confirmed the final tally, and Kershaw nodded. "The Eminent Domain petition is granted. These proceedings are closed."

Gloria exchanged a quick look with Stu Eckstein. Both of them nodded, and Gloria pressed a button on her wristcom.

N-o-o-o-o-o-o-o-o-o-o-o!!!!

The Voice sounded primal and savage, like the cry of a thousand tortured beasts. It shook the Emporium and reverberated in the breasts of frightened men and women.

YOU . . . MUST . . . NOT . . . HURT . . . ME!!!!!

Fear and awe permeated the room. Judge Kershaw's mouth dropped open and his bushy eyebrows arched skyward. Thomas Shoop instinctively grasped Maddie Mitchell's upper arm, and Ozzie Hanratty's eyes looked like saucers. At the corporates' table, Myron Vigo kept looking around in search of the source of this unexpected petition. Young Rankus looked utterly spooked, as if he were hearing the reproach of his grandfather from beyond the grave. At the media table, Bishop Arkwright wore an expression of beatific sanctity, like a Crusader who had finally found the Holy Grail.

YOU . . . MUST . . . NOT . . . HURT . . . ME!!!!!

And suddenly, the Emporium began to shake. A low rumble coming from the anteroom gradually grew in volume and intensity. People gasped and cried out, a few women screamed, and they all leaped to their feet and began searching for the nearest exit. They tumbled over each other in a mad dash to the doors. Petra started to rise, but Gloria clamped her arm and pulled her back to her seat. "Wait," she said calmly.

The human tide flowed past them and out the main door. Media reps stood fast, imaging the scene, until they were infected themselves and joined the rush. Judge Kershaw stepped down from his riser and, attempting to maintain his dignity, walked briskly toward the door, his two clerks running interference. Whores, bar girls, bartenders, gamblers, boomrats, grifters, speculators, big shots, and small fry all swelled the exodus, until, barely a minute after it had begun, Gloria was all but alone in the Emporium's main room. Petra, with Pug Ellison hugging her, Stu Eckstein, a few Bugs, and the imperturbable and newly wealthy Slim Jim Zuni remained with her. Then, with unspoken accord, they walked to the door.

In the anteroom, the source of the rumble was immediately obvious. The plasma recharger was vibrating furiously, shaking the entire building. Eckstein looked at it and nodded his head in satisfaction. "Yep," he said. "I think we should all get well away from this building."

The Bugs charged out into the street and began herding people away from the Emporium. Petra and Pug followed. Slim Jim Zuni smiled at Gloria on his way out. She should have been annoyed with him, but for some reason she returned the smile. Gloria exited with Eckstein, and together, they strolled after the retreating crowd. Off to her right, she noticed a similar retreat from the environs of City Hall. As she walked over the wooden planking, she saw that the water in the ubiquitous mud puddles was sloshing around, and the mud itself was trembling.

The mob instinctively halted a couple hundred meters away from the Emporium. People stopped, turned, and stared, waiting to see what would happen next. They didn't have to wait very long.

With a loud sizzle and a static discharge that made hairs stand on end, the Emporium and City Hall suddenly gave birth to two dazzling beams of plasma that shot upward into the gray skies, drilling holes through the low clouds and disappearing in the distance. The brilliant, blue-green columns of concentrated energy were so intense that it hurt to look at them, yet it was impossible to look away from the spectacle. The awestruck onlookers felt the ground shaking beneath their feet and clutched one another as if Judgment Day had come.

"What is it? What is it?" a woman cried.

"It is the Spirit," Bishop Arkwright declared. "The Spirit, in righteous wrath and glory!"

"It's the fuckin' rechargers, is what it is," a boomrat countered. "Just look at them bastards." But he was ignored.

"Look!" someone shouted. He pointed toward the ridgeline to the east of town. There, pencil-thin beams of plasma were shooting upward at odd angles, like random, drunken searchlights. Someone else turned to the west and saw the same thing happening on the ridge across the river. Above, the clouds began to spin in darkening whirlpools and eddies as the superheated air responded to the assault.

"Save us! Save us!" A woman's desperate cries captured the inner feelings of all except a few. Gloria looked at Eckstein, who merely frowned and gave a little shake of his head.

"Blessed Spirit!" Bishop Arkwright intoned. "Blessed Spirit! We see Your power and Your glory! We hear and understand Your message! We beseech Thee, Blessed Spirit, spare us that we might spread Your sacred word! We shall not forsake Thee!"

And suddenly, it was over. The plasma beams abruptly vanished, and air rushed in to fill their ionized trails. A thousand thunderclaps boomed across the valley, shattering every window in Greenlodge and knocking people off their feet with their force. And then, silence.

City Hall collapsed into a heap of smoldering rubble. The anteroom of the Emporium had vanished, along with one of its walls; clouds of bluish vapor billowed outward from the building, as the new fire-prevention system proved its worth. The ground stopped trembling, and the apocalyptic skies smoothed into tranquility.

"We thank Thee, Blessed Spirit!" cried Bishop Arkwright. "Thy will be done."

chapter **28**

GLORIA SAT ALONE IN THE MIDDLE OF THE
battered Emporium, nude and half-drunk, a dirty glass
and a bottle of Scotch her only company. She looked
around at the deserted balcony, the empty rooms, the
vacant gambling tables, and sighed. "Bare, ruined
choirs," she said aloud.

Three days had passed since the plasma eruption,
and in that time, everything had changed. The boomworld was no more.

Following the spectacular blast ("Even better than I
expected," Eckstein had told her), dominoes had fallen
in rapid, ordered succession, and now her mission to
Sylvania was all but completed. She had won.

"Whoopee," she said, holding up her glass in a
solemn salute to herself. She downed the Scotch in a
single gulp and poured some more.

Eckstein and his geologists had gone out in the LASS
to take samples the day after the Eminent Domain hearing, and returned that same afternoon with the results. He
reported to Imperial Governor Bosworth, Judge Kershaw,

and the Eminent Domain victors before a small throng of media reps and interested onlookers in the main room of the Lodge.

"Samples from along the ridgelines east and west of the river were remarkably consistent," he told them. "The average impurity level was 185 Parts Per Billion, in a range from 160 PPB to 220 PPB."

Joe Pollas and the reps from Excelsior and Servitor groaned.

"As distance from the epicenter increased," Eckstein continued, "impurity levels declined. But even a hundred kilometers inland, which was as far as we went, the average was still 65 PPB. We found no sample anywhere with an impurity level less than forty PPB."

"And your conclusion?" asked Governor Bosworth.

"The inescapable conclusion," Eckstein said with an air of finality, "is that the entire Fergusite layer has been destroyed."

Pollas jumped to his feet and pointed an accusing finger at Gloria. "You did this, you fucking bitch," he roared. "I don't know how, but I know it was you!"

"Mr. Pollas, please control yourself," said Governor Bosworth.

"You did something to those rechargers!" Pollas insisted, still glaring at Gloria.

"Me?" Gloria asked, the essence of purity and innocence. "I don't even know how they work!"

"Then you hired somebody to do it! I'll get to the bottom of this, VanDeen. That's a promise!"

"Oh, really," interjected Bishop Arkwright. "You are being preposterous, Mr. Pollas! Next, I suppose you'll claim that Ms. VanDeen was responsible for the Voice, as well. Perhaps she's a ventriloquist!"

"I wouldn't put it past her," muttered Myron Vigo.

"Gentlemen," the bishop continued, "I can understand that you are upset. Your losses in this affair must have been enormous." Sherwin Lund answered that with a combination snort and moan, but the bishop went on, undeterred. "Nevertheless, you must accept the truth of what we all witnessed. The Spirit, in Her incarnation as the Voice, acted to protect this world, just as She once acted to protect the Earth itself! Even now, word of this miracle is being propagated throughout the Empire, and billions of the faithful will take it as a sign that the Spirit is with us always, as She promised. The events we witnessed will become a new chapter in the Book of the Spirit, and those who were not here will envy us."

"Bullshit!" Pollas snarled.

"Oh, ye of little faith." Bishop Arkwright sighed. "You are in pain now, but in time, that pain will fade, and you will be comforted by the blessings of the Spirit. Have faith, Mr. Pollas, have faith!"

"If I may interject a more worldly note," said Judge Kershaw, "may I now assume that the petitioners no longer intend to execute their claim?"

"Judge," said Gaspar Norfleet, rising to his feet, "you may now assume that we are getting the hell out of here. This place is worthless."

"Not entirely," said Stu Eckstein.

Norfleet looked at him. "How so?"

"Only the contiguous Fergusite layer was destroyed. That makes large-scale extraction operations pointless, of course, and it also puts the highboys out of business. But the riverrats will be unaffected by what happened. They are recovering Fergusite that had already broken off from the main layer, so none of it would have been touched by the plasma discharge."

"And how much of it is there?" asked Sherwin Lund.

"Not much," Eckstein conceded. "Certainly not enough to go after it with an Extractor. That would be like hunting mosquitoes with a battleship. In fact, I would think that the most cost-effective way of recovering that Fergusite is the way the riverrats are already doing it. Small-scale placer mining. Panning for it in the rivers. And even though it's not entirely pure, I think it would be good enough to use for unmanned vessels, like couriers and messengers. The riverrats ought to turn a nice little profit."

"Then maybe we should execute our claim after all," Lund suggested to Norfleet.

"Servitor didn't get into this to turn a 'nice little profit,'" Norfleet replied with disdain. "Anyway, if we took those claims, we'd just have to turn around and hire the riverrats to work them for us. Screw it. I've got a yacht waiting in the harbor. You want a ride back to Palmyra?"

"With pleasure," said Lund. "Just let me get my bags." Lund looked around at the barons of the Lodge. "Gentlemen," he said. "Thank you for your hospitality. And if you ever get back to Earth—stay the hell away from me." With that, the representatives of Excelsior and Servitor departed from Sylvania, millions of crowns poorer for their efforts.

BY COMMON CONSENT, THE MEETING BROKE UP. Young Claude Rankus III shyly approached Gloria. "Ms. VanDeen," he said, "I apologize for Joe Pollas and the others. They're pretty upset by all of this. They took a huge loss."

"And you aren't upset?" Gloria asked him.

"To tell you the truth," said Rankus, "I think I'm relieved. If it had been up to me, I'd have voted no on the petition. But, well, the family . . ."

"I understand."

"Grandfather was right. This is a very special place. It meant a lot to him, and it means a lot to me. I'm going to stay on for a while, and see if I can get the Lodge back in shape. Find a new overseer to replace Thawley, hire some new staff. And I'm going to have a talk with Governor Bosworth about forming a new local government. I imagine that you Dexta folks will be leaving now."

"Most of us will be gone tomorrow," Gloria affirmed. "What about Pollas and Vigo and the other trustees?"

"I think they'll be leaving in a couple of days," said Rankus. "And to be honest about it, I'll be glad to have them out of the way. They don't . . . *appreciate* this place the way they should. But I think you do, Ms. VanDeen. I know you had an unpleasant experience here, but I hope you won't consider it inappropriate for me to extend you an invitation to return, anytime you like."

Gloria smiled at the young man. "You never know," she said.

BUT SHE DID KNOW. SHE WOULD NEVER COME back to this place, and would try very hard to forget that she had ever been here. The Scotch wasn't helping much in that effort, but perhaps a little more . . .

"Drinking alone?"

Gloria turned her head and saw Slim Jim Zuni standing next to her table.

"Ah," she said. "Why aren't you on Palmyra by now, counting up your winnings?"

"Thought I'd stick around for a while," he said. "Mind if I join you?"

"Be my guest. Only one glass, though. But you colorful boomworld types drink straight from the bottle, don't you?"

"Sometimes," said Zuni, sitting down and helping himself to a slug of Scotch. He took a long, appreciative look at Gloria's naked body, then met her eyes and smiled. "You're pretty colorful yourself, you know. Elba was a grand old broad, but I liked the Emporium even better with you in charge. What happens to it now?"

"Funny you should mention that," Gloria said, pausing to sip some more of her drink. "Just got a note from headquarters, via messenger. The Dexta Comptroller has ordered me, pending resolution of our mission on Sylvania, to dispose of the Emporium as expeditiously and economically as possible. It seems that there are certain Members of Parliament who are not entirely pleased to discover that Dexta is operating a bawdy house."

"So?" Slim Jim asked. "What are you going to do?"

"I have to find a buyer who doesn't mind a huge repair bill and the fact that most of the clientele is deserting the planet in droves. You see the harbor this afternoon? There's a whole fleet of transports out there, and highboys are fighting each other for berths on 'em."

"Riverrats are staying, though," Slim Jim pointed out.

"Good for them," Gloria said. "But none of them is rich enough to afford this place. Maybe if they formed a consortium. Maybe if some smart young man got them organized . . ." She trailed off. Sad thoughts of Ted Oberlin filled her head, and she sought to chase them away with more booze.

"Maybe I'll buy it myself," she said. "I can afford it. I was born rich, y'know."

"I know," said Slim Jim.

"And I was born a whore, too. Did you know that? It's true. These special genes I've got? Do you know how they were created in the first place? Seems that three or four centuries back, some rich sultan on Suliman IV decided that it might be nice to have a bunch of custom-designed harem girls. So he hired some genetic sculptors, and they came up with the ol' S-Complex, just what the sultan ordered. O' course, you can't keep a good thing like that a secret, can you? So pretty soon, other people were getting access to the S-Complex. And one of them was one of my ancestors, so here I am. Born to be a whore. Maybe I really should buy this place and stay here and run it. Althea kept telling me I should work the rooms, but I never got around to it. Too bad."

"That's the booze talking," Slim Jim said. "You'd be wasted here, Gloria. The Empire needs you more than the riverrats do."

"Fuck the Empire," Gloria said. "If the Empire knew what I just did, they'd lynch me."

"You mean, if they found out what you were up to in Room 9?" Slim Jim grinned at her.

Gloria's eyes widened. She slammed her glass down on the table, sloshing out Scotch. "Jim! You can't—"

"Relax, Gloria. It's none of my business. I just happened to notice, is all. Your secret, whatever it is, is safe with me."

Gloria stared at him for several moments. Twice, she started to say something, but stopped. What *could* she say?

"So," Slim Jim said to break the tension, "everyone else is gone?"

Gloria poured some more Scotch and took a swig. She nodded. "All the Dexta people took off on the Cruiser this afternoon. Except Dina Westerbrook. In a couple of days she and I will take available transportation to Palmyra and go home on the Flyer."

"And your friend Stu Eckstein?"

"Hitched a ride on the Cruiser. Had to get back and report to the Imperial Geological Survey."

"And Althea and the girls?"

"She left, most of them stayed. She got them lodging around town."

"She took good care of them," Zuni noted. "It's a shame she left. I could have used her."

"*You* could have used her?"

"Yup," said Slim Jim. "I've decided I want to buy the Emporium."

Gloria shook her head for a second, trying to clear away cobwebs. "I don't get it," she said. "Why would you want the Emporium?"

Slim Jim slid back in his chair, propped his legs up on the table, and helped himself to another slug from the bottle. "I like it here," he said. "Feels like home. Oh, I'll hire someone to run it for me, but it would be nice to have someplace to come back to. My own table, a place to deal a few hands of five-card stud, knock back a few drinks. Home."

"Well," Gloria said after a moment's thought, "you can't have it. I told you, *I'm* buying it. A little paint, a little plaster—a new wall—and it'll be as good as new. Gloria's Knocking Shop. Come on in and hump the hostess. It's the perfect place for the perfect whore."

"Why are you being so hard on yourself, Gloria?" Slim Jim wondered. "You got what you wanted here, didn't you? You won."

Gloria cocked an eye toward Slim Jim. "You know how many men I killed on this planet?" she asked him. "I'll tell you. I killed even more men than I fucked."

"You didn't kill anyone," Slim Jim said sharply. He brought his feet down and slid his chair over next to hers so he could look her in the eye. "You can't blame yourself for what happened at Pizen Flats."

"Can't I? Why the hell not? If I had been a little smarter, if I had handled things better, if I hadn't been so damned sure of myself, Gus Thornton and Ted Oberlin and all those people would still be alive."

"Maybe," Slim Jim agreed after a moment. "And maybe if you'd played things different, even more would have died. Gloria, you can't spend your life beating yourself up over how you played your cards in the last hand. It's the *next* hand that matters."

"Hah!" cried Gloria. "Listen to the gambler-philosopher."

"Yes, listen to him. You can't change what happened, Gloria."

"Maybe I can," she said.

"How are you going to do that?"

"Not change it . . . but make it come out . . . differently. Better, maybe."

Slim Jim raised an eyebrow. "Do I want to know how?"

"No," she assured him, "you don't." She swallowed some more Scotch.

"Well, anyway," Slim Jim said, "I want to buy the Emporium."

Gloria shook her head. "Told you, I'm buying it."

"Tell you what, we'll cut cards for it. Winner gets to buy the Emporium. Loser leaves town and gets on with his or her life. Deal?" Slim Jim removed a deck of cards from his vest pocket and slapped it down on the table.

Gloria stared at Zuni, stared at the deck. "No," she said at last. "Winner gets to buy the Emporium *and* fuck the loser's brains out. I go first." She reached for the deck and lifted off a single card. She held it against her breast and didn't look at it.

Slim Jim lifted the next card, looked at it, and flipped it onto the tabletop. It was the three of clubs.

Gloria smiled boozily, then peeked at her card. "Deuce," she said, and quickly slid the card back into the deck. She spread her legs and leaned back in her chair. "Emporium's yours. So am I."

So Slim Jim knelt before her and began collecting his winnings. Soon, Gloria was gasping in ecstasy, as Slim Jim brought her to one shattering climax after another. And for the first time all day, she didn't think about what she was going to do the next morning.

GLORIA STOOD AT THE LAKE OGUNBAYO DOCK in the early-morning mist, flanked by two Imperial Marshals. Clad only in thin white shorts and an unzipped windbreaker, she let the cool, moist air rouse her from the depths of her hangover and sleepless night. She watched in silence as the departing barons approached the dock, followed by a small army of baggage bearers. Joe Pollas, Myron Vigo, Sidney Taplin, Rahim Ogunbayo—and Raul Tellemacher. Perfect.

The party stopped and Myron Vigo came forward. Gloria held out her pad to him, and he glanced at it. The warrant was a parting favor from Judge Kershaw, who didn't quite see the point of it, but wasn't inclined to argue about it.

"You just won't quit, will you, Ms. VanDeen?" Vigo

said as he handed the pad back to her. She slipped it into the deep pocket of her windbreaker.

"No," Gloria said, "I won't. Please place all your baggage on the dock and open it so the Marshals can inspect it. And Mr. Pollas, the warrant covers your yacht, as well."

Pollas gave her a sour expression, then pressed a remote to open the hatch of his yacht at dockside. Gloria stepped inside, followed by Pollas. "I don't know what the hell you expect to find," he said.

"Evidence tying you to the massacre at Pizen Flats, of course. You didn't think I was just going to let you walk away from that, did you?" Gloria began looking around at random inside the yacht, opening drawers and cupboards, lifting cushions, checking the undersides of chairs.

"This is just harassment," Pollas told her.

"That's right. Get used to it. Maybe people will forget about the massacre in time, but Dexta will never forget that you were also responsible for assaulting two of its officers." She turned to face him. "And I guarantee you, Pollas, *I* won't forget it."

"Vigo?" Pollas called. "You hear that? Are you going to let her get away with that?"

Vigo joined them inside the yacht, with Tellemacher following him in. "Yes, I heard it," Vigo said patiently, "and yes, I'm going to let her get away with it. Relax, Joe. She's just playing out her final scene with us. It's not enough for her that she destroyed the Fergusite and cost us a fortune. She needs to make it as personal as possible. Isn't that right, Ms. VanDeen?"

"Believe whatever you want, Mr. Vigo," Gloria said. "It's just the five of you going? No pilot?"

Tellemacher gave a short, sarcastic laugh. "Joe doesn't need a pilot. He's the best pilot in the Empire. Right, Joe?"

"I'm fully qualified," Pollas said simply. "Why? Were

you planning on suspending my license as part of your harassment?"

"It's a thought," Gloria replied.

"Yeah," said Tellemacher, "you'd better check to make sure he's really qualified. It's a real tough job, isn't it, Joe? You must have to press, what, five or six buttons between here and Palmyra?"

Pollas seemed annoyed by his friend's needling. "If I press the wrong one, Raul, instead of decelerating and docking at Palmyra Orbital, we'll just zoom off into the galaxy."

"Yikes!" cried Tellemacher.

"As I recall, Ms. VanDeen," said Vigo, "you've already conducted a thorough search of this yacht. What can you possibly hope to find at this late date?"

"Maybe a telltale heart? Who knows? Get comfortable, gentlemen, this may take a while. I intend to be very thorough."

Gloria spent the next hour prying into every nook, alcove, and compartment of the yacht. Vigo and Pollas followed her around for a while, but finally grew bored and retired to the main lounge and left her alone to continue her relentless probing. Meanwhile, on the dock, the Marshals turned every piece of baggage inside out. Finally, the bags were repacked and loaded aboard, and Gloria announced to the five travelers in the lounge that she had completed her search.

"Was it good for you, too, Gloria?" Tellemacher asked with a leer.

"It was satisfactory," she said.

"You didn't find the evidence that wasn't here," said Pollas. "Big fucking surprise. Now get the hell off my yacht so we can leave. I don't want to see you again until I meet you in court, VanDeen—when we sue you for damages. I still think you were behind that business with the plasma, and I'm going to prove it someday. You think you're going to harass us? Just wait till you see how we harass you!"

"I'll look forward to it," she told him. "In fact, I'll even give you some help. I'll tell you the truth if you tell me the truth." Gloria pulled off her windbreaker and tossed it out onto the dock. Then she slipped out of her shorts and shoes and threw them out, as well.

She held her arms out to her sides. "No concealed weapons, no recording devices," she said. "Now close the hatch so we can talk in private."

"Don't trust her!" cried Pollas. "She could have a bug in her teeth!"

"Yeah," said Tellemacher. "I think we ought to search her as carefully as she searched us. I volunteer."

"That won't be necessary," said Vigo. He was holding out his own pad and waving it back and forth across Gloria's naked body. "She's clean. Close the hatch, Joe, and we'll have our little talk."

Pollas frowned, but pushed a button that closed the hatch.

"I still think we should search her," Tellemacher insisted, "just to be safe."

Vigo sighed. "She would like nothing better," he pointed out. "Remember what she did to those four allegedly strong and competent men in the ski lodge. Sorry to disappoint you, Ms. VanDeen, but we will give you no excuse to vent your wrath. And if you are planning on making up an excuse, just remember that witnesses on the dock saw you strip and ask that the hatch be closed. That would make assault rather difficult to prove."

"No doubt," Gloria conceded. "But that's not what I had in mind. I just wanted to get to the bottom of things before we part. No one will ever know what we say here, so we can all speak the truth. I'll start."

She looked directly at Pollas. "You're right," she said. "I *am* responsible for what happened to the Fergusite. We used the two rechargers to drill shafts down to the Fergusite layer, then hit it with a huge overload of energy that spread throughout the layer. I don't know the technical details, but I'm sure you can figure out what happened."

"I knew it, I knew it!" cried Pollas.

Vigo nodded. "And the Voice?" he asked.

"That was just Old Abel, the hermit who lives up in the hills. He's been doing his Voice act for years, but I managed to enlist him. It seems he was an audio engineer before he came to Sylvania. He's got bugs and resonators planted all over the valley."

"That old bastard!" exclaimed Ogunbayo. "Why, I used to give him a handful of crowns whenever I saw him in town. It just goes to show you that people like that have no sense of gratitude."

"Very clever," said Vigo. "And may we know the reason why you felt compelled to do all of this, Ms. VanDeen?"

"It was necessary," Gloria said. "If that Fergusite had been put into widespread use, accident rates would have skyrocketed and confidence in interstellar transit would have been undermined. Planets would have turned inward and depended on their own resources. Trade would have declined, and the very fabric of the Empire would have been threatened."

"Interesting," said Vigo. "And yet, I know for a fact that the Emperor does not share your fears."

"The Emperor," Gloria declared, "is a selfish, shortsighted ass. And I know *that* for a fact!"

Vigo chuckled. "Yes, I suppose you would, at that. So, may I assume that your sabotage was conducted not at the Emperor's behest, but that of the redoubtable Norman Mingus?"

"You may," said Gloria. "And now, it's your turn to tell the truth. Tellemacher, I already know that you betrayed Petra, so don't even try to deny it."

Tellemacher simply shrugged.

"What I don't know," Gloria said, "is which of you decided on the massacre at Pizen Flats. You didn't trust Grunfeld to manage it himself, so you brought in some outside help, in case it became necessary. And when the

Pizen Flats group got organized and started refiling their claims, you realized that you could lose the Eminent Domain vote. So you gave the go-ahead signal for the massacre. Who gave the signal? Was it you, Vigo? Or was it you, Pollas?"

Sidney Taplin stepped forward. "Actually," he said, "it was me. I'm not as loud or flashy as Joe, or as slick as Vigo, but I generally get my way. The whole thing was my idea, and the others went along with it."

Gloria nodded. "And which one of you killed Rankus?"

"Thawley did the actual shooting," Vigo said. "We were doing Claude a favor, really. He was in pain, and losing his grip."

"And you paid off the Thawleys on Palmyra, didn't you?"

"They knew too much and were no longer needed," said Taplin.

"Of course," Gloria agreed. "All right, gentlemen. Just one final question. Have any of you lost any sleep over this? Do you feel the slightest twinge of conscience over all the people you've killed?"

There was an awkward moment of silence. Then Rahim Ogunbayo said, "They were only boomrats. They didn't matter."

"They were *people*!" Gloria snapped.

"That's a matter of opinion," said Taplin blithely.

"There are people, Ms. VanDeen," said Vigo, "and then, there are *people*. That's one thing I've learned in over a century of practicing law. The boomrats may have been colorful and lovable individuals—although personally, I doubt it—but as a group, they were simply an impediment to progress."

"And profit," Gloria added.

"One and the same," said Vigo. "A word of advice, if I may presume, Ms. VanDeen. If you are going to play the game at this level, you need to understand that personal morality simply doesn't apply. All of us"—he spread his arms to encompass his friends—"are quite decent people. We give to charities, we endow hospitals, we are kind to our families and pets. But we don't confuse personal decency with economic necessity. Men such as ourselves built this Empire, Ms. VanDeen, and we have run it for centuries. We will continue to do so, and you and Mr. Mingus and your little Office of Strategic Intervention cannot change that immutable fact. Accept that, and you will have an easier time of it in the future. Forget about Pizen Flats, Ms. VanDeen. It simply doesn't matter."

"It matters to *me*," Gloria told him, grinning fiercely. "You remember *that*, Mr. Vigo. And the rest of you. The moment will come, I promise you, when each of you will pay for what you did at Pizen Flats. And when that moment comes, I want you to think of me."

Gloria looked at each of them in turn, then pivoted sharply, smacked the hatch control with her palm, and stomped out onto the dock. A moment later, the hatch closed behind her.

She stood on the dock and watched as the yacht engines activated and the vessel swung out into the lake. Its main engines fired and in moments it was airborne, streaking upward into the gray skies of Sylvania. Gloria gathered up her clothes and walked back to her skimmer to return to the Emporium.

"... AND WHEN THAT MOMENT COMES, I WANT you to think of me." Pollas laughed out loud as he shut off the playback on Vigo's pad.

"That stupid bitch!" Pollas chuckled. "She strips down to prove *she's* not recording the conversation, and it doesn't even occur to her that *we* would."

"I wonder," said Vigo thoughtfully. "Ms. VanDeen is many things, but stupid isn't one of them."

"She just wanted her big moment, her dramatic final scene," said Tellemacher. "And naturally, she wanted to play it in the nude."

The five of them were gathered in the lounge as the yacht sped through the featureless, colorless haze of Yao space. In a few hours, the computer would shut down the Ferguson Distortion Generators, the yacht would burst back into normal space, and Pollas would assume manual control and decelerate for rendezvous with the Palmyra Orbital Station. Until then, they had nothing to do but savor their unexpected gift from Gloria VanDeen.

"Are you sure that recording will be admissible?" Taplin asked Vigo.

"It ought to be," Vigo replied. "Of course, if we play it in court, Ms. VanDeen will simply claim that she was just making up stories to get us to confess to crimes we never committed."

"But those stories can be checked," Pollas pointed out. "All we have to do is go back to Sylvania and find some of those bugs and resonators. And grab Old Abel."

"And that's what troubles me," said Vigo. "She would certainly have been aware of that. And yet, she told us." Vigo looked around the interior of the yacht, as if he expected to see something that shouldn't have been there.

"Oh, relax, Myron," said his old friend Ogunbayo. "Ms. VanDeen simply made a mistake. And we shall profit from it."

"She doesn't make many mistakes," said Vigo.

"I'll tell you a mistake *we* made," said Tellemacher. "We should have searched her when we had her standing here naked. Damn, I sure would have enjoyed searching her. You know, I think we were probably the only men on that whole damn planet that she never fucked."

Pollas laughed. "Maybe you're right, Rowdy. We probably could have taken turns screwing her right here, and she would—what was that?"

There was a soft popping sound and a muffled hiss. Everyone looked around.

"Shit! Are we losing pressure?" Tellemacher wondered.

"No, it came from over there, in the aft galley. I don't—*oh my God!*"

A thin, pink haze was drifting forward from the kitchen. The five men watched it approach them, watched as fabrics and fibers began to disintegrate before their eyes as the haze advanced.

And then Myron Vigo understood.

The moment had come, and he said, "VanDeen."

chapter 29

GLORIA WALKED SLOWLY THROUGH THE FOREST
at the base of the falls, nude as she always was here, feeling the special magic of the place once again, even though she knew there really was no magic. It was nothing more than a forest and a falls, trees, rocks, and water. There was no Voice and, she now assumed, probably no Spirit, either.

And yet, the place itself was its own reason for being. To human senses, it didn't really matter whether there was magic here or not. The natural did not require the supernatural to explain or justify it. It was what it was, and that was enough.

Gloria felt oddly at peace with herself, considering that by then, she had committed cold-blooded murder. If the timer had gone off as scheduled, half an hour ago Vigo, Ogunbayo, Taplin, Pollas, and Tellemacher had died horrible deaths. She wondered why she didn't feel something.

"Special circumstances," she said to herself. Under the *Imperial Code*, the death penalty could not be invoked unless there were special circumstances involved in a crime. Mass murder qualified. The massacre at Pizen Flats qualified. Justice had been done, she assured herself.

It was called Toxgon, Arkady Volkonski had told her when she asked him about it that night at the Emporium. It had been developed more than a century earlier as a means of decontaminating sites that had been attacked with certain biological or chemical weapons. The superoxidant compound broke down every organic molecule it encountered, reducing them to nothing more than harmless atoms of carbon, oxygen, nitrogen, and hydrogen. Its job accomplished, the Toxgon broke down, leaving no trace.

Since Toxgon, in itself, could be a powerful weapon, its use was strictly regulated and access to it was restricted. But it could be found in the inventory of hospitals on worlds like Palmyra, where biological weapons had been unleashed in the war with the Ch'gnth Confederacy, just four decades earlier. Every now and then, a previously overlooked contaminated site was discovered, and the Toxgon was needed.

Joe Pollas had gotten Toxgon from the hospital his family endowed, and had used it to remove every trace of Petra's presence on his yacht. Clever and foolproof.

But when Gloria returned to Palmyra and confronted Dr. Hamdoon and administrator Suharto about the missing Toxgon in their inventory, they admitted that they had given a packet of it to Pollas. They admitted it because Gloria had assured them that she would see to it that their unfortunate and highly illegal lapse would never see the light of day. In return for her lenience, she required only a Toxgon packet for herself— for the investigation of other crimes.

The Toxgon packet was about the same size as a deck of cards. It was self-detonating and had its own timer. She carried it aboard the yacht in the pocket of her windbreaker, and had no problem finding a place to hide it. Vigo and Pollas were worried about what she might find, not what she might leave behind. It had been easy.

"When I was in training," Arkady had told her, "taking a course on decontamination procedures, they showed us a vid of an accidental Toxgon release. A security cam caught it in a laboratory where a Toxgon packet detonated prematurely. The shields closed immediately, of course, trapping five people inside the lab."

Arkady had paused at that point. He frowned and shook his head at the memory of the vid. "The Toxgon," he continued, "killed those people from the outside in. First it decomposed the outer layers of their skin. And their eyes. Then the deeper layers of the skin, right down to the bones, then the bones themselves. When they breathed it in, it went to work on their lungs and they began coughing up blood. They were still alive, you see. Nothing vital had been affected yet, so they lived until they bled to death, as their bodies melted away. It was the worst thing I ever saw. Worst way to die you can imagine."

Gloria stopped and leaned against a tree for a moment as she remembered Volkonski's words and thought about what must have happened inside the Pollas yacht.

Gloria VanDeen: judge, jury, executioner. Avenging angel.

Personal morality didn't matter at this level, Vigo had told her. People didn't matter, Ogunbayo claimed. Very well, then.

But justice mattered. Murder had been committed, and the murderers had been punished.

Except, she reminded herself, Tellemacher was not a murderer. He'd had nothing to do with Pizen Flats. But he had betrayed Petra, and that betrayal would surely have led to her death if not for the fortunate intervention of their friends from the Emporium. So Tellemacher was as guilty as the rest of them.

In any case, he was as dead as the rest of them.

For a brief moment, Gloria thought she was about to vomit.

She caught herself, took a few deep breaths, and rubbed her eyes. "I can live with this," she said.

"What can you live with?"

Gloria looked around and saw Old Abel standing a few meters away. She shrugged and managed to smile at him. "With whatever I have to," she said.

Abel thought about that for a few moments. "That pretty much applies to all of us, doesn't it?" he asked.

"Some of us more than others," Gloria replied.

Abel raised an eyebrow. "You worried about what we done here?"

"No, not about that. We've saved Sylvania, Abel."

"For now, anyway," he said.

"No," Gloria said, "permanently, I think. When I get back to Earth, I'm going to suggest to Charles that he turn Sylvania into an Imperial Park, with a waiver that will permit the riverrats to keep working their claims. He'll be furious about what happened, but I think he'll go for it. That would bring in tourists, which would help defray the cost of the Orbital Station."

"Tourists?" Abel sniffed. He didn't look happy about the prospect. "I suppose they'll be coming here to the falls."

"Some of them," Gloria agreed. "Would you rather have Extractors?"

"I'd rather just keep the place to myself."

Gloria grinned at him. "You're a selfish old bastard, aren't you?"

"Damned right, I am. But you're welcome to come here anytime you want."

Gloria shook her head. "I don't think I'll be coming back this way, Abel. In fact, I'll be leaving tomorrow. I just wanted to see the falls—and you—one last time."

"Well, I'm glad you did. But I ain't gonna like it when them tourists start showin' up, I can tell ya that."

"You'll have to get used to it, Abel. In fact, they're

already here. A shipload of religious pilgrims arrived from Palmyra just this morning. The Spiritists are all agog over what happened here—which is lucky for us. If people are convinced that the Voice was a manifestation of the Spirit, the Emperor won't be likely to investigate everything that happened here. That would cost him Spiritist support, and he'd never risk that. Of course, the people who come here expecting to hear the Voice aren't going to hear it, are they, Abel?"

Abel stared at the ground for a moment, then said, "Naw, I 'spect not."

"You know that you have to gather up all your bugs and resonators, don't you? We can't risk having them discovered."

"Yeah," Abel said, "I know. I'll do it, I guess. Wouldn't want either one of us to get in trouble. But first, I want to let the Voice speak one last time. I just need to think up the right words."

"I know the right words," Gloria said. She leaned close to him and whispered them in his ear. Then she gave him a long, heartfelt kiss good-bye.

THE NEXT DAY, UP AND DOWN THE VALLEY, IN the streets of Greenlodge, in the meadows of Overhill, along the cliffs, and deep in the forests, coming from everywhere and nowhere, the Voice whispered,

Thank you!

About the Author

C.J. Ryan lives and works in Philadelphia.

Be sure not to miss

THE FIFTH QUADRANT

BY
C. J. RYAN

Now that Gloria VanDeen has provent her own merits, she is about to face her toughest mission ever. For Gloria is suddenly caught in the midst of a vicious turf war, fighting for her personal and professional survival against terrorist assassins and vengeful bureaucrats, as she untangles a web of intrigue and corruption from the Empire's past that threatens to destroy its future. . . .

Coming in Fall 2006

THE FIFTH
QUADRANT
On Sale Fall 2006

THE LIGHT OF THE SUNS BEAT DOWN ON THE baking streets of Cartago like a curse. One of them was small, blue, and hot; the other was fat, red, and less hot. They were separated in the sky by about the width of a fist held at arm's length, and Cartago whirled endlessly about a point somewhere between the two blazing orbs. They cast twin shadows in the streets, which angled away from one another slightly, as if reluctant to admit they knew each other.

Gloria VanDeen followed her host and his entourage through the swarming streets, enjoying the color and bustle and the singsong entreaties of the bazaar merchants. Exotic, fan-tailed phoenixbirds could be hers for only ten crowns, or perhaps seven. Silken scarves and golden bangles and cotton caftans of the highest quality would only enhance her astonishing beauty, and at a price so low she would feel guilty for taking such advantage of the poor but honest merchants of Cartago; but the honor of being permitted to offer garments and jewelry to grace the famous form of Gloria

VanDeen would more than offset the financial loss. The most beautiful woman in all the Empire surely deserved no less than the finest craftsmanship and artistry in the entire Sector—nay, the entire Quadrant!

"I would buy you something as a souvenir," Praetor Ulmani said to her, "but that would surely cause a riot. The merchant whose wares you wore would become insufferable, and his competition, unable to bear their shame, would doubtless kill him."

"Then I suppose it's best that I wear nothing," Gloria said with a smile. "I wouldn't want to be responsible for a tragedy."

"Spirit forbid it!" Ulmani grinned at her. Since nothing—or very nearly nothing—was precisely what Gloria was wearing, he spent a long moment staring at her. Her soft, flowing, nearly transparent garment rested lightly on her shoulders and descended in narrow vees of sheer white fabric, front and rear, shielding her from the suns but not from the hungry eyes that surrounded her. Her flanks and legs were entirely bare, and the garment swirled mischievously with each movement to reveal her firm, round buttocks and golden pubic nest.

Gloria took a deep breath and reveled in the moment. There were times when being Gloria VanDeen was just so damn much fun that it should have been illegal. She smiled and waved happily to the throng in the streets, then let Ulmani take her elbow and usher her along.

The people of Cartago, like their Praetor, had many reasons to be grateful that Gloria VanDeen had come to their world, and Gloria was well aware that her stunning beauty and breathtaking sexual presence were not the least important. Without those attributes, it was doubtful that she would have been able to fulfill the mission that had brought her here.

On this, the thirteenth day of January in the year 3218, Standard Calendar—just three days after her twenty-fifth birthday—Gloria VanDeen was the most famous, popular, and (quite possibly) important woman in an empire that spanned a sphere of space two thousand light-years in diameter and was home to some three trillion sentient beings. The fact that she was the former wife of the man who was now Emperor Charles V was of some importance, as was her position as head of the Office of Strategic Intervention—the newest action arm of the Department of Extraterrestrial Affairs, the sprawling bureaucracy that administered the Terran Empire. Alone, either one of those facts would have made her a woman of some consequence; together, they made her a potent force within the Empire. But it was her beauty, brilliance, and courage that had won the hearts of the masses and made her, as was often said, the Sweetheart of the Empire.

At moments like this, Gloria was outrageously happy to be exactly who and what she was. She had just brought her mission on Cartago to a triumphant and altogether satisfactory conclusion. And for a change, the intervention had been brief, bloodless, and relatively simple.

Cartago was a thirsty world, where a small population of some five million lived on the margins of a globe-girdling desert. Just 194 light-years from Earth, the planet had been settled some 800 years earlier in pre-Imperial days. In later years, it probably never would have been colonized at all, but in that first era of interstellar expansion, Earthmen were not yet very particular in their choice of new worlds. If a planet had oxygen in its atmosphere and a mean surface temperature somewhere between the freezing and boiling points of water, it was a candidate for settlement. Cartago qualified—if only just.

Over the centuries, the slowly growing population had splintered into what amounted to tribal groups, although the ethnic, cultural, and religious orientations of the three main tribes differed little. The only differences of real consequence concerned water and access to it. The Mountain Tribe controlled the flow of the precious liquid that trickled down to the dusty plains and the lands of the Eastern and Western Tribes. Accordingly, the Mountain Tribe had always selected the Praetor who headed the planetary government, such as it was. The coming of the Empire had remarkably little impact on existing arrangements on Cartago, and generations of Imperial Governors and Dexta bureaucrats were content to let the natives work things out for themselves.

In recent years, however, the elders of the Eastern and Western Tribes had—for Spirit knew what bizarre reasons—taken to sending their brightest sons and daughters back to Earth to be educated in The Law. Having nothing better to do when they returned to their homeworld, the young barristers began suing the other tribes over the only thing that mattered on their world—water. Thus, there had been angry protests, boycotts, insults, threats, and finally, the sequestration of water that had once flowed freely from the slopes of the central mountains. The Imperial Governor had been unable to persuade anyone to see the light of reason, and the tiny Dexta establishment on the planet had thrown up its arms in despair.

So Norman Mingus had sent Gloria to Cartago.

Cartago was the fifth intervention for Gloria and OSI, and by far the easiest. Gloria hadn't even bothered to take along any staff; Cartago was just two days away from Earth via Flyer, and so help was relatively close at hand should any prove necessary. None did.

In less than two weeks on the planet, she had met with a handful of young lawyers, a clutch of tribal elders, and Praetor Ulmani, adroitly resolving their conflicts through a combination of judicious bribes and personal persuasion. The Dexta Comptroller would probably grumble about the bribes, small though they were, but Gloria had thoroughly enjoyed her brief sojourn on Cartago. She had charmed, beguiled, and bedazzled everyone who mattered, as she usually did wherever she went. Displaying and exploiting her beauty were a standard *modus operandi* for Gloria, and in this age of Spiritism, few saw anything shameful in it.

Resolving the conflicts on Cartago had been so easy that Gloria seriously wondered if the whole mess hadn't been cooked up by the young lawyers simply to lure her to their world. Probably not, she conceded; on a desert world, no one played frivolous games with water. Still, her fame and reputation had reached the point that she had to beware the Heisenberg Effect; her mere presence was often enough to alter the terms of any equation.

At the moment, her presence in the streets of Cartago was altering the normal routine of the bazaar at searing mid-day, when energy levels and activity normally reached low ebb. Praetor Ulmani kept his grip on Gloria's elbow while his entourage of aides and security men plowed a path through the increasingly excited crowds. They could have taken an air-conditioned limo skimmer directly to the restaurant, but Ulmani had calculated that it could not hurt his popularity to be seen escorting Gloria through the teeming streets of his city. Gloria didn't really mind being paraded through the streets as if she were one of Ulmani's hunting trophies; she was willing to let him get whatever political mileage he could out of the affair. He was a nice enough man and probably as good a leader as the planet needed. She was content to let him have his big moment; all that really mattered was that she had solved Cartago's little problems and would soon be returning to Earth.

The outdoor restaurant was just ahead. Security men were already clearing a path while the maitre d' stood before a large table in eager, fawning anticipation. Gloria impulsively decided to give everyone—not least of all Ulmani—one last reason to cheer before they settled in for their luncheon. She turned to face Ulmani, pulled him close, and gave him an incendiary kiss. The cheers were deafening. Gloria released her hold on the astonished Praetor and grinned at him. "Your people adore you," she said.

"After this," Ulmani replied, "they may start worshipping me!"

Gloria winked at him. "Or me," she said.

They made their way through the wrought iron gateway that delineated the restaurant, greeted the proprietor, and moved to the reserved table. One of Ulmani's aides pulled out a chair for her, and Gloria had just begun to bend to be seated when the blue-green bolt of plasma crackled through the air just above her. The characteristic plasma thunderclap followed an instant later, as air rushed in to fill the ionized trail of the discharge; and just after that, Gloria heard the pained, startled moan from the aide standing behind her.

Before she could fully register what had happened, three security men were firing back, their plasma beams converging on a head and shoulders just visible on the rooftop across the street. The head and shoulders vanished in green fire, and the triple thunderclap echoed through the suddenly silent streets. As quickly as that, it was over. Gloria smelled burnt hair.

She looked around and saw Ulmani's aide slumping backward against the white stucco wall of the building. Flames flickered along the torn sleeve of his garment and he stared in open-mouthed wonder at the inch-in-diameter trench of blackened meat that now grooved his upper arm. Behind him, there was a smoldering hole in the wall.

Comprehension slowly dawned, and Gloria reached upward and ran her fingers through the singed tunnel that had scorched through her thick blond mane, just above her scalp.

I've been shot in the hair, she thought. *How odd.*

GLORIA DIDN'T HAVE MUCH TIME TO DWELL ON the events of Cartago, however, for no sooner was she back on Earth than she was officially declared an Avatar of Joy—a sort of secular saint of Spiritism, a religion that had no saints. The ceremony was held in Rio. She'd had no intention of seeing Charles while she was in the city, but an Imperial invitation was impossible to ignore.

The limo deposited Gloria at the entrance to the Imperial Horticulture Gardens on the grounds of the Residence. Here, exobotanists had assembled a unique collection of plant species from all over the Empire, and had somehow gotten them to grow in harmony without annihilating each other or the native species of Earth. The result, one critic had noted, looked as if Salvador Dali had taken up gardening.

Gloria wandered though the gateway, past a bright blue hedge and under the drooping boughs of a quaking willow from DeSantos IV; when she brushed against its fronds, they drew back as if in fright. She spotted Charles strolling along a pathway between a fragrant, carnivorous gluetree from somewhere in the Pleiades Cluster and a pygmy sequoia from a high-gravity world that was all of four feet tall. The Emperor smiled and nodded at the sight of her and casually walked onward in her direction.

"What's this?" he asked, pointing at her. "Clothing? On a Visitation Day? I would have expected better from an Avatar of Joy."

"It may be a Visitation Day, and this may be Rio," Gloria replied, "but back home in Manhattan, it's still January."

"Indeed. Tell me, have you had any snow there yet? The Imperial Climatologist tells me we'll see it in our lifetime."

"Not that I've noticed. But I hear they had a little up in Poughkeepsie last year."

"Something to look forward to, then. What fun, waiting for an Ice Age." Charles stopped in front of Gloria and held out both hands to her. She hesitated a moment, then took them in hers. They held each other and stared in silence for what felt like a long time.

Charles, now twenty-eight, was looking more like an Emperor with each passing year. His medium-length dirty-blond hair was artlessly tousled over the tops of his ears, and his closely trimmed beard emphasized rather than concealed the arrogant thrust of his chin. His nose was characteristic of the Hazar Dynasty, rather long and bony, and his watery blue eyes seemed to radiate condescension. He was still slim and fit, and was tall enough to look down on most people with lofty nonchalance. He was dressed in casual splendor and looked quite comfortable with himself.

It had been nearly a year since Gloria had seen him face to face. Upon her return from Mynjhino, Charles had seen fit to award her a Distinguished Service Medal; having been embarrassed and frustrated by her during that episode, he had concluded that the only way to deal with her performance was to reward her for it. On the other hand, her service on Sylvania had inspired no award, only icy silence.

Charles finally released his grip on her hands and gave her an appraising once-over with his eyes. She was clothed, true, but only minimally, in a pale blue wrap dress that was loosely fastened at the waist, exposing vistas of breast and belly to his appreciative view.

"You've done something to your hair," he said at last.

"Well, something was done to it, anyway," Gloria admitted. Her hairdresser in Manhattan had performed some creative first-aid on her damaged 'do following her return from Cartago, and her long, Dura-Styled mane now flowed halfway down her back in apparent good health.

"So I heard," Charles said. "Dammit, Glory, if Mingus keeps sending you to these two-crown shitholes, sooner or later you are going to get seriously hurt. And for what? So a bunch of provincials can water their fucking lawns?"

"People live on those shitholes, Charles," Gloria responded. "They have rights and needs, the same as anyone else in the Empire. Dexta does what it can to see that they receive the respect and attention they are due."

"Spoken like the career bureaucrat you've become," Charles snorted.

"Thank you," Gloria smiled. "That's the nicest thing you've said to me in years."

Charles shook his head in evident disgust. "I cannot fathom why you are at Dexta. I never could. It's a barbaric environment, as I'm sure even you would admit, considering everything that was done to you when you started out there. And now you've become Mingus's Girl Friday, which I find appalling."

"I'm sure *you* would."

"He's a hundred and thirty years old!"

"A hundred and thirty-one," Gloria corrected. "Why, Charles, are you *jealous*?" She snickered at the thought.

"Please, don't be disgusting. If you are fucking the old coot, I'd rather not know about it."

"Actually," said Gloria, "I'm not. By his choice, not mine, I hasten to point out."

"Wise of him," Charles said. "He's too old to handle an Avatar of Joy." Charles looked upward toward the treetops and the sky and shook his head. "An Avatar of Joy, Spirit save us! You know, don't you, that if it weren't for the damned Spiritists, you'd probably be spending the rest of your life on a prison world for what you did on Sylvania?"

"Me?" Gloria asked innocently. "What did *I* do?"

"You know damned well what you did. You ruined a quadrillion crowns' worth of Fergusite! Only I can't touch you for it, because of the fucking Voice and the idiot Spiritists who think the whole thing was divine intervention, instead of a plot—a goddamn conspiracy—by you and Mingus. Don't deny it, Glory. I don't know how you managed that business with the Voice, but—"

"Oh, ye of little faith!" Gloria laughed.

Charles seemed about to respond, but stopped himself abruptly and reeled in his rage. He walked down the path a few paces and pointed at a large, gnarled tree a few meters away. "Know what that is?" he asked.

"Beats me."

"It's a glashpadoza tree. The native species on

Belonna V believe that the glashpadoza absorbs all of the sins of the clan that grows it. That's why it's so hellishly ugly." He turned to look at her. "Would you care for a cutting?"

"Are you suggesting that I need my own glashpadoza tree?"

"Don't you?"

Gloria considered the question seriously. She had committed many sins on Sylvania, and the business with the Voice and the Fergusite was far from the most serious of them. A spaceship with five evil men in it had never reached its destination, and only Gloria knew the reason.

She looked again at the tree. "I might have a good spot to grow one of those at my place on Long Island," she said finally.

"I thought you might," Charles said. "I'll have the Imperial Gardener see to it."

Charles went over to her, stared into her face for a moment, then carefully put his arm around her shoulders and drew her closer to him. She didn't resist.

"I know more about what happened there than you think I do," he said softly. "I'm not saying you were wrong. If it had been me, I'd have done the same, or worse, probably. But tell me, Glory, are you planning to make a habit of that sort of thing?"

She looked up into his eyes. "What if I am?" she asked.

"Then do it right," he said. "Don't just play at it. Don't think you can go around dispensing justice and righteousness, ad hoc, on behalf of Dexta, because you can't. Sooner or later it will catch up with you, and not even Norman Mingus—not even *I*—will be able to save you from the consequences. If you're going to do it, do it right."

"What do you mean?"

"Don't do it as a Dexta drone, Glory. Or even as an Avatar of Joy. Do it as Empress!"

• • •

GLORIA WAS TAKEN ABACK BY CHARLES'S PRO-
posal, although not completely surprised by it. A year
and a half ago, just before she left for Mynjhino, he had
made it clear that he wanted her back. But she had long
since chosen another path, and had no intention of retreating into Charles's waiting arms

They had married young, and divorced young. At
the time, Charles was seventh in line to the throne, then
sixth after old Darius finally died, and seemed unlikely
ever to be Emperor. He seemed unlikely, in fact, ever to
be much of anything other than a wealthy, privileged
wastrel. He had persuaded her to suspend her education, and together they had spent much of their marriage gadding about the Empire in his luxurious yacht.
But in her travels, Gloria had become fascinated with
exosociology, the study of the lives and cultures of the
Empire's many denizens, human and otherwise. When
she decided to return to school and continue her studies, Charles had absolutely forbidden it. So she left him
and never looked back.

More than two years later, after Gloria had completed her studies and joined Dexta, a botched coup
known as the Fifth of October Plot had killed Gregory,
his two sons, and three of his nephews, leaving the Imperial throne to Charles. Gloria had sighed in relief at
her narrow escape from having become Empress. The
last thing she wanted was to be a useless, ineffectual or-
nament to the reign of Charles V. She drew immense
satisfaction from her work at Dexta, and would have
been miserable if condemned to spend her life in ceremonial playacting.

She broke away from Charles and began walking
down one of the Garden pathways at a brisk pace.
Charles followed along behind her, apparently content
to give her some space.

Empress! Spirit, why did he think she would want to
be Empress? She had more real power now, as head of

the Office of Strategic Intervention, than most Empresses ever dreamed of possessing. There had been an unbroken line of forty-seven male Emperors, of course, dating back to Hazar the Great in 2522, 696 years ago. Unlike the kings and potentates of antiquity, producing male offspring was no hit-or-miss proposition for the Emperors of the Terran Empire. Empresses were simply the wives of Emperors, and not rulers in their own right.

Oh, five or six of them had obtained considerable power, being married to weak or dimwitted men, but that was the exception rather than the rule. Some Emperors had done without Empresses altogether, preferring to sire their offspring with a series of Imperial Consorts.

"I know what you're thinking," Charles said from behind her. "But this would be different. I'd give you real power, Glory."

Gloria stopped so abruptly that she skidded forward a bit on the crushed stone of the pathway. She whirled around and faced Charles.

"What is that supposed to mean?" she demanded.

"Just what I said. Real power. We'll work out the provisions in detail, put it in writing, sign it, and publish it. I wouldn't be able to back out even if I wanted to."

She stared at him, took a couple of steps toward him, then stopped and stared at him some more, her eyes narrowing in suspicion. "What are you up to, Chuckles?"

He grinned at her. "No good, I assure you. No good at all. But since you insist, I shall reveal to you the details of my nefarious plot."

Charles closed the distance between them and put his hands on her shoulders. "What I intend," he said, "is to wed and bed the most beautiful and popular woman in the Empire so that we can fuck each other like crazed minks whenever we want. And what's more, I want that woman to give me the benefit of her very great intelligence, creativity, and courage in ruling an Empire of three trillion sentient beings, every one of whom would be thrilled and delighted to have her for their Empress. There, you see? An evil plot, if ever there was one."

"You're serious, aren't you?"

"Entirely. You'd be, if you like, my co-ruler. I would retain primacy, of course—the laws would require that in any event. But you would have full authority in virtually any area that you prefer. Spirit, Glory, I have no interest in doing half the things I'm required to do, anyway. Believe me, I'd *welcome* sharing the load with you. And the people would love it. Together, we'd be the best rulers this old Empire has ever seen!"

"And . . . ?" Gloria prodded. She wasn't ready to buy into this fantasy just yet.

Charles removed his hands from her shoulders and stepped back from her. He nodded and said, "And . . . I'm under increasing pressure these days to produce an heir, one way or another. I could find an acceptable Consort easily enough, but I'd much prefer to do it with you. Host-mother, of course, so you needn't trouble yourself with a pregnancy. And it really is necessary, Gloria. I mean, you know who's next in line of succession at the moment, don't you? Cousin Larry. I know what you think of *him*."

"Larry?" Gloria groaned. "Lord Brockinbrough the Detestable?"

"The very one. How did you describe him that time? Old enough to be my father, unscrupulous enough to be my brother, and immature enough to be my son. Wonderful line, that. Even Larry appreciated it. Anyway, I really need to cook up a more appropriate heir, and there is no DNA I'd rather entwine with mine than thine."

Gloria frowned, looked at the ground, chewed her lower lip for a moment, then looked back up at Charles. "And . . . ?"

"And," Charles said with a laugh, "your approval numbers in the polls are better than mine. I don't want to spend the next century competing with you, Glory. I'd rather pool our resources. And there's one more *and*."

"Which is?"

Charles wrapped his arms around her, pulled her to him, and kissed her with Imperial urgency. She responded with urgency of her own, like a good Avatar of Joy. Moments later they lay sprawled in the grass beneath the gnarled limbs of the glashpadoza tree.